CHANTAL ROOME

Print ISBN 9781777707620

ebook ISBN 9781777707637

To the ladies who read my stuff way before anyone else.
Thank you for being so thoughtful in your comments and careful in your observations. Amie, Ashley, Lorraine, Lindsay, and
Maggie, you guys made this book possible.
Thank you so much.

Creepy Andrew and a Pity Party

Ryder

"CAN I TELL YOU again how happy I am you two worked out your differences," I say around a mouthful of prime rib. "Your weekly dinners are the only time I eat well all week."

Ever since Alex and Connor reconnected, and then made it through the bullshit that was a groupie drugging and trying to rape Connor a couple of months ago, Alex has been hosting weekly family dinners at their house. She's a professional chef and loves cooking. And I am a semi-professional eater who is more than willing to eat any of the delicious things she makes.

My dad wasn't much of a cook while I was growing up. His specialties were mac and cheese and takeout. I never went hungry, but the food probably could have been healthier. It's not his fault, though. Being stuck raising two young boys all alone because their mom wants nothing to do with them is tough. He did the best he could with us. It's really hard to compete with an actual chef.

"I'm happy you all come every week and give me a chance to feed you. It's been tough since I haven't been working. Who knew taking ten weeks off would have such an impact on my employability?" Alex is serving up the extra Yorkshire puddings she's pulled from the oven. I immediately put my plate up to grab a couple of those crispy little golden puffs of goodness.

Maybe it's a good thing Dad couldn't cook like this. I'd never have been able to maintain my girlish figure.

"How is your hand feeling now that you've had your cast removed?" Denise asks. She's sitting opposite me, next to her clean-cut looking doofus of a boyfriend. Dude hardly ever talks, unless he whispers something into Denise's ear. She never looks pleased with what he's said, either. The guy gives me a weird feeling, but I can't put my finger on why. Mostly, he gives me the creeps.

"So much better. I can shower without help now, which is nice. I can't believe they made me keep it on for nine weeks."

Connor comes up behind Alex and runs his hands around her waist as he pulls her toward him. "Oh babe, you know I'm still going to help you in the shower."

"Get off me, perv." Alex laughs while pushing Connor away.

They've come a long way in the ten weeks since Alex broke her hand defending Connor from a groupie. It was subconscious since she didn't know Connor had been drugged, but she beat the chick so hard she fractured her hand and saved Connor from sexual assault. They're so happy together it's gross, but in a good way.

I hope to one day find a love like they have, but since I'm only interested in one person and she is currently dating a stupid asshole named Andrew, I don't think that's likely to happen. You could say my crush on Denise is the reason I have a problem with Andrew, but it's not. Well, it's not the only reason, anyway. He's not quite right.

I look across the table at Denise. She's got her long black hair tied up in a red bandana with her long bangs hanging down over her forehead. It goes great with the tight jeans and flannel shirt she's wearing tonight. She looks like a pin-up queen out for a casual stroll. That idiot Andrew leans over and whispers in her ear while I'm looking. Denise looks at him and shakes her head a little before he whispers to her again. She looks away from him and rolls her eyes while letting out an enormous sigh.

"Well, I hate to say it. We're going to have to get going now. I've got early meetings tomorrow, and there are some things I need to get sorted tonight in preparation." Denise stands and places her napkin beside her still full plate. She spent more time wiping her fork with her napkin than she did eating. Every time she took a bite, she'd make a face and then wipe her fork again. It was weird, yet oddly adorable. "Thank you so much for dinner, Alex. It was delicious, as always."

"You're leaving already?" I stand when Denise does, a remnant from when I was a kid and my brother, Hunter, and I would spend half of every summer vacation with my grandmother. She drilled into me the importance of being a gentleman. I may be an asshole, and I may drink too much, but I still use my manners, especially with women like Denise. Standing when she does is the least I can do.

"Yes, Ryder," she says, a look of irritation on her face. "Can you please try to behave tonight? I don't have time to bail you out of jail again."

Okay, that happened once. However, she has had to rescue me from other towns, public parks, private homes, and the occasional possibly haunted hotel. Like I said, I drink a lot more than I probably should.

"I will be on my best behavior tonight, love. Just for you." I wink and give her a little bow. That's probably too over the top, but it gets a laugh from her, so it's worth it.

"Good." Andrew sneers in my direction. "I plan to keep her well occupied tonight."

Ugh, he is such a creep.

"Yeah, we'll see," is all Denise says. She looks a little uncomfortable. "See you all later."

Denise and Andrew leave, and the rest of us stay to enjoy our dinner.

Alex looks over at me, checking if I'm okay. She knows I have a thing for Denise, and she knows I'm doing my best to stay out of her business with Andrew. What she doesn't know is how hard it is for me to see them together every week at family dinner. The way he acts makes me want to punch him in his stupid math teacher-looking face.

"That was a weird." Aiden is sitting to my right. He's noticed my crush too, but he hasn't come right out and said anything. "I'm not sure I really like Andrew."

"Me neither," Alex says, still looking at me. "Why is he always whispering in her ear? She always looks uncomfortable when he does it. There's something weird about him."

"Agreed." I put my napkin on my plate. I've had three helpings already. There's no way I could fit anything else in my stomach.

"I have crème brûlée for dessert," Alex offers. "I'm so excited to try my new torch."

"Leave it to my girl to want to play with fire for the sake of dessert." Connor's pulled Alex down to sit on his lap, and he's kissing along her jaw while she tries to stand.

"I'm going to have to pass, Alex. I couldn't eat another bite if I tried." I'm already going to need to open the top button on my jeans the second I leave. I'm overly full, but it was totally worth it.

"Well, I'm going to get a few ready, anyway. Connor, can you help me?" Alex gets out of Connor's grip and she walks out of the dining room.

"You guys can see yourselves out." Connor jumps out of his chair and runs after Alex, stopping to throw her over his shoulder. "Leave the mess," he calls out over his shoulder while running out with Alex giggling the whole way.

"Yeah, so... I don't think dessert is on the menu anymore, guys." Aiden laughs.

Travis is already on his way out, leaving me and Aiden at the table. Alex's friend Becca had to work tonight, shooting someone's Sunday wedding, and Johnny and Devon weren't able to make it, either.

"See you, Trav."

"Bye guys," he says without turning around.

Aiden waves at Travis before turning to me. "Sit for a minute."

"Um, okay?" I say, taking my chair again. "What's up, man? Everything alright?" Aiden is the oldest member of our band, and he's also the quietest. He doesn't normally talk unless he really has something important to say.

"I know how you feel about Denise," he says to me. "And I also know how we all feel about Andrew. There's something wrong with that guy."

"Right? But what can we do about it? Denise is a grown woman. She can make her own choices."

"Yes, she is grown, and she can make choices. But tell me this. Have you ever presented yourself as a choice? She's never going to choose you if she doesn't even know you're an option."

"Geez, man. You're not pulling any punches today, are you?"

"Actually, I am," he says. "If I weren't pulling punches, I'd tell you that your drinking and fucking around isn't helping you get over her like you think. And getting over her isn't what you actually want, even though you think it is. I know that's why you're doing it, even if you won't say it. You're a good guy, or at least you would be if you'd stop acting like such a fuckup. So stop being a fuckup and tell her how you feel."

"Well, shit." I run my hands through my hair and my tongue pokes out to play with my lip ring, a nervous habit I can't seem to shake. "I can't tell her something like that. She has a boyfriend. It wouldn't be right."

"Normally, I would agree with you. But I get a bad feeling from that guy. I think Denise might be keeping him around because she feels like she's run out of options. I overheard her talking on the phone one day, upset about the fact that she's thirty-six already, and she's unmarried. I guess her mom's been after her about it."

"She can't marry Andrew." Just the thought of it makes me feel sick to my stomach. The three helpings of prime rib with all the fixings don't help either. "It doesn't seem like she even likes him."

"That's what I'm saying, man." Aiden gives my shoulder a little squeeze. "Talk to her. You might not get to be with her, but maybe hearing she has other options will get her away from that guy before something bad happens. If we all feel the same way about him, it means something."

"He probably has a few bodies in his freezer or something." I laugh bitterly. It's supposed to be a joke, but Andrew is so creepy it wouldn't surprise me if he had bodies hidden somewhere.

On my drive home after dinner, I find myself parking in front of the liquor store. I'm not brave enough to go talk to Denise, but I also can't think about her with Andrew. A bottle of vodka sounds like good company for the night.

When I get home, I head straight to the couch with my vodka. Why dirty a glass? I drink straight from the bottle while I search for something to watch on Netflix, but nothing gets my interest, so I turn off the TV. It's totally normal to sit in the dark and drink alone, right?

No wonder the guys think I have a problem.

If I'm being honest with myself, I do have a problem, and it's gotten progressively worse the longer Denise has been with Andrew. That guy is so wrong for her, but she doesn't see it.

Not that I'm a better choice, no matter how I feel about her. I'm such a fuckup that even if I got her to go out with me, she'd leave me, eventually. It wouldn't be the first time.

My brother and I were kids when my mom left. I was six, and Hunter was three. I was hiding behind the couch when she came downstairs with a suitcase and told my dad she was leaving. Had I not been so curious, I wouldn't have heard what she told him as she walked out the door.

"I love you, Tom," she told my dad, "But I can't do this with those kids anymore. I never wanted them, and I still don't. I can't be their mother. I won't put off my life any longer because you wanted children. Goodbye. Don't look for me." And then she left.

She left because of us, me and my brother. Luckily my brother hadn't heard what she said, and he was too young to remember if he had. And I never told him about it. Even at six years old, I knew that would hurt him too much. I didn't even tell my dad I'd heard it. He told us she had to go take care of her sick sister. Even after the way she left us, he didn't want us thinking badly of her. But I never forgot what she said. I never forgot that when she left, she left us kids not my dad. Who abandons a child?

I had a few girlfriends when I was younger, but I always dumped them before they could dump me. After a while, I stopped dating and stuck to casual sex instead. Seemed to be an easier way to go about it. I never had to worry about anyone leaving because it would never be more than one night, anyway.

And then I met Denise. When she walked up to me and the guys after a show we played at a friend's house party, I was instantly attracted to her. Her ice-blue eyes looked right through me, like I didn't even exist, and the need to make her acknowledge me consumed me. Even back then, she wore a flower in her long black hair, pin-up girl style, and had a take charge attitude. Before she even started talking, I decided I would take her home that night to see what was under her wiggle dress and whether her take charge attitude transferred to the bedroom.

Obviously, that didn't happen.

She told us, "You guys have a great sound, but you won't get anywhere playing house parties. I'm going to represent you. I'll get you better gigs and together we'll take this thing to the next level." She was twenty-one then, and she had balls of steel. After that speech, I knew I'd never be happy with just one night. If I took her home, I'd never be able to get enough. And that was too risky for me.

I tried to convince the guys we didn't need her. And like an asshole, I did it right in front of her. Thankfully, the guys convinced me she was right. She'd had no clients before, but we took a chance on her, like she took a chance on us, and now here we are. Next level, exactly like she said. The price has been my never-ending heartache, because I've been in love with her since that day. A bargain, really, considering all she's done for the band.

So now I'm sitting here again, drinking by myself, wondering what it would be like if Denise actually loved me back. But I know she doesn't. I've done enough stupid shit in the last fifteen years to ensure she would never take a chance on me now. Instead, I get to sit here alone, drinking a toast to her happiness with Andrew, even though it means I will never get a chance.

Fucking Cheers.

2

Breakups and Barfing

Denise

AFTER ANDREW WHISPERED IN my ear during family dinner at Alex and Connor's place, again, I wasn't all that interested in having him come in and 'keep me well occupied', as he hinted to Ryder earlier. He's never made much of an effort with my friends at all, and it's really starting to bother me. Every time he leans over to whisper in my ear, my skin crawls. I have asked him to stop doing it and to say what he wants to say, but he continues with the whispering. It probably has something to do with how he's always trying to get us to leave places early, or saying something rude about one of my friends. But it's fucking annoying.

"Okay, goodnight," I tell him as I practically leap out of his vehicle. I don't even lean in for a kiss first, which gets an irritated huff from him.

"No kiss?" He pins me with a suspicious look. "Is this about Ryder?"

What the hell? Why would that even be a question?

"No, of course not." I lean in the door. "It's about you whispering in my ear again and insisting we leave before I was ready."

"Your clients are... unsavory." The look of disgust on his face leads me to believe unsavory was the nicest way he could put it. "They're not the type of people I would normally associate with, and I don't think you should, either. They're honestly kind of trashy, Denise."

Well, that's news to me. He's never really gotten along with them, but this is the first time he's ever expressed this kind of distaste.

"Are you fucking serious right now?" I'm barely able to keep my voice down, but I continue quietly so I don't disturb my neighbours. "They are my friends, and they are all good people. There is nothing trashy about them."

He snorts out a laugh. "Oh come on now, Denise. They're musicians. They drink, they smoke, they're all tattooed and pierced. If they weren't wealthy, they would be the definition of trashy. Associating with them makes me look bad. If any of my accounting clients ever saw me with them, I'm sure they would drop me in a minute."

"How did I not notice how stuck up you are?" I huff in disbelief. "How did you ever bring yourself to lower your standards enough to get together with me, I wonder?"

"I didn't lower them necessarily. I always saw your potential. But I was hoping you would change the way you dress, at least when we are together. Your parents are nice upper-class people, Denise. When they introduced us, they assured me you would eventually settle down, become more like them. I understand you dress the way you do because of your job, but you can't honestly think old band t-shirts are the most professional item to be paired with skirts? Or that those shoes you wear are the most feminine you could choose? They look like they belong in a dominatrix's closet."

I'm completely floored. I didn't know he hated the way I dress. I like to consider my look to be rocker-chick-meets-pin-up-girl with a little extra edge. And I love the way I dress. Even if my shoes do look like they belong to a dominatrix. Actually, it's probably at least partly because my shoes could belong to a dominatrix that I love them so much. They are heels, though, and people usually consider heels to be feminine.

"My shoes? Do you mean the heels I wear all the time? How are heels not feminine?"

"You know what I mean. They're so... *rock-and-roll* looking. Big, flashy, sometimes they even have metal bits on them. Women should be dainty. Submissive. You always look like you're daring someone to take you on."

I stare at him, eyes wide, mouth gaping in surprise. This is not the man I thought I was involved with, not at all. And right now I almost feel like daring *him* to take me on.

"Yeah... I'm going to go inside now. I'll talk to you later sometime. I think I need some time to think all this over." Before he can say anything, I slam the car door and run up the stairs to my house.

As I grab my keys from my purse, I hear him yelling my name from the open car window, but I refuse to turn around. Instead, I unlock the door, go inside, and lock it again right behind me. I was serious about needing time, but I'm pretty sure I've already made my decision. He thinks my friends are trashy, doesn't like the type of people I work with, hates the way I dress, and is rude to the people I care about. The only thing I need time for is packing up the few things he has at my place and thinking about how to word the break up.

I refuse to stay with someone who likes nothing about me. The last thing I need is someone trying to tell me who to spend time with and how to dress. Thank you very much. My parents did enough of that when I was growing up. I'm a grown ass woman and I can take care of those things my damn self. I should have known better than to agree to go out with someone my parents set me up with, I guess. Even after all these years, they're still trying to turn me into Debutante Barbie.

Once inside the house, I get changed into some comfy joggers and a loose tank, ready to get to work packing up Andrew's stuff. I have no patience for a man who has been with me for almost a year, hoping I would change myself the entire time.

I'm nobody's renovation project.

Andrew has very few belongings here and before long, I have one small box of stuff all packed up for him. I'll call him tomorrow to come over so I can break it off with him and he can take his stuff when he goes. No sense in prolonging the inevitable.

I'm starving since I didn't get to eat much at Connor and Alex's place. My fork tasted like it had soap or something on it, so I barely ate three whole bites before Andrew wanted to leave. I fix myself a cup of tea, grab a snack, and get settled in to watch something on TV. After far too long scrolling through my choices on Netflix, I settle on *The Dirt*. Nothing like a little Mötley Crüe debauchery to remind me how good I have it with my boys. Now anyway.

Sleeping Dogs went through a bit of a hard partying phase in the first few years, but it was never outrageous. The worst thing I can remember is walking in on Ryder fucking a groupie in the women's bathroom at Rough Mix, in the early days. It had to have been one of the first few times I'd ever booked them there. And it was a blessing in disguise, seeing Ryder bending a girl over the sink. Up to that point, I had more than a little crush on him.

It took longer than I'd like to admit getting over that heartbreak. Andrew was the first actual boyfriend I had since I'd realized Ryder would never settle down, and if he ever did, it definitely wouldn't be with me. I spent almost fifteen years throwing myself into my work, making Sleeping Dogs the sensation they are today, and trying to deny the feelings I had for Ryder. I know I'm not the one responsible for their talent, but

I got them in front of the right people and booked them into the right venues. That counts for something.

Fifteen years turning myself into the person I am now, a person who I love everything about, and the first guy I take a chance on doesn't even like me, apparently. I'm not normally one of those people who says fuck my life, but... fuck my life.

I stay up and watch *The Dirt* for a little before deciding to turn in for the night. I'll need a good night's sleep to deal with Andrew tomorrow and I haven't been feeling well for the last little while. Probably from working too hard. I usually wind up sick at the end of a tour and this illness feels like it's been coming since then. I'm not looking forward to the conversation with Andrew, but I refuse to stay with someone whose feelings for me depend on me changing who I am and how I dress.

WHEN I WAKE UP in my bed, it feels like only a few minutes later, but a glance at my phone tells me it's already after nine in the morning. I slept for over ten hours, but I still feel like I haven't slept at all. I must be getting sick.

I am a firm believer in the concept of eating the frog, getting the worst tasks completed first, so I text Andrew to come over. Might as well get the shittiest part of my day over with as early as possible, so I can move on to something better. Like watching the rest of my movie from last night. Or buying more dominatrix shoes.

Denise- Come over as soon as you can. We need to talk.

There, short and sweet. Well, not exactly sweet, more like short and to the point. He must have been waiting for my message, because he texts me back almost immediately.

Andrew- on my way

He'll take at least twenty minutes to get here, so I drag myself to the bathroom to have a quick shower before he arrives. I'm midway through shampooing my hair before my stomach roils with the sudden, unavoidable need to vomit. I jump out of the shower and throw myself to my knees on the bathmat where I spend the next few minutes naked, dripping sudsy water, and throwing up into the toilet.

I guess that settles it then. I'm not *getting* sick, I *am* sick.

I flush and quickly rinse my hair in the shower, forgoing conditioner, opting instead to dry off and dress in my comfiest joggers and a big Sleeping Dogs t-shirt from the last tour. Andrew is sure to be thrilled with this attire if he hates my skirts and band tees so much. There's nothing feminine about these baggy sweatpants and this oversized t-shirt.

The doorbell rings, announcing Andrew's arrival, right as I'm emptying my bathroom garbage can to bring to the living room in case I feel an overwhelming need to vomit again. I carry it with me when I go to let Andrew in.

"Hey," I mutter, turning and heading back to the couch. "Come sit. I'm sick so not too close." That's convenient too, since I have no interest in being close to him, anyway.

"Oh, okay," he says while lowering himself into the armchair opposite the couch.

"So I'm going to say this. We need to break up." It's then I feel my mouth filling with liquid, telling me I'm about to throw up.

Good thing I brought my trusty trash can. I grab it off the floor and forcefully vomit up the rest of last night's snack.

"What? Why?" Andrew seems surprised, which doesn't make much sense to me after last night. He had to have been able to tell how unimpressed I was with his behavior. Plus, in my mind, this has been a long time coming. I probably wouldn't have been able to deal with his rude whispering for too much longer.

I grab a tissue from the box on the coffee table and wipe my mouth. "Really? You have no idea why—" but before I can finish my sentence I'm throwing up again, and Andrew takes that as his cue to leave.

"I'll call you later to talk about this," he says as he walks toward the door. "I don't think this is the right time to be having this conversation. You obviously have other things going on." And then he's walking out, slamming the door behind him.

"What a dick," I mutter into my trash can. "Didn't accept my breakup and then didn't even offer to help me when I am clearly sick."

I lie back and settle in for what I'm assuming will be a long day of throwing up when the doorbell rings again. I lean forward to get up, but it sets me on another round of vomiting. Whoever is at the door knocks and then opens it. I guess Andrew didn't bother locking it.

"Hello? Anybody home?"

Ugh, what the hell is Ryder doing here? Like I don't have enough to worry about today. He better not be here to tell me he got himself into some kind of trouble again.

3

Couches and Comfort

Ryder

I WALK INTO DENISE'S place to find her bent over on the couch with her head in a bucket. She looks up at me for a second, and she seems like she's about to say something, but then she's got her head back in the bucket, hair hanging dangerously close to the splash zone, the sounds of retching replacing the greeting she was about to offer me.

"Holy shit. Are you okay?" I walk over and look around on the coffee table before I find what I'm looking for. I grab the hair elastic and pull her hair up onto the top of her head before tying it into a weird ponytail/bun thing. Good thing I used to have long hair and know my way around a hair tie.

"Thanks," she mumbles. "Can you pass me a tissue?" She gestures to the box on the coffee table.

I grab a tissue and wipe her mouth for her. "Can I get you something? Ginger ale? Crackers? Advil?" She must be hungover from whatever she and Andrew drank after they came back here last night. "How much did you drink last night?"

"Ha!" She laughs a little. "Nothing to drink, plain old sick. I think it's a delayed version of my typical post tour illness. It's been threatening since we got home and I guess it's decided that now is the right time. And yeah, a ginger ale would be amazing. There's some in the fridge I think."

I go into the kitchen and grab her ginger ale, along with a cup of ice and a few crackers on a plate.

"Here you go," I say, putting all the items onto the coffee table. "Want me to put something on TV for you?"

"Sure," she says. "I was watching *The Dirt* last night before I went to bed. Maybe put that on so I can watch the rest of it."

"Oh, *The Dirt*, hey? Got a thing for salacious rock star stories?" I tease while turning it on like she asked. "Can we start at the beginning? I haven't seen it yet."

"Um, sure, I guess so." She sounds a little confused, but maybe that's because she's talking into a bucket. It makes her voice sound a little strange. Like Darth Vader, but without all the heavy breathing.

I lean back on the couch and start the movie over at the beginning.

"Want me to rub your back a little? My dad used to do it when I was sick as a kid and it always helped me to feel better." It's probably not the best idea, considering the reason I came over in the first place was to confess my love for her, but I should be able to control myself. The puke bucket isn't exactly doing it for me. Vomit never has been one of my kinks.

She looks up at me, an unspoken question in her eyes. She probably wants me nowhere near her. I know she thinks I'm a man whore, even though it's been years since I behaved that way. I suppose all the partying would lead someone to believe I was still sleeping around, though, so it's not like I can blame her for thinking that. Especially since it's not exactly like I discourage it.

I take a deep breath, about to let her off the hook before she has to make up a reason for me not to touch her, when she answers.

"That would be nice, actually. Thanks Ryder." She turns and looks at the screen. Stunned, I reach over, and start rubbing her back in soft circles. After all these years dreaming about Denise, I can't believe I'm finally touching her. Sure, I'm rubbing her back because she feels sick, but still. I'm touching Denise!

She makes a little moan of appreciation which does things to my downstairs, leaving me trying to adjust myself discreetly. I guess the puke bucket isn't as much of a deterrent as I thought. I don't stop rubbing her back, though. I've never had the chance to be this close before, and I'm not about to fuck it up now. I'll rub her back until my arm falls off, if that's the way I get to keep touching her.

"So why did you come over?" Denise twists to look at me, holding her bucket tightly. "You didn't do something dumb last night that I'm going to have to deal with, did you?"

"No, not this time." I laugh. "I actually went home last night." And drank an entire bottle of vodka by myself in the dark, but I'm not about to tell her that. I was coming to tell her how I feel, but I can't bring myself to do it. She's sick. It's not the right time. "So where's Andrew this morning? Why isn't he here taking care of you?"

"Oh, yeah... It's fine. You don't have to stay." She sounds disappointed. "I'll be okay on my own."

"Oh, no. I don't mind being here for you at all." There's nowhere I'd rather be, actually. "I figured he'd want to be here taking care of his sick girlfriend, is all. He probably wouldn't appreciate me doing it in his place, anyway."

She laughs a little. "He was here this morning before you got here, actually." She takes a small sip of her ginger ale before continuing. "We had a fight last night, and I had him come over this morning so I could break up with him."

WHAT? This is the best news I've heard in ages. I barely stop myself from jumping up off the couch and pumping my fist in the air a la John Bender at the end of the *Breakfast Club* movie.

"Are you okay?" I try not to sound as excited as I feel. "What happened? You guys have been together for what, a year?"

"Ugh. I can't believe I wasted a whole year with him." She puts her bucket down and leans back, effectively forcing my arm around her. Not that I'm not complaining. "I'm sure you've noticed all of his stupid whispering when we're all together?"

I have noticed that. We all have. I nod, encouraging her to continue.

"Well, he does it when he wants to leave early. Which is apparently all the time, because he has issues who I spend my time with."

I probably could have guessed that. The guy always seemed a little straight laced for the rest of us. Not a tattoo or piercing in sight. Hell, the guy could barely dress casually, always looking like he's about to run off to a meeting at the office or go golfing with his lawyer or teach math to middle schoolers.

"Not only that," she adds, "he also doesn't like the way I dress. Get this. He says it's not *feminine* enough."

"What?" That surprises me. "You wear skirts and heels pretty much every day. How much more feminine can you get?" I hope she doesn't catch on that I notice what she wears every day. More than noticed, I actually have favorite outfits. I could probably list off five different pairs of shoes that give me a semi every time she has them on.

"That's what I said. But apparently the heels aren't a feminine style, and pairing skirts with band tees isn't professional. He basically thinks I look 'too rock-and-roll'." She makes air quotes with her fingers.

"Too rock-and-roll?" I have to laugh. "He knows you manage a rock band, right? How else would you dress?"

"I honestly don't know." She sighs. "But I like how I dress now. I'm not changing myself for him."

"Good for you; you're perfect. You don't need to change for anyone. And for what it's worth, I love the way you dress. You always look amazing." This might be a bit much for this conversation, but I need her to know how great she looks when she wears what she likes. "You should change the way you dress because *you* want to. Not because Andrew is looking for something... different. If he wants you to change so badly, then maybe it's not you he really wants."

"Yeah, that's kind of what I was thinking, too." She looks over at me, turning her body in my direction. "I feel so stupid for wasting so much time on him, you know? I'm not exactly getting any younger."

I must have a look of shock on my face because Denise laughs and adds, "I'm thirty-six. That's not young, especially since I'm a woman."

"That's not old, Denise. And even if it were, what does it matter? You have a good life, right? With a job you enjoy, and friends who love you." Some of us a little more than others, but I can't tell her that now. "Everything will fall into place when it's meant to. Hell, look at Connor and Alex."

"Yeah, I guess." She frowns. "I guess I always thought I'd be married and have kids by now..."

Oh, it all makes sense now. I pull her towards me and put my arm around her again.

"Women are having kids older these days. You still have lots of time. Don't worry about that. For now, focus on feeling better. Things will look different when your stomach isn't trying to empty itself every few minutes."

She snuggles in closer to me and rests her head on my shoulder.

"Yeah, you're right. Let's watch the rest of the movie."

I'm not about to ruin this moment, so I keep my mouth shut and nod. I've dreamt of sitting here like this with her countless times. Okay, my dreams featured a lot less vomit, but still. My heart feels like it's about to hop out of my chest and run into the kitchen for a snack. I won't tell her how I feel right now, but after a little time has passed, I will. I can't take the chance she'll find another Andrew, or another anyone, for that matter. I've tried to get her out of my head for years and it hasn't ever worked. It's long past time for me to come clean. I hope I haven't ruined my chances already by being such a fuck-up for the last fifteen years.

4

Shirts Off, Flirts On

Denise

I MISSED THE END of the movie again because I fell asleep against Ryder. He must've fallen asleep too because at some point we wound up laying down on the couch together. I wake up lying partly on top of him with my head on his chest and my leg thrown over both of his. I also have my arm wrapped around him like I'm holding on for dear life, which I'm not, because I'm tucked snugly in between him and the back of the couch. This moment makes all the extra money I spent buying this ridiculously over sized couch worth it.

"Hey, Ryder." I lift my head to look at him and whisper, "Wake up. We must've drifted off."

"Hmmmm, what?" he mumbles, sounding half asleep still. He wraps both arms around me and pulls me against his chest, reaching a hand up to press my head back down. "Shhhh, five more minutes."

A yawn forces its way out of my throat and I realize I can't argue with that. More than that, I don't want to argue with it. I'm more comfortable than I've been in a long time. That, and all the throwing up I did took a lot out of me. Five more minutes would be heaven.

Closing my eyes, I imagine what it would be like if Ryder were sweet like this all the time. He's been so good to me today, and there are worse things to be doing than sleeping pressed up against his hard body. I'm not sure what he's been up to lately, but I can appreciate the increased muscle mass that's come along with it. He's always been sexy to me, but now he's even more so. I squeeze him a little again, letting my hand slide up under the bottom of his shirt slightly, enjoying the feel of his skin against mine. All these years I've dreamed of Ryder, and lying here with him is so much better than anything I ever imagined.

By the time we wake up again, it's mid-afternoon and I'm starving. My stomach is no longer protesting the thought of food, so I take that as a sign I'm feeling better.

Ryder is playing with my hair, twirling the loose strands around his fingers, and it feels amazing. I lie here pretending to still be asleep because I'm not ready for it to stop. Once he knows I'm awake, we'll sit up and move apart and we'll go back to how we were before. Friends. And coworkers. Him, the fun-loving party-boy, and me, the serious adult who bails him out of trouble. I don't feel bad about feigning sleep if I get sweet Ryder to myself for a few more minutes.

Too bad my stomach has other plans for me. It gurgles, then makes itself known with a loud rumble.

"Shit," I whisper.

Ryder chuckles a little. "I thought you might be awake." He surprises me by not letting me go right away. And I gotta say, I like it. I like it even more when he places a gentle kiss on my head before slowly sliding us both up into a sitting position. "I can't remember the last time I slept so well."

"Yeah, me neither." Holy shit! Ryder kissed me. It was on the top of my head, but still. My stomach flip-flops, but it's butterflies this time. I don't feel sick anymore at all. I lean back and look at Ryder. When I notice his shirt I cringe a little. "Ugh, Ryder? I'm so sorry. I totally drooled all over your shirt."

He looks down at the large wet spot right where I'd been resting my head on his chest. He laughs. "It's fine. It'll dry."

"Um, yeah. Maybe you'd better let me wash it? I was throwing up before I leaked saliva all over you, remember? You're drenched in watered down vomit."

An exaggerated look of horror crosses his face before he laughs and quickly reaches behind his head, pulling his shirt off in one quick motion. "I forgot about that," he says, while holding onto his shirt. "Tell me where the washing machine is and I'll throw this in."

I reach out and take the shirt from him while already walking away to empty my bucket. I'm not letting him wash it, not after I'm the one who drooled all over him. "I need to do a load, anyway. It's no trouble." Before he can protest anymore, I get up and walk through the kitchen into the laundry room. I wasn't lying about having a load of laundry to do. I probably have several, actually. I wait as long as possible to wash clothes because it's my least favourite household chore. I throw Ryder's t-shirt in with an armload of assorted casual clothes, add some soap, and start the machine.

"All started," I call out as I walk out into the kitchen. "Shouldn't be too—" My mouth drops open and I stop dead at the sight of Ryder standing in my kitchen, shirtless, his jeans hanging low on his hips. Holy shit, since when does Ryder look like that? He's got muscles on top of muscles and I swear my face is on fire from looking at him. He even has a sexy V pointing into the front of his pants. I don't think my brain is working right because my mouth is moving, but no words are coming out. Not to mention, there's a suspicious heat flooding my panties. I'd fan myself if I could do it without him noticing. That's not likely, though, considering he's looking right at me.

"How about you go grab a shower and I'll order us something to eat?" he finally asks, a smirk on his face. I'm sure he noticed me ogling him. How could he not? I wasn't exactly being subtle about it. My eyes damn near popped right out of my head, for crying out loud. "What do you feel like?"

My stomach rumbles loudly, shaking me out of my half-naked-Ryder induced stupor. He laughs at the noise it makes.

"Whatever will get here the fastest?" I laugh. "I think my stomach is threatening to eat itself if I don't get some food into it ASAP."

"You got it, babe." Babe? What is happening right now? The temperature of my face kicks up a few notches. Maybe I have progressed to the fever part of this illness? "Go get cleaned up and food should be here by the time you're done." He looks at me with a small smirk. "But don't take too long or I'll have to come in there after you."

My mouth opens and closes a few times, trying to make words happen, but I have nothing to say. Maybe I should test how long is too long, to see if he follows through with his threat?

Suddenly, an inexplicable surge of confidence floods my body. "I like to take long showers," I say with a wink as I walk past him on my way to the bathroom. "I'll leave the door unlocked."

This time he's the one left with his mouth hanging open. Good. Two can play that game.

5

Sustenance and Secrets

Ryder

SHIT. SHE CALLED MY bluff. I was messing around, saying I would come into the shower to get her. Why'd she have to say she'd leave the door unlocked? She can't be serious.

Can she?

My dick definitely hopes she's serious. With the way it's sucking up all my blood flow, I'm surprised I can think at all. Better to focus on ordering the food than to keep thinking about her naked in the shower. Water running over her skin, cascading over her perfect tits—Fuck! *Get it together, Ryder.* She's still not feeling well. Now is not the time to be fantasizing.

I go back to the living room to grab my phone so I can order something to eat. I'm not going to actually get into the shower with her, but I might try to snuggle with her on the couch a little more. I still can't believe I was lucky enough to get to hold her while she slept. She seemed so peaceful. I lied about how good my sleep was; I spent most of my time watching her. Even when my arm fell asleep under her, I didn't move. I didn't know when I would, or *if* I ever would, get another chance to lie with her like this, so there's now way I'll cut it short for anything. It was definitely nice when she woke up but pretended to still be asleep, though. Or when she went back to sleep because I asked for five more minutes.

My phone is on the coffee table where I left it. I pull up the food ordering app and decide on soup and sandwiches. This way, if Denise feels sick again, at least she'll have something easy on her stomach to eat. Probably be a lot easier to eat soup than a big burger or pizza if she has a stomach flu. While I'm at it, I order her some Gatorade too. It seemed like she'd been throwing up for a while this morning, if how tired she was is any sign, and the electrolytes will do her good.

Look at me being so thoughtful. I ought to get a boyfriend of the year award. I'm not exactly her boyfriend, though, am I? With that sobering thought for company, I sit on the couch and feel sorry for myself while looking around at Denise's townhouse.

She has interesting tastes in decorating. Lots of horror movie posters in fancy frames. And she has what looks to be an impressive collection of skulls in assorted shapes, sizes, and colors displayed in a china cabinet, of all things. The cabinet is matte black, and the color, combined with the ornately carved legs and doors, gives it a dark, Gothic look. It's interesting because I'd never really peg Denise as a fan of horror or scary things. Then again, I've never been in her townhouse for long, so this is my first chance to get a good look at what she likes to surround herself with.

Getting up and moving to a small room off the living room, I notice she has a home office set up in there. She does most of her work from home or on the road, so it makes sense she would have an office.

Continuing my tour of her house, I notice that besides the horror movie posters, she also has lots of small pictures in tiny frames. Some square, some round, some oval, all ranging in size from a few inches to around eleven inches. Looking closely, I can see they're little pictures made of threads, like embroidery or cross-stitch, or some other sort of grandma craft. Except these are nothing like any grandma I've ever met would make. I mean, my Gran totally *would*, I don't think she knows how. There are skeletons, skulls, conjoined twins, anatomically correct hearts, something resembling a head in a jar, and so many more. It's like an old-fashioned circus of oddities is forever memorialized in string and placed on her walls.

Past the living room is a short hallway leading to the stairs. Under the stairs, I find a small half bath which I stop to make use of. Checking myself out in the mirror, I find myself glad for my trips to Pops' gym. My muscle definition is coming along nicely, and Denise definitely noticed. She noticed, and she liked it. Maybe it's a good thing she drooled on me in her sleep. I'm not actually grossed out like I pretended to be earlier. It seemed like a good chance to be half naked around her so I could show off my hard-earned body. I'm not making a move right now, but it can't hurt if she has me in her mind, right? And I know for a fact I look better without a shirt on than Andrew. He's more of the dad-bod kind of guy. Not that there's anything wrong with that, but Denise was definitely interested in what I was showing her earlier. I'm not complaining about getting to show it to her for a little while longer yet, while we wait for the laundry.

After I finish checking myself out and using the toilet, I flush and wash my hands quickly. A sudden scream from upstairs breaks through the silence of the house. Something is wrong and Denise is screaming. I run out of the half bath and straight up the stairs. The first door I try is the bathroom, and it swings open. It's a good thing she left it unlocked, after all.

"Denise," I call out as I open the door, "are you okay? I heard a scream."

She has one of those glass encased shower stalls separate from the bathtub, and through the glass doors *I. See. Everything.* I stop in my tracks and can't move.

"Hot!" she yells, pointing to the opposite end of the shower, where the handle is located.. "It's so hot. Turn it off. Just turn it off, please."

Oh shit, this must be an older building. When I flushed the toilet and washed my hands downstairs, I changed the water temperature in her shower. Besides noticing how gorgeous her body is, I see she's standing as far away from the spray of water as is possible in the enclosed space. She's burning in there, and it's my fault. I open the shower door and reach in to turn the water off for her.

"Shit! I'm so sorry Denise. I wasn't thinking, and I used the bathroom downstairs. Are you okay? I didn't mean to..." I trail off and I can't help myself. I look at her and I can't look away. She's not even trying to cover herself from sight. She's so confident, and it is such a turn on.

"Are you going to stand there and stare, or can you pass me a towel?" she asks as she stretches a hand out to me. "I was almost done. I was enjoying the heat. Before it became like lava, anyway."

Or was she waiting for me, I wonder?

Shaking my head to clear the nudity induced stupor, I look around until I find her towel hanging on the back of the bathroom door. I grab it and stretch my arm to give it to her, but I still can't seem to avert my gaze. Just like with her sleeping on me earlier, I sort of want to commit this sight to memory in case I never get to see it again.

"Thanks," she says, taking the towel from my hand and wrapping it around her body. She steps out of the shower stall and onto the bathmat beside it, causing me to step back into the vanity behind me. She stands there, looking right at me, her impossibly blue eyes staring directly into me. I see a flicker of something, like interest maybe? But then the moment ends.

"I think I have it from here." She gestures to the door. "I'll be out in a few minutes."

"Oh, right. Yes. Sorry." I step out into the hallway. "And sorry again about almost burning your skin off. I wasn't thinking."

"It's fine. Not the first time it's happened." She smiles, letting me know she's really fine. "Don't worry about it. It's already forgotten."

I nod in acknowledgment and close the door behind me. I can't believe I saw her naked. This has the potential to be awkward, but I refuse to let that happen. I'm brainstorming ways to laugh it off while on my way down the stairs when the doorbell rings. Perfect timing. Food will provide the perfect distraction.

I bring everything into the kitchen and place it all on the counter. I portion the chicken noodle soup out into two bowls I found in the cupboard and put a sandwich on a plate for each of us. The sandwiches aren't anything crazy either, turkey and cheese, but it's a perfect comfort meal. The only way it would have been better is if I could have made it for her myself. We'll have to save the home-cooked meal for another time, though. If there is another time. This day has been so out of the ordinary, and so amazing, I'm treating it like a one-off and savoring every second.

"That smells delicious. I don't know if I've ever been this hungry before." Denise is walking into the kitchen, pulling her wet hair up into a bun on top of her head. She looks perfect, dressed in casual leggings and a loose tank. She's not wearing her usual full make-up either, and even though it's different, I love this look as much. I'd love to imagine this softer look is for me; that she's letting her guard down a little. She's always so tough and in control, it's nice being able to see her relax sometimes.

"Nothing too crazy," I tell her, pointing out the plates and bowls. "Turkey sandwiches and chicken noodle soup. I wasn't sure how your stomach would feel, and I didn't want you to push it with something heavier."

"That sounds perfect." She grabs half of one sandwich and takes a huge bite. "Want to try to watch the movie again?"

She wants me to stay! "Sure, I'd love to," I say, with what is probably a little too much excitement considering the look she gives, but whatever. She wants me here and I'm thrilled about it.

I grab both plates and one bowl, gesturing for her to grab the other bowl, and walk into the living room. After I put everything down on the coffee table, I run back to the kitchen and grab the Gatorade I got for Denise. Even if she doesn't keep any food down, I want to make sure she at least drinks that. I pour it into a glass with some ice and a straw and place it on the coffee table. I grab my soup as I sit beside her on the couch.

"What's this?" she asks as she grabs the drink. She's already started the movie over for us.

"It's Gatorade. You were throwing up for a while. I heard it's good to drink after you get sick, to balance your electrolytes. Or something like that anyway." She's staring at me now, and I feel a little embarrassed. I don't want her thinking I don't trust her to take care of herself. She's more than capable of looking after herself, but I wanted to be the one to take care of her this time.

"That's so unbelievably thoughtful." Her voice quavers. It's so slight, I'm not sure I actually heard it. I put my bowl down and look at her. Her eyes look shiny, and she's looking up at the ceiling like she's trying not to cry. "Thank you," she whispers.

"Hey, hey. It's okay." I take her plate and put it on the coffee table so I can pull her into a hug. "I wanted to make sure you were okay and comfortable. I don't want you to be sad."

"Oh, I'm not sad," she says, looking at me again. "No one has ever taken care of me like this. It's so nice."

"Not even your parents?" I know she grew up with both of her parents. "When you were sick as a kid?"

She shrugs. "My parents worked a lot. They were busy and had lots to do. When I got to be about nine years old, I stayed home alone when I was sick. They left me food I could heat in the microwave and I would lie on the couch and watch TV."

That's... so sad. Even though I only had my dad when I was a kid, he always took a day off work to stay home with us whenever my brother or I were sick. And we didn't have the money to spare for that. I can't imagine being a kid and having to stay home alone while sick.

"I'm sorry you had to do that," I tell her, handing her soup to her. "From now on, I am going to be your nanny when you're sick. Whenever you need to be taken care of, you call Nanny Ryder, and I will come and look after you until you feel better. Now eat up. You need to get some food in your belly."

She smiles as she takes a spoonful of soup. "You say that now, but when I'm calling you in the middle of the night interrupting one of your hook-ups, asking you to come look after me, you're going to be pissed."

I choke on my soup. "You don't have to worry about that."

"Oh?" she questions. "Yeah, I suppose you wouldn't answer in that case."

Fuck, I hate she thinks I'm still like that. It's not like I don't deserve it, though. The first few years after we met, I didn't want to be in love with her, and I did everything I could to distract myself from it. And by that I mean, I did every willing woman I could find. Here we are, fifteen years later, and I'm more in love than ever, so obviously *that* didn't work.

"No." It's time for me to come clean, which is hilarious. For who else would 'come clean' mean confessing to *not* sleeping with a bunch of random women? My life is nothing if not fucked up. I take a deep breath and begin. "I've been pretty much celibate for years. I put on a show, and let everyone think I take all these women home, but I usually send them home in a cab if we ever get to my place. They never even make it inside. More often than not, I leave them at the club, or bar, or wherever. I go home alone."

It's her turn to choke on her food now. She coughs a little more than I did, though, so I pat her on the back while I grab her a tissue. She dabs at her mouth once she has the coughing under control, but then she laughs. When she notices I don't join in, her smile drops.

"You're serious?" she asks. "You always have women around you. You're the playboy of the band. Everyone knows if a groupie wants one of the guys from Sleeping Dogs they should go for you because it's a sure thing."

"Yeah, and you'd be surprised at how tricky it is to keep up the charade. The ladies get pretty upset when the 'sure thing' turns out to be a 'no way'. Let's say I have a lot of respect for how women have to deal with men who don't want to hear the word no. I'm no saint; I've had a few hook-ups, but nowhere near as many as I've let everyone believe."

I've never been drugged like Connor was, but I've had a lot of women try to talk me into sleeping with them, or try to get started on me without my active participation. The groupie who was trying to get her mouth on me before the last show of our last tour comes to mind. It's really hard to maintain a playboy image when you're trying to say no in front of a bunch of other people. I was so glad when Connor stormed in and shut that whole thing down.

"I don't even know what to say to that, Ryder. We've all thought you sleep with every woman who offers." She looks thoughtful for a minute, then she grabs my hand and looks into my eyes. "I'm truly sorry, Ryder. You didn't deserve that."

"Of course I did." A sardonic laugh bursts out of me. "The first couple of years I *was* like that. And I let everyone keep believing it even after I lost interest in that life. It's my fault you all didn't know any different. I acted that way to ensure you all still kept believing it. But..."

"But what?"

"But I want it to stop now." I take a deep breath and let it out slowly. I wasn't planning on having this conversation now. In fact, I've tried to talk myself out of it more than once today already, but here we go. "I let everyone think that because I thought it would be best if you thought that, Denise. When we first met, I knew you were amazing, and I wanted you. But then you became the band's manager, and I knew it would be best if I stayed away, kept things professional. I was so young and dumb back then, I thought sleeping with other women would make me forget those feelings. But it didn't. I never forgot them."

She looks at me, mouth open wide, eyes open even wider; I don't even think she's breathing. She stares quietly for what must be an entire minute before I say something.

"Are you... are you okay?"

She shakes herself a little and stands up. Bending down, she picks up the trash can she was using earlier when she was throwing up. "I need to clean this," she says before scurrying away.

Well. That went about as well as I expected. Good job, Ryder.

6

A Little Friendly Advice

Denise

WHAT THE HELL WAS that? Did Ryder confess he had feelings for me? He said he had feelings for me way back when we first met, and if I heard correctly, he still has feelings for me now. And I ran away like a scared little kid when he told me. I spent all these years fighting back feelings for him, forcing myself to watch as he became the biggest man slut in the band so the feelings would leave. And for what? He wasn't even sleeping around most of that time? And he was doing it to hide his feelings for me? What is even going on right now?

Looking for answers, I call the one woman who knows both me and Ryder, who may be able to help.

I grab my phone and dial Alex's number, glad I saved it after she had to quit the chef's job. I guess it would have been hard to cook with a cast on. Thankfully, she answers after a few rings.

"Hi Denise, what's up?"

"Hi Alex, do you have a minute? I think I need some... advice? Or something?"

"I sure do. The guys are in the studio. How are you feeling? Ryder messaged me earlier to say he was hanging out at your place because you were super sick. And, you know, because of Andrew."

"Oh, yeah, I'm feeling much better, thanks." At least I won't need to tell anyone about Andrew; Ryder already took care of it for me. "That's not really what I want to talk about, though." I give her a brief rundown of my conversation with Ryder, and I don't think she's ever sounded happier.

"He finally told you! Yay! It's about time. I've been hinting at it since I met him. Maybe now he can stop drinking too much and acting like such an idiot. What did you say to him?"

"What do you mean, 'he can stop drinking too much and acting like an idiot'? Wait. Are you saying Ryder's been drinking so much because of me?" That's... I don't know *what* that is, but it leaves me with a weird feeling in the pit of my stomach.

"Oh, you know," she says, like it's common knowledge. *"He's been pining after you for so long, and he's watched you with Andrew all this time. I think he was drowning his sorrows or something. I'm not completely sure on that part. You'd have to ask him for the actual answer."*

"I didn't know," I say. "I thought he was sleeping with all those women this whole time. I never would have thought his behaviour had anything to do with me."

"Really? You never noticed every time you said you had a big date or something with Andrew, Ryder would do something stupid and you'd be called away?" Well shit. Now that I think about it, yeah, that did seem to happen a lot.

"But why wouldn't he say something? Why act like a jerk instead?"

"Well, see, I have this theory. I came up with it after years of having boyfriends who cheated on me and thought they could get away with it. Are you ready for it? Here it is: boys are dumb." I burst out laughing and she joins in. Once we've calmed down a little, she continues, *"But seriously, he had feelings for the manager of his band. His incredibly capable and effective manager who was actually getting results. He didn't want to risk that by making things awkward with you."*

"Ugh… it would have been easier if you'd let me think he's dumb. It's so much more confusing since his reason was a good one."

"Denise." Alex sounds serious now. *"It really doesn't matter if he was dumb or if he had a good reason. What matters is how you feel about him. This is not about what he wants and when he wants it. This is about you and what you want to do with this information."*

"Why are you making so much sense? I thought you were a chef, not a life coach." I chuckle. "I had feelings for him from the first time we met. But I thought he wanted to have a rock star life, which I found out today was really a distraction technique for him. And watching him with all these women over the years has been rough. I worked really hard to get over the crush I had on him, and get myself to a place where I wanted to try seriously dating. And we all know how that turned out."

"How did that turn out?" Alex asks.

"That was Andrew. Who has apparently been hoping I would change into a different person the entire time we were together."

"Wait. You never dated anyone seriously before Andrew?"

"Nope." I say, popping the 'P' a little at the end. "I had some flings and short-term things, but with my job, and travel, and with being around the guys all the time, it was really hard to find someone who was there for the right reasons. I had a few guys who wanted to use me to get into the industry, some who were Sleeping Dogs fanboys, and some who were too jealous to deal with me being around the band all the time."

"Well, that explains why Andrew appealed to you, I suppose. He is nothing like that at all. He's as far from rock-and-roll as you can get."

"Yeah, but it turns out even he wasn't around for the right reasons. My parents promised him I would change. I was some sort of fixer upper for him. Looking back, my parents probably set us up so he could fix me. They've always seen me as some sort of broken commodity. The Lathans aren't exactly proud of who their daughter is. They expected more return on their investment in a child, I suppose."

"Sounds to me like you have some thinking to do." Alex suggests. *"And I would recommend never taking your parents' recommendations for dates ever again. They have terrible taste in men."*

I laugh. They do have terrible taste in men. "You're right. Again. I need to think this all through for a bit. Thanks for the talk, though. You've opened my eyes to a few things I hadn't thought about."

"Anytime, call me. I'll talk to you soon, okay? Get some more rest."

"Okay, Alex. Bye."

I hang up my phone and wonder what to do now. I should go back downstairs and talk to Ryder; I sort of left him hanging after bolting when he said he had feelings for me. But I'm not ready to face him yet. I'm too tired to make sense of my own feelings, even though I've already had the best nap of my life today.

I pull back my blankets and crawl into my bed. I'll have a little nap here and go down and talk to Ryder after. He can watch the movie without interruption and I can get some rest and then we can get into it. Yeah, that's the best plan.

I turn onto my side and tuck my blanket up under my chin, already drifting off to sleep by the time I've made that decision.

Wisdom from the Elders

Ryder

I WAIT AROUND DENISE'S place for about an hour before deciding I should go. After cleaning the mess from our leftover dinner and making sure the living room and kitchen are in order, I look for a way to leave her a note. I find a pen and a notepad in a drawer and jot something down.

DENISE,

I'M SORRY I MADE
YOU UNCOMFORT-
ABLE. THAT WASN'T
WHAT I WANTED.
DON'T FEEL LIKE YOU
NEED TO SAY ANY-
THING TO ME ABOUT
IT. I WANTED TO TELL
YOU HOW I FELT BUT
MORE IMPORTANTLY,
I WANT US TO RE-

MAIN FRIENDS. AND I STILL EXPECT YOU TO ASK ME FOR HELP NEXT TIME YOU'RE SICK. NANNY RYDER IS A FRIENDSHIP SER-VICE, NOTHING MORE.

– RYDER

With that done, I find my keys and phone and get out of her place, locking the door behind me. It doesn't dawn on me until I'm outside that my shirt is still in her washing machine. I walk out to my car, shirtless, in the rain. This day can't get any worse.

No, that's not right. Most of this day was amazing. I had a great time with Denise until I opened my stupid mouth and told her about my feelings like an asshole. She'd broken up with her boyfriend before spending hours throwing up. Only I would think that was a great time to confess to liking her. Stupid.

Before I realize it, I'm leaving the liquor store, another bottle of vodka in my hand. It's a good thing they know me there, or they wouldn't have let me in without a shirt. I guess I know what I'm doing tonight. Again. One of these days I may need to investigate this drinking issue. But today is not that day.

Once home, I go inside and repeat last night's routine of looking for something to watch on TV before settling on sitting in the dark with my vodka. I probably should have gone to the studio instead. I'm sure the rest of the guys are still there, but right now I need to drink myself into oblivion and forget about how I scared Denise away.

I drink deeply from my bottle, ignoring the burn of the alcohol as it travels down my throat, and I look around my apartment. After seeing Denise's place, I realize how not lived in my apartment feels. The problem with that is I've lived here for years. I have no art, nothing making this space feel like it's mine. There's nothing other than leather furniture and a TV set up in the living room. My bedroom isn't much different, but instead of couches it has a bed and dressers.

Maybe that's something I can do, get my apartment to feel more like it's my own. If Denise ever talks to me again, I'm going to ask her where she got those embroidered pictures. I think it might be cool to have some of those. And tomorrow I can go check out some local art galleries and see if anything catches my eye. I could probably hire a decorator, but I'm not interested in getting my place into any magazines. I want to make it more comfortable to live in.

I'm sitting there thinking about what I can do to make this place a little more like a home when my phone buzzes in my pocket. I nearly drop my bottle trying to get to it, hoping it's Denise.

Nope, Connor.

Connor- Hey, are you busy two weeks from now, on Saturday?

I never have actual plans. What is he even bothering to ask for?

Ryder- Not busy. What do you need?

Connor- I need you to spend the day with Alex and Becca, keep her away from the house until 5 or so.

Ryder- Yeah, sure. What do you want me to do with them?

Connor- Becca is going to get in touch. You can figure it out with her. I have enough to plan.

Ryder- Oh? Gonna tell me what's up?

Connor- I'm proposing to Alex. You better not fucking tell her.

Ryder- Shit, congratulations man. Your secret is safe with me. I'll get it figured out.

Connor- Good. See you tomorrow?

Ryder- I'll be there

He doesn't respond again after that.

I put the lid back on my bottle and bring it to the freezer. If I promised to be there tomorrow, I should slow my drinking for tonight. Instead, I grab my laptop and order some new stuff for the apartment.

After browsing a bunch of different furniture and decor sites, I realize I am completely out of my element and give up. I ordered a couple of art prints I liked and a dining set, though. That has to count for something, considering I didn't even have a table before. I'm making progress. I grab the vodka from the freezer and take a deep drink in celebration.

After ordering myself some dinner, I settle in to finally watch something. I'm not having much luck concentrating on the screen, though. My mind is preoccupied with thoughts of Denise. It felt so right laying there with her while she slept. Even the teasing was fun. I'm kicking myself for messing it all up by telling her how I feel. I planned on waiting until she was feeling better. Why the fuck didn't I stick to my original plan?

The food arrives, and I still haven't settled on anything to watch, my mind too caught up in thoughts of Denise to concentrate. I wolf down my dinner and make a spur-of-the-moment decision to hit the gym. Grabbing my gym bag, I head out the door before I can talk myself out of it.

"Hey Pops, you miss me?" I yell as I walk through the door after a short drive. It's already almost eight p.m. but Pops pretty much lives here, so I'm sure he's around here somewhere.

"Hey, kid. What're you doing here this late? Don't you have some party to be at or something?" He's walking down the stairs from his office, which is an elevated space with a cage around it where he can look over the entire gym. I mean, he has a desk, so it is an office, but with chain link fencing instead of actual walls.

"It's a little too early for the good parties," I tell him as I walk over, "but I'm trying to cut back on that, anyway. Maybe Alex has been a good influence on me or something." I smile. Alex is Pops' granddaughter, and that's how I met him, even though Connor has been training with him for years.

"Good for you, son. Alex tells me how you've been a real good friend to her. She cares about you. I'm sure she's real proud to hear you're finally getting your shit together."

"Well geez, Pops, don't hold back or anything." I laugh while I clap him on the shoulder. "You got the energy for some training, or is it about your bedtime? I know old folks like you usually need to go to bed pretty early. Or did you have a nap in your chair after dinner?"

Pops bursts out laughing and punches me in the arm. "Yeah, yeah, you little shit. Get warmed up and get your gear on. I'll meet you in the ring when you're ready. I'ma give you a good beating for that comment."

I rub my arm where Pops hit me; for a seventy-five-year-old man, he still packs a hell of a punch. Hell, who am I kidding? He probably hits harder than I do and I'm thirty-four. "Them's fighting words, gramps. I won't hold back because you're practically mummified," I call out. "Don't blame me if there's nothing left of you but dust after this." I head into the locker room to change before he replies. Connor usually comes dressed to work out because, as the lead singer of Sleeping Dogs, he's the most recognizable member of the band. I'm the lead guitarist; so far I almost never get recognized. Unless I call attention to myself, anyway.

I strip down and get into my training gear, compression shorts with training shorts over top and a moisture wicking shirt, and my wrestling boots. Going back to the main part of the gym, I hit the treadmill for my warm up. Pops usually has me jumping rope, but I'm really feeling like I need a run tonight.

Twenty minutes, and a lot of running later, I join Pops in the ring. He's got my gloves for me and helps me strap them on, then gets his pads and we start my workout. He leads me through different punching combinations, focusing on that for the evening. I'm a mediocre fighter, but I usually do much better with my workouts than I'm doing tonight.

"Alright kid." Pops puts his hands down, showing me he wants to take a break. "What is your problem? It's like you're not even here tonight."

"I'm good, Pops, let's keep going." I punch my fists together a few times while I do a little boxers' shuffle, hopping from foot to foot.

"No way, kid. You're barely paying attention. If we kept going, I'd have to smack you in the head every time I caught you with your mind elsewhere. You'd wind up with a concussion. I can't have that on my conscience."

I sigh. There's not much point trying to hide stuff from Pops. He's got the kind of insightfulness that comes with age. My Gran is the same way.

"In my experience," he continues, "this kind of distraction only comes from love problems. So here's what's going to happen. You go shower, 'cause I can't stand the stink of you. Then you come up to my office and we'll sort this out."

"No really, Pops. I'm fi—"

"I don't want to hear it," he interrupts. "Shower, change, get your ass to my office. In that order. Now get!"

"Okay, okay." I do what he says. You can't hide stuff from Pops and you definitely can't argue with him.

My grandmother is wonderful and loving, not to mention hilarious, but I kind of wish I also had a grandfather like Pops in my life. My grandfather passed before I had the chance to meet him, though, so I adopted Pops as my own when Alex introduced us. It hasn't seemed to bother him yet and I don't plan on doing anything to mess it up.

I knock on the door of Pops' office, and then I walk right in.

"Alright son," Pops points at a chair opposite his, "sit, and tell me what's bugging you."

"Fine. But only because I want to keep coming around here and I'm worried you won't let me if I don't answer you."

"Oh good. So you're not as dumb as you look. Now stop stalling."

"Okay, let's cut it short, shall we? I have a thing for Denise, have had for years, and I told her today and she freaked out. I'm kicking myself now."

"Denise? That's the band's manager girl, right? The one who wears those super sexy high heels all the time? Doesn't she date that nerdy looking guy though?" That's right. I forgot Pops has been to a few of Alex's family dinners, so he's met Denise and Andrew before.

"She broke up with him." I say. "He apparently had issues with those sexy heels, along with a lot of other things. She said he made her feel like he'd never been interested. That he'd seen her as some kind of renovation project."

"Okay, so let me get this straight. You found out they broke up and then immediately told her how you feel?"

I spend few minutes explaining how the day went, starting with showing up to talk to her, finding out she was sick and that

Andrew wasn't there to take care of her because she dumped him, right through to the end where I confessed my feelings and she disappeared.

Pops is quiet for a minute before he says, "So you decided not to tell her, and then you told her anyway? You had a smart thought and then your dumb thoughts took over?"

I laugh. "That's one way to look at it, I guess. It felt so right laying there with her in my arms I think my brain short-circuited or something. I thought I needed to get it out there and it wasn't until I said it I realized what a huge fuck-up it was."

"Have you talked to Alex about this? She might have some insight. She's probably a more reliable source on the inner workings of the female mind than a seventy-five-year-old man is."

"Not yet. She knows I have feelings for Denise, but I haven't talked to her about today. You think I should?"

"I think you should talk to Alex and stay away from Denise for a bit. She dumped a loser who she thought she'd be with for a while. She needs to be on her own a little before she can even think about someone else."

"Fuck Pops, you're killing me." I know he's right, but I don't want to wait. I had a tiny taste of what being with Denise could be like and I know I can't give it up without feeling like absolute shit about it.

"Listen, what you do is up to you, but let me tell you one thing. If this girl means to you what I think she does, a few months of waiting won't change anything. You said you've been waiting years already. What's a little longer when it comes to love?" Pops looks to the side of his desk, where an old photograph of a beautiful young woman sits, and he takes a deep breath. "Love doesn't go away, no matter how long you wait."

We sit quietly for a few minutes. He's right, of course. I know he's never loved anyone other than his wife, even though it's been years since she died. And Connor and Alex didn't even see each other for twenty years, and they still loved each other when they met again. If Denise and I are meant to be, then waiting a little longer won't make a difference.

"You're right again, Pops," I say, startling him out of his thoughts. "But I'm sure you know that already." I smile at him as I stand up. "I'd better be going now if I want to make it to all of those wild Monday night parties." I give him a little wink at that last bit, making him chuckle.

"Alright, you little shit, get out of here. Come back and see me when you're ready to concentrate on your workout."

"Sounds good, Pops. Thanks for the chat." I wave as I leave his office and head down the stairs. Despite what I said earlier, I have no intention of hitting any parties tonight; I head straight home instead. I sat around with Pops for so long it's nearing eleven o'clock. That's a lot earlier than I would normally attempt to sleep, but I figure if I want to make a go of this 'getting my shit together' thing, that's as good a place to start as any.

The early bird gets the worm and all that shit, right?

8

Well, That Explains the Puking

Denise

I WAKE UP TO light pouring into my bedroom through the open curtains. I guess I didn't sleep long after all. I was so tired when I lay down after talking to Alex I assumed it would be dark by the time I woke up.

I suppose I'd better go down and see if Ryder is still here or not. Not that I know what I will say to him if he is here. I still don't know what I'm going to do about his confession of feelings for me. I had assumed that ship had sailed and I've worked hard to accept that nothing would ever happen between us. To find out now he's been feeling the same way all these years is a little too surreal.

I'm barely at the top of the stairs when the nausea overtakes me. I turn and run into the bathroom, barely making it to the toilet before I puke. What the fuck? I was feeling so good before my nap; I thought I was better. I guess not though, since I'm here puking again.

I'm sitting on the floor in front of the toilet, waiting for the nausea to subside, when I hear the doorbell. Shit, talk about bad timing. But I'm sick so whoever it is can wait or leave. They ring the bell a few more times before finally giving up. Good, I don't really want to deal with anyone today, anyway.

Just then, I hear my phone ring from where I left it in my bedroom. I have a feeling the person calling is the same person who was ringing my doorbell, so I force myself to get up. I grab the same trash can I used earlier, in case, and go grab the phone.

"Hello?" I didn't even look to see who was calling this time.

"It's Alex, I'm at your door. Come let me in. I brought breakfast," she says before hanging up without even giving me a chance to respond. I take my phone and my bucket and go answer the door.

"What do you mean, you brought breakfast?" I ask, finally cluing in to what she said on the phone. "It's too late for coffee." I say as I eye the tray of drinks she's carrying along with the bag of food. The smell of it is making me feel nauseated again, so I step back.

"Girl, what?" she says while she brings everything into the kitchen. "It's like ten in the morning. It's practically brunch time, but I figured mimosas weren't a good idea after you were so sick yesterday."

Ten in the morning? I look at the time on my phone. She's right, it is morning. That means I slept all evening and all night, for around sixteen hours, maybe more. I can't even remember if I got up to the go the bathroom.

"Holy shit," I say. "I knew I was tired after I talked to you, but I didn't think I was tired enough to sleep right through to today."

"You've been asleep since we got off the phone yesterday? I thought you said you were feeling better?" She pulls out breakfast sandwiches and bowls of fruit from the bag she brought. The sandwiches smell weird but the fruit bowls look amazing, so I grab one of those and start eating it.

"I thought I was feeling better too, but when I woke up now, I started throwing up again." I pick up my bucket from the floor beside me to show her. "I was throwing up when you rang the doorbell, so I had to bring a trash can in case of emergency."

She looks so thoughtful for a minute, I can almost hear the gears turning. Her eyes take me in. She looks me up and down before speaking.

"So you were sick when you woke up yesterday?"

"Yup," I say around a mouthful of pineapple. This fruit is so delicious I might have to eat the other bowl too.

"And you were sick this morning when you woke up?" She's waving her hand like she's hinting at something, but I'm in no mood for guessing games today. "And you haven't been feeling well for a while either, have you?"

"Yeah, why? What's your point?"

"Denise." She looks at me seriously and takes my fruit bowl and puts it on the counter. "You've been feeling off for a couple of months? You were sick. In the morning. Yesterday and today? Sick. Morning." She raises her eyebrows and opens her eyes wide while looking into my eyes. She shrugs a little, as if to say, 'get it?'

But I don't get it. And I want my fruit back.

"Alex, you better come out and say it," I tell her while I stuff a whole strawberry in my mouth. "I don't know what you're trying to say."

"Morning sickness, Denise. I think you're knocked up."

"What? You're insane. No, I am definitely not pregnant."

I think she would have been more likely to believe me if I hadn't chosen that exact moment to be sick again. I'm so glad I thought to bring the bucket down with me, otherwise I'd be throwing up right onto the counter.

"Yeah, sure babe," Alex says to me, then grabs her keys from the counter. "Tell you what, you sit here and relax. See if you can eat some more, and keep it down, and I'll run to the drugstore.

For a pregnancy test. For you. Because you seem pretty pregnant to me."

"Ugh, fine," I say, with my head still over the bucket. "But grab me an anti-nauseant while you're there. Because when we find out there's no baby, I'm going to need to stop throwing up so I can get back to work."

"You got it," she says, already on her way out the door. "I'll ask the pharmacist if it's okay for pregnant women to take before I buy it, though."

"I'm not pregnant!" I yell at the already closed door.

I finally broke up with Andrew. I can't be pregnant now, because that would seriously suck.

"WELL, SHIT." I'M LOOKING at two pink lines on the third pregnancy test I've taken since Alex came back from the drugstore. "I really am knocked up," I whisper to myself.

"Can I come in?" Alex says through the bathroom door.

I peed on the last stick and then waited for my result instead of going back to the kitchen like I did with the first two. Now Alex is as nervous about the result of this last test as I am. It's no surprise she's here at exactly the right time to see the result. I bet she set a timer on her phone.

"Yeah, come in."

"So?"

"You were right." I look at her, my eyes already filling with tears. "I'm going to have a baby."

"Oh," she says and sits down on the floor and puts an arm around me. "So now what?"

"I don't know," I say. This changes everything. "I have to tell Andrew."

"Yeah."

"And I probably should give him another chance?"

"Is that what you want?"

"I want my baby to have a dad. Andrew deserves to be involved in the kid's life. We broke up. Maybe I was too hasty? He never really tried to change me. And he came to family dinners at your place even though he's not a big fan. So he tried, right?"

Alex takes a deep breath and leans back against the bathtub. "I can't make this decision for you. And I can't even give you much advice. I had both of my parents until I was sixteen. Connor grew up with only his mom, but she is a whole different type of person than you. If anyone would know about being raised by a good single parent, it's Ryder. Maybe you can talk to him?"

I laugh through my tears. "Yeah, that would go over well. 'I know you told me you had feelings for me, but can you give me some advice now that I'm having someone else's baby?' I don't want him to know about this."

"Well, he's going to find out eventually, you know. He's not blind. And if he keeps paying as much attention to you as I know he has been, he's going to know well before you start to really show."

"Life really is a bitch. I thought Andrew was the one who could finally make me forget about Ryder. And he turned out to be so different from what I thought. Although I should have seen this coming, considering it was my parents who introduced us. And now Ryder says he has feelings for me and, boom, I'm pregnant with Andrew's kid. I feel like someone somewhere is laughing at me. I must have done something bad in a past life for this one to be so fucked up."

Alex laughs at me. "I know it seems like a lot right now, but I have a feeling this will turn out better than you could have hoped. From what the guys say, you are great at controlling everything around you, but I suspect maybe you need to let go of some control in this situation. You're going to need to find your inner flexibility for this to go smoothly."

"Ugh, you don't know me at all." I smile at her. "I don't have any inner flexibility."

She gives me a sad smile. "I'm pretty sure having a baby will change that real quick."

She wraps an arm around me, and I lean into the hug. I need the comfort right now.

What the hell am I going to do?

9

Sweet Stolen Moments

Ryder

"So, has anyone heard from Denise this week? Is she still sick?" It's family dinner Sunday at Alex and Connor's and I haven't heard from Denise since last week when I told her how I feel about her. I've sent a few texts, but she hasn't responded at all and I'm a little worried. I'm so close to going right to her place and checking on her, although I've been trying to give her some space since my confession.

Alex glances over at Connor before answering me. "Uh, yeah. She's still not feeling well. She might be sick for a while, from the sounds of it."

Damn it. She hasn't called me to look after her like I told her to. I don't like the thought of her having to look after herself when she's sick. I know she's more than capable, but I want to take care of her. If I hadn't screwed it up by telling her about my stupid feelings, I wonder if she would have taken me up on my offer?

"Have you been to see her, Alex?" I ask. "Does she need anything?"

"I think she's okay for now, Ryder. She said she'd try to make it for dinner today, though, so you probably can ask her your-self." Alex looks at me with a sad smile. She guessed how I felt about Denise back before I was on my best behaviour. Well,

Alex didn't know me when I was really bad, so all she's seen is a little partying. I'm practically reformed now, considering I drink mostly at home by myself. And I'm going to the gym too, so I'm pretty much a model citizen.

"Why are you so concerned anyway, man? You're not normally concerned with anything other than the next party and the next chick." Johnny laughs at me. Fucker.

"Hey Johnny? Shut up." Connor says in my defence. I can't even hide the look of shock on my face. When was the last time anyone defended me? "Ryder's been working on that, in case you haven't noticed, so leave him alone."

At that moment Devon and Travis walk in carrying pizza boxes.

"Dinner is served," Devon says, before placing the boxes onto the dining room table. He looks over at Connor. "Tino says you're still a sketchy fuck. Sorry, dude."

Everyone at the table bursts out laughing. Tino owns the place where we always get our pizza now, and he has also known Alex for years. When Connor was trying to track down Alex a couple of months ago, Tino saw him creeping around the neighbourhood. Then he decided Connor was a sketchy fuck because he'd gone into the pizza place and asked for her information. Tino is way too protective of Alex for that to go over well, and he's been calling Connor a sketchy fuck ever since.

We all think it's hilarious. Connor? Not so much. He's been trying to change Tino's mind with little to no success.

"What the fuck?" Connor looks over at Alex. "I thought you were going to talk to him for me?"

"I tried." Alex tries to suppress a laugh. "But he says he doesn't trust my judgment anymore since my boyfriend is such a sketchy fuck." A hysterical laugh breaks free from her mouth. Everyone else at the table joins in, all of us laughing at Connor's expense.

"What's so funny?" Denise asks from the entry to the dining room.

She's here. And that fucker, Andrew, is with her. What the hell?

"Oh. Hi, Denise." Alex stops laughing and greets her, glancing at me when she notices Andrew is with her. "We're teasing Connor because Tino at the pizza place still calls him a sketchy fuck."

"Ha! Classic." Denise chuckles a little, and Andrew doesn't even smile.

"Hi Andrew," I say. "Why are you here?"

"Ummm..." he doesn't say much before Denise interrupts.

"Ryder, can I talk to you in the kitchen for a second?" She widens her eyes and jerks her head toward the kitchen before leaving Andrew standing there and walking away.

"Have a seat, Andrew," Alex tells him while I get up and follow Denise into the kitchen. "Help yourself to some pizza. We have a wide variety. I'm sure there is something here that is up to your exacting standards."

I laugh as I move out of earshot. That was definitely a dig against Andrews' distaste for all of Denise's friends. She must've told Alex about it at some point.

What I really want to know is why that asshole is here? Denise seemed pretty confident she didn't need a boyfriend who viewed her as a renovation project. So what changed her mind?

"Ryder." Denise is standing on the far side of the kitchen, but she is still keeping her voice low. "Please don't get after Andrew tonight."

Denise is wearing a fucking flowy pink dress with low heels. Her makeup is soft, and she looks so different from her usual bad ass self. This must be the kind of look Andrew approves of. She looks beautiful, as always, but she doesn't look as comfortable as she usually does. And from what she told me the other day, I know she based this change on what Andrew wants.

I don't want to worry about keeping my voice down. "Let's talk outside," I say as I walk to the door. I open it and hold it for her as she walks through, stumbling a little on nothing.

"Fucking shoes," she mumbles.

"I'm sorry." Denise doesn't even wait for the door to close behind me before she begins. "I need you to be nice to Andrew. Try to forget he doesn't like you guys."

"I don't give a fuck what Andrew thinks of me, or anyone else in there." My voice comes out louder than intended, so it's a good thing we came outside. "I care what he thinks about you. I thought you dumped him? Because you realized it wasn't actually you he wanted? Isn't that what you told me the other day when I was at your place, taking care of you when you were sick?"

"It's important for me to give him another chance, Ryder. And it's not really your business, anyway."

"I'm your fucking friend, Denise." I run a hand through my hair. "And I think you know I want to be more than that." I know she felt something the other day, too. She let me hold her for hours while she slept, for fuck's sake. That has to mean something.

"You have no right to ask anything of me!" Her eyes flash with anger while she pokes me in the chest with her index finger. "I have watched you hook-up with countless women for *years*. Years that you did everything you could to make me think you were fucking every woman you could get your hands on. You put on an act so I would still believe you were sleeping around even after you'd stopped, if what you told me the other day is true. You don't get to tell me *now* that you have feelings for me, and expect me to drop everything in my life and come running. Who the hell do you think you are?"

"Whoa, whoa." I gently take her hand from my chest. "You're right. I'm sorry. I expect nothing, and more importantly, I deserve nothing, Denise. But I know how angry you were the other day. I know you didn't want anyone who would expect you to change yourself. And now here you are, a week later, and you've changed yourself and taken him back." I gesture at her outfit.

"That's my business, not yours." She stomps away to the other end of the deck and drops into a chair near the outdoor fireplace.

I follow and sit directly in front of her on a stool. Leaning in close, I grab the arms of the chair and pull her so close her knees press against the stool between my legs. She glares at me, her ice-blue eyes flashing.

"I'm sorry I told you about my feelings the other day," I say. "It was not the right time. That wasn't fair to you. I got caught up in how easy it was to spend time with you, and how it was what I've been dreaming of for years without believing it was even a possibility. But I couldn't bear the thought of seeing you find another Andrew without at least trying to see if you could feel for me what I feel for you. "

"I *had* those feelings, and you found a new girl every night while I looked on." She looks down at her hands in her lap. I can't stop myself from taking them both in one of mine and reaching to touch her cheek with my other hand. She looks up at me again, and I can swear her eyes are glistening now. She looks like she's on the verge of tears. "I don't know what you want from me, Ryder."

"I want everything, Denise." I breathe while sliding my thumb across her lower lip. "I want you to be mine."

I know it's wrong, and I know I shouldn't, but I can't stop myself from leaning closer. She licks her lips as I approach slowly, giving her plenty of time to turn away. When she doesn't move, I kiss her gently. My heart beats faster as Denise's breath quickens against my lips. I taste her lower lip with my tongue and she answers with a soft moan. Taking that encouragement, I part her lips with my tongue, deepening the kiss. Denise shakes her hands free from mine and grabs the front of my shirt, pulling me closer, kissing me back roughly.

I reach down between us and lift her legs over mine, dragging her onto my lap so she's straddling me. Someone could come out here at any moment, but I can't bring myself to stop. I reach one hand up into her hair and the other to her ass so I can pull her onto my hard cock; I want her to feel what she does to me. I close my fist in her hair, tilting her head back, and I kiss along her jaw until my mouth is against her ear.

"I want you so fucking bad, Denise." I grind my dick against her. "Can you feel how hard I am for you?"

I kiss down her neck and run my tongue along her collarbone, listening to her gasp. The heat from her pussy warms me through my pants, and I might die if I don't find out how wet she is. I move my hand from her ass around and up underneath her dress, teasing the edges of her panties with my fingers. I kiss my way back up to her mouth, teeth grazing her bottom lip before I kiss her deeply. My fingers find their way to the front of her panties and I growl low in my throat.

"Oh god, babe. You're so wet for me." I slide my fingers under her panties and through her slick heat. I brush my thumb against her clit and she moans into my mouth, pressing closer to me, chasing the friction she needs. My thumb makes soft circles around her clit, and her breath catches.

"Please Ryder," she whimpers.

"Do you like that? Do you want more?" I don't think I can ever get enough of this woman. The noises she's making are shooting straight to my dick, making me uncomfortably hard.

"Yes, yes, more." She grabs my hair with both hands and pulls me into a deeper kiss.

I slide two fingers into her while continuing to work her clit with my thumb. She rides my hand with abandon, bucking against me, while my fingers massage that spot inside that I'm not sure anyone before me has ever found.

"That's it, baby," I growl in between kisses. "I want to feel you come all over my hand. Can you do that for me?"

I feel her pussy clench around my fingers, and I push a little harder on her clit, moving my thumb in tighter circles. I squeeze my fist in her hair, pulling her head back to expose her neck. As I feel her orgasm approaching, I bend my lips to her neck, finding the pulse point and licking it with my tongue, nipping at her with my teeth.

A wave of wetness rushes over my fingers as she clamps down on me. Denise throws her head back, a low moan coming from deep in her throat as I continue to coax her orgasm from her. While she comes, I gently bite and suck on her neck, adding a little pain to make the pleasure that much sweeter.

When I've finally wrung every drop of her orgasm from her, and she's panting with her release, resting her head against mine, I kiss her lips again. I slip my fingers out of her and slide my hand out of her panties. My other hand is still in her hair and I use it to pull her head back, so she's looking at me. I make her watch as I put my hand to my mouth and lick every bit of her come off of my fingers.

"You taste so good, babe." Her eyes widen as she watches me. "When I finally get to eat your pussy, I'm going to take my time and enjoy every second."

I lean forward and kiss her again, sliding my tongue into her mouth, tasting her like it could be the last time, because, honestly, it could. These moments, no matter how sweet, were stolen, I know that. But for now, she kisses me back, and it's perfect.

Until the door to the deck open and Denise jumps off my lap and back into the chair.

"Hey guys?" Devon is peeking out the door. "Andrew is looking for Denise. I think he wants to go home or something." He rolls his eyes. I'm not surprised Andrew wants to go already. He doesn't like any of us, including Denise.

"I have to go," Denise says to me, "I... I don't... I have to go." And with that, she pushes her chair back away from me, gets up and goes back into the house.

"You coming, man?" Devon asks from the doorway.

My dick is so hard there's no way I can go back in right now without getting called out for it. Better if I leave from here.

"Nah, man," I say. "I'm going to go home, I think. I'll walk around the house, though. Don't want to risk seeing Andrew again, you know?"

He winks at me. Shit, he probably saw a little more than he should have. "I got you. See you soon, buddy," he says before going in and closing the door behind him.

I stand up and adjust my dick in my pants. Fuck, I'm pretty sure I've never been this hard in my life. But holy shit, Denise is so fucking sexy when she comes. I'll be picturing that when I jerk off later. Hell, I'll probably picture that every time I jerk off for the rest of my life.

Checking my pockets for my keys and phone, I go down the stairs to walk around the house. The last thing I want is to see Andrew and Denise leaving after I made her come. Although... No, that wouldn't be fair to Denise.

No matter how hilarious it would be to see Andrew's face when he realized it.

10

Frilly Pink Dresses and Mystery Ramen

Denise

I CAN'T BELIEVE I let that happen. How could I let Ryder get me off, sitting outside at Connor's place while Andrew waited for me in the house? I wouldn't normally behave that way. It's like I can't control myself ever since Ryder told me how he feels.

It was the best orgasm of my life, though. I think I may have blacked out a little. And Ryder is an amazing kisser. My fingers touch my lips before I even know it's happening.

"What are you smiling about?" Andrew asks from the passenger seat. Devon was right. Andrew was looking for me because he wanted to leave. So much for him making more of an effort. Of course, maybe it had something to do with me disappearing with Ryder pretty much as soon as we got there.

"Nothing," I say, before changing the subject. "I thought you were going to try today? I clearly did," I say as I gesture to my ridiculously frilly pink dress and understated makeup.

"Yes, well, I didn't say I wanted to hang around with those people without you." He says *those people* like they're diseased or something. Maybe he's afraid of catching tattoos. Or a personality. Heh.

I'm regretting calling Andrew and saying we could give this another try. He doesn't know about the pregnancy yet though, and I'm thankful for that. I want to see if we can compromise enough to have this baby as a couple or if we'll be working out some kind of co-parenting agreement for when the baby comes.

"Sorry about that," I lie. I'm glad I'm driving, so I don't have to look at him while we talk about this. Despite being great at business negotiations, I am terrible at lying. "I had some contract stuff to talk over with Ryder and wanted to get it out of the way."

"Contract stuff?" Andrew asks. "Like what?"

"You know I can't discuss that with you, Andrew. It's confidential." Plus, that is not at all what was going on and I'm definitely not telling him what really happened. I probably should feel guilty about it, but for some reason I don't.

He huffs. "I don't see why I can't know. I'm your boyfriend, plus I signed the stupid NDA so I could come to these dinners with you. That should prove I'm trustworthy."

I shake my head; we've had this conversation before and I'm not doing it again. Hopefully, he'll drop it and we can ride the rest of the way to his house in peace.

"You do look much better than normal today," he says after a few minutes of silence. "Those earrings you're wearing aren't exactly dainty, but they're not too bad."

I release an exasperated breath. It took a lot for me to swallow my pride and get into this pink dress and the low heels. This is not an outfit I would ever have chosen for myself before, but I wanted to make this work with Andrew. He's making it incredibly difficult with his nitpicking my earrings now.

"What's wrong with my earrings?" I ask, rolling my eyes.

"Well, you know," he gestures at them, "they look thick, and the hoops are so big. They look a little too rock-and-roll. Or like you're one of those freaky people with gigantic holes in their ears."

What the hell? I *am* one of those freaky people with gigantic holes in their ears. Okay, so they're not much bigger than a normal earring would be, but they are stretched a little. Has he really never noticed before?

I ignore his comments and keep driving. The sooner I can drop him off, the better. I'm getting a little irritated with him right now and if I want to take a shot at this, I need some time away from him.

But what does it say about me that being away from him is the best way to make this work?

I'm turning into the parking lot of his apartment building before he even knows we were going there. I pull up right in front of the door to drop him off, and he turns to look at me.

"Aren't you going to come up? We could, you know..." He waggles his eyebrows, hinting at sex.

The last thing I want right now is to 'you know' with Andrew. Especially after the incident with Ryder out on the deck. I don't think I could handle having a disappointing sexual experience so soon after such an amazing one. Plus, I need some time to sort all that out in my head before I do anything else with anyone.

"I have a lot of work to do tonight." The lie comes more easily this time. "You're still coming with me next Saturday?" I almost hope he says no.

"Umm, yeah? Remind me again?"

"It's the engagement thing for Connor and Alex."

"Ugh. Right. That." He rolls his eyes. "Yeah, I'll come with you. We'll work out the details." He leans over to kiss me and I give him my cheek.

"Oh, I'm not fully over whatever illness I had this week. I'd hate to pass it on to you." Really, I don't want anything erasing the memory of Ryder's kiss. My lips tingle thinking about it.

"Oh yeah, that makes sense. Okay then." He opens his door and steps out of the car. "See you soon?"

"Yeah, sure thing." I stomp on the gas and drive away the second he closes the door. My body is itching to leave, almost like it can't stand to be around Andrew for another minute.

It's going to be tricky to work things out with Andrew if I can't even be around him. I need to try, though, for the sake of the baby. Right?

By the time I get home, I'm starving. I should have stopped to pick something up so I wouldn't have to cook, but I was a little preoccupied. This wouldn't even be an issue if Andrew had kept up his end of the bargain and stuck around at Alex and Connor's for a decent amount of time. I could have eaten some of whatever amazing thing Alex prepared today, instead of scrounging around at my place looking for something to eat.

I'm eating for two now, for crying out loud. Not that he knows yet. In fact, the only other person who knows so far is Alex, and that's because she figured it out before I did.

I still can't believe I was sick in the morning for days and I didn't even put two and two together. Pregnancy brain must be a real thing, because something like that wouldn't normally slip by me. I'm usually quite good at noticing details.

The doorbell rings as I'm opening the fridge to look for something edible. Who is that? I'm not expecting anyone.

I look through the peephole (because a woman who lives alone can never be too safe) and all I see is a teenager holding a brown paper bag. Opening the door, the delivery guy hands me the bag and tells me to have a great day. Inside is my favourite ramen from the little noodle shop near Rough Mix. The timing couldn't be better, since I'm starving, but I can't trust ramen that shows up mysteriously. Can I? I mean, it is my favourite.

I'm putting the bag in the kitchen, trying to decide what I should eat, when my phone buzzes with an incoming text.

Ryder- I figured you'd be hungry since Andrew made you leave before you ate. I stopped to grab myself some noodles on my way home and figured I'd send you your favourite.

Dammit! That is so nice.

Denise- That's very thoughtful. Thank you.

Ryder- You're welcome. You didn't call Nanny Ryder to take care of you this week while you were sick, so I'm doing it now.

I can't believe he was actually serious about that. After him looking after me so well the other day, it sucked going back to doing it myself. But I couldn't exactly call him to come look after me while I was having morning sickness because of another man's baby, could I? Not after he told me he had feelings for me. That wouldn't have been fair at all.

I'm even more disappointed in my behaviour today because of that. He was so great when he was, uh... 'talking to me' out on the deck. Best orgasm of my life. How am I going to make things work with Andrew when I know Ryder can blow my mind with his hand? Especially since with Andrew, I usually need to get myself off.

But that's the way it has to be. I can't let anything else happen between me and Ryder. Even if I can't make it work with Andrew, I can't imagine Ryder would want to tie himself to a pregnant woman anyway. He's still a party guy, after all. And nothing cramps your style quite like having a kid.

11

She's Making it Work... With Him

Ryder

DENISE SHOWING UP TO Alex's family dinner with Andrew was not at all what I was expecting. I can only blame my behavior on the shock of seeing her there with him. After she told me they broke up, I thought that was the end of them. It never would have occurred to me she would want to make it work with him after that.

And the dress she was wearing. She looked so uncomfortable in it. I don't know if anyone else noticed because she dragged me outside as soon as she arrived, but I could tell she wasn't happy with it. Maybe I should text Alex to see if she knows what's up. It sounded like she'd been talking to her during the week sometime, so it's probably my only shot.

Ryder- Hey, any idea why Denise brought Andrew today? I thought they broke up.

Alex- That's not my place to say. But you should probably ask

her if you want to know. Where
did you go, anyway? Devon said
you left, but I didn't see you
leave.

Ryder- I went around the house
after I talked to Denise. I
didn't feel like coming back inside. What do you mean I should
ask her?

Alex- I know she has her reasons, but I can't tell you what
they are. You'll have to ask her
if you want to know.

Ryder-Did you know I told her
how I feel?

Alex- She mentioned that.

Ryder- Then why the hell would
she try to make it work with
Andrew? I felt something when

I spent the day there. And I'm pretty sure she did, too. It makes no sense that she'd run back to him after what she told me.

Alex- Like I said, she has her reasons. Call her. If she wants you to know, she'll tell you.

Ryder- Did you notice her dress?

Alex- Yeah, that was weird. Didn't really seem like something she would normally wear.

Ryder- That's what I thought too.

Ryder- Okay. I'll call her. Talk to you later.

I don't know if I really should call Denise. But I can't stop myself and before I know it, the phone is ringing. She picks up on the third ring.

"*Hello?*"

"Hey," I say. "It's Ryder. I was hoping you had some time to talk? Maybe I could come over?"

She sighs into the phone receiver. "*I don't think that's a good idea, Ryder. At least not you coming here.*"

"Okay, well, we can talk on the phone now. I mean, If that's good with you?"

She doesn't answer, but she doesn't hang up either, so I take it as a sign to continue.

"Why did you bring Andrew today? I thought you dumped him because you didn't want to change for him?"

"*I know. But after I got over being mad, I realized maybe I should try to compromise.*"

"What about him? He wanted to leave as soon as you got there today. You didn't even get to eat first." I'm frustrated and I'm sure she can hear it in my voice.

"*What the hell would you expect?*" she says after a pause. "*I went outside with you and left him there alone for half an hour. He's already jealous of you, and me disappearing with you made him uncomfortable.*"

"What do you mean, he's jealous of me? He has no reason to be jealous. He's the one who's with you, not me." I hate the sulky way my voice sounds. I'm the one who has a reason to be jealous, not him.

She laughs, like I'm the dumbest person she's ever met. She sighs deeply before explaining it to me. "*He's jealous because he knows he's the first boyfriend I've had since I met you. He's jealous because he knows I've been hung up on you for almost fifteen years. He's seen the way I still look at you when you're on stage, how I can't look away when you're in the room.*"

"You..." I can't even say anything. Is she saying she's felt the same way for all these years? That can't be right? She said she was over that.

"He's seen my heart break every time you left the bar with someone. Every time I had to rescue you from your latest bad idea." She says through tears. *"He's jealous because he knows he can only ever hope to be second place with me, despite all that."*

I'm silent, thinking over what she's said. It sounds like she's been dating Andrew this whole time, knowing she really wanted me. And I've been stupidly trying to forget her, thinking I'd never be able to be with her.

"I want you to be with me." I confess. "What do I need to do? I don't want to run away anymore, Denise. I love you. And I think you love me, too."

She's crying now and I want to go to her.

"I can't love you, Ryder. I need to make it work with Andrew. I'm sorry."

All the air rushes from my lungs as she hangs up the phone. She's still going to try with Andrew.

I fucked up everything.

I walk over to the freezer and get the bottle of vodka. It's not the healthiest coping mechanism, but it's going to have to do.

12

How Did Alex Get So Smart?

Denise

RYDER SAID HE LOVES me.

He loves me and I told him I can't love him back.

How did I get myself into this mess? I can't believe after all these years of taking care of everything, one little slip up has made this much of an impact on my life.

I'm having Andrew's baby.

I have never really gotten over Ryder.

Ryder confessed his love for me.

How can I possibly try to work things out with Andrew when I know how Ryder feels? When I know how I feel?

Being pregnant is causing me so many issues right now, but I already know there's no way I'm not keeping this baby. I was telling Ryder how I'm not getting any younger, so I'm sure he'll understand my need to try with Andrew once he finds out I'm having his baby.

If that's even the right move. Maybe I should call Alex with this recent development? She's the only person I've told about the pregnancy so far, and I need someone to talk to.

She picks up immediately, almost like she was expecting my call.

"Hey Girl, how are you doing? How's the nausea?" she asks as soon as she picks up.

"I've been better, actually. Do you have time to talk?"

"*For you I do.*" I can hear the smile in her voice. "*Let me get into another room.*"

"Okay, thanks. You're the only one who knows about my situation, so you're the only one I can talk to right now."

"*Alright, I'm ready. Tell me what's going on. You sound upset.*"

I take a couple of deep breaths before launching into the story. I leave out the details of exactly what Ryder and I did on the deck, but other than that, I tell her everything. Old feelings, new feelings, my desire to cut Andrew out of my life because he's not right for me, my fear of the baby not having a father, my fear of allowing Ryder's feelings to get to me even though I know nothing can come of it; all of it.

"*Wow,*" she says after a minute. "*That is a lot.*"

"Yeah, it sure is."

"*Okay, let's break this down into more manageable parts. Would you stay with Andrew if it weren't for the baby?*"

"No," I say without hesitation. "I had already broken up with him before I found out I was having this baby. I can honestly say I wouldn't be trying to compromise if it weren't for the baby."

"*Okay, that's good. Do you think you need a live-in partner for you to take care of a kid?*"

"Well, no. It would be nice to not be the only person waking up at night, though."

She laughs. "*Yeah, I could see that.*"

"But I suppose I could do it myself. Or hire a nanny to help."

"*Right. You are the most capable woman I know, and I guarantee you when the guys find out about the baby, you'll have more help than you could ask for, anyway. This baby is going to be a band baby whether or not you like it.*"

It's my turn to laugh now. I've been so caught up in the Andrew question I forgot to consider how many honorary uncles this baby is going to have. These guys have been some of my best friends for fifteen years. I won't lack for support if I need it. Plus, Alex is in our lives now, and she's already helped me so much.

"You're not wrong about that."

"Okay. So I conclude you don't need Andrew around for this, nor do you want him around for you. He can be a father to the baby without being your boyfriend. You don't need to change yourself for someone for this kid to have a dad. He'll have several uncles, and an amazingly awesome auntie, if I do say so myself, to help you when you need. You should only keep Andrew as your boyfriend if you want him that way. And it sounds to me like you don't."

"Wow, don't hold back on my account." I joke. "Tell me how you really feel."

"Well, since you asked," she says, *"I don't really like Andrew. He seems sneaky when he's around us. He never wants to talk, doesn't take part in conversations, and can't even speak up when he wants to leave. What's with the whispering? It's weird."* She's teasing me a little, but I know it's true. He is a little strange and the longer we're together, the more I see it.

"Okay fine, you're right. I give." Alex has really broken this down for me. Andrew can be a dad without being my boyfriend, and there is nothing wrong with that. I don't need to change my mind about the breakup because I'm having his baby.

"Now for Ryder," Alex says. *"He's had feelings for you for a long time. And now he's saying he loves you?"*

"That's what he said on the phone a little while ago. But I told him I can't love him; that I need to work things out with Andrew."

"Right, but we've established you don't need to work things out with Andrew at all, so let's forget him for now. He sucks. We can focus on Ryder for a minute. How do you feel about him?"

"I can't love him. I'm having Andrew's baby. It wouldn't be fair to Ryder to have feelings for him now."

"Denise, are you purposely not listening to me?" Alex asks, sounding a little frustrated. *"I asked you how you feel about him, not how you feel about being pregnant. Forget that for now. How do you feel?"*

"I... I don't know. I've thought about nothing but him for years. But I worked so hard to push it all away. How can I let myself feel those things now? How can I believe he won't go back to how he used to be? I guess I could let myself love him, but I don't think I should. Does that make sense?"

"About as much sense as anything else." she says, taking an audible breath. *"But you need to realize if you love him, you don't need to keep yourself away. He's a grown man who can decide for himself whether a baby is a deal-breaker for him. But don't hide from love because you think he shouldn't want that. Tell him and let him make that choice."*

"Ugh. That makes sense. I don't think it's fair to him. Especially now that he's told me he loves me. I wouldn't want him to feel obligated because he's already said that. He needs to know he can still turn away."

"Admittedly, I haven't known you guys for long, but I don't think that is something you need to worry about. But it is something you have to risk if you want to try. That's not something anyone can try to talk you into or out of."

"Thanks Alex." I feel better, even if I don't have all the answers yet. "I knew I was right to call you."

"Anytime Denise. I mean that. Whatever you need, we're here for you."

"Thank you. I'll talk to you later. Bye."

"Bye."

I feel a little better now that I've talked to Alex. I guess I need to talk to Andrew, but I'm not ready to do it yet. He doesn't need to come to the engagement party this weekend, though, so I text him.

Denise- Hey, don't worry about coming to the engagement party this weekend. This isn't going to work out after all. I'm sorry. I'll call you next week sometime. I have something I need to talk to you about.

Andrew- K

Huh, that was a lot easier than I thought it would be. I figured he'd have questions, but at least now I won't need to see him around my friends again. I'll talk to him next week and we can work out the baby stuff. For now, I think I need to relax. Maybe even take a nap.

Who knew growing a baby would make me so tired? At least I'm not one of those women who has morning sickness all day. The mornings this last week were more than enough of that nonsense for me.

13

Better Coping Mechanisms

Ryder

I'M SITTING ON THE couch feeling sorry for myself, nursing my bottle of vodka, when I hear a knock at the door. I was planning on drinking it quickly but I couldn't bring myself to do it. Denise has never been mine and all the drinking I've done has never made me forget her, so clearly *that* method doesn't work.

"Hey, dumb fuck." Connor walks into my place, with Devon close behind. "Alex told us to come check on you."

"I'm good," I say. "You can leave now." I don't need their shit at the moment.

Devon sits on the couch beside me.

"That was a pretty intense conversation you were having with Denise today." He tells me while he takes my vodka and puts the lid back on. "Anything you want to say?"

"Nope." I'm not volunteering any information to these two. The less they know, the better.

"Okay, well, here's how I see it." Devon passes the bottle to Connor, who takes it to the kitchen. "You've been in love with her for years, but you've been doing everything in your power to not be. How am I doing so far?"

"Shut up."

"Okay cool. I'm on the right track." Devon smiles at me, the asshole. "What you don't realize is she's been in love with you for as long. Everyone thinks I'm the security guy, but I see everything. She's been in love with you for years. And your antics have hurt her more than anyone."

"I know!" I jump up off the couch. "You think I don't fucking know that already? Believe me, want to make it up to her, but she told me she can't love me. I've ruined it and I can't go back. She wants to try with Andrew for some fucking reason."

"Actually." Connor is looking through my fridge, so it's a little harder to hear him. He grabs out a few beers and brings them to us in the living room. "Alex told me before she sent me over here that Denise is no longer interested in trying with Andrew. It was a momentary lapse in judgment, apparently." He uses his lighter to pop the caps off the beer bottles and passes one to me and Devon before sitting down in the armchair opposite the couch. "So you can get that twist out of your panties if that's what your problem is."

"Fuck off, Connor." It feels good to be the one saying that to him for once, for how often they say it to me. "It doesn't matter if Andrew isn't an option for her. She still doesn't love me."

"She said she *can't* love you, not that she doesn't. Don't be dense." Connor looks like he knows something I don't. "She has something going on right now, and it's taking up most of her time. Alex won't tell me what it is, because Denise doesn't want to burden us, I guess. But I assure you, drinking your way to the bottom of every vodka bottle in the city won't help you get her."

What could Denise have going on? Is it something with the label and our new album? Maybe she's thinking of taking on other clients, even though we pay her enough that she can stick with only us. She's kind of like Devon that way. We pay them based on how much we value them in our lives, not the going rate for their role.

"So anyway, we're here to check on you and make sure you're not dealing with this unhealthily." Connor tells me. "So finish up your beer, then we're going to head to the gym to see Pops. He'll put you through a workout and talk you down. Alex seems to think you need to continue with being more responsible if you want Denise to give you a shot."

"The gym sounds good, but I really don't think Denise will give me a shot either way. I've been too much of a fuck up for too many years. It's not the same as you and Alex. You guys were completely off each other's radar. Denise has had a front-row seat to my stupidity. And I've broken her heart with it so many times over the years there's no way she'd want to subject herself to the possibility of more. Did you know Andrew is her first boyfriend since she met me? She told me that. She told me Andrew has been jealous because he'll only ever be second place in her eyes. Because I am first, but she can't love me. I fucked myself by doing what I thought was the right thing."

"Yeah, well, nobody ever said you're not a dumbass." Devon punches me in the leg and laughs. "But even dumbasses can fix their mistakes. There's hope for you yet."

Connor finishes his beer and puts it on the coffee table. "Grab your shit and let's go. You're stressing me out with this. I need a workout too. We can spar." He walks toward the door.

"What?" I'm surprised. I didn't know he would consider sparring. "What about your pretty face? Aren't you worried you'll ruin it?"

"Haha, hilarious," he says sardonically. "Besides, you'd need to hit me to actually make a mark. Get your shit. I'm having a smoke."

"You heard him," Devon stands up. "Grab your bag and let's go. We don't want to keep him waiting. Plus, all joking aside, I think you need to work out some frustrations before you can think clearly about this. Sparring with Connor will be good for you. But you better hit him in his stupid, pretty face, to make him shut up." He laughs as he walks out the door to wait with Connor.

These guys have been giving me a hard time for years, but I really couldn't ask for better friends. Them, and Alex, since she's the one who sent them.

I wonder if that means Denise called her after she talked to me? How else could Alex have known I'd need someone to come and talk me down? I didn't think I was that upset when I talked to her on the phone before I called Denise.

I grab my stuff and meet them outside. Devon drives us over to the gym in the band's Escalade. Well, I think it's technically Connor's, but Devon is usually the one driving.

"Pops, you old bastard. Where are you?" Connor yells out when we walk in the door. With us, at least Pops doesn't need any kind of doorbell. We always call out for him as soon as we walk in, letting him know we're here. "Ryder needs an ass kicking, and Alex told me to give it to him."

"I've been saying that ever since I met the kid. It's about damn time." Pops laughs from behind the front desk. "Go get changed and warm-up then we'll get down to business."

"This is gonna be good." Devon is chuckling at me as we walk to the locker room. "Connor's been training with Pops for years. You're going to regret agreeing to this."

"Is that so?" I ask, putting my bag down on the bench in the locker room. I quickly take out all of my piercings and strip down to my bare ass.

"Ah fuck, dude." Devon yells at the same time as Connor says, "Warn a guy, would you?"

"Oh, come on, guys," I say, sticking out my pelvis and making my dick flap back and forth against my legs. "I thought we already established that y'all love seeing my dick?"

I jump up on the bench and turn my ass toward them before bending over to grab my shorts out of my bag.

"*Heurrghh*," Devon gags, but I'm pretty sure it's fake. "I *do not* love seeing your dick and I most *definitely* do not love seeing your balls or your asshole."

Connor laughs. "Put those away, man. How am I going to fight you with the sight of your rusty bullet hole burned into my brain?"

I step off the bench and slip into my compression jock shorts. There's no way I'm sparring without some kind of protection for my junk. That's reckless.

"Damn, you figured it out. My evil plan is to blind you with my nut sack and asshole, then submit you with an armbar." I consider pulling on the training shorts I usually wear over the top of the compression shorts, but I feel like these guys deserve the spectacular view that is my ass in spandex. You're welcome. Instead, I grab my mitts and my mouth guard and head out. "See you out there."

Grabbing a jump rope off the wall, I walk to an open area and start jumping. Soon Connor joins me, and Devon heads over to the free weights area to get some lifting in before we get started.

Once we're both warmed up, we go over to the ring and call Pops over.

He checks our gear, raising an eyebrow at my shorts. "Getting into spandex now?" he asks.

I laugh. "Yeah, Pops. Connor won't stop looking at my ass. I figured I'd make it easy for him."

A small crowd of other gym goers has gathered around the ring. I guess this fight is going to have an audience. I wasn't really planning to pull out all the stops, but with this many people, I sort of feel like I need to teach Connor and Devon both a lesson. Connor may have been training with Pops for a long time, but what they don't know is I'm not completely inexperienced with MMA. I did a lot of martial arts training when I was a kid, specifically Brazilian Jiu Jitsu, and that's exactly how I'm going to win this fight.

Pops explains the rules to us and gives us the signal to fight. As I expected, Connor comes in strong with his punches, clocking me with a few good ones before I put him on the defensive. Within a matter of seconds, I have him down on the ground and I'm in full mount. He attempts to throw me off, but before he can really move, I've flipped over to the side and put him in the armbar I warned him about in the locker room. The only thing left for him to do is tap out, which he does almost instantly.

Not even a full round. Damn, I still got it. I smile to myself.

"Where the shit did *that* come from?" Connor asks while he rubs his arm. Armbars never feel good, and Connor is going to feel this one for a few days. It's a good thing he tapped out so quickly.

"Oh, didn't I tell you I used to train in Brazilian Jiu Jitsu? It must've slipped my mind when you said you were going to give me an ass-kicking. If I recall correctly, though, I warned you about that armbar." I laugh as I grab the bottle of water Pops is offering me. "It's not my fault you couldn't stop thinking about my balls."

"I can't believe how quickly you got me, man." Connor shakes his head. "I didn't know you could fight like this."

"To be fair, if I hadn't gotten you to the ground quickly, you would have had a better shot. I'm not as skilled with stand-up fighting as I am on the ground. I could teach you some stuff? I used to teach some of the little kiddies at my gym when I was younger."

"Fuck off. Really? People let you instruct their kids?"

"What? Like I can't take charge of a class of little kids? You really have no faith in me. Kids are awesome, and they love me. Never mind," I say, taking a big drink of my water, "I'll teach Alex instead and then she can kick your ass when you need it."

"No way, man, she's tough enough as it is. She doesn't need any more training." Aww, poor Connor. He actually looks a little afraid. I have to admit that I am, too. I saw Alex's hands after she beat up Connor's would-be rapist. Alex hit that girl so hard she broke her own hand, and, if the rumors were true, she also broke the girl's face.

"I think that's a great idea, Ryder," Pops says seriously. "And when you have time, I'd actually like to talk to you about helping me out with some of the self-defence training I'm offering to teen girls in local schools. BJJ would be an excellent skill for them to learn."

"Wow, Pops..." I'm actually a little taken aback at his trust in me. "That means a lot to me. I'll call you later and we can talk about it. I'd love to help."

Look at that. One little fight, and Connor and Devon have already given me some new coping mechanisms.

Maybe this hasn't been a complete shitshow of a day after all.

14

Confirmation and Coffee

Denise

WAITING IN THE OFFICE of my OB/Gyn is certainly eye opening. There are women here in all stages of pregnancy, as well as some women who have small babies, and some women who look a little older than me who could be here for anything.

I was surprised but happy when I called yesterday and the nurse could squeeze me in for an appointment today. I was expecting to have to wait a week or more. I don't want to tell Andrew about the baby until I've had confirmation from the doctor, you know, in case I had three false positives from those pee stick tests.

The nurse has already had me pee in a cup, so I will get a result from the doctor once I'm called in to see her. I'm a little nervous even though I'm sure I already know the test will say. But what if I'm not pregnant? The more time I've had to think about it, the more I like the idea of having a baby. I wish the situation were a little different, but it's not like I'll be the first woman to have a baby without a partner. Plus, like Alex said, this kid will have tons of uncles and an amazing auntie to help. I will have a village, likely a better one than many moms have.

"Denise?" The receptionist calls me and I stand up. She leads me to an exam room in the back. They decorated the walls with anatomically correct illustrations of the female genital organs

86

and there is even a 3-D model of a cross-section of the same sitting on the doctor's desk. Besides those, there are advertisements for different types and brands of birth control interspersed amongst cheesy, worn out posters of people holding babies. It's outdated and a little boring.

I'm planning the logistics of making her an embroidered version of the anatomically correct uterus when there is a knock on the door. Without waiting for an answer, the doctor walks in.

"Hello Denise, what can I do for you today?" she asks as she picks up my chart. "It says here you think you're pregnant? What makes you think that?"

"I took three home pregnancy tests, and they were all positive."

"Well," she says with a smile, "that certainly narrows it down then, doesn't it?"

I laugh nervously. "Yeah, it does. Circumstances with the father have changed, so I wanted to get confirmation from you before I tell him."

"Well, the urine test we did when you checked in says you are indeed pregnant. Congratulations."

"Thanks." I'm not surprised, but hearing it from a doctor makes it feel a little more real.

"Have you been having any trouble with nausea?" she asks.

"A little. I was feeling off for several weeks and then I threw up in the morning for about a week or so, but it seems to have calmed down already."

"That's completely normal," she says. "There are going to be some other things to watch for in pregnancy with a woman of your age."

She explains all the possibilities which could happen with what they apparently call a 'geriatric pregnancy'. So that's fun. From a slightly increased risk of miscarriage to an increased chance of stillbirth after twenty weeks. There's also the possibility of a premature birth being more likely. And let's not forget the increased chance of birth defects being present.

I may not need a partner to have a baby, but I wouldn't mind having someone to share this anxiety with. So many women are having their babies older and older that I didn't really consider a pregnancy at my age would be much different from any other pregnancy.

"Well, that all sounds fabulous, doc," I tell her, my voice practically dripping with sarcasm. "Now tell me the bad news."

"I know it sounds daunting," she says gently, "but these are not the likeliest of scenarios. The best thing you can do to mitigate the risk is to eat a healthy diet, take your prenatal vitamins, get light exercise, and really take care of yourself. Stop at the desk on the way out and the nurse will give you some pamphlets and book recommendations so you can learn more."

"Sure thing," I say, standing up. "Thanks for squeezing me in today. Have a good one."

I stop at the reception desk and the nurse loads me down with pamphlets. She also writes a list of books and websites that will help. I need all the information I can get. This pregnancy seems to get more complicated by the minute.

On my way home, I stop at the bookstore to pick up a few of the books from the list. It's clear some of them are more informative and some of them are more for entertainment. I appreciate the nurse taking the time to consider I might need some cheerful content along with the dry facts.

While I'm here, I pick up a couple of wedding magazines for Alex. She doesn't know she's getting engaged this weekend, but I think I will invite her over next week to go through the magazines and talk about her for a change. We don't know each other well and she has been such a good friend throughout this pregnancy already. I want to make sure she knows our friendship goes two ways; I'm not here for what she can give me.

Plus, I'm awesome at organizing things. I'd love to help her with wedding planning.

I'm walking to the register, juggling a stack of books and magazines, when I spot Ryder standing in line at the cafe in the front corner of the store, looking better than ever. Why does the man have to look so sexy all the time? I don't want him to see me after what went down between us the other day, and I especially don't want him to see me with this stack of pregnancy books. My eyes scan my surroundings and spot an empty shopping basket sitting on top of a display of books, and I grab it for myself. I wrestle my pile of books into the basket and arrange the magazines on top, effectively disguising the books. And in time, too.

"Denise?" Ryder's gravelly voice cuts through the noise of the store, causing me to jump a little, even though I was expecting it. Looks like he gave up on ordering coffee in favour of coming over to talk to me. "What are you doing here?"

I turn around and hold up my basket a little. "Grabbing some wedding magazines and books. I'm thinking I will invite Alex over next week after she's officially engaged. We can have some food and go through them so she can start planning her wedding."

"That's a great idea," he says, looking directly into my eyes. My breath catches at the intensity of his gaze. "You should get Becca to join you, too. I'm sure she'll be in the wedding party so you might as well get her help right away. Don't let her get away with slacking off." He laughs. "I didn't know you and Alex were such good friends. It's nice to see you have some more women friends to do stuff with. It must be hard hanging around with a bunch of guys all the time."

It's my turn to laugh now. "Well, there is something to be said about the improved smell that comes with women friends.

Being on a bus with a bunch of stinky guys for months at a time brings new meaning to the word 'fragrance'"

"Hey, I'm one of those stinky guys, and even I have to agree with you. The tiny shower on the bus is not as effective as I would like. Plus, when we all need to wait around to use it, the smell of us soaks into all the bus's upholstery. I'm almost happier we rent a bus when we need one, so we don't have to deal with getting rid of the smell ourselves."

"Yes but, if you had the money to buy your own bus you'd probably also have the money to stay in hotels more often. Then you'd have the chance to scrub off really well after shows and the bus wouldn't ever get too smelly." I may have put some thought into this over all the weeks I've spent inhaling the scent of six sweaty dudes on a bus.

"Hmmmm, that's definitely something to consider." His eyebrows scrunch up a little. "Do you want to grab a coffee with me? We can sit and talk?"

"Ummm." I'm not sure this is a good idea. But at least in public, I don't have to worry about having a repeat of the other day. I *should* be able to control myself if there's an audience. "Yeah, sure. That sounds nice. Let me go pay for my stuff." I hold up my basket again. "And I'll meet you there. Grab me a peppermint mocha please, with extra whipped cream?"

"You bet. See you in a few minutes."

I take my basket to the checkout and have the cashier double wrap my pregnancy books, to make sure Ryder won't be able to see them through the bag. He'll need to know eventually, but I am not ready for that conversation today. Whatever we are talking about, I can guarantee it will not be what is currently growing in my uterus.

By the time I get back to the cafe, Ryder has already bought our drinks and found us a table. I don't see him right away because I'm expecting him to still be in line, so he has to call me over.

"Denise," he calls out loudly enough to be heard over the noise of the coffee shop. "Over here." He's halfway standing up and waving me over.

I push through the crowd and go to the table where he's sitting. Why do they make these places so small? There's hardly any room between tables and this place is packed. I'm surprised Ryder found us a place to sit, to be honest. He probably had to swipe it as someone was getting up.

"Hey, thanks." I say, picking up my mocha and taking a small sip to test how hot it is. I made the mistake once of taking a big sip, letting the coolness of the whipped cream fool me into thinking the temperature of the drink was acceptable. It was only when the burning hot liquid burned my tongue and the roof of my mouth that I realized that was not the case. It was a painful lesson to learn. It happened at my friend Xena's coffee shop, Bump & Grind, too, so it's not like I would even sue. It was lucky for her, though, it happened to me instead of an actual customer.

"Still doing the test sip, hey?" I forgot Ryder was there when it happened. He's the one who ran back into the coffee shop to get me a cup full of ice water to help cool my mouth.

"Oh yes," I reply with a small smile. "I will *never* make that mistake again. Did you know the roof of my mouth actually peeled? It peeled! And it apparently wasn't even that severe of a burn. I'd hate to know what a worse one feels like."

"I didn't know that. But you ate smoothies for a while after it happened, so I probably should have realized something was up. You like your food too much to subsist on a liquid diet without a reason."

I laugh a little. "I suppose that's true, isn't it? Thanks again for sending over the ramen the other day. It was delicious."

"Oh yeah, you're welcome." He runs a hand through his hair while he looks down at the table. "Listen, about that day... I've been meaning to apologize, but I wanted to give you some time first. What I did was incredibly inappropriate. I am so sorry I put you in that situation. You were there with Andrew, and that's not my business. I had no right to start something with you, especially not like that."

Holy shit. I was not expecting that at all. Ryder apologizing was probably the last thing I expected he would want to talk to me about. But I can't say I don't appreciate it.

"Forgiven and forgotten," I say, much to his relief if the look on his face is anything to go by. "You were looking out for me as a friend, with the Andrew thing, and then it got way out of hand. Let's not talk about it anymore, okay?" Not that I really minded when it got out of hand. That was the best orgasm of my life.

"Okay, sure. If that's what you want. But Denise, and please forgive me for this, too. I think you deserve better than Andrew. If he doesn't love the amazing woman you are, right now, like this," he gestures toward all of me, causing my skin to flush, "then he shouldn't get to have you at all. You're perfect and you deserve to have someone who understands that and loves you the way you are."

I grin before I can stop myself. It feels good, but a little weird to have Ryder describe me this way.

"You have nothing to be sorry for with that, Ryder. You're right. I deserve better than that. I wish I'd figured it out sooner, before all this went down. But I did finally figure it out." He looks up at me with a smile. "I realized I didn't actually want to try again with Andrew after all."

"Does this have anything to do with the pink monstrosity you were wearing the other day?" He chuckles, lightening the mood.

In between laughs he adds, "You look gorgeous in anything, but shit! You looked so uncomfortable in that."

I join in his laughter. I did look ridiculous. Like another version of myself entirely. "I know, right? I felt like I was in a different body, not different clothes. And those shoes! I could hardly walk in them. I either do sky high heels or flat sneakers, there is no in between."

"I noticed that too. I don't understand how you can walk in those," he points down at the platform stilettos booties I'm currently wearing, "but not in those other ones with a much lower heel."

"It doesn't make sense to me either, but it's the way it is." I shrug. It's nice talking to Ryder like this. When he's not doing the whole party-boy routine, he's actually a good guy. I hope we'll be able to stay friends when he finds out about the baby. I would hate to learn that he's my friend only when he thinks there's a chance for something more. Because I can't allow that to happen, not with a baby on the way. That wouldn't be fair to him, no matter what Alex thinks.

"Well, as nice as this visit has been," Ryder says before drinking back the last of his coffee, "I told Alex's Pops I'd go down to the gym today to talk about me teaching a couple of classes."

"What? You're going to be a trainer at the gym? Is that safe? Are you even qualified?" I never really considered Ryder to be an athletic sort of guy, so to say I'm surprised Pops wants him to teach a class is an understatement.

He laughs. "It's my best kept secret, apparently. I'm not sure how it never came up, but I actually used to teach Brazilian Jiu Jitsu before we started the band. Pops found out the other day and asked if I would be interested in donating some time to teach his teen girls' self-defence class a little. He says they could use it. I guess the granddaughter of a friend of his was nearly raped a while back and since then Pops has been teaching self-defence to teen girls for free. That's not something I would say no to."

"That's amazing, Ryder." He keeps surprising me. "I'm really impressed. Not only because you're some secret martial arts master, but that you'd volunteer to teach girls how to defend themselves. That's really awesome."

"It means a lot to me that you feel that way, Denise. But I figured, since I don't want to go back to the way I was behaving, I may as well be useful instead. This way I can use knowledge I already have to teach the people who need it the most."

"Well, good for you. I'm really proud of you." I'm standing now too, clinging to my bag of books, my heart fluttering strangely because of this new Ryder. "But I'll let you get going. I've got some stuff to do as well, so I should get to it."

We say our goodbyes and then each go our separate ways.

Who would've thought Ryder would happily volunteer his time to teach girls self defence? It's not something I could have ever imagined. I'm glad he's taking himself seriously for once. It'll be great for him, but maybe I won't need to worry about bailing him out of trouble while I'm pregnant. I'd hate to drag my enormous belly out somewhere to rescue him in the middle of the night. I might need to assign all future midnight rescues to Devon, in case.

15

Party Plans and Girl Time

Ryder

SEEING DENISE AT THE bookstore the other day was the highlight of my week. Not even Pops asking me to help with the self-defense classes came close. We had a normal conversation after I apologized for my behaviour. I still want her to be mine, but instead of trying to chase her down, I'm focusing on being the type of man who is worthy of a woman like her.

Denise has been cleaning up my messes for years. She does everything for the band, and everything for everyone else around her, too. My plan is to become someone she trusts to take care of her.

I've spent the days since I've seen her working with the guys in the studio. I've written a couple of songs I think might even make it onto the album. Connor is a better lyricist than I am, but I think I impressed with what I've come up with. It's amazing how much work we've been able to get done with me being sober. And with me actually showing up. I wasn't aware of how much I was letting these guys down until this week, and do I ever feel like an asshole for it. Luckily we've all been friends for so long, or they probably would have already kicked me out of the band. I couldn't have blamed them either. I was definitely not carrying my weight.

Today is our last day in the studio before Connor's surprise proposal to Alex. He booked Rough Mix for a private party and invited all of Alex's friends. Alex's best friend Becca and I are responsible for keeping her occupied tomorrow while Connor gets everything ready.

Becca sent me a text the other day to tell me what she has planned. Apparently we'll be spending the day at a spa. Manis, pedis, waxing; you name it, we're doing it. Wait when they find out I called and had us all booked into a group session. I don't mind the odd beauty treatment, and I won't let them put me in a separate room because I'm a dude. Unless Alex or Becca have an issue with it, anyway.

I tried to get Denise to come too, but she has some appointment she can't get out of. Too bad. I'm sure she'd have enjoyed my suffering as much as the other two are sure to. I plan to get the full stripper wax, top to bottom, front and back. Don't let it be said I won't do anything for a laugh. My grooming routine is usually a little more private, and I usually prefer a trim to wax, but since I know it'll make the ladies laugh, I'm going to give it a go. How bad can it be, right?

"Hey, Ryder, got anything new for us today?" Connor asks while the other guys grab drinks from the kitchen.

"Not yet, man." I tell him. "I've been spending a lot of time with Pops this week."

Connor felt my proficiency with Brazilian Jiu Jitsu first hand the other day when we sparred and I submitted him with an armbar in less than a minute. He was impressed to hear I'm going to be helping Pops with his teen girls' self-defence classes.

"How's that coming along? Alex said Pops is excited. What about you?"

"I can't wait to get started." I've surprised myself with how much I've been looking forward to it. I even grabbed a book about coaching girls when I was at the bookstore the other day because I really don't want to screw this up. "It's nice to be giving back to the community. I never thought I would be the kind of guy who volunteers my time, but here we are." I laugh.

"I gotta say, I really like this 'new and improved' Ryder. You're as funny as ever, but you're a lot more focused too. I hope this new Ryder is with us to stay."

"Me too, man. I'm not getting any younger; it's time I grow up. I need to be the type of guy a woman can count on, instead of another idiot looking to get his dick wet."

"Speaking of women, how are things with Denise? You guys work things out yet?"

Fucking Connor, jumping right to the crux of the issue.

"Not that it's your business," I say with a pointed look, "but we're friends again. I'm leaving it at that for now. She broke up with Andrew, again, and she doesn't need me sniffing around." Not that I wasn't already waiting, but this time I'm going to give her more time. "She forgave me for my ill-timed confession last week, and that's enough for now."

Connor looks at me with a small smile on his face, nodding his head a little. "I'm impressed man. That is the smartest thing you have said about it. Be aware, though, if you screw this up, we're taking Denise in the divorce." He snickers.

"Believe me, I know." I nod while laughing, too. "She's amazing. I'd keep her over me too, if I had to choose."

"You are so whipped." Devon is coming back into the studio, Travis, Aiden, and Johnny trailing along behind him. Devon is almost six inches taller than each of the others and the way they're following him now makes him look like the pied piper. I wonder if he's going to lead all these guys into a lake and drown them? Nah, I can't see Devon doing anything so sinister. As scary as the guy looks, he's basically a giant teddy bear. To people he likes, anyway. Cross his friends and that's another story entirely. "I can't wait until you two are actually together to see what kind of purse she'll use to carry your balls in."

"Laugh it up, fuckers," I tell them all as they laugh. Not surprisingly, the only one not laughing is Connor. "Lady love comes for us all, and one of you assholes is sure to be next."

That sobers them up a little. They're all around the same age as me, which makes us all late bloomers in the love and commitment department. Not necessarily when you consider our career choice, but amongst the general population. Most people have had a serious relationship or two by the time they reach our age. Which means we're all due.

"Speak for yourself," Johnny says. "I'm not ready for that kind of relationship. I'll keep my balls where they are, thanks."

"Yeah, sure pal." I may have been preoccupied and drunk for the last little while, but I can see the way he looks at Becca when he thinks no one is watching. And he may or may not notice she's looking at him the same way. "I'll expect my wedding invitation in the mail soon."

"Oh, that's right." Travis turns to Connor. "Tomorrow's the big day. You all ready? What time do you need us there to help you set up?"

We spend the rest of the day going over the details of Connor's proposal to Alex. Listening to those guys talk, I'm glad I got tapped for 'distract Alex' duty. I'd way rather get the full body wax I have planned than set up hundreds and hundreds of candles. I'll take hanging with the girls over that sort of tedious manual labour any day.

"I can't believe you actually got waxed, Ryder," Becca laughs. We're sitting on the patio of a pub down the street from the spa, enjoying some appetizers and a couple of drinks before we all head our separate ways. "You should have seen that poor girl's face when she realized Ryder Sullivan, world famous lead guitarist for Sleeping Dogs, was up on her table with his ass in the air, waiting for her to wax his butthole." Tears are running down her face as she pictures it again.

"Who thought a group appointment was a good idea? I think I need to have my eyeballs bleached after that." Alex laughs too.

"Forget your eyeballs. I had her bleach my asshole. She didn't seem to mind when I asked her out." I didn't really ask her out. Telling Alex I did is part of my 'keeping her occupied before her surprise proposal' plan.

She spits her drink out, getting most of it on the table. "You did not! You asked her out? What did she say?"

"I'm picking her up at seven tonight," I lie. "I need to get home so I can get ready."

"What do you even need to get ready?" Becca asks. "You've waxed your junk and bleached your asshole. You should be good to go."

"I'll have you know I like to look good for my dates. Plus, I need to shower and make sure the bleach and wax are gone. Wouldn't want her to encounter any of it when she's not at her day job." I wiggle my eyebrows suggestively. I'm actually going to have a shower and change before the party. Maybe make up some plans for my upcoming classes at the gym.

"Such a gentleman." Alex jokes.

"I always take care of my lady friends," I say. "And with that, I'm out. See you guys at family dinner tomorrow. Thanks for inviting me to join you today. I love a good girls' day." I give both women hugs and then I'm gone.

Maybe I'll call Denise after my shower? To talk, like friends do sometimes. I bet I can make her laugh pretty hard with stories of my spa appointment today.

16

Marathon Peeing and the Wonders of Peenjazzling

Denise

SATURDAY COMES TOO SOON and before I know it, I'm hanging around the medical lab with the most uncomfortably full bladder I've ever experienced in my life.

Ryder invited me to join him and Becca while they distracted Alex at the spa today, and while I'd much rather be doing that, I don't want to put off this ultrasound. Today I will find out exactly how far along I am, and I may even get a picture of the baby. Maybe I can get two, so I can give one to Andrew when I talk to him next week. I haven't set up a day to do it yet, but I know it won't be until later in the week. I'm not ready to talk to him yet.

My eyes are on the nondescript clock on the wall as I wiggle and shift around in my seat. I'm trying to sit on the sides of my thighs because it seems to relieve some of the pressure on my bladder. All I want to know is, why do they tell you to drink so much water before you come if they're going to make you wait so long before they see you? If I don't get called soon, I'm going to be sitting in a puddle of my own piss, and I certainly won't be happy about it.

"Denise? We're all set for you." Finally, the ultrasound technician calls me. She leads me to a darkened room and gives me a gown to put on. "Take off your shirt and bra and put this on. You can leave your pants on. We'll push them down out of the way. When you're done, open the door a crack and I'll come back in."

She leaves me to my own devices and I get into the gown in what I imagine is record time. Leaving the door open a crack like she said, I go back and sit on the edge of the bed on the far side of the room. It's pretty spacious in here, which does nothing to distract me from the thought that most women who come for an ultrasound have someone with them.

At least, that's how I always imagined it would be. Me, lying on the bed while the tech moved the wand over my goo-covered belly while my husband looked on with tears and love in his eyes. It's cool though. I'm a bad bitch. I got this. The tears threatening to fall from my eyes have another opinion, but I don't have time for that now. I can cry later, when I'm back home alone.

"All set, Denise?" the tech asks from the doorway.

"Yup," I say back. *I left the door cracked, didn't I?*

"Okay," she says, coming back into the room. "Just lie back there and I'll get you all set up." She lifts the gown up to under my boobs and pushes the top of my pants down so far I bet she can see the top of my landing strip. That was always a bone of contention with Andrew, too. He thought I should be hairless. I thought adults shouldn't be hairless and refused to wax completely.

The technician tucks a towel in the top of my pants and squirts a pile of disgustingly warm goo onto my belly.

"It's so much better now that we keep this stuff warm," she says, making conversation. "It used to be so cold all the women would jump up off the bed." There's no way this girl is old enough to remember that. But then again, what do I know? I don't actually know when they started warming the stuff.

She grabs the wand and starts pushing and rubbing it over my belly.

"Oh man, I have to pee so bad." I laugh. "I hope I don't wet myself on this bed."

"Oh honey," she says to me, never taking her eyes off the screen in front of her, "it wouldn't be the first time and it definitely won't be the last. As soon as I get the images your doctor needs, you can go to the washroom, and we'll finish up when you get back."

"Oh my god, thank you. I feel like I've been holding it for days."

"I know, it's terrible. You'd think with technology being what it is, we wouldn't have to do it this way anymore. Sadly, a big ol' bladder full of liquid is the best magnifying glass we can hope for when it comes to looking at the fetus."

She makes a few more passes with the wand, stopping and clicking on her keyboard every few seconds before she puts it down. She reaches over and wipes my belly with the towel she's tucked into my pants.

"There you go, you poor thing. The bathroom is across the hall. Come straight back when you're done and we'll finish up and get you a picture." The smile she gives me is big and bright. That's reassuring. I was a little concerned she'd see something worrisome that she'd need to tell the doctor about. You know, thanks to this being a 'geriatric pregnancy' and all.

In the bathroom, I pee for a good thirty minutes. Okay, probably not, but it sure feels like I was peeing for a long time. And damn, did it ever feel good. I'd heard having an ultrasound wasn't the most comfortable experience, but who knew it was this bad? Who'd have thought holding your pee would be such a hardship? They ought to warn people.

Once I'm back in the room and settled on the bed, the rest of the ultrasound goes quickly. The baby is being shy so I don't find out the sex, but I do find out I'm right around twelve weeks along. I can't believe it's so far already. I must've been really busy the last few months to not realize I was feeling weird and missing my period.

A few more minutes and I'm on my way out the door, two copies of my ultrasound tucked into my purse.

It's getting close to dinnertime, but if I play my cards right, I should be able to go home and catch a nap before I need to get to the bar for the proposal party. I can't wait to see Alex's face when she realizes she's there for her proposal and not a small show like Connor is telling her. I wonder if he's going to sing to her? It would make sense if he did, considering he's the lead singer of Sleeping Dogs and all. I'm sure Alex will love it either way, but I think it would take a lot more than a pretty song to woo me.

Oh, who am I kidding? If the right guy sang me a song, sent me an email, or even bought me a hot dog at a baseball game I'd probably come running. If I didn't have this baby to think of, that is. The baby comes first now.

I get in my car, and begin my drive home, when my phone rings. It connects to the hands-free feature of my car's stereo system when I answer.

"Hello?"

"*Hey, Denise. It's Ryder.*" Speaking of the right guy.

"Hey, what's up? How's the spa day going?" I still can't believe Ryder is spending the day at the spa with Alex to keep her distracted while Connor gets his proposal plans all set up.

He chuckles quietly before he says, "*Well, I have a lot more respect for male strippers and the lengths they go to for beauty.*"

"Well, shit," I laugh. "I guess you'll need to rethink your plan of stripping if this whole band thing doesn't work out."

"Absolutely. There's no way I can commit to full-body hairlessness if these are the methods required."

"Tell me you didn't wax your chest?" I snicker as I picture him going full *40-Year-Old Virgin* and screaming out 'Kelly Clarkson' like Steve Carell's character.

"I waxed my everything," he says, *"and I do not recommend it."* I can see him pushing his lower lip out in a big pout.

Uncontrollable laughter bursts out of my mouth and tears stream down my face. I'm picturing Ryder writhing in anguish as a big, mean lady slathers him in hot wax and rips it off while he cries. It's so hard to see through my tears I'm forced to pull off the road and into the parking lot of a small diner.

"Oh yeah, thanks for laughing at my pain. I won't forget this next time you get your asshole waxed and bleached and are looking for sympathy."

That makes me laugh harder. Tears run down my cheeks and drip onto the steering wheel as I bend over, holding my stomach. My breath comes in gasps, and my laughs are nothing more than open-mouthed wheezes at this point. I can't remember when I've ever laughed this hard.

I take a few minutes before I can get myself under control and catch my breath. Ryder waits patiently on the phone the whole time, an occasional chuckle from him my one sign he's still there.

"What are you doing before the party?" I ask, on a whim. "Want to grab an early dinner with me, or do you need to go help Connor finish setting up?"

"Fuck that!" Ryder exclaims. *"I have already sacrificed all of my body hair for this proposal. I'm not planning to do anything more but have drinks, play his song, and say congratulations. So yes, I'd love to grab dinner."*

That gets another chuckle out of me. "I was laughing so hard I had to pull over and I'm here at a diner. Do you know where Maggie's is? On a hundred and eighth Street, downtown?"

"I know where it is. I'll meet you there in about fifteen minutes?"

"Sounds good. See you soon." I say before disconnecting the call.

I can't believe I asked Ryder to meet me for dinner. Why would I torture myself like this when I know I can't start anything with him?

He made me laugh so hard though, and I could really use the good cheer right now. It's not fair to either of us really, but it's so hard to think straight when I have such a good time talking to him. The invitation to dinner was out of my mouth before I even knew I was thinking about it. Last I knew, I was going home to nap before the party, and then suddenly I was asking Ryder out to eat.

Getting out of my car, I go into the diner and find us a place to sit. I choose a booth in the front window and I sit facing the door so I can see when Ryder comes in. The server brings me menus and I ask for a chocolate milkshake. I've been craving one forever. Okay, not really forever, just since I walked in here and saw this place is apparently home to 'Westborough's finest double cup milkshake'. So I've been craving it for all of three minutes, but, hey, pregnancy cravings are intense and forceful and not to be denied. At least not when it's the only liquid courage I can have before I face Ryder. Not that this place looks like it serves alcohol, even if I'd been able to have some.

I look over the menu while waiting for Ryder, and I hear a buzz from my cell phone. Shit, I hope he's not cancelling. I flip over my phone to look. Nope, it's Andrew.

Andrew- What are you up to? Want some company for dinner?

What is he thinking? He knows the party is tonight.

Me- No thanks, getting ready before heading out to the party tonight. I'll talk to you next week.

Andrew- Oh right, that's tonight. Okay, I'll talk to you later.

I put my phone on silent, and I'm putting it into my purse when I see Ryder pull into the lot. He parks next to my car and gets out. I can't help but check him out. His dark jeans hug his ass and quads and a grey, well-worn, looser fit, v-neck t-shirt shows a hint of the muscles I saw at my place. He's wearing black Chuck Taylors like he usually does and has mirrored aviator sunglasses shielding his eyes. The man looks practically edible.

I wave him over when he looks around to find me, and I see his face light up when he sees me. Andrew never looked that happy to see me, not once in our entire time together. How sad is it I was going to settle for that? That I was going to attempt to make that work? I'm shaking my head at my stupidity when Ryder makes it to the table and takes a seat across from me.

"What's wrong?" he asks while hooking his sunglasses into the front of his shirt. "Why are you shaking your head?"

Before I can answer, the server arrives with my milkshake. My enormous double milkshake. There's enough here for me, Ryder, and the table sitting across the aisle from us.

"Wow! This thing is huge. Want to split this with me?" I ask Ryder.

"Sure, it looks amazing. I saw the sign on the way in, and I was going to get a one, anyway. Now that I see the size of it I think it's better if I share with you." He looks at the server. "Can I get a cup of coffee too, please?"

She nods her head while fluttering her eyelashes at him, which sends a shock of jealousy through my body. *He's mine!* I say in my head before I can stop myself. That's not even right, anyway. He's not mine. He can't be mine. This baby is mine, that's all.

"So what's good here?" Ryder asks while opening the menu?

"No idea," I say. "I've never been here, I pulled in when I couldn't see to drive because I was laughing so hard I was crying. I figured it was as good a place as any. Dinner wasn't even on my mind before that; I was on my way home for a nap."

"A nap? Are you still not feeling well?" The concern in Ryder's eyes makes me like him a little more.

"Just tired." I say, wishing I could tell him the truth right now. But I want to tell Andrew first, before anyone else finds out. That seems like the right thing to do. "Plus napping is awesome."

"That is a fact," he says, still looking over the menu. I've already decided on a greasy cheeseburger with fries and gravy. Good old-fashioned diner food. "I like to get up early, but I also like to stay up late. The way to do both is to nap. You probably still have time for a quick nap after this, if we eat fast. You could probably get in a good hour and a half to two hours."

I grin. "I like that you think an hour and a half is a quick nap. I never understood these people who think twenty minutes is a nap. How do you even fall asleep that fast? And who feels rested after such a short time? Sounds like bullshit to me."

"Right?" Ryder puts his menu down as the server arrives with his coffee. She places a napkin down and then puts his cup on it, but off to the side a little. "You ready?" he asks me.

Ryder and I both place our orders, and he lifts his coffee cup to take a sip. He makes a face before reaching over for the cream and sugar, adding one of each to his cup. I get a closer look at the napkin when he does, and I see the server has written her name and phone number on it. Guess that's why she put the cup off to the side. Right as I'm debating whether to call Ryder's attention to it or not, he notices it, too. He smirks and scrunches his eyebrows a little before grabbing the napkin, using it to wipe up the condensation from my milkshake, and then crumpling it up into the little creamer container he used for his coffee.

"That was pretty rude of her," he says to me when he notices I've watched the entire thing. "She doesn't know we're friends and not on a date. Pretty insensitive if you ask me."

That's so thoughtful. A stranger had once given Andrew her phone number, and he put it into his pocket because he 'didn't want to hurt her feelings'. Even after hours of arguing, I still could never convince him my feelings should be more important than those of a stranger.

"I don't really blame her," I say. "Have you seen you? I'd be tempted to shoot my shot too." My face heats at the admission. I can only hope the heat doesn't correspond to visible redness.

"Oh, really?" Ryder's voice drops dangerously low, taking on a sensual tone not entirely appropriate for a family diner. "You like what you see?"

Flirting; that's what this is. Ryder is flirting with me and I'm loving it. I'm having someone else's baby. I shouldn't be doing this, but I can't seem to make myself stop. Ryder has been all I've ever wanted for so long even this baby isn't easily driving those feelings away. A little flirting is pretty harmless, really. Nothing bad can come from it, right?

"Well, I can't deny I'm interested in seeing the results of your waxing experiment," I deflect with a laugh.

He groans, running a hand over his face. "Ugh, it was the worst. I don't understand how some women do it all the time. I thought I was going to die when the waxer got to the 'good bits'. That's the last time I use my body like that to get laughs."

"You did that to get laughs?" Well it worked, because I'm laughing again. "Does it look funny? Did you get a design or something?" I'm picturing him naked with a little, pink, heart-shaped patch of pubic hair above his dick and it's simultaneously disturbing and kind of hot, so my laughs are tinged with a hint of hysteria.

"Haha, very funny," he deadpans. "I called ahead and had us all booked into the same room. The hilarity was from Becca and Alex witnessing my pain, not from getting myself vajazzled. No wait, that's for vaginas. What's it called for a penis? Pejazzled? Jazzledicked? Dickjazzled? No, wait. I know. It's peenjazzled, isn't it?" He waves his hands like he's trying to refocus. "Whatever. That's not the point. The point is, I did not get rhinestones anywhere on, or near, my junk."

"Stop, stop! I can't take it anymore." I gasp through laughs, hands on my belly again, and tears streaming down my face. "I can't breathe."

I'm still laughing a few minutes later when the server brings our food out. My cheeseburger and fries look amazing, but Ryder's talk of peenjazzling has me too distracted to eat yet. I take a few more minutes to calm down enough to take the first bite. It's the best burger I've ever had. Why have I never been here before?

"This is delicious." Ryder points at his own burger. It's a bacon chili cheeseburger, and it must be a good one because it's making a gigantic mess of his face. "We need some more napkins."

"Should've saved the server's phone number. You could have used it to wipe your face." I say while passing him my napkin.

"Is that a hint of jealousy I detect?" Ryder says as he wipes his mouth. "Never mind, don't answer that."

Poor guy looks a little broken-hearted. Maybe it's as hard for him to be here as it is for me.

"Yeah, it is." His head pops up at my confession, his eyes searching mine for answers.

"Denise?"

"I have no right to feel jealous, but I do all the same."

He heaves a sigh and leans back in the booth. "This situation is complicated for both of us. I am glad you asked me to join you for dinner, though. I enjoy spending time with you away from everyone else."

"I enjoy spending time with you, too, Ryder. I feel like I can relax when I'm with you. It's rare I get to relax." I admit. "Plus, when you're off doing something else I find I'm always worried you'll need me to come and get you out of trouble." Teasing him a little breaks the tension and we both laugh.

"I'm sorry about that. I promise to find better things to do with my time from now on."

We sit quietly for a few more minutes, each of us finishing as much of our meals as we can. If there's one thing Maggie's Diner does right, it's portion sizes. Everything is on scale with the milkshake, with each meal giving us enough food to feed two or three people. I excuse myself to the restroom and when I get back to our table, I see Ryder has already paid the bill.

"You didn't have to buy my dinner, Ryder, but thank you."

"You're welcome. Thanks for inviting me," he says as we leave the diner and walk to our cars. We both hesitate in front of our vehicles, Ryder with his hands in his pockets and me playing with my keys. "See you at the party, then?"

"Yeah, see you later," I say, walking around to my door and getting into my car. Ryder does the same, giving me a wave before he starts his car and drives off.

I suddenly really don't want him to go.

Fuck it. It can't hurt to pretend I deserve him for one day, can it?

17

Naps and Proposal Mishaps

Ryder

"Hello?" I say, answering the phone through my car's hands-free connection.

"*You want to come to my place before the party?*" It's Denise. I left her in the parking lot of that diner and she's already calling me. If you saw me smiling right now, you'd think I'd lost my marbles. No one smiles this widely when they're alone in a vehicle unless they're a little nutty.

"I'd love to, on one condition."

"*What's that?*" she asks, the suspicion clear in her voice.

"We need to nap. All that talk of napping earlier left me looking forward to having one, and I think you need one too."

She laughs. "*Yes, that sounds perfect.*"

"Okay, I'll meet you at your place."

"*See you soon,*" she says, then disconnects the call.

Good. Now I have a ten-minute drive to get this stupid grin off my face. And to convince my dick to calm down a little, if that's even possible. The thought of sleeping next to Denise has him all sorts of excited.

Driving to Denise's place also gives me time to think about what I plan to do once I get there. As much as I want to do more, I think it's best to stick to the nap like I said. Not only did Denise look like she could really use one, I'm hoping I get the chance to hold her like I did last time. I don't think that physical contact is what she invited me over for, and I will not go for anything more than holding her while she sleeps. I can't deny that being able to touch her was my primary motivation for asking to nap with her, though. And thinking about touching her makes my dick painfully hard. Which won't go over well. He needs to calm down.

I drive around for a few extra minutes, so by the time I get to Denise's, my smile is less crazy looking and my dick is at a much more manageable rigidity. Thanks to my extra driving time, she's beaten me here, so I park behind her in the driveway. I get out of my car and take a deep, calming breath. *You can do this,* I tell my dick. *We're not here to get in her pants. We're here to nap, and to be a good friend. That's it.* Nothing like a little pep talk to keep the ol' cock in line, am I right? I hope it works.

"I'm here," I call out after knocking and letting myself in.

"I'll be right down," she yells from upstairs. "Grab yourself a drink from the fridge if you want."

"Do you want me to get anything for you?"

"No, thanks."

I get myself a soda from the fridge and bring it back to the living room. Sitting on the couch, I look around her townhouse and remember that I was going to ask her about that string art that she has up everywhere. I'm still working on making my apartment feel more like a home, but acquiring enough art that I like is proving difficult. I don't want to buy a bunch of stuff that I don't really love.

"Hey." Denise comes around the couch to sit beside me.

"Nice shirt." I smile when I see she's wearing the shirt I left in her laundry last week. "It looks sort of familiar."

She chuckles a little. "Oh yeah, sorry. Found it in the laundry and claimed it. It's so comfortable."

"Well then, it's yours. It looks better on you anyway." It's way too big, hanging to the middle of her thighs, but I love how she looks in it. Because it's mine, and it makes me feel, a little, like maybe she's mine too.

She lowers her eyes a little before looking up at me. "I've never had a nap date before," she says quietly. "So how does it work?"

I think for a second, my tongue pushing my lip ring from side to side. I can't come right out and say that I want to hold her while she sleeps, even though I want it more than anything, so I settle on giving her options. "Well, we know we're going to nap. It's up to you how that will look." She nods. "Last time I was here with you, we slept on the couch, so we can do that again. Or I can nap on the couch and you can nap in your bed." She looks into my eyes, urging me on. "Or we can both nap in your bed. But whichever option you choose, we need to make sure we set an alarm so that we make it to the party on time. I don't think either of us wants to miss it."

"You especially," she laughs. "Considering you made the ultimate sacrifice to keep Alex occupied."

I laugh along with her.

"Yeah. That full-body wax probably wasn't the best idea I've ever had. I can admit that now."

I lean forward to grab my soda from the coffee table, taking a long drink to calm my nerves. I meant it when I said it was up to her, but I am really hoping she picks one of the two options that gets me closer to her. Even if we wind up on the couch again. As long as I get to hold her, I'll be happy.

Suddenly, she stands up and reaches out to take my hand. I let her pull me up off the couch and follow as she leads me down the hallway and up the stairs. When we get into her bedroom, I look around.

"There's more room here." She gestures to her king-size bed. "We'll both be more comfortable this way."

She pulls back the duvet and climbs into bed, sliding over to the far side, leaving room for me. Without making a big deal out of it, I reach behind my head and pull my shirt off before undoing my jeans and dropping them to the floor. She's seen me naked before so I shouldn't be so nervous to be standing here in my boxers, but I am. It's one thing for me to be naked and acting like an idiot in front of the guys when she happens to be there. It's another thing entirely being nearly naked, half hard (*what did I tell you, dick? Get it together*), and getting ready to sleep in a bed with someone as sexy as Denise. I wonder if this is what stage fright feels like? I've never experienced it before, but I imagine it can't be much worse than this.

I sit on the edge of the bed and pull off my socks before laying down and pulling the duvet up to my waist. I can feel Denise shift to look at me. She chuckles a little to herself.

"You're going to end up pulling that lip ring right out if you don't stop wiggling it around with your tongue."

"Nervous habit," I say, turning to look at her. "To be honest, I'm not really sure what I'm supposed to be doing right now, and it's freaking me out a little."

"We're napping. Close your eyes and go to sleep. Simple." She smiles at me, making little crinkles appear at the corner of her blue eyes.

"Very funny, smartass." I shake my head at her and grin. "I mean, am I allowed to touch you? Like, hold you, not anything more."

She smiles again, looking up at me through her lashes, and I feel a sense of hope building in my chest. She quickly flips her body, so she's facing away from me, and then reaches back to grab my hand. She uses it to pull my arm over her, scooching her body back against mine, so I'm spooning her.

"There," she says. "No more freaking out. Now sleep."

This is more than I could have hoped for. I move my other arm up and over her head, which lets me get even closer to her. I snuggle in a little closer yet, tucking my face right into her hair, and I inhale as deeply as I can. Maybe I'm weird for loving the smell of her hair so much, but I can't get enough. It smells of coconuts and summer.

Denise has laced her fingers with mine and she's tucked our hands up by her breasts. The trouble is that she has her hand over the top of mine, so she's essentially holding my palm to her breast. It's not helping the situation in my pants at all.

The feel of her breast under my hand, together with the smell of her hair, and feel of my body around hers, combine to give my dick the wrong idea. I meant what I said about not trying anything else, so with my erection growing by the second, I carefully slide my ass backwards. Hopefully, I've moved far enough away she won't feel me getting harder and harder, even if it feels ridiculous to have my ass sticking out this far.

Denise's breaths tell me she is relaxing into sleep. Her grip on my hand loosens as her body sinks into the bed. I want to stay awake and enjoy this moment, but having my arms around her like this, with her so warm, soft, and relaxed, has me floating away into unconsciousness with dreams of Denise dancing in my mind.

I WAKE UP SLOWLY to the feel of my lip ring moving back and forth. Opening my eyes, I see Denise has turned over and is facing me now. Her left hand is raised, and she's moving my lip ring with her fingers, a small smile on her face while she does so.

She must sense that I'm awake because she doesn't move her eyes before saying, "I can see why you mess with it so much. It's kind of fun."

"It really is," I whisper, not wanting her to stop touching me. My heart is pounding through my chest. She must be able to feel it shaking the bed.

My hand is flung over her waist, resting where her ass curves out from her lower back. I glide my hand from her back to her side, gripping her hip gently before sliding up to rest my hand under the hem of her shirt, feeling how soft the skin of her waist is. She moves her eyes up to meet mine, her hand moving from my lip up to trace my left eyebrow.

"What happened to these?" she asks, noticing that I've removed my eyebrow piercings. "Why'd you take them out?"

"I took them out when I worked out with Connor the other day and didn't bother to put them back in. I wasn't really feeling them anymore, anyway. Plus, it's a hassle to remove them all every time I have a class to teach at the gym. I kept the lip ring because it's fun to mess with."

"Hmm, I see." She slides her hand up to tangle into my hair. Her fingernails scratch my scalp gently, sending tingles down my neck. If I stay completely still, maybe she'll do this forever, because it feels fucking amazing to have her touching me like this.

Her tongue darts out, wetting her lower lip, before she grips my hair and pulls my lips down to meet hers. She gives me one soft kiss before resting her open lips against mine and using her tongue to move my lip ring from side to side. A low moan escapes my throat before I can stop it.

Denise pulls back, a little, to smile and whisper, "It's more fun if I use my tongue."

Fuck staying completely still. That was before she kissed me. I'm not sure what's changed her mind, but I'm too far gone already to question my good fortune. I close the distance between us and kiss her again. My tongue slips in and she opens her lips more, deepening the kiss. She grips my hair tightly in one hand, sending a barrage of scorching tingles along my scalp, while her other hand presses against my chest. I pull her toward me, unable to get close enough as we face each other on our sides.

"Yes, Ryder. More," she moans into my mouth. "I've wanted you for so long. I can't stay away any longer."

I push her onto her back without breaking the kiss, my body following as I move her, coming to rest in the space she's made for me between her legs. Needing some relief, I press my hard cock against her, feeling the heat of her pussy through the fabric of our underwear. She whimpers in response, pressing herself closer to me.

I explore her mouth with my tongue while I push her shirt up, interrupting the kiss to take it off. Holding myself up over her, I see her eyes blown with lust. Her pupils are so large her eyes look almost completely black, with a small ring of light blue surrounding them. She looks like a goddess with her impossibly black hair fanned out over the pillow and her lips swollen from our kisses.

"You are so beautiful." I lean down and whisper in her ear. "The most beautiful woman I've ever seen. You wouldn't believe how many times I've dreamed of you like this." I take a breath and say, "This is so much better than I ever dreamed."

I kiss down the line of her neck and across her collarbone. My hands roaming her body while my lips kiss a different path. She grips my hair in her fists, following my movements all the while. I trail my lips down her breast, stopping to pull a pebbled nipple into my mouth. She meets the light grazing of my teeth with a gasp that quickly turns into a moan, one of her hands releasing my hair to reach up behind her as she arches her back to push herself to me. I squeeze her frantically, trying to memorize the way her body feels in my hands. I already don't want this to end.

Her body shivers as I dance my tongue along her smooth flesh, and I feel my breath heat her skin. When I make it to the line of her panties, I sit up and pull them down her legs and off her feet. I look back up and see her looking at me, still with me in this, so I lower myself and string kisses along her right leg, from the top of her foot upwards. I cross over the apex of her legs, hearing her groan as I purposely miss the spot where she needs me, and kiss down her left leg to the top of her foot. As my kisses reach her toes, I slide myself off the bed, pulling her along with me until she reaches the edge of the mattress.

Kneeling on the floor at the end of the bed puts me on a level with her pussy.

"God, this pussy, babe." I groan against her inner thigh as I kiss and lick my way closer to her center. "So pretty, so perfect." I place a kiss right over the firm nub of her clit and her body bucks in response.

"I've been waiting to taste you forever." I tell her, before licking from her glistening entrance upward. "After you let me touch you the other day, I knew I'd never be happy until I could feel you come on my tongue. And I am going to be so happy today, babe." When I reach her clit this time, I suck it directly into my mouth, fastening myself against her. I massage her with my tongue, flicking, licking, and sucking until grabs my hair with both hands and pulls me closer.

"Oh god, Ryder." I can feel the way she moans my name right down to my balls. "Don't fucking stop."

She rides my face, thrusting her hips up toward my mouth. Her body shudders and she grabs my hair tighter, pulling my face even closer, as her orgasm takes hold and doesn't let go. She throws her head back, eyes closed, as a low moan escapes her mouth. Sucking and licking her until the pulsing of her orgasm slows, I finally release the suction grip I have on her clit and focus on licking around her slowly, savouring the taste of her orgasm on my tongue.

"Fuck, Denise," I say against her pussy. "You look so gorgeous when you come. I'm going to make you do it again for me now, okay?"

She nods eagerly, looking at me through hooded eyes. Damn, she's beautiful.

I kiss down her thigh again, reaching for my jeans and grabbing a condom from the pocket. I throw it up on the bed beside Denise and slowly kiss my way back up her body before taking her mouth in mine again. We kiss slowly, taking our time, savoring each other. I'm holding Denise's face in my hand, my fingers tangled in her hair, while she runs her hands up and down my back.

Our kiss grows deeper and more heated until finally Denise is pushing my boxers down with her hands. I sit back so she can push them down farther and she moves her body all the way back, kneeling up on the bed in front of me. Turning us around, she pushes me back on the bed and works my boxers the rest of the way down my legs before kicking them to the floor to join her panties.

"Condom?"

I feel around on the bed until my hand finds the condom I threw, and grab it and tear it open. Denise takes it from me before I can put it on, though. Straddling my legs, she places the condom on the tip of my cock, squeezing my shaft with one hand, and I nearly lose control. She raises one eyebrow at me before sliding her body a little further down the bed. She licks her lips, leans all the way down, and rolls the condom down my dick, using her mouth. I immediately feel the tingling start at the base of my balls, my orgasm threatening to come much too soon.

"Holy shit. Fuck. Denise, That is so fucking hot."

She strokes me with her mouth a few times before releasing me and sitting up again, a smile on her perfect lips.

"You like that, do you?"

"Oh babe, I don't think there's anything you could do that I wouldn't like, but that is a definite front runner for my favorite."

She crawls up my body, licking along the V muscles that make up my adonis belt, and I secretly thank my workouts with Pops for giving her something to kiss. She continues to kiss up my torso, stopping when she gets to a barbell through one of my nipples.

"Oh, I like this." she says, before gently pulling the whole thing, nipple and barbell, into her mouth, flicking it with her tongue. A tingling current shoots to my dick, making my balls tighten.

I moan a little louder this time. "Oh, I like that too." I breathe. "Don't forget about the other one." I grab one of her hands and bring it to my other nipple, encouraging her to play with it, too.

She pinches and pulls one nipple while rolling the other over her tongue before releasing both and taking me in a deep kiss again. Her tongue takes charge of mine, kissing me so passionately I nearly lose my breath.

"Shit, Denise, baby."

She continues kissing me and reaches down to grab my hard cock with one hand. She lines me up and slowly slides her pussy down over me. A guttural sound escapes my throat as she lowers herself inch by agonizing inch. Once I'm completely inside her, she releases our kiss and moans loudly into my mouth.

"So good," she says with the moan. "How do you feel so fucking good?"

She rocks her body, grinding her clit against me, chasing another orgasm. I grip her hips and raise mine in time to meet hers, keeping her pace. She opens her eyes, pupils still completely blown, and looks straight into my own. I'm afraid she'll see my love for her plainly written on my face, so I sit up and take her lips in a kiss.

Gripping her with one arm and balancing on the other, I flip us over and put myself on top, needing to control the pace or I'll come too soon.

"You feel too good," I say against her mouth. "I can hardly control myself."

"So don't," she whispers. "Let go. I want to feel you."

"Not until you give me another one, babe. I need to feel you to come on my dick." I thrust a little harder before reaching down and putting my thumb over her clit and letting my body grind it against her as I slide in and out of her warm pussy.

"You're so fucking wet, babe. It feels amazing."

"Shut up and fuck me harder, Ryder," she groans before grabbing my ass with both hands and pulling me into her.

I pull back and slam back into her, hard; fucking her slow, but rough.

"Like that? Is that what you like, babe?" I murmur into her ear between thrusts. "You like it when I fuck you hard?"

Her answering moan tells me all I need to know. I continue to slam into her until I feel the walls of her pussy squeezing me, her orgasm nearing. Her moans get louder, her nails digging into my back as I pump into her, forcing her release from her body.

When her moans soften, and the pulsing from her slows more, I pull out and flip her over.

"Up on your knees, babe," I say roughly, my voice like gravel. I grip her hips and pull her back until her face is in the pillow and her ass is in the air. "Yeah, like that. Fuck, you look so hot like this. You're practically dripping, you're so wet." I bend down and shove my face right in her pussy, licking every drop of wetness that I can get.

"You taste delicious," I say, straightening my body, lining my cock up with her entrance and slamming into her again, "but I think I'll die if I don't get to come inside you right now."

She groans again and pushes her ass back against me, forcing me to fuck her faster and harder. I reach down and grab her hair, twisting it around my hand, and pulling as I fuck her.

"You feel so good, Ryder," she says on a breath, her head pulled back by the hair twisted around my fist. "Oh. Don't stop." An orgasm rips through her body, forcing her to clench around my dick, and my orgasm catches me by surprise, filling the condom with jet after jet of come.

"Oh, fuck," I groan as I come, pumping a few more times before stilling against her. She continues to clench her muscles around me, extending my orgasm more than I ever thought possible, milking every drop from me. When it finally subsides, I slide out and remove the condom, tying it off, and dropping it to the floor to deal with after. I lean over and kiss her shoulder, pulling her down and wrapping her in my arms.

God, I love this woman.

I'm so fucked.

"Be right back, babe." I roll out of bed and pull my boxers on. After disposing of the condom in the bathroom trash can, I go down to the kitchen and grab two bottles of water from the fridge. I run back up the stairs to Denise's room, bottles in hand.

Denise has put my shirt back on and is laying on top of the blankets, her long legs left naked. Putting the bottled waters on the bedside table, I jump onto the bed beside Denise, making her bounce up into the air, earning me a giggle. Fuck, her laugh is sexy. I could listen to it all day. I wrap my arms around her, nuzzling into her neck, kissing her while I throw one leg over hers and squeeze her in a full body hug.

"I thought you might be thirsty," I say, leaning back and grabbing a bottle of water without letting her go completely. I pass it to her and take the other bottle for me. "I know I am." One of my arms is stuck underneath her, but I refuse to let her go, making it pretty much impossible to open my water. Luckily, Denise notices and twists off the top for me.

I drink back three quarters of the water before putting the bottle on the nightstand. Denise has already put hers down and is looking at me, her face unreadable. Using my knuckle under her chin, I tilt her face up to me and press my lips to hers. My tongue reaches out to explore the seam of her lips before she opens to me, allowing me to kiss her more deeply. I pull back from her lips and place chaste kisses on both cheeks, on her eyelids, and lastly, on her forehead. I lean back, pulling her to me so she's laying with her head on my chest. Even after what we shared, I'm scared she's pulling away. Something is preventing her from being all here with me, and I need to know what it is. I don't think now is the time to discuss it.

"That was amazing, Denise." I finally say. "When can we do that again? I vote we skip the party and stay here and do that all night. Deal?"

She laughs and smacks me lightly. "Yeah, right, that'd go over real well. We can't skip our friends' surprise proposal and engagement party. Especially after all the trouble you went through."

"Yeah, I suppose you're right." I push my boxers down and cup my balls. "What do you think, by the way? Nice and smooth right? I'd show you my waxed and bleached butthole but I have a feeling we're not there yet. That's probably more of a second nap date kind of activity."

"Oh my god, Ryder." She laughs, pushing off of me and sitting up. "We are definitely not at a butthole viewing level of comfort in our relationship." She reaches down and caresses my balls, feeling their hairlessness, forcing a groan from my throat while all the blood in my body moves to my dick, getting ready for another round. "These do feel pretty nice though."

"Don't get too used to it. I am *never* doing that again. Not only does the hot wax hurt like a son of a bitch, but ripping the wax off is a whole other level of pain. And then, after all that, the chick slapped me every time she pulled a strip off. I'm all for a little rough stuff but having my balls slapped around like that... Yeah, no thanks." It hurt like no pain I've ever felt before and for some unknown reason I got a little hard while it was going on. I'm not telling Denise that part, though. That seems like a little TMI, even for me.

"What the hell, Ryder? Did you not ask what waxing was like before you agreed to it? What were you expecting?" She's laughing hysterically again, tears coming to her eyes. If it's anything like she experienced earlier today, it's no wonder she had to pull over.

She gets up and goes into the walk-in closet and I follow behind her, not bothering to pull up my boxers. While she flips through skirt and dress options, I wrap my arms around her from behind and rest my chin on her shoulder. I press my hard cock against her ass. With boxers pulled down and her wearing only my t-shirt, it's skin on skin and it feels amazing.

"You're going to get me all riled up and leave me hanging like this?" I tease.

She pushes back against me. "Yup," she says, "I hear having blue balls builds character."

"Hey." I spin her around and wrap my arms around her again. "I'll have you know I have plenty of character." She reaches her arms up and puts them around my neck. I can't see how my life can get much more perfect than it is at this minute. "I've been waiting for you for a long time, Denise. My balls have been plenty blue. Plus, right now they're black *and* blue. You know, from all the slapping."

She bursts out laughing at that, and I can't help but smile. Fuck, I love this woman. I can't imagine going back to the way things were between us after this. And that's why I do what I do next.

That, and I'm an idiot.

"I love you, Denise," I blurt. "Marry me?"

"WHAT?!?!" She stares at me, eyes wide and unblinking.

Oh shit, I fucked up. Turns out waxing my entire body is the *second* dumbest thing I've done today. Who would've thought?

18

Proposals and Pants-Party Puppets

Denise

"WHAT?" HE CAN'T BE serious. "Did you ask me to marry you?"

"Yes?" Ryder is standing in front of me, in my closet, in his boxers. He cringes a little when he answers.

"Was that a question? Are you asking me if you proposed to me while standing in my closet in your underwear? Correction, standing in my closet, *halfway* in your underwear." He's standing there with his dick and balls popping out over the waistband of his boxers, looking like some kind of upside down bug-eyed pants-party puppet with an enormous nose. I can't tell if I'm super freaked out that he proposed, or if I find the circumstances hilarious. I think maybe I want to laugh, but I also want to cry a little, or maybe do both at the same time? I'm not too sure. What I am sure of is that we don't have time for either of these reactions. We have a party to get to.

But I will definitely need to talk to him about my pregnancy sooner rather than later. It was already going to be a weird enough conversation, considering I couldn't keep it in my pants. But having sex *and* a proposal hanging over our heads while I tell him? Not exactly how I imagined that conversation would go down.

"Yes?" Ryder says again, while pulling his boxers up to cover his dick properly. "I mean no, I'm not asking you if I proposed. I did. And yes, I am standing here in my underwear. I don't suppose you'd consider forgetting about it?" Ryder is holding my arms while he looks at me. His eyes go from looking at me to looking at the ceiling to looking like he wants the floor to swallow him whole. He's adorable, in a 'crazy person who proposes to a woman the first time he sleeps with her' kind of way. Imagine what the tabloids would think of Sleeping Dogs' party boy ladies' man if they could see him now.

"Look Ryder," I say, taking a breath. "We need to get ready and get going or we're going to be late. But after what's happened here today I think you and I need to talk."

"Ouch," he says, dramatically grabbing his chest over his heart. "So that's a no?"

"That's a no to forgetting it entirely. But we can forget it for now." I wish I could remember it forever. I wish I had the luxury of taking it seriously and actually saying yes, regardless of his state of dress during the proposal. But I have to remember that it wouldn't be fair of me to trap Ryder in this pregnancy with me. That's not his responsibility. "We can talk about this later. Okay?"

"Yeah, that works." He leans down and kisses me. "Can I take you to the party? You know, since you won't marry me?" He laughs nervously.

"I'd like that." I smile, fighting back tears. Fucking pregnancy hormones. They're making this so much harder than it needs to be. "Can you give me a few minutes to get myself sorted here?" I ask before quickly turning around so he can't see my tears.

He rests a hand on my shoulder before walking out of my closet. I watch as he pulls on his jeans, pick up his shirt and socks, and leaves the room. I take a deep breath and fan my eyes to stop the tears before they have the chance to turn my entire face red. Why am I even crying? Because he asked me to marry him? Because he can't possibly be serious? Or because I really want to say yes but know that I can't?

Ugh, what a mess this is. I still have to tell Andrew about the baby. How would that even work? He's always been jealous of Ryder. I can imagine the jealousy he would feel if I tried to be with Ryder while having his baby. It would be better for all of us if I tell Ryder we can't continue. Especially for Ryder. I can't let my own feelings interfere with what is best for him. It would be selfish to let him love me, knowing I have a baby on the way. It's bad enough that I slept with him, I can't let him think more is possible.

This baby is my responsibility. Not his. I'll tell him tonight that we can only be friends. No matter how much it hurts me.

"Wow!" Ryder stands up from the couch when I come into the room. "You look incredible."

"Thank you." I'm wearing a simple black belted dress with red stiletto booties. I'm already getting a tiny baby bump, although so far it looks like I'm bloated, and most of my other dresses weren't fitting right. But thanks to my expert make-up application skills, you can't even tell I was bawling my eyes out in the shower less than half an hour ago. "Are we all set?"

He leans over and kisses me, a soft brush of his lips, but my knees still go weak. Ryder kissing me is enough to make me swoon, like those silly girls in the movies. Who knew that stuff was real?

"Now I'm ready." He smiles down at me. How can he look so good when he's wearing the same jeans and t-shirt he's had on since the diner? It should be a crime to be so sexy and distracting.

Even his messy sex hair looks better than if he'd taken the time to style it.

He takes my hand, lacing his fingers with mine, and leads me outside, waiting with me while I lock the door. He opens his car door to let me in, passing me the seat belt before closing the door and walking around to the other side.

Okay, girl. You got this. Tell him the two of you can't be involved. Explain that it's best you be friends. Tell him you never want to have mind-blowing, toe-curling, scream your lungs out sex ever again.

Gah! I will never have good sex again. Damn you, Ryder. If it weren't for you, I wouldn't have even known what good sex was.

I shouldn't have agreed to let him take me to the party. Now I will need to find another way home. I can't imagine he'll be too happy with what I have to say. Not after all the amazing sex we had and the fact that he proposed to me not much more than an hour ago.

"Ryder?" I say to get his attention. I can do this. "I think we need to talk about what happened."

"Okay," he drawls, glancing at me from the corner of his eye.

"I had an amazing time with you today." I want to make sure he knows. "And you have made me feel more special, and cared for, than I have in a long time and I want to thank you for that."

"But?"

"But, I think, with so much going on right now, it's best if we stay friends." There, I said it. And it's hurts so fucking bad.

"What? What do you mean, 'stay friends'?" He raises his voice, but he doesn't sound angry, surprised. "I may have been jumping the gun a little asking you to marry me, especially considering I was standing there with my dick out, but I still meant it when I said I love you. I love you, Denise. And I know you feel something more than friendly feelings toward me."

I'm fighting tears again. I can't seem to blink my eyes fast enough to keep them away. I fan my face with my hands while trying to simultaneously search in my purse for a tissue. Ryder notices what I'm doing and reaches over to open his glove box, taking out a small package of tissues and handing it to me.

"Thanks." I say through sniffles. I dab my eyes with a tissue and take a few deep breaths. "I broke up with Andrew," I say. "Connor and Alex are getting engaged. You guys have an album to write and record. The timing isn't right for us." *Not to mention the fact that I'm having another man's baby and that wouldn't be fair to you*, I add in my head.

Ryder says nothing, doesn't even glance in my direction, he keeps driving. He drives us all the way to Rough Mix and parks in the side lot, all without saying a single word. When he turns off the car, he comes around and opens my door, holding out his hand to help me up. Ryder drives a gorgeous Camaro. It's easy to get into but not so easy to get out of, so I'm grateful for the help.

Before I can go more than a couple of steps, Ryder closes the door behind me, grabs me by the waist, and backs me up toward the car. He notches his hips against me, grinding me against the door, letting me feel the hard line of his cock through his jeans. I told him we can only be friends. How is he hard right now? My breath catches when he leans down and takes me in a deep kiss. He reaches one hand up into my hair, tilting my head where he wants me, and his other hand grabs my ass hard, pulling me closer to him. I can't resist. My arms reach up of their own accord, my fingers tangling in his hair, while my tongue dives into his mouth, matching him in his eagerness. It appears I have zero willpower with Ryder now that we've been intimate. I was telling him we can only be friends and now my tongue is in his mouth. We make out like teenagers at a movie theatre for several minutes before he finally pulls back. His hands move back around my waist, and he rests his forehead against mine.

"I have waited fifteen years for you, Denise. I know I love you, regardless of what is happening now, or whether you think the timing is right. And I am pretty sure that you love me back, but I won't presume to speak for you." He stops talking to wipe a tear from my eye. "I will give you some more time to get used to the idea, but I am not giving up. We will be together, because we love each other. And because when we are together, everything finally feels right." He pulls me in for another kiss, and it feels like he's pouring all of his love into this one, like he wants to imprint himself into my mind. And it's working. I lose all track of time and space, melting into him, kissing him like I'll never see him again.

"What the fuck is going on here?" Someone yells in our direction. Ryder pulls away and looks around. He sees Andrew at the same time as I do.

"I thought you told him not to come?" Ryder whispers to me.

"I did. I don't know why he's here."

"What the fuck is this, Denise? You're cheating on me with him?" Andrew yells as he stomps closer to us.

"Andrew, I broke up with you, remember?" Did he somehow not understand me when I told him that? "And I told you not to come tonight. What are you doing here?"

"I wanted to talk to you," he says. "And I knew you would be here tonight, so I came."

"This is pretty inappropriate, Andrew. Even for someone with your lack of social skills. You can't really think it's a good idea to confront your ex-girlfriend at an engagement party for her friends, can you?"

"Fuck off, Ryder. This isn't any of your business. This is between me and Denise."

"Hold up. You don't get to talk to Ryder like that." I jab my finger at Andrew before turning back to Ryder. "It's okay, Ryder. I can handle this. You can go ahead inside and I'll see you later. Thanks for driving me."

"Are you sure?" he asks. "You'll be okay with him?"

"There's nothing to worry about." I say in a reassuring voice. I'm pretty sure it will be okay, at least. "We'll be there in a few minutes."

Andrew relaxes noticeably at my use of the word 'we'll' regarding going inside. Ryder, on the other hand, tenses up. Still, he leans down and kisses my cheek.

"I'm not done with you yet," he whispers, so only I can hear. His voice is low and dripping with desire, and my legs clench with the rush of memories from what we did this afternoon. I am so screwed. "Andrew." Ryder nods as he turns and walks to the front of the bar.

I don't give Andrew a chance to say a word.

"And you," I say, pointing angrily, coming short of poking him in the chest. "You know it was wrong to come here. Completely inappropriate, not to mention rude. If you wanted to talk to me, you could have called. However, since you are here now, you may as well stay. Don't make a scene or I'll have Devon remove you, alright?" He nods his agreement. "You can drive me home after and we can talk then. There's something important I need to discuss with you, and I suppose tonight is as good a time as any. This doesn't mean that we are together, though. Because we are not." And with that, I turn and walk to the front of the bar as well, leaving Andrew to scramble along behind me, trying to catch up.

19

Voicing Suspicions

Ryder

I'M SITTING WITH BECCA when Denise and Andrew come in the doors at Rough Mix. They were out there for a couple of minutes after I left, and if I know Denise at all, she spent the entire time giving Andrew shit. Dude deserves it too. Who crashes an engagement party to talk to his ex? That's over the line.

"Are you doing okay?" Becca is trying to get my attention.

"Hmmm, what?" I say, when I finally catch on, that she's talking to me. "What did you say?"

"I asked if you are okay? How're all the waxing sites feeling?" She's chuckling while she asks, so I feel confident that my mission to make Alex and her laugh today was a success. But her mention of the waxing sites reminds me of the feel of Denise's hand on my balls when she was testing how smooth they are, which of course brings back the erection that was finally subsiding.

Awesome.

Being with Denise means I'll be walking around with a twenty-four seven boner. Can't say I'm complaining though, because I'll also get to ask her for help in relieving them. Pretty sure I come out on top in this scenario.

Unless she's on top, that is. Heh.

"Ryder? Are you listening?" Becca is waving her hand in front of my face. Guess I drifted away there for a second.

"Oh, yeah, sorry. Yeah, everything feels fine." I tell her honestly. "I was sore for a bit, but I got over it quickly."

I look around and find Andrew and Denise again. She's walking around, mingling with everyone, and he's following her like a puppy. He doesn't even say hello to anyone. I wish he would leave, but Denise must have some sort of plan, or she would have made him go before she came in.

"Hey, man." Aiden is pulling up a stool beside me. "Did I see you out in the parking lot with Denise not too long ago?" He wiggles his eyebrows at me, already knowing the answer to his question.

"Oh, I want nothing to do with this dude convo," Becca says, grabbing her drink and standing up. "I'm going to go talk to Marcus and Domenic. See you guys later."

"So?" Aiden is waiting for an answer. "What's going on? And if something *is* going on, what is that shitstain Andrew doing here with her?"

I wasn't planning on saying anything about what happened with Denise today, but before I can stop myself, I say the stupidest thing I could possibly say. "I asked her to marry me today."

"WHAT?" Aiden nearly falls off his stool, catching the beer that he knocked over in his surprise before it rolls to the floor. "What do you mean you asked her to marry you?" he adds in a whisper.

"I mean, I was standing in my underwear in her closet while she was choosing what to wear tonight, and I told her I love her and want her to marry me."

"What the fuck, man? What did she say?"

"She said the timing isn't right for us, and that it's better if we're friends." I sigh and run my hand over my face. "And she laughed. A lot."

"Ouch, that hurts."

"Yeah, that's sort of what I said too."

"So what did I see in the parking lot? That didn't look much like ' friends' from where I was standing. At least, you've never had your tongue down *my* throat or your hand on *my* ass quite like that, and I'd like to think we're pretty good friends."

Aiden laughs when I reach over and pinch his ass.

"That's only for my very special friends." I say, my mood lightening. "If you play your cards right tonight, I might let you kiss me after the party."

"Okay, but really," Aiden says seriously, "What is Andrew doing here with her?"

"I don't know. She told him not to come, and he showed up. She said she had it taken care of. She's a grown woman, and I'm sure she has it handled. You know Denise, she's always in control of the situation."

"Of course she has it handled," he says. "But she shouldn't have to. He's crossing over into creep territory now, man. And it seems to me, if you're trying to be her man, you could take care of this for her. Or at least be there to back her up when she takes care of it. She doesn't see Andrew the same way we do. I don't think he's going to go away quietly after the party tonight."

"Fuck," I know he's right. But I don't want to step in and try to save the day when I know Denise can handle pretty much anything. And I don't think Andrew is anything to worry about. If Andrew *is* dangerous, though, I wouldn't be able to forgive myself if I didn't do everything I could to help her. "How do I do this? I don't want her thinking that I don't trust her to handle herself."

"I don't really know, man. You'll figure it out, though."

Right then, Connor's voice comes through the speakers. "Alright assholes, and Pops, thanks for joining us here tonight. I got word that Alex is almost here, so we're going to turn the lights down. If you all could move along to the tables set up along the outside edges of the bar now and stay as close to the walls as possible. I don't want her to know you're here until after the proposal. Okay, go to your seats now and this will all get started shortly."

"That's our cue. I'm going to get Denise to a table we can see from the stage," I tell Aiden. "Can you keep an eye on her too?"

"You got it. I'll go let Devon know too." Aiden grabs his beer and goes up to his drum kit on stage, stopping to talk to Devon on the way.

"I missed you." I whisper into Denise's ear when I get to her. Even five minutes away feels like too much. "Can we go back to your place after?" I lead her to a table that is close to the stage, right in front of where I will be standing.

She leans in close, her lips brushing my ear in a way that makes me think it's not an accident. "I have something important to talk to Andrew about, so I asked him to drive me home. I will call you when we're done talking though, to say goodnight."

Like hell I'm letting her go home alone with him. "I can come with you," I tell her. "In case he acts like he did in the parking lot."

"I think that was because he saw us kissing," she says, her lips right against my ear, sending shivers straight down my spine. "He was fine after you left."

I reach around behind her, placing my hand at the top of her ass, and I lean in closer to whisper in her ear. "Okay, if you think everything is fine, then I trust you. But I will be waiting for your call, and I can't promise I won't be in my car nearby, so that I can say goodnight in person." I keep my face near hers and lick the outer shell of her ear before gently kissing the hollow behind her jaw until she shivers.

"Cold? Want me to go grab you a sweater?" I ask when I lean back, a knowing smirk on my face.

I watch as she struggles to compose herself. "No," she squeaks out, "I'm fine."

I love knowing that I'm getting to her like this. Not the right time, my ass. Something else might be going on, but there's no denying that she is as crazy for me as I am for her. I may have agreed to give her some time, but I'm going to be as close to her as she'll let me be during that time. Needing to touch her again, I reach under the table and trace lazy patterns on her thigh with my fingertips.

Andrew is glaring at me from across the table. I lift my chin at him.

"What's up, Andrew? Having a good night?"

He doesn't answer me, looks at Denise. I don't like the way he's looking at her. Like he thinks they're still together. She was pretty clear outside when she told him she'd already broken up with him. He's not getting the message. I pull my arm away from her leg and put it around her shoulder, which gets me another glare from Andrew. I don't think he much likes my answering smirk.

When the door to the bar opens and I see Alex silhouetted against the light from the street, I turn away from Andrew. I don't want to rush my friends' special moment but I want this to be over with so I can get more time with Denise. I know she plans to talk to Andrew after the party, but I plan to be next in line for her attention as soon as she's done.

"Time for me to get up there," I whisper into Denise's ear with another kiss on her earlobe. "I'll be back soon." I jump up on stage, grab my guitar, and move off to the side where the rest of the guys are waiting.

Connor's proposal is romantic enough, I guess. He declares his undying love for Alex amidst an ocean of candles. We help him out by playing a new song that he wrote for her called

Meant to Be and I doubt there is a dry eye left in the place by the time he's done.

If I ever want to propose to Denise, I'm really going to have to step it up.

Hold up! What was that? If I want to propose? I proposed to her in her closet before we came here tonight. Of course, that proposal slipped out. But I have been obsessed with her for so long that it makes sense I would eventually propose. If she really will have me, anyway. I know I'm acting like she will right now, but that doesn't make it a reality.

Tonight, after she talks to Andrew and sends him on his way, I will tell her how I feel. I'll tell her the full extent of how I feel. I've told her I love her but it doesn't feel like enough. If I can make her believe that I really love her, and really want to marry her someday, maybe she will agree to give us a chance, to give me a chance. I know I can be the man that she deserves, if she'll let me prove it.

Now if I could figure out *how* I'm going to prove it.

A Party Crasher and a Knight in Shining Armor

Denise

CONNOR'S PROPOSAL TO ALEX is lovely, and the party afterward is fun. It would probably be more fun, though, if I weren't pregnant and exhausted. And if Andrew and Ryder weren't trying to kill each other with death glares while I sit between them.

Not that I mind Ryder trying to scare away Andrew, necessarily. It's going to make it that much harder when I tell him we can't be together after all. I just hope I'm strong enough to withstand his rejection. In my heart, I want him to want me anyway, but that's a dream. What man, especially one with Ryder's history of partying, would want a woman who is having another man's baby? I know he says he's changing, but it's one thing to be a little more responsible. It's another thing entirely to take on being the father of a baby that isn't his.

"You going to be okay if I leave you for a minute?" Ryder leans over and whispers into my ear. "I want to go talk to Alex and Connor."

I nod my head. This is perfect. It will give me the chance to get Andrew to drive me home without Ryder trying to butt in. I want to get this conversation with him over and done with.

We'll eventually need to come up with a plan for him being able to spend time with the baby, but for now, I want to tell him that the baby exists. And that even though that is the case, we will not be getting back together.

Alex has been darting glances over at me and Andrew occasionally while she's been accepting congratulations from everyone. I'm sure she's wondering what the hell he's doing here. I still can't believe he thought it was a good idea to crash this party to talk to me, even after I told him not to come. Not something he thought through, I'm guessing.

I don't feel bad about ducking out early. I can already see from the way Connor is eyeing Alex that they won't be here for much longer, anyway. The desire is plain on both their faces. I'm sure they'll be out of here shortly to go home and celebrate privately.

I stand up and wave at her, pointing to the door to let her know I'm leaving. I'll call her later and congratulate her. She waves back and nods to let me know she understands.

"Andrew, can you drive me home now?" I ask. "I need to talk to you about something private."

"Oh, thank god," he says. "I was wondering when you'd finally want to leave this place. I feel dirty being in this dive bar."

I roll my eyes while Andrew gets up from the table. I won't miss dealing with this. Of course, he's going to have to be okay with the baby being around my friends, but I'm sure he will understand that I would never bring a baby around anything dangerous. Then again, I never thought Andrew disliked almost everything about me, so I'm not sure I really know him well enough to say that.

I walk to the door of the bar, trusting that Andrew is following right behind me. I don't feel great about sneaking out on Ryder while he's busy, but this is the only way he'll give me the privacy I need for this conversation with Andrew. I'm so nervous about telling him that my stomach is all knotted up. I was on birth control, and this shouldn't have happened, but we always knew there was still a chance that I could get pregnant. When we were together, we said we would deal with it if it came up. Now that we're not together, I'm not sure how Andrew is going to feel about it.

Andrew parked near the building and I go to let myself in as soon as he presses the unlock button on his key fob. He frowns at me when I reach for the door handle before he does.

"I was going to open that for you," he pouts, before walking around to the driver's side of the vehicle.

"It's fine," I say once he's in the car. "I can open my own door." I don't want to give him any encouragement. The last thing I need is for him to think that opening my door means we're together again. With the way he's been acting lately, I wouldn't put it past him.

After a short drive in total silence, Andrew is pulling into my driveway. I'm out of the car and halfway up the steps before he's even turned the car off. I'm not interested in putting this conversation off any longer. We need to get this sorted out soon, so he has to know about it.

I unlock the door and go inside, leaving it open for Andrew to follow behind me.

"Have a seat." I say, pointing at the armchair as soon as he comes in. "We need to talk."

"Yes, we do," he says, sitting on the couch and patting the seat beside him for me to join him, but I sit in the armchair instead. I don't want to be any closer to him than absolutely necessary. "I've been thinking and I think I can deal with your friends and their crazy lifestyles if you agree to dress like a proper lady, and give up all this rock-and-roll style you like to wear."

I burst out laughing. What the hell is he thinking?

"I didn't ask you here for a relationship negotiation, Andrew. We broke up, and we are staying broken up. That's not why you're here." I take a few deep breaths to calm myself. It wouldn't do for me to laugh in the middle of what I have to say to him.

I pull a copy of the ultrasound photo from my purse and hold it out to him. "There is no way to soften the blow on this, so I'm going to say it. I'm pregnant, Andrew."

At first he says nothing at all. He is so quiet that I'm not sure if he even heard me. That's how little reaction he has to what I said. Then suddenly he's jumping up off the couch.

"WHAT THE FUCK?" he shrieks. "How did this fucking happen? You said you were on birth control."

"I'm guessing it happened in the usual way," I snap, slamming the ultrasound down on the coffee table. "How do you expect me to answer that?"

He paces in front of my coffee table, hands pulling roughly through his hair.

"I can't believe you would do this to me!" Andrew is raising his voice, yelling so loudly now that I'm sure the neighbors can hear him. He grabs the ultrasound picture and shakes it at me. "How do you even know this is my baby? People like you are always sleeping around. It could be anyone's." He grabs the picture in both hands and rips it into pieces before throwing it in my face.

"Excuse me? *People like me?*" Tears are pooling in my eyes, but I don't think I've ever been this angry. They are absolutely tears of rage. "I never cheated on you, Andrew. How can you even say that to me?"

Andrew walks over to one of the gallery walls where I've hung some of my embroidered artwork and old photos. Standing with his hands on his hips, he faces the wall. Suddenly he reaches out and swipes nearly every frame off the wall, shattering the glass and breaking the wood.

"I can't believe you would be stupid enough to let this happen!" He's screaming now, his face red, veins sticking out in his neck. "What kind of dumb bitch can't take birth control properly?"

He comes over to where I'm sitting in the armchair and grabs the lamp from the end table. He then swings it over his head and smashes it down on the floor beside me, sending shards of glass flying. I jump up, but I trip on the coffee table, stumbling into the couch.

"Stop!" I scream. As I right myself to a sitting position, and Andrew takes a step toward me, Ryder comes storming in through the front door.

"Alright asshole, I think that's enough."

21

Didn't See That Coming

Ryder

I ONLY WENT OVER to see Alex and Connor for a minute, to say a quick congratulations and let Connor laugh at my waxing fiasco, but when I look up again, Denise and Andrew are gone. My head swivels frantically, trying to find them in the crowd, but all I notice is Aiden calling me over.

We meet in the middle of the room.

"Denise and Andrew left. I saw them drive out of the parking lot now." Aiden is already walking toward the door. "I got a weird feeling, man. I think we should go after them."

I hurry to catch up. "You really think so?" Andrew weirds me out, but he's not dangerous. Is he? "They're going to talk. Denise said she was going to call me when he leaves her place."

Aiden stops at the door before pushing it open. "I know that, Ryder," he says. "But I'm saying I have a bad feeling about this. And I've been in this kind of situation before. Would you rather we listen to my gut and have nothing be wrong? Or not listen, and have something happen to Denise?"

"Okay, fine. You're right. Let's go." I pull my keys out of my pocket while we walk to my car. "But if everything is fine, you're leaving and I'm staying."

Ten minutes later, we're getting out of my car in front of Denise's townhouse. As we're walking to the door, a loud crash comes from inside the house. Holy shit, Aiden was right. Andrew is nuts! I sprint to the door, reaching for the handle, when Andrew's voice explodes through the door.

"I can't believe you would be stupid enough to let this happen!" That fucker Andrew is yelling at Denise, and I can hear her crying. "What kind of dumb bitch can't take birth control properly?"

HOLD UP! What the hell? Denise is pregnant?

I hear another crash and burst through the door, charging into her place.

"Stop!" Denise screams as she sits herself up on the couch, and Andrew takes a step in her direction.

"Alright asshole, I think that's enough." I jump over the back of the couch and get myself between them. Denise has tears running down her face while she looks down at the floor. "You need to go home and cool down before you say something you can't come back from." I may not like the guy, but Denise felt something for him once and if she really is having his baby, she probably wants him in the picture.

Holy shit. Is Denise really having his baby?

"You're going to let him kick me out?" He clearly meant this question for Denise, but I'm the one who answers instead.

"She's not letting me do anything. I'm doing this for you before the neighbour calls the cops, and you get arrested. So go." I point to the door. "You can talk to Denise tomorrow after you've both had some time to think."

"He's right, Andrew. Go home. Call me tomorrow." Denise is still looking at the floor, watching the tears fall in puddles at her feet. Fucking Andrew, how dare he make her cry like this?

"Fine." Andrew grabs his coat and walks out the door, slamming it as he leaves. I'm right behind him, following him out to the driveway.

Aiden is on the porch, watching us. I'm going to make sure Andrew gets in his car and leaves. Seems that he doesn't like how closely I'm following him, though, and before he gets to his car, Andrew spins around and steps right into me.

"It's yours, isn't it?" He spits at me. "That slut has been after you the entire time we've been together. She's probably been fucking you on the side since the beginning. You and him—" he gestures to Aiden "—and the rest of the trash in your band!"

"Look, asshole." I grab him by the front of his shirt and push him against the side of this car. "You better not let me hear you talk about her like that ever again. Denise has been faithful to you, so if she says that baby is yours, it's yours." I slam him against his car to drive the point home. I lean close, my forearm resting against his throat, and I say quietly, "Besides, I can guarantee if she had been sleeping with me, she'd have been so satisfied she wouldn't haven't bothered with you in the first place."

That's when Aiden reaches around me and grabs Andrew from my grip. "Alright, Ryder. That's enough for tonight. I think Andrew gets the point now. Don't you, buddy?" He looks at Andrew for confirmation, but instead of answering him, Andrew rubs his throat and glares at me.

"Why don't you go in and check on Denise?" Aiden says. "Before Andrew here makes you do something you regret."

"Yeah, that's probably a good idea. I promised her I wouldn't get into any more trouble. She has enough shit going on now and I won't be the one giving her more to worry about."

I take my keys out of my pocket and give them to Aiden. "Make sure he leaves, and then take my car and go home. I'll take a cab if I need a ride later."

It doesn't escape Andrew's notice when I say 'if I need a ride' and not 'when I need a ride'.

"I knew you were fucking her," he says, a cruel sneer on his lips.

He doesn't have time to react before my fist smashes into his face, causing an instant nosebleed.

"I told you to shut up. She dumped you, who she does, or does not fuck, is none of your business anymore. Now fuck off. You've caused enough trouble here for one night." I look at Aiden. "I'm going in. Take care of this?"

"Definitely. You know how I feel about abusive pieces of shit like our friend Andrew here. I'll deal with this, no problem. Devon is already on his way."

At least Andrew finally has the sense to look scared. When Devon and I took care of Alex's ex-boyfriend a little while back, he didn't know how much trouble he was in until parts of him were broken and he required a hospital visit. Devon doesn't look kindly on those who hurt his friends. He'd befriended Alex, and he took pleasure in hurting her ex, so who knows what he'll be like protecting Denise. He's known *her* for fifteen years.

Things are not looking good for Andrew.

Once inside, I lock the door behind me and walk over to the couch. I flop my ass down beside Denise and pull her into a hug.

"Well, normally after a situation like this I'd suggest a drink, but something tells me that's out of the question." I say with a small smile.

22

A Good Friend

Denise

THANK GOD FOR RYDER showing up when he did. I still don't think Andrew would have actually hurt me, but I'd also never seen him that angry before. I know we didn't plan this pregnancy, but we were together for a while and we're both in our thirties. It's not like having a baby now would devastate his career like it will mine. It's tricky to be the manager of a band at the best of times, never mind when you're pregnant or when you have a kid.

"So." Ryder is sitting beside me, his arm around my shoulders. "Do you want to talk about it?"

"What more is there to talk about?" I ask, while wiping the remaining tears from my face. "I guess you heard the news?"

"Yeah, I may have heard Andrew screaming something about birth control when I was about to knock on the door. So... you're having a baby?"

"How'd you guess?" Sarcasm has always been my default mode, why should this time be any different. "You win the big prize! Surprise, it's a brand new baby." I joke with a cynical laugh. If there is anyone less suited to parenthood than Ryder, I can't picture it. He's a thirty-four-year-old man with the mentality of a sixteen-year-old boy. He's not exactly a bastion of stability. Yet another reason that we can't be together, even if he still think that's what he wants.

He looks at me, shocked. Well, would you look at that? I made Ryder Sullivan speechless. This is certainly a day for the history books. First, my mild-mannered, accountant ex-boyfriend throws a hissy fit and trashes my house, and now Ryder Sullivan has no words. Will wonders never cease?

"Uhhhh," he says, while looking around the room at the mess.

"Relax, Ryder, I'm joking. I know you're not ready for that kind of commitment, regardless of what you've been thinking recently. Who wants to be saddled with a kid that isn't theirs, anyway? I have no interest in doing that to you."

"It didn't seem like Andrew was thrilled with the idea of having his own kid. You guys have never talked about what you would do if it happened?"

"That's part of what I don't understand. We have talked about it." I sigh and lean into Ryder a little more. I feel guilty for using him like this, but I could really use the comfort he's offering. He is one of my oldest friends, after all. "It's not like I planned to get pregnant, but we'd both agreed a long time ago that if it happened, it happened. He completely freaked out and blamed me when I told him."

"That's ridiculous," Ryder snorts. "It's not like you impregnated yourself. I'm pretty sure you lack one set of the required parts for such a thing to occur."

"Not to mention that isn't something that happens in humans, even in those with both required sets of parts." I smile. Ryder can always make me laugh when he wants to.

"Right? Plus, how would that even work?" He turns to look at me, a mischievous grin creeping across his face. "I'm sure plenty of women who would be thrilled at the ability to have their own babies with zero input from men. Think of the problems you would solve if you'd somehow figured it out."

"See, these are the real questions we should be asking. This is where science lets us down. Who cares about space when we need answers to important questions like these?" This conversation is getting silly, but it is working to cheer me up.

"I'm pretty sure I missed my calling." Ryder laughs. "I should have been a scientist instead of a guitar player. I could be studying what would be necessary for solo reproduction and how to make it happen instead of playing music on stage."

"Yeah, the world is definitely poorer for not having Ryder Sullivan, the scientist, in it."

Ryder pulls me close again, keeping his arm around me. I lean my head against him and inhale deeply. He smells like the outdoors, a mixture of earth and pine, and the aroma calms me. We sit like that for several minutes, with me inhaling his intoxicating scent while he holds me and runs his fingers along my upper arm.

"I don't want to tell everyone yet," I finally speak, pulling myself out of my reverie. "I'm not ready for them to know." I don't need their judgment. This is the most irresponsible thing I've ever done, and I can't stand to see their disappointed faces. I'll already have to deal with my parents at some point. I don't need to get it from all sides.

"I will do whatever you need me to, Denise." Ryder still has an arm around me, but he's also holding both of my hands in his. I never noticed before how big his hands are. I can feel his calloused fingertips touching my palms, and the tickling sensation is making it hard to focus on what he's saying. "But I should probably tell you that Aiden came with me tonight. He and Devon will make sure that Andrew goes home and stays there. So everyone may already know. But you should also know that none of us would ever judge you."

"Huh?" I say, still distracted by the feel of his hands on mine. "Aiden and Devon are here?"

"They're outside. And Aiden heard Andrew say that the baby is mine, so he knows you're pregnant. I won't say anything until you're ready though."

I'm about to say something when a huge yawn escapes my lips. Today has been so eventful. I think my body is about ready to shut down, and go into some sort of recovery mode, and let me tell you, I am here for it.

"But it's not your baby, though. Apparently it's my baby, since Andrew doesn't want to claim responsibility." I yawn again. I'm having a hard time keeping my eyes open.

"Come on, babe," Ryder says, standing up and holding out his hand. "Let's get you to bed. I have a feeling this has been a long day for you."

I reach up and take his hand, letting him help me off the couch. He laces his fingers through mine and pulls me up the stairs to my bedroom. The bed is still the mess that we made of it before we left to go to the party earlier. It's hard to believe that was today.

Ryder is right, this has been a very long day.

"You go into the bathroom and wash up and I will get the bed all made up, okay?" Ryder guides me out of the room. "Where are the clean sheets?"

"Linen closet outside the spare room, right there." I point to the door in question.

I shuffle into the bathroom. Looking in the mirror, all I can see is my puffy red face staring back at me. I make quick work of brushing my teeth and washing my face, pulling on Ryder's t-shirt again after I'm done. It really is the most comfortable shirt, and not because it still smells like him. And if I can't have him, at least I can wear his shirt and pretend. Until I wake up tomorrow morning and I'm forced to deal with what happened tonight, that is.

How could Andrew be so cruel? For someone who professed to love me, he sure seemed to exude hateful feelings tonight. I never would have expected that type of reaction from him. He was furious. Like, foaming at the mouth furious. I am so lucky Ryder got here when he did. If only he could have been here a few minutes earlier. Maybe he could have stopped Andrew from breaking all my stuff.

I must've had twenty-five or more pieces of embroidered artwork, plus another ten or so pictures hanging on that wall that he destroyed. I'm going to have so much glass to clean up tomorrow. And then I'll have to go find all new frames for everything. It took me years of shopping at vintage stores and thrift shops to find the ones that I had. Replacing those won't be easy.

Walking back to the bedroom, I see Ryder has already finished changing the sheets and is fluffing up the duvet now.

"Thank you, Ryder." He turns to face me at the sound of my voice. "You've been so helpful tonight." I wish I could hug him again, but now that he knows about the pregnancy, I really need to keep my distance. If I'd been keeping my distance this whole time, it would probably be easier to stay away from him now that he knows.

He surprises me by coming over and wrapping me in his arms. Tears well in my eyes as I wrap my arms around his waist, getting as close as I can. How am I going to be able to keep my distance when he's here in front of me, offering exactly what I need?

"Time to get into bed, babe. You're dead on your feet." Ryder turns and pulls the covers back, motioning for me to get in. "Is it okay if I lie with you for a bit?"

"You... you want to be here with me? Even though I'm pregnant?" I blurt, shocked. I really thought he would turn and run as soon as he found out.

"I want nothing more than to hold you while you sleep, if you'll let me. We can worry about the rest later. Tonight I want to comfort you after this crazy day."

My stomach drops. Oh. Right. He's being a good friend, comforting me when I'm obviously upset. I should have realized he wouldn't actually still want me. And I should be glad about that. It will make it much easier to stay away from him knowing that it is back to not even being a possibility.

So why does it hurt so much to hear him say it?

"Sure, Ryder. Thank you."

I climb into the bed and slide to the other side, turning to face away from him. I hear the sounds of him changing behind me. He'll probably get down to his boxers again. Because *that's* what I need. A reminder of exactly what I can never have again. I feel the tears welling up as Ryder's weight pushes the bed down behind me. He fixes the blankets over us and then reaches over my waist, pulling me against him. He holds me with one arm while he plays with my hair with the other.

As I focus on keeping my breathing even, silent tears trail down my face, soaking into my pillow. This needs to be the last time I get to feel Ryder's muscular arms around me. I can't handle him being so close when I know I can't have him.

Eventually I run out of tears and my breath steadies itself without my interference. Sleep finally takes me, dreamless and dark, allowing my body the rest it so desperately needs.

23

Clean Up on Aisle Three

Ryder

DENISE CRIES HERSELF TO sleep while I hold her. After the day she's had, I can't say that I blame her. The things I heard Andrew say to her should never be said to the mother of your child. How could he not want to have a baby with this beautiful, smart, strong, amazing woman? I know if I were lucky enough that Denise was having my baby, my reaction would have been a lot different. I wouldn't have screamed at her or called her a slut, for starters. Nor would I have broken anything in her house.

Speaking of things that Andrew broke, now that Denise is asleep, I'm going to take care of that stuff for her. She has enough going on. The last thing she needs to worry about is cleaning up that mess. I slip my arm out from under hers and slide off the bed, careful not to disturb her.

Grabbing my clothes from the floor, I tiptoe out into the hallway and close the bedroom door. I pull my clothes on before going downstairs to the kitchen. In the small closet near the front door I find the cleaning supplies I'm looking for and pull out the vacuum, a couple garbage bags, and an empty cardboard box. I put my shoes on and get to work.

Andrew really did a number on this place. I clean up the glass from the lamp, then I get to work picking up Denise's artwork. None of the prints or string art pieces are damaged, thankfully.

I'm sure Denise will appreciate that. But there are a few pieces of what looks like a ripped up picture. It's mostly black and white and I have the feeling that I've seen it before. I collect all the pieces and put them in the office, along with the other artwork.

Most of the frames themselves are fine, but the glass panes are all broken. After putting the wooden frames in the box, I tidy all the large glass shards and finish up with a vacuum. Last, I vacuum the furniture and wipe all the tables and bare floors with a damp rag to get any tiny shards that might be left behind. I really don't want Denise getting hurt by Andrew's stupidity.

When I bring the garbage out to the big outdoor garbage can, I see Devon hanging out in the Escalade in the driveway. That's odd.

I go to knock on his window, but he's already seen me coming and gets out of the truck to talk.

"How's she doing?" he asks.

"She's finally sleeping." I tell him. "I finished cleaning up all the broken glass and crap from the shit that Andrew broke. Not sure if you've ever noticed, but Denise has lots of artwork up on the walls? Well, it looks like Andrew tried to knock all of it down. There must be like fifty different pieces that he ripped off the walls. Plus, he broke a lamp."

"Fuck. What an asshole. Denise works really hard on those embroideries that she does. He had to have known that he was ruining something important to her."

"She makes those? That's amazing." At least now I know where I can get something like that for my place. *If* she would make me one. Not that she's going to have much time for that, with a kid on the way. "What are you doing here, anyway?" I finally get around to asking.

"There's a bit of a problem." Devon clears his throat and rubs a hand on the back of his neck. "Andrew lost us on his way home."

"What do you mean, he lost you? He went all Fast and Furious on you, drifting around corners, and gave you the slip?"

He laughs, but nods at the same time. "Essentially, yeah. That's exactly what he did. Who knew he could drive like that? Math nerd's got skills. Aiden is driving around, hoping to catch sight of him. I figured I'd come back here and wait, in case he shows up."

"You really think he'd come back here? He knows I'm here. He can't think that I would actually leave tonight after what he did?"

"I don't know, man. I never thought he'd do half the shit he's done lately, if what Aiden tells me is true. Did he really accuse Denise of sleeping around? And say that her baby is probably yours?"

Shit. I should have known Aiden would tell Devon. "Yeah, he did. But look, Denise doesn't want everyone to know about the pregnancy yet, so don't say anything, okay? She'll tell everyone when she's ready." I don't think she'll care that Devon knows already, but Denise asked me not to tell yet. This is going to change a lot of things for her, and for the band, and knowing how she likes to plan everything out, this probably has her freaked right out. We'll all be here for her, but I think she's a little worried about how everyone will react.

"Of course, man. Aiden only told me because he asked me to come help deal with Andrew. I won't say anything to anyone else."

"Thanks. And thanks for keeping watch on her tonight. I'm going to go back in, and I will be here until morning. You want to come in? You can probably sleep on the couch and still protect the place."

"I don't know, man. I don't fit so well on couches." He laughs. He is bigger than most couches by quite a bit. When I remind him that Denise has a nice oversized couch, he agrees to come in.

"Let me grab some bedding for you." I tell him as I head up the stairs. "Grab a drink from the fridge if you want."

The linen closet holds extra sheets, blankets, and pillows, so I grab Devon everything he'll need and go back to fix up the couch.

"I cleaned this pretty thoroughly," I tell him as I put the sheets on. "You don't need to worry about glass or anything. And you should be warm enough with the blankets, but if you need more, the linen closet is upstairs, past the bathroom. There's a half bath over there." I point to the bathroom under the stairs. "But for god's sake, don't flush if you hear the shower upstairs running. I nearly boiled Denise alive last week when I did that."

Devon quirks an eyebrow at me, a smirk on his face. "What?"

"You're pretty comfortable here," he says. "Want to tell me what's up with you and Denise?"

"Nothing is up. At least, nothing that we've had the chance to talk about yet. I was hoping to talk to her tonight, after she talked to Andrew, but you know what happened with him, so..."

"So you put her to bed and cleaned up down here. And now you're playing host to me, in her place, and what? You're going up to sleep with her, in her bed? That doesn't sound like nothing." He smiles. "Sounds like maybe you two are finally figuring out your shit. As long as you're sure you know what you're getting yourself into. You can't mess around with a pregnant woman, you know."

"Fuck off, Devon. I would hope you know me better than that." I turn and walk to the stairs. I sure hope he doesn't think that I would do that to Denise. As if I would mess around with her. Even before I knew she was having a baby, that's not something I would have done.

"Goodnight, Ryder." He singsongs to my back as I climb the stairs. "Take care of that woman up there. I'll keep an eye out for that fuckface, Andrew."

"Get some sleep, asshole." I shout down the stairs. "I can't deal with you when you're like this."

As I open the door to Denise's room, I can hear Devon's laughter drifting up the stairs. He's a dick sometimes, but I'm glad he's here. Andrew may have proven useless to Denise, but even without him, she's going to have more support than she can handle. Everyone in the band is going to be behind her completely. And me too, if she'll let me.

I strip down to my boxers and crawl into bed beside Denise. She automatically rolls over in her sleep, turning to face me, and lays her head on my chest. A plan forms in my head as I lay there stroking Denise's hair. I know I told her I wouldn't mention the pregnancy to anyone else, but after tonight I think most everyone in the band will know, anyway. She needs to know that we won't let her go through this alone.

I grab my phone from the nightstand and write a quick text to Alex and Aiden. I'll need their help if I want to pull this off on such short notice. I suppose I should feel bad for bothering Alex tonight when she's celebrating her engagement, but I waxed my entire body for her entertainment. She can deal with this one minor interruption.

Finally ready to sleep, I bend and kiss Denise's hair, smelling that coconut scent again. It reminds me of summers at the beach when I was a kid. Gran would take us out during our visits and she'd slather us in coconut scented sunscreen every hour, it seemed. My brother and I would play in the water or sand all day, only taking breaks to eat, or get our sunscreen reapplied.

The smell of Denise's hair reminds of those days, days that were both too short and endless all at the same time.

It's memories of the beach that invade my mind as I fall asleep tonight. I feel Denise stir on my chest, but my dreams pull me under before I fully wake.

24

Breakfast out of Bed

Denise

THE LIGHT COMING THROUGH the window is bright even through the lids of my closed eyes. I wake up slowly, memories of last night coming back to me in flashes. Yawning, I stretch my body out, taking up the whole bed starfish style. That's my first clue that Ryder left.

I sigh to myself. I knew this was coming, so I guess it shouldn't surprise me he's already run screaming from me. I am the one who doesn't want to burden him, after all. He stayed for a while last night to comfort me, like he said. Whatever was happening between us isn't happening anymore.

No, this is good, Ryder being gone. I'll be able to focus on getting ready for this baby and figuring out what my life is going to look like after this. I'm kidding myself if I think I can continue to manage the band with a baby, at least not in the hands-on way I have been until now.

Reluctantly, I get up out of bed, pull on some yoga pants, and head downstairs in search of coffee. A loud snore coming from the direction of the couch makes me jump. What? Ryder stayed but slept on the couch? Why bother laying down with me if he was going to get up and sleep down here?

I come around the front of the couch to wake him up, and I'm surprised to see Devon stretched out there, not Ryder. What the hell? When did Devon come in? And why is he sleeping on my couch? I guess it's a damn good thing I bought the extra big couch, though. Devon barely fits on it as it is. He'd have been sleeping on the floor last night if I had anything smaller.

I let him keep sleeping and turn back toward the kitchen. I'm sure he's here for a good reason, and if he's still asleep, then he probably needs it. He'll appreciate the coffee when he wakes up.

My coffee maker sits in a prime location on its own coffee bar. It's a regular drip coffee maker, but I bought a fancy one that grinds the beans for me and brews it all in one shot. I'm particular about my coffee, insisting on buying it from a local shop called Bump & Grind that roasts its own beans. My reason for going there isn't that they have the best beans, though. My friend, Xena Cross, owns it.

Xena and I hardly have time to see each other anymore. I should really call her and tell her about this whole baby business one of these days. She's one of the funniest people I know, so I'm sure she'll help me realize the lighter side of this whole situation. Though she may be fun most of the time, don't call her Warrior Princess. She's gotten so much shit over her name her entire life that she's more than a little touchy about it. It suits her though, because she's definitely tough like a warrior and spoiled like a princess.

I'm chuckling to myself as I go through the motions of getting the coffee going when I hear the front door open. My heart starts pounding out of control. Shit, I really hope that's not Andrew coming in. Thank god Devon is still here. Fucking Ryder. He should have locked that door when he left. After what Andrew did here last night, I don't trust it to be unlocked for any length of time, ever again.

Before I can yell for Devon, Ryder comes around the corner with a tray of drinks and several bags of food. With a sigh of relief, I finish getting the coffee ready. It takes a few focused breaths before my heart returns to normal, though.

"Hey, babe," he says, leaning over and kissing me on the cheek. He puts my keys on the counter beside me. "Sorry. I borrowed your keys so I could lock the door behind me. I went and got your favorite coffee from Bump & Grind. Xena says hi, by the way."

I've bought all the guys coffee from Bump & Grind before, so they know I love it. I've even brought Ryder there for coffee many times in the last few years. Usually when he needed sobering up after being rescued from whatever stupid situation he'd gotten himself into. He's quite familiar with my obsession with their coffee, and he knows Xena knows me.

"I was thinking of her as I was getting the coffee going," I say. "Did she tell you how long she was going to be there? I really should call her. It's been way too long. And I could use another girlfriend, especially now."

"She didn't say, but I'm sure if you called her soon, she'd still be there. The place was packed when I left though, so maybe give her a bit." He stops in the middle of taking food out of the bag to look at me. "Did you know she had a sword behind the counter? She threatened a customer with it when he called her Warrior Princess. Dude looked like he was about to piss himself as he apologized."

"Yeah," I tell Ryder, laughing. "I bought it for her years ago when she complained to me that people still call her 'warrior princess'. It's a replica of the one the character used in the show. So now when someone calls her 'warrior princess' she pulls out her sword and goes warrior princess on their ass."

"What?! How does she not get arrested for that?"

"It's realistic looking foam rubber. There's no way it could cause any damage. Plus, her brother, Kaden, is a cop. He keeps his ears open for calls coming in about her. From what I hear, the Westborough police are all too familiar with Xena and her fake sword."

"You have some strange friends." Ryder says as he continues to pull the food from the bag. "I didn't know what you'd want, or how your stomach would feel this morning, so I bought some of every breakfast item on the menu. We've got eggs, we've got pancakes, we've got bacon, and we've got a bunch of other stuff, too. Choose what you want first, and Devon and I will take care of what's left."

"Hey! I'll have you know you are one of my strange friends. Probably one of the strangest, if we're being honest." I slap him in the arm, making him drop a breakfast sandwich. "Besides, I like my friends." I open a container and grab a piece of bacon, smiling as I bite off a piece.

"I like your friends too, babe." He smiles at me and squeezes my ass. "And I like you."

Before I can react, Ryder is striding into the living room to wake up Devon.

"Time to wake up, sweetheart," I hear him say.

"What the fuck, man! Get off of me."

I come around the corner in time to see Devon throwing Ryder off the couch and onto the floor.

"Oof," Ryder exhales sharply when he hits the ground. "I was trying to make it a good morning for you." He laughs without getting up.

Devon gets off the couch and walks over to where I'm standing.

"It would have been a much better morning if I didn't wake up to you humping my leg like a dog." He chuckles. "At least you're wearing pants this time."

"Hey." I look around, finally realizing that the mess from last night isn't there anymore. "Where did all the stuff go? The stuff that Andrew broke?"

Someone cleaned up while I was sleeping. Which is amazing, because I was not looking forward to that at all. There was so much broken glass, and so many pictures and pieces of artwork thrown all over the place. It must've been tough to clean it all. And now it looks like it didn't even happen. If it weren't for all the picture hooks still on the walls, you wouldn't even know that anything was missing.

Ryder jumps up off the floor. "Oh, yeah. I cleaned it up last night after you fell asleep. If I'd known *this* asshole"—he points to Devon—"was sitting outside in his truck, I'd have made him help."

I'm stunned. I wouldn't have expected something like this from Ryder. And my hormones must be making me crazy, because the thought of him cleaning up for me has tears welling in my eyes. I try to blink them away before anyone sees them, but Ryder notices immediately.

"Awww, don't be sad," he says, coming over and pulling me into a hug. "I saved all the artwork and all the pictures. I even saved most of the frames. It's mostly the glass that was broken."

Devon disappears into the kitchen. Probably because my tears make him uncomfortable.

"Thank you, Ryder. I can't believe you did that for me." I don't know what else to say. "It took me years to do all that embroidery, and even longer to collect all those pictures. Thank you so much."

"You are more than welcome." Ryder is still hugging me and my tears are soaking his shirt. His shirts are not safe around me, apparently. Vomit-laced drool and tears seem to soak them at every turn. "The gallery will have new glass panes ready in a couple of weeks. They're extremely backed up or they would finish sooner. Sorry about that."

I pull back from the hug a little and look at Ryder. "You brought my frames to have new glass cut?"

"Well, yeah," he says, letting me go, and turning to take care of the bedding on the couch. "I also brought the few frames that were broken to see if they could repair any of them. They're not sure about that part, though, because the wood was so badly splintered. They said they would call to let me know as soon as they have it figured out."

Who is this standing in front of me, and what has happened to Ryder? I was dreading dealing with the frames more than anything else. And now I don't have to, because Ryder has already taken care of it all for me.

And now he's folding up all the bedding that Devon used last night.

"I don't even know what to say, Ryder. Thank you doesn't seem like enough. I wasn't looking forward to sourcing new frames for all those things. Not to mention how much I didn't want to clean up that mess." I hiccup a little laugh through my tears.

"I told you I would take care of you," he whispers, loud enough for me to hear. "I didn't mean when you were sick." He leans over his pile of blankets and kisses me gently on the lips before I can pull away. My heart jumps into my throat.

"Oh, okay," I say lamely, before changing the subject. "I'm starving. Let's go see what else you brought for breakfast before Devon eats it all."

"I heard that," Devon yells from the kitchen. "I'll have you know I was waiting for you before I got started, but now I'm going to dig in."

"Hey asshole," Ryder yells back, "Denise gets first choice, so keep your giant fingers out of there until she's gotten her breakfast." He takes the pile of blankets into the laundry room and comes back to join us.

"I was kidding, dickface. I'm getting coffee right now."

Devon is grabbing his coffee from the tray that Ryder brought from Bump & Grind. Even though they act like they hate each other, they really care. A lot of bands in this business hate each other after so many years together, but these guys have always been more like brothers than anything else.

I hope they can all stay as close to me now that I have a baby on the way and I won't be as involved in their day-to-day lives anymore.

25

My Girl is Hurting

Ryder

DENISE SEEMS A LITTLE off today, but I don't blame her. After what Andrew did last night, I have to say that I'm feeling a little off, too. I have a little plan in the works for how to take her mind off of it for today, but she'll still need to figure out what to do about Andrew now, too. I'm not comfortable with the thought of Denise being around him alone anymore, but even with what he did last night, I'm not sure I can convince her to have someone else around if she meets him again.

"Aiden sent me a text after you guys went to bed last night," Devon says around a mouthful of pancakes. "Andrew still wasn't home by three, so he went home and went to sleep. He wants to know what you want to do now, Denise."

Denise raises her eyebrows and her eyes go wide. She doesn't answer right away, choosing instead to take another bite of the breakfast sandwich she selected from the assortment of breakfast options I brought. Devon and I continue with our own breakfasts, giving her time to think it over. It's not like this is a simple situation. There must be so many things going through her head.

"I don't even know what I can do," she says, finally. "I need to make a list of what my options are, I guess."

"You could try to get a restraining order against him?" I suggest. "He was pretty violent last night. I'm not sure it would work though, since it was an isolated incident." I stop myself, shocked I didn't think of this before. "Wait. Is it an isolated incident? Has he done anything like this before?"

"No, no, of course not. This is the first time. The other stuff is the stuff you know about. The whispering instead of talking in front of you guys, and not liking the way I dress."

"We weren't being smart last night. We should have called the police right away. Then there would have been a record of his behaviour. I think for now we need to wait and see. Maybe he'll come to his senses?" I shrug my shoulders. I doubt he'll come to his senses, but you never know. He does have a kid in this scenario, after all.

"Do you really think he'd come back?" Denise drinks some of her coffee. She's going to need to limit caffeine with a baby on the way. I might have looked up a few things about pregnancy this morning while I was waiting for our breakfast.

That's why I ordered her a decaf at Bump & Grind. She probably wouldn't be too happy with me if she knew that, but I had Xena use our names to label the cups. There's no sign of what's in them at all.

Of course, I had to explain to Xena why I was getting Denise decaf, and even though I swore her to secrecy, I'm almost positive that won't last long. I'm hoping she can wait until the party tonight, but I doubt she'll be able to. If I know what's good for me, I'll confess to Denise sooner rather than later.

"I didn't think he had it in him to do something like that in the first place," Devon says, "so I'm probably not the best judge of whether he'll be back. You should talk to Aiden. He's always had a bad feeling about Andrew; his instincts about him were spot on."

"That's true," I say to Denise. "Aiden is the reason I came straight here last night instead of waiting for you to call. He saw you guys leave and his gut told him something was up. I almost tried to talk him out of it; I told him you said you'd call when Andrew left. But he convinced me it was better to trust his gut and be wrong than to assume everything was fine and be wrong about that. And he was right."

"I guess I should call Aiden then." Denise looks around for her phone.

"Maybe you should let him sleep for a bit first. And I'm sure Devon wants to get some sleep in his own bed for a while, too. Your couch is big, but it's still a couch."

Devon looks between me and Denise. I'm trying to get rid of him, but not be too obvious about it. Hopefully, he catches on.

"Yeah," he finally says. "I didn't get much sleep before this asshole was jumping on me and humping my leg this morning."

"Oh, fuck off," I laugh. "You loved it. That's the most action you've gotten in years."

"You're not wrong about that." Devon grabs one of the breakfast bags. "I'm taking the rest of the pancakes and bacon with me, though, since you're kicking me out."

Well, I may not have been obvious, but that sure was. Thanks a lot, Devon. Denise laughs.

"I'm kicking you out for your own good," I say. "Denise might need you back here later to keep her safe. You need to be fully rested to be effective. It's all about your health and Denise's safety. I'm kicking you out because I care." I give him my cheesiest, shit-eating grin, and he can't help but laugh.

"You're good, I'll give you that." He grabs his keys from the coffee table in the living room on his way to the door. "See you guys later."

I follow him to the door and lock it behind him.

"I think it's probably a good idea to keep that locked from now on. What do you think?"

"Yeah, that's what I was thinking, too. I was a little pissed this morning when I thought you'd left without locking it behind you."

I move to the couch, motioning for Denise to come with me. She sits, but not right next to me like I'd hoped she would.

"Ryder." Denise is looking down at the floor. "Thank you for looking out for me last night. If you and Aiden hadn't shown up, I'm not sure how far Andrew would have gone. I've never seen him like that. He was... it was... fuck..." She trails off, tears in her eyes again.

I slide over beside her and pull her against me.

"Shhhh, babe, it's okay." She leans her head down on my shoulder. "I know that you're surprised at what he did. Hell, I'm fucking shocked, and I didn't date the guy for a year." That gets a little chuckle out of her. "I can't imagine how it feels to have someone you cared about for so long have such a complete personality transformation. I never would have expected Andrew to have any fight in him at all."

"I didn't expect that from him either." She lets out a shuddering sigh and sags into me further. "I didn't think he'd be so upset over a baby. We always knew it was a possibility. Maybe it's the timing of the whole thing? Because we broke up before I told him?"

"Maybe, but he's still in the wrong here. You didn't deserve to be treated that way, to be screamed at and called names. And he shouldn't have broken your stuff either. He should have been able to control his temper better than that, even if it upset him. That was completely uncalled for."

We sit in silence for a few minutes. Aside from our breath, the only sound is the ticking of the eyes and tail from her vintage Kit-Cat Klock. Good thing it wasn't on the same wall as the other artwork that Andrew broke. I remember when Denise found it in a little vintage shop last time we were home. She was so excited to get that creepy thing that she had it professionally cleaned and restored. She even ordered parts from the original company.

"Listen, Ryder," Denise finally looks up at me. "I'm sorry that you finally got the courage to tell me how you feel and this is how it's turning out."

"You have nothing to apologize for, Denise. Nothing. I was the stupid one who waited this many years to realize what I feel for you isn't going away. It was perfectly normal for you to have a relationship with someone. I have no claim on you. Nothing that is happening is your fault."

"Well, to hear Andrew tell it, I'm the idiot who couldn't take birth control properly."

"Denise, Andrew is the idiot. I'm sorry that you have to find out this way." I smile at her while pulling her against me again.

"Yeah, well, that idiot is the father of this baby growing in me. How do I deal with that now that he's revealed himself to be a giant asshole?"

She's right. That will make this situation a lot harder on her. Not for the first time since I found out she was pregnant, I find myself wishing this baby was mine. My heart tightens at the mere thought of Denise having my baby. I've never really thought much about being a father, but with her, I want it all.

"What do you want to do?" I have a thought. "Have you checked your phone since last night? Has he tried to call you?"

"I haven't checked it. I sort of lost track of my purse in all the fuss last night. I had it when I came in, because I took out an ultrasound picture to show Andrew. That was before he flipped out and ripped it to shreds, though."

Recognition lights through me. "Oh shit, that's what that was." I run into the office where I put all the artwork and pictures when I cleaned up last night, and come back with the little pile of ripped up pieces of picture. I also bring her purse, which I'd found on the floor beside the couch, and put in the office as well. "I knew I'd seen it before. These pieces were mixed in with everything else I found last night when I was cleaning up. I'm sorry, but it looks like there's no way to fix this."

She takes the pieces from me and puts them on the coffee table. Then she reaches for her purse and digs through it for a minute, before coming up with her phone in one hand and another picture in the other.

"I had the ultrasound technician print two pictures, because I thought Andrew might like to have one." She's looking at it with a small smile. "Do you want to see it? You don't have to, I thought maybe—"

"Are you kidding me? Of course I want to see it," I interrupt. "Show me that baby."

The way she grins when she passes me the picture makes my heart skip a beat. As soon as I see the black-and-white image, my lungs stop working and I can't catch my breath. I sit down, hard, and stare at the blob in the picture. I've never been much of a baby person, but this isn't any baby. The most perfect, beautiful baby that I've ever seen is laying there, all curled up like a little bean. Before I can do anything, I feel the tears welling up in my eyes. *What the hell? I'm crying?*

"Oh my god, Denise. He's beautiful. Look at this baby." I turn the ultrasound so she can see it again. "This baby is in here." I reach over and place a hand on her belly, like she doesn't know. God, I'm an idiot. This amazing woman is growing a human being inside her body, and I'm sitting here telling her about it like she doesn't already know. I knew she was strong, but this is something else. I can't stop looking between her and the picture.

"Ryder, you're crying?" Denise's eyes look a little watery and when she blinks, the tears spill onto her cheeks. "Why are you crying?"

I laugh a little. "I'm not sure. You're ... you're the most amazing woman, Denise. And you are doing something truly beautiful. You're growing a baby. I'm so happy for you."

I reach forward and pull her towards me, my hand on the side of her face. I place my lips on hers, kissing her gently. Slowly, I caress her lower lip with my tongue, urging her to open for me. She meets my kiss eagerly, her tongue sliding against mine. We spend several minutes savoring each other's taste, taking our time. This amazing woman is way too good for me, and yet here she is, kissing me back. My dick and I both appreciate this amazing turn of events.

I'm about to pull her upstairs to bed when the doorbell rings, followed immediately by a series of loud knocks, causing us to jump apart.

"I know you're here. Your car is in the driveway. Let me in, Denise. I need to have words with you."

Oh, shit. It's Xena.

"Ummm, Denise? I'm so sorry. There's a chance that I may have told Xena you're pregnant when I got you decaf coffee this morning."

And if my plan works out, a few more people will know about the end of the day too. I hope Denise isn't too upset with me when it's all done.

26

Warrior Princesses and Plans

Denise

"HEY XENA, GLAD YOU came by," I say as I open the door and let in my oldest friend. "I hear Ryder has been spilling secrets in the name of keeping me away from caffeine."

Xena walks in and drops her purse by the door, kicking off her shoes at the same time.

"I had to drag it out of him," she says. "I was thinking I'd have to get my sword, but the man finally wised up when I threatened to add shots of espresso to your coffee."

Ryder stands up, looking like he's not sure what to do with himself.

"Well, I guess I'll get going now then." He says while patting his pockets for his keys. "How long do you think you'll be hanging around here, Xena?"

"Oh, I'd say for a couple of hours at least. Why?"

"I want to be sure that I'm back before you go, that's all. I'm sure Denise will tell you the details, if that's what she wants." Ryder walks over and kisses me, like it's the most natural thing in the world and we do it all the time. Oddly enough, it almost feels like we do. "I'm going to talk to Aiden about this, to see if he has any ideas about what your next steps should be. Call me if anything happens, okay?"

"I'm sure everything will be fine"—He gives me a disapproving look—"But yes, I will call you if anything happens."

"That's all I ask. See you ladies later." He kisses me again, deeper this time, and it feels like a promise. A promise that zings right to my lady parts. "Don't forget to lock the door behind me."

Once Ryder leaves, Xena and I head to the couch and sit.

"Alright, we're going to talk about whatever that"—she gestures to the door Ryder left through—"is all about later. For now, what's this I hear about you being knocked up? And why am I hearing about it from Ryder?"

She looks a little hurt, which surprisingly makes me feel pretty good. I knew we were friends, but I thought we'd drifted apart in recent years. Apparently, I've been in hiding, and she's been missing me, too.

"I've missed you," I tell her, pulling her into a hug. "I'm sorry I haven't been around more."

"Yeah, yeah, I've missed you, too. Don't change the subject."

"Okay, so I have some news," I say. "It might come as a surprise, but I'm pregnant!" I make it sound like I'm announcing it to her for the first time, widening my mouth into an 'O' and throwing up some jazz hands. May as well try to tell her, like I originally wanted to, before Ryder opened his big mouth.

"What? You are?" Xena pretends to be shocked, catching on to what I'm trying to do. "That's amazing. Congratulations!"

"Thank you. Do you want to see the ultrasound picture?" I ask, while already reaching for it on the coffee table. "I got it yesterday. They said I'm about twelve weeks along."

"Gimme that baby." Xena snatches the picture out of my hand. "Oh, look at this little beauty," she says, her mouth turning down into one of those frown smiles reserved for things that make you so happy you're sad. "Auntie Xena is going to spoil you so bad. But you have to promise not to tell your mom," she whispers to the picture.

"Hey, stop making plans to corrupt my fetus. I'm sitting right here." I joke.

"Shhh, never mind your mom. Auntie Xena will corrupt you real good. I'm going to teach you all the best swear words." She laughs as she puts the ultrasound back on the coffee table. Xena has been known to string together some pretty hilarious and nearly nonsensical expletives when she's angry.

"So. You and Ryder? You finally snagged him? Good for you."

Xena has known about my crush on Ryder since the beginning. She was with me at that house party the night that I approached the band and declared that I was going to be their manager. It wasn't much later that she opened Bump & Grind and both of our increasing workloads kept us apart more than I would have liked.

"I wouldn't say I've snagged him."

"Well, he kissed you goodbye before he left for a couple of hours. Plus, there's the whole 'you're having his baby' thing to consider. And he came into the shop this morning to buy you coffee, and I assume all the bags from the diner mean he also bought breakfast. That sounds an awful lot like you snagged him to me."

"Yeah... about that. This isn't Ryder's baby. Although things would probably be a hell of a lot easier if it were."

I give her a quick rundown of the events from last night, and by the end of the story she's hopping mad, and even more convinced than ever that Ryder is now mine. She seems to have completely ignored the part where I said it wasn't fair of me to encourage things with Ryder when I'm having someone else's baby.

"First things first. Where does this donkey-humping son of a rabid badger Andrew live? I think I need to pay him a visit with an actual sword, not the replica you bought. Or maybe I can get Kaden to go over and arrest him?" Xena pulls out her phone and taps at the screen for a minute before putting it on the couch beside her and continuing. "No wonder Ryder wanted you to make sure the door was locked."

"Yup, that's why. I guess Andrew lost them somehow. It was three in the morning before Aiden finally wound up going home to get some sleep. And I already told you Devon slept on my couch last night."

Xena's phone chimes with a notification, and she grabs it to look at the message.

"Kaden says he can't arrest the guy, but he says you need to call it in if the guy does anything else."

"I didn't say you should ask him that. I know he can't arrest Andrew."

"Yeah, well, I figured my brother being on the force should give me some perks. It's not like I've ever had a speeding ticket forgiven."

A disbelieving look crosses my face. "You mean the fact that you never get arrested, or even questioned, when you pull a sword on someone in the middle of your coffee shop isn't a perk?"

"No, of course not. That's the cops having common sense. No one wants to take on the bitch with the sword." She laughs. "Especially not one who has as impressive a physique as I do." She flexes her nearly non-existent muscles. This girl is barely five feet tall and has a tiny little body. If she didn't have boobs, she'd look like an eleven-year-old boy.

"Oh yeah, for sure, Xena. They're scared of you." I laugh in spite of myself. It's been a stressful few days and having my friend here to joke with is really helping. I still have to deal with all my problems, but at least I can not worry for a bit while she's here.

"I know," she says. "I'm a badass. They know better than to fuck with all this." She gestures to her entire body. "I like to call it 'Short Bitch Energy'. Like 'Big Dick Energy', but deceptively cute and super deadly."

"Well then, I'm glad you're on my side. I'd really hate to have all that SBE directed at me."

"But seriously. What are you going to do about Andrew? Where's your list? Let me see what you have so far."

Xena knows me well enough to know that I like to make lists whenever I face a big problem. And this is the biggest problem I've ever faced, so she obviously assumes I have a list started already. But I don't.

"I haven't had the chance to start a list yet," I tell her. "But I think I should start one now."

I grab a notebook and pen from my office and sit on the floor by the coffee table. Opening my notebook to the next clean page, I write 'What to do about Andrew' at the top and underline it. I start with number one.

"One. Wait until he does something else and then call the police."

Xena is reading my page from her spot on the couch, and she scoffs at this option.

"May as well cross that one out right now," she says. "Because that will not work for me. And I don't think it's a smart move."

"I know, but it's an option, so I have to write it down. That's how this list works. Write every option down, cross out the obviously shitty ones, and then pro and con the rest."

"Exactly. I'm telling you, this one is shitty, so you should cross it out."

"Can't," I say. My listing process is incredibly detailed. The guys in the band think I'm a little too particular about some things, but they definitely aren't complaining when the checks are rolling in after I make the best deal for them. "I have to do the crossing out after I've exhausted every possible option I can think of. It doesn't work if I don't do it in order."

"Okay, crazy lady." She laughs at me. "We'll make a mental note to cross that out later, then."

I tap the pen against my lips while I try to think of another possibility. The options in this situation seem so limited. I wonder if it's because I'm too close to it to see a solution?

"What if you had someone 'send him a message'? You know, the kind that comes at the end of a fist, or a boot?"

Leave it to Xena to suggest violence. She is the one who likes to threaten people with a sword for teasing her about her name, after all.

"I'll write it down, but I really hope I don't have to go that route. I was with Andrew for a year after all, and he is the father of this baby. We'll need to be in each other's lives for the next eighteen years. Why make it more of a strained relationship than it already is?"

I write her suggestion as number two and follow it up with my own number three.

"I'm adding, 'call his parents and get them involved'."

"You think he would listen to his parents?"

"I think so. Andrew is concerned with what is right and proper and he defers to his parents in everything. They're nice enough people, besides being like my parents, so I think they'd be of some help in straightening this all out."

"Okay, be real with me. Do you really want to straighten this all out?" Xena gets up and goes to rummage through the fridge, coming back with bottles of water for each of us. "Like, wouldn't it be a lot easier if Andrew wasn't in the picture at all? Write 'get Andrew to sign all his rights away'."

That's actually not a terrible idea. If Andrew signed his rights away, he'd never have to pay child support, but I'd also never have to deal with him ever again. After what he did last night,

I'm not sure how comfortable I would be leaving my baby with him for visitation, anyway.

"That's my favorite idea so far. It would be so much easier if Andrew would go away. What are the chances that he does that on his own, considering he doesn't even think this baby is his?"

"That's it!" Xena jumps up off the couch, her finger pointing up as though she's shouted 'eureka!', and not 'that's it'. "What if you tell him he was right? That it's Ryder's baby? Then you and Ryder get married and bing, bang, boom, you get Andrew out of your life and Ryder into your bed all in one go."

When I was telling Xena about recent events, I neglected to divulge the fact that Ryder and I had already been in bed together. And I certainly didn't tell her about his impromptu naked proposal.

"Well," I draw out. "Ryder has been in my bed already-"

"WHAT!? Why didn't you lead with that? Or at the very least, you could have told me about that before telling me about Andrew being a dickhead. You need to tell me everything. When, how, where, all the details. Go." She gestures while pulling her legs up to sit cross-legged on the couch, getting comfortable, waving her hand that I should start now.

"You will get general details, not specifics." I say, chuckling. "You know how sex works, so I'm not giving you the blow by blow."

"Oh, my god! There was blowing? How was it? Did you have to unhinge your jaw like a snake when it's eating something large? I've heard rumors about him. I need confirmation from a reputable source." She leans forward, eager for whatever answer I can give her.

"What the fuck? No. First off, a snake's jaws don't actually dislocate to swallow prey. That's a myth. They have stretchy ligaments that connect their jawbone to their skull, rather than the jawbone hooking in like ours do." Nothing like needing to give a spontaneous snake anatomy lesson to make me thankful for the National Geographic channel. "Also, what!? That's such a disgusting thing to imagine. Someone's jaw coming unhinged to suck an enormous dick? Gross."

She laughs, leaning back again. "Okay then, go on."

I get her caught up to speed, glossing over the details but telling her about the deck incident, as well as the sexy nap time before the party. And then I drop the bomb. I don't mention the fact that Ryder wasn't entirely in his boxers, that he was standing there with his dick and balls still on display from showing me the results of his waxing session, but I do tell her he was in his underwear.

"Ryder proposed yesterday."

"I—what—he did—holy—what did you—is this rea—Gah!"

Oh, fuck. I think I broke Xena.

Thank god the doorbell rings before I have to put her back together.

27

Denise > Super Mario

Ryder

"HEY MAN, WHAT'RE YOU doing here? I thought you were staying with Denise today?" Aiden greets me as he opens his door. I clearly woke him; he's still wiping sleep from his eyes. "Come on in. Want coffee?"

Turning away before I can answer, he heads back into his house, going straight to the kitchen. He busies himself getting the coffee going while I look around. I haven't been in Aiden's place in a while, but it's the same as it's always been. Family pictures on the walls, comfortable furniture, big ass TV taking up almost the entire wall, and tons of video games.

Aiden has every console you can imagine. It's the one thing he'll rush to buy when the latest version comes out. He'll keep his old phone until his screen is so cracked he can't even see through it, but as soon as the latest Xbox is available he has one. Everyone has their thing I guess.

I can't say I wouldn't be happy playing some old school Super Mario World on SNES sometime. It makes me feel like I'm really a kid again, instead of acting like one all the time.

"So, tell me what's happened since I left last night." Aiden comes back into the living with a cup of coffee for each of us. I take a spot on the couch while he sits in a well-worn recliner. I guess I know where he sits when he games, if the looks of that chair say anything about it. "How is Denise doing?"

Aiden doesn't like to talk about it, but he is intimately familiar with domestic violence. When he was younger, before he met the rest of the guys, his dad would take his anger out on him and his mom. When Aiden turned eighteen, he moved out, and within three months, the rest of his family was gone. They were in a horrible car accident and no one survived.

I didn't know Aiden before that, but it doesn't take a genius to know that it changed him. He's volunteered with local women's shelters for as long as I've known him. And since we started making real money with the band, I know he donates sizeable sums of money to domestic violence initiatives in the city. He takes any hint of violence or aggression against women and children seriously, almost personally.

He's never said it to me, but I sometimes wonder if he blames himself for the accident. Not that he should, of course. I know that if it were me, I probably would feel guilty.

"She's doing okay, considering," I finally answer. I've been staring off into space, thinking about Aiden's family for so long that he probably thought I fell asleep with my eyes open. "Her friend Xena—you know the chick who owns Bump & Grind?—she's over there visiting with Denise right now. I accidentally on purpose let slip that Denise is pregnant when I went to grab coffee and breakfast this morning so I could invite her tonight. Anyway, Xena went over to give Denise the third degree. I figured I'd come see you, and check if you'd made any progress on my request from last night, and leave them to their girl talk."

"Good thinking. And you're aware at least some of that conversation is going to be about you?"

"Yeah, I'm aware. Yet another reason I needed to get out of there and leave them to it. Plus, I really wanted to talk about this

Andrew thing with you. I know you have contacts experienced with this type of situation, so I thought you might have some ideas of what Denise can do about this."

Aiden puts his cup down on the end table beside the couch and gets up to grab his phone from the kitchen counter.

"I texted some people last night before I went to sleep, but I haven't checked if anyone got back to me yet. Some asshole woke me up and forced me to make him coffee."

"Yeah, yeah, fuck you too. And thanks for the coffee."

"You're welcome."

Aiden swipes through screens on his phone, the look on his face alternating between small smiles and outright grimaces. So good news and bad news.

"Well, it looks like it's going to be like we thought. There's not much that can be done about Andrew, legally, since this is the first incident. They're not together and they never lived together so this situation sort of straddles a line between domestic violence and stalking. And either way, the laws don't really work in favor of the victims. I mentioned how he showed up at the party when Denise told him not to, which is what made my friend think of the stalking aspect. But for the other stuff, for tonight, that is all taken care of. Alex texted me too, and she has her part under control."

I think that over while I sip my coffee. At least tonight is squared away. That's one less thing to worry about.

"So, if we can't do anything legally...?"

"We might have to look at our illegal options." Aiden shrugs, giving no indication that he is concerned about being involved in illegal activity. Which is a relief, because I would hate to be committing crimes alone. At least this way, if we get caught, we can bunk together in prison. Silver linings, and all that.

"What kind of illegal options are we talking about here?"

"Well, you know I try to focus my energies on embarrassing and inconveniencing people when I go for revenge, but Andrew doesn't seem like he would take kindly to a giant inflatable penis on his lawn. But I also don't think he needs killing, at least not yet, so we can take that off the table. Wait, let me grab some paper to write this down. Denise has a good point about list making. It really helps you organize your thoughts." Aiden gets up and rummages around in some drawers in the kitchen, coming back with a pen and a notebook.

He sits back down, and flips open the notebook. Then he looks at me, waiting for a suggestion. Good thing we've already taken killing Andrew off the table. It wouldn't do to have it in an itemized list of options on how to deal with him. It would certainly be a damning piece of evidence.

"So when Alex had a problem with her ex-boyfriend, Devon and I took him for a walk and beat some sense into him. That could be an option. Maybe beating the shit out of Andrew would convince him to stay away from Denise?"

"I'll write it down," Aiden says, scribbling on the notepad, "but Denise being pregnant with his baby complicates things a bit."

"Yeah, you're right. We'll all have to be around each other for a long time if he ever gets his head out of his ass and acknowledges that the kid is his."

"Wait." Aiden's face splits into a huge grin. "What if he doesn't have a reason to get his head out of his ass?"

Great, now he's speaking in code. Like that's helpful.

"Okay," I drawl. "Now try that again. But this time, make sense."

"Ugh, sometimes you are as dumb as you look, man," he teases. Apparently I'm ridiculously good looking or something, so people often assume I'm dumb. I'll take it, though. Makes it easier to fuck with them when they think I'm too dumb to do anything.

"Fuck off. Just explain what you mean. Your brain is working on Aiden wavelengths. We're not all old dudes who think in hieroglyphics." I laugh. Making fun of Aiden being an old man is one of my favorite things.

"I'm not old," he says. "I'm aged, like a fine wine."

"Yeah, whatever you say, gramps. Tell it to the Volvo station in the driveway."

"Hey! I'll have you know that car is a classic. But we're getting off track. I'm saying, what if Denise tells him that the kid isn't his? That she was mistaken? He already thinks the kid is yours. What if she let it slip 'accidentally' that it really is yours?"

"How would that work? Do you think he'd believe her? Better yet, what makes you think she'd even go for it?"

"Well." He thinks for a second, tapping the pen on the notepad. "I guess not enough has happened for her to really consider it a viable option. She's only seen the one incident from Andrew. You and I have had a bad feeling about him since the beginning. And I think we both know that this won't be an isolated incident. Good thing I have no problem keeping an abusive father away from his child by whatever means necessary."

I scrub my hand over my face and let out a sigh. Of course I know that it most likely won't be an isolated incident, but for Denise's sake, I wish it were. I wish Andrew would be a decent human being about this and work something out with her. Whatever will make it easiest on her, that's what I want.

"That's enough of that for right now," Aiden says, putting his notepad and pen down. "Let's get some video games going and get our minds off this for a bit. What do you say?"

"Sounds good, I was thinking how I'd love to play some Super Mario World."

Aiden gets up and grabs both of our coffee cups. "Get us set up and I'll grab more coffee."

We play video games for a while, the time draining away as we relive the games of our youth. Sometimes it's nice to go back to what you know. And when it's a nice straightforward game like Super Mario, it's even better. It's comforting in a way.

"Oh, shit!" I suddenly remember that Xena was only staying for a couple of hours. "How long have I been here?"

Aiden looks at the time on his phone. "A couple of hours, for sure," he says. "Why?"

"I told Denise I'd be back before Xena left. I gotta go. Thanks for everything. I'll see you later? Alex is still doing dinner, right? Or should I order something?"

"Not sure, man. She didn't mention that in her text. I imagine she had a pretty late night with Connor, so she might not want to cook. I'll get in touch with them and take care of it. You go take care Denise."

"That sounds good. I'll talk to you later, then."

I jog from his door to my car. I can't believe I lost track of time. The chance of something happening to Denise after Xena leaves and before I'm back is minimal, but it's not zero. I don't think I'd be able to forgive myself if Andrew showed up while I wasn't there, all because I was playing video games with Aiden.

No matter how much I love Super Mario, I love Denise more.

She has nothing on his mustache, though.

Visits with a Tiny Dancer and a Princess

Denise

"WELL, IF IT ISN'T the little Princess." Devon has a surprised smirk on his face when he sees Xena sitting on the couch. "What are *you* doing here?"

Saved by the doorbell. Devon rescued me from Xena's impending breakdown over my revelation that Ryder had proposed to me in my closet. She seems adequately distracted now, so maybe we won't need to talk about it again. It's not like Ryder was actually serious, anyway. Even if he was, he sure won't be now that he knows about the baby.

"I could say the same to you, Tiny Dancer. Why are you showing up at my bestie's house? Are you following me?" She squints at Devon, hands on her hips.

"What am I missing here?" I ask, looking back and forth between them. "I didn't know you guys knew each other."

"Oh, we go way back. Isn't that right, Tiny Dancer?" Xena prompts.

Devon shoots Xena a dirty look before elaborating, "Yeah, I used to hang around with her brother Kaden a lot back in the day. Before I met you guys, I was a—I was considering becoming a police officer. Little Xena here always had a huge crush on me and wouldn't leave me alone. She was such a pest, constantly mooning over me, drawing my name in hearts in her notebook. You know, kid stuff."

"Ugh. You asshole. That is not how it was at all, and you know that, Tiny Dancer. Plus, you're not that much older than I am."

"Why do you keep calling him 'Tiny Dancer'?" I ask, my curiosity getting the best of me. "He's certainly not tiny, and he definitely can't dance. I can't believe I didn't know you two knew each other. What a small world."

"Can't dance?" Xena bursts into peals of hysterical laughter, losing her breath almost immediately from the force of her laughs. "You don't know about his—"

"I think that's enough for now, Xena." The way Devon says 'Xena' leads me to believe there is something going on here. Something that I am for sure going to find out about later. "Let's not start talking about stuff no one needs to hear about. But to answer your first question, Denise is my friend, and I came to talk to her."

"Oh, yeah sure. Got it." Xena backs down. This keeps getting more and more interesting. When I get my shit sorted, I'm going to be looking into this further.

"So anyway, what are you doing here, Devon?" I better break the tension before things get out of hand. "I didn't know you'd be coming back so early. You went home to sleep not that long ago."

"I couldn't sleep that well, and I wanted to come and check on you. I had an idea that I thought could help with the Andrew thing and I was hoping to talk to you about it."

"Oh? Let me grab my list. Come sit. Grab a drink from the fridge." I sit back on the couch, grabbing my notebook from the coffee table where I left it when I answered the door.

Devon goes to the kitchen, and Xena leans over and whispers to me.

"Don't think I forgot about Ryder proposing. We'*ll* talk about that later."

Shit.

"So what's your idea, Devon?" I have my pen ready, and my notebook open to the list I started with Xena.

"Well," he starts, opening his soda and taking a drink, "what if you called Andrew and said you were mistaken? That the baby isn't his? Then you wouldn't have a reason to ever see him again. And it's not like you'd be alone with this baby. I guarantee you will have more help than you could ever want from me and the rest of the guys. And Alex."

"Ahem."

"Oh, sorry. And Princess here too." Devon adds when Xena clears her throat at his forgetting to mention her.

"You bet," Xena adds. "I will do anything you need, and more. I can make laundry my bitch, I make a mean cup of coffee, and I know how to order takeout like nobody's business."

"Speaking of takeout." Devon looks around. "What's for lunch?"

"We had breakfast not that long ago," I say. "And you brought home a bunch of pancakes and stuff. I'm eating for two, so I know why I'm hungry, but how are you hungry already?"

He laughs. "Have you seen me? I burned all that food off walking to my truck. It takes a lot of food to keep this temple in tip-top shape." Devon does some bodybuilding poses a la Hulk Hogan, and I think I see Xena's heart stop.

Oh yeah, I really need to know what happened between them. Why, after all these years, has she never mentioned that she knew Devon? It seems a little fishy.

He's not wrong about why he's hungry, though. Devon is six and a half feet tall, and at least two-hundred-seventy-five pounds. A muscular two-hundred-seventy-five pounds. It makes sense that he would need a lot of food to sustain that.

"Fair point. Should we order something? Go out? What do you guys want to do?"

We have lunch delivered and soon we're sitting around my kitchen table enjoying the best sushi I've tasted in ages. It could be the fact that I was craving it that makes it taste so good, but either way, it's delicious.

"So, what did you think of my idea?" Devon asks, expertly maneuvering his chopsticks with his giant fingers, trying to snag my last shiitake mushroom roll while he has me distracted.

"Nice try, Tiny Dancer." I may as well use Xena's nickname for him, even if I don't know what it means. Yet. "You're not stealing the last shiitake roll from the pregnant lady, are you?"

He looks at me, shocked when I use my own chopsticks to snatch the roll right as he's about to eat it. I quickly shove it in my mouth before he recovers, smiling at him through teeth full of seaweed and rice.

"That's gross," he laughs. "Celebrate your petty victory after you're done chewing your ill-gotten gains, you heathen."

Xena and I both howl with laughter, our senses of humor obviously not very refined. My mouth is still full and I have to fight not to choke on my food while I laugh. Seeing how hard we're laughing has Devon joining in, and in no time the three of us are trying desperately to catch a breath between our guffaws. Tears are streaming down Xena's face, I've given up and spit my food into my napkin for safety's sake, and Devon has his head down on the table while his shoulders shake with silent laughter. It's not like it was even that funny, but we're all laughing like we've lost our minds. Must be the effects of sleep deprivation.

I imagine we're quite the sight for Ryder when he walks in at the exact moment our laughter is at its most hysterical.

"Looks like I missed the party," he says, the grin on his face coming through in his voice. "What's so funny?"

The three of us look up at where Ryder stands in the doorway, trying to get the laughter under control, when Devon looks over at my half-chewed shiitake roll sitting on my napkin.

"All—that—and you—didn't even—eat it?" He barely gets the words out in between snorts of laughter. Which, of course, sends Xena and me both into another uncontrollable fit of giggles.

Rather than try to make sense of the situation, Ryder grabs a plate from the cupboard and sits in the empty seat at the table. He loads up his plate and eats silently while looking at the three of us, the howling hyenas we are, with a grin on his face.

"At least *he* grins with his mouth closed when there's food in there." Devon chokes out through labored breaths, which starts us laughing all over again.

Ryder has the chance to finish his plate, clean up the dishes and leftovers from the table, start the dishwasher, and drink an entire soda, before the three of us have calmed down enough to make any sense.

"Now, can someone tell me what happened?" Ryder asks again.

Of course, as is usually the case, the explanation lacks the hilarity of the initial situation, so Ryder ends up shaking his head at us with a little smile on his face.

"Well, I'm glad you all are having fun at least," he says before sliding his chair over to sit closer to me. Xena catches the move right away and wiggles her eyebrows at me. That bitch doesn't miss a thing. "So babe, far be it from me to tell you what to eat, but... I was looking up pregnancy stuff and apparently one of the main things you shouldn't eat, other than caffeine, is sushi."

"Whoa, hold up there, my guy." Xena stands and leans over the table as far as she can, and points at Ryder with a chopstick as though it's a switchblade. "I'm rooting for you two and all, but don't be telling Denise what to do with her own body or

I swear to god, I will stab this chopstick so far up your peehole you'll be pissing toothpicks for a month."

"Whoa, whoa, whoa, calm down Princess." Devon reaches out and slowly takes the chopstick from her hand, easing her back in her chair. "That's not what he was doing. Right, Ryder? There's no need to threaten the man's urethra."

Ryder's face is completely pale, and he looks a little sweaty. I doubt the thought of chopsticks in his peehole is something he enjoys.

"Huh? Oh yeah, no, that's not what I meant at all. I was trying to be helpful. But I'm sure Denise already knew about the sushi thing, anyway. I didn't mean to imply that she wasn't making the best possible choices for herself." Good save, Ryder.

I leave the table for a moment, coming back with a stack of pregnancy books. Sitting back in my chair, I put the pile down in front of Ryder.

"This is my collection of pregnancy books. Remember when you saw me at the bookstore? Well, this is what I was actually buying. I had picked up a couple of wedding magazines for Alex, but I used them to hide the rest of what was in the basket." I motion to the books. "But I haven't gotten around to reading them yet. They've been sitting in my office. So if you want to share things you've learned, then by all means, please do. Just know that I won't automatically listen to your advice."

I sit back down and Xena reaches across the table to grab the book on top of the pile. The classic *What to Expect When You're Expecting.*

"I'm pretty sure we all know what to ultimately expect. You're going to push a baby out of your vag, and it's going to hurt like a motherhumper." Xena shudders. "Then you're going to spend the next five years wiping its ass and trying to stop it from eating stuff off the floor."

"Wow, thanks for that beautiful, and thoughtful, review of childbirth and motherhood," Ryder snarks. "I'm not sure Denise needs to worry about the pain of childbirth yet, though. She still has to grow the baby until it's big enough to come out and see us. Let's give her some time to get used to that before we scare her with the details."

Ryder has somehow slid his chair right next to mine without me noticing, and I feel his arm wrap protectively around my shoulders. I lean in reflexively, forgetting that I'm not supposed to be encouraging his attempts to be closer to me. It's almost as though, when he's this close, my body betrays what my brain logically knows. *'Oh, I shouldn't trap Ryder into a relationship with me. I'm having another man's baby,'* says my brain. Then my body reacts to his touch without my consent. I need to get this under control, so I slip out from under his shoulder and scoot my chair away a little. We're going to have to talk about this soon.

I can't let myself fall any more under his spell.

"Thanks, Ryder," I say, to soften the blow of my obviously moving away from him. "I will learn about the horrors of childbirth eventually, but for now I want to worry about how fat my ass is going to get, and whether I'll be able to find maternity clothes that I actually like that will fit it."

"Okay, okay. Point taken," Xena apologizes. "How about I take on researching maternity clothes and I'll find you some stuff that will work for you?"

"Yes, thanks. That would be a much better use of your time." I point at the pile of pregnancy books. "I'm sure these books will tell me all the horrible stuff that I will need to know."

Devon pulls his phone from his pocket and looks at the screen.

"I need to get going," he says while standing and taking his plate to the sink. "Johnny needs my help with something. You going to be okay here?" It doesn't escape my notice that he directs this question to Ryder, but I'm not going to make a big deal of it. I know they're all concerned that Andrew might come back. They want to make sure I'm not alone if that happens.

"We'll be fine." Ryder answers.

"Yeah, I gotta get going too." Xena stands up beside Devon. "Walk me out, Tiny Dancer?"

"Sure thing, Princess."

Xena comes over and hugs me. "I'll call you soon."

"Yeah, that sounds good. It was so good to see you today. I'll try to get around to the shop more often, too. I want to see this sword in action."

Ryder and Xena both laugh, and Devon looks confused. He really must not have seen Xena in quite a while if he doesn't know anything about the sword.

"Come on, Tiny Dancer. I'll explain it to you on the way out."

They both wave and head out, Ryder following behind them to lock the door.

"So, Aiden thinks he knows what you can do about Andrew."

Looks like we're going to talk about this some more, after all.

It's Not a Trap if I Want to Go

Ryder

I GET UP AND reach for Denise's hand, and she avoids it. Something's up.

"Is everything alright?"

"I think we should talk, Ryder." She won't look me in the eye. Whatever it is she wants to talk to me about, it can't be good. She doesn't seem to like it much, anyway.

"I'm not sure I want to hear this," I admit. "You seem upset."

"Let's go to the living room."

I follow her and watch as she takes a seat in the armchair. I was hoping to put less space between us, not more, but whatever she needs to feel comfortable is what I'll give her. If that's space, well, then... she'll have space.

"So..." She still hasn't looked at me. Her hands are in her lap, and she's playing nervously with her fingers, tapping them against each other. "I'm going to have a baby."

I look at her, waiting for the rest of whatever it is she's saying, but she continues to look down at her hands.

"No! Really?" Probably not the most helpful thing to say, but I'm not sure where she's going with this, and I'm trying to lighten the mood.

She laughs at me a little before finally continuing. "Fine, I deserved that."

"No, you didn't. I wanted to make you laugh. You seem upset? Is there anything I can do?"

She takes a deep breath and looks up at me. "Ryder, you've been amazing through this whole thing."

"I told you, I'm here to take care of you. Whether that's when you're sick or when you're pregnant, or even when your ex comes into your house and screams at you and breaks your stuff."

"That's what I'm trying to tell you, Ryder. I can't let you take care of me. It's not fair to you."

"What do you mean, it's not fair? All I've wanted for so long is the chance to be with you. Taking care of you when you were sick, and helping you these last few days, has been my pleasure. It's been an honor, really. I don't understand why you would think that's not fair."

I move to the end of the couch closest to her and reach out to place a hand on her knee. Without missing a beat, she removes it. Uh oh.

"Ryder, we can't keep doing this. I'm having someone else's baby. I can't force you into this position. It feels like I'm trapping you. That's what's not fair."

Ah, finally she gets to the point. But is it because she doesn't want to trap me or because she doesn't think I can be the man that she needs? Either way, I know she wants me, and if she weren't having a baby, then this wouldn't be an issue right now.

Which means it's not an issue.

I meant it when I said I would be lucky if Denise were having my baby, but I would also be lucky if she let me be with her when she has this baby.

"It's not a trap when I walk in willingly, with my eyes and heart wide open."

I stand up and pull Denise up with me, wrapping my arms around her. It seems like she wants to slip away for a moment, but then she relaxes into my embrace, wrapping her arms around my waist and resting her head on my chest. I hold her for a little longer before leaning back to look in her eyes.

"I may have spontaneously proposed yesterday, and, okay sure, that may have been rushing things a bit. Even if it wasn't, it certainly wasn't done in the way that you deserve, and for that, I'm sorry. But I still want to be with you. Even now, knowing that you are having someone else's baby, I still want to be with you. Because to me, this isn't someone else's baby." I place one hand on her stomach. "This is your baby. And *everything* about you is amazing, baby included."

I pull her back into my arms, her face resting against my chest. I can feel her tears through my shirt. What am I going to do to make her see how serious I am?

"I don't want you worried about whether you are being fair to me. I want you to think about doing what is going to make you the happiest. Because whatever makes you happy, makes me happy. Understand?"

She nods her head against me, answering without words.

"Good." I pull back again and wipe the tears from her cheeks. "Now, we've had enough depressing conversations for one day. Okay? Let's do something." I kiss her on the forehead. "I'm not complaining about how amazing your ass looks in those yoga pants, and you already know how much I love seeing you in my shirt, but why don't you go get dressed and come somewhere with me for a bit? There are a couple of things I need to do. And after, we can go over to Alex and Connor's place for family dinner."

She nods again and takes herself upstairs to get dressed. I pull out my phone and make arrangements for what we're doing. I didn't actually have anything planned, but Denise needs a distraction and I know the perfect place to go.

I hope it doesn't blow up in my face.

30

Baby Shops and Big Hearts

Denise

AFTER A QUICK SHOWER, I throw on my favorite navy floral summer dress with a flared skirt (it has pockets), a lightweight cardigan, and a pair of bright orange platform wedge sandals. Luckily it wasn't a hair washing day, so I didn't need to dry it. I curl my bangs slightly under and pull the rest of my hair back into a sleek high bun, finishing the look off with a huge flower pin in yellow, pink, and orange. Taking a page from Alex's book, I forgo my usual full face of makeup, instead using some mascara and lipstick. Ryder said he had stuff to do. I don't want to make him late for whatever it is, and I feel like I've taken long enough already.

"Wow! You look beautiful." Ryder is waiting for me at the bottom of the stairs. "I feel like I should take you to do something better than to run some errands with me."

"Oh, yeah, thanks. I figured I should wear the things I like for as long as possible before nothing fits me anymore. It seems like everyday I try something on and can't get it zipped or buttoned." I had to squeeze into this dress a little today, so I better enjoy wearing it because I'm sure it won't happen again.

"Xena is on that for you, remember?" Ryder says while leading me to the door with his hand on the small of my back. Funny how such an insignificant gesture can cause my belly to flip-flop like it's full of giant butterflies. "Before you need to worry about fitting into your clothes, she'll have an entire bad ass maternity wardrobe for you to approve. It seems like she's taking that job seriously. I bet she has stuff for you to look at already."

I grab my purse from the hook by the door and look around for my keys so I can lock up.

"I've got your keys already," Ryder says, holding them out to me. "Is there anything else you need before we go? Maybe you should bring something to do? You might have to sit around for a little at one of our stops, and I don't want you to get bored."

"Oh, okay. Hold on a sec." I go into my office and grab my project bag for my embroidery. I've barely started on the piece that I want to give my OB/GYN and today could be a good chance to get some work done on it.

"Got it." I step out onto the porch and wait while Ryder locks the door behind me. When he takes my bag from me and offers his elbow to help me down the stairs, I look up at him and smile. No matter how much of a crazy party boy he's been in the past, he's always been a chivalrous guy. He opens doors for people, stands when a woman arrives or leaves the table, and has decent enough manners for a guy who pretty much always gets what he wants without having to ask. He leads me to his car, opens the door for me, and passes me the seat belt and my bag before closing the door and going around to the driver's side. It's weird being taken care of like this, but I like it when it's Ryder.

"So, where are we going?" I ask when he's backing out onto the street in front of my house. "What do we need to get done today?"

"It's a surprise," he says. "You're going to have to wait and see." He has a slightly evil glint in his eye, because he knows how much I hate surprises. Surprises mean I don't have control of a situation, and I hate not being in control.

"That is completely unfair, Ryder." I'm not proud of it, but I may pout a little. "You know I don't like surprises."

"I promise you'll like this one, babe," he says with a laugh. "It'll be fun."

I cross my arms over my chest and huff out a breath as I push myself back into the seat. "It better be fun. I could be napping my afternoon away, you know?"

He's laughing at me again. "You can probably have a nap at one of our stops if you're tired. And we can skip dinner at Alex and Connor's too. Or you can nap there. I have a bedroom there, remember, and you're welcome to it anytime."

All the guys have bedrooms at Connor's place. He has a studio in his house and the guys spend so much time there that he had part of his walk-out basement converted to extra rooms for the guys. I've never bothered going down there, though. Something about invading their space like that didn't feel right to me. Especially when Ryder was still giving everyone the impression that he was sleeping with anyone with a vagina. I may have been trying to push my feelings away didn't mean I wanted to see the proceedings in person.

"I might take you up on that," I say. "We're not skipping dinner, though. I think I want to tell everyone else about the baby tonight." I glance at him from the corner of my eye, trying to get a read on what he thinks of that. I'm not sure why his opinion matters so much to me regarding this, but it does.

Ryder is parallel parking on a narrow street downtown. This street is known for small boutique shops that carry unique items of all varieties. Things that you can't find in big box stores. And most of them stay closed on Sundays, so I can't figure out what Ryder could possibly have to do here today.

"I think that is a great idea, Denise." He's already taken off his seat belt and turned to face me. "Once you see how much support you have from all of us, hopefully this Andrew thing won't seem as serious. You know we all have your back, and we'll all help in any way we can." He grabs my hand and places a kiss on my knuckles. My breath catches at the feel of his lips on my skin. He's probably too sexy for his own good. And he's *definitely* too sexy for *my* own good.

Before I can answer, Ryder is out of the car and opening my door for me. When takes my hand and helps me out of the vehicle, I sigh. Yeah, being taken care of is nice sometimes.

"Here we are," he says, pointing to a door that has a 'closed' sign clearly displayed. "Let's go."

"Ummm, Ryder?" I say as he walks up to the door. "They're closed. It's Sunday, remember? Everything on this street is closed on Sunday."

"Normally, yes." He takes his phone out of his pocket, presses some buttons, and holds it up to his ear. "Hi, we're here," he says into the phone after a few seconds.

"What is going on?" I ask him.

An older woman is at the door now, opening it from the inside. "Ryder! It's so good to see you," she says as she pulls him in for a hug. "And you must be Denise." She comes out to hug me, too. "I've heard so much about you. Come in. I can't wait to see what you two pick out. Come, come." She turns and walks back through the door Ryder is now holding open.

Once inside, Ryder introduces the woman to me. "This is Lana," he explains. "She was my neighbor when I was growing up. She used to watch me and my brother when my dad had to work late or when he picked up extra shifts. This is her store."

I turn and take in our surroundings. It's a baby store. A high end baby store.

"Oh, you shush, boy." She smacks Ryder on the arm. "This is Ryder's store," she tells me. "He found it and bought it when my old job laid me off. He lets me run it."

"You know that's not true, Lana. We've been over this." Ryder sounds like he's had this conversation more times than he'd like. "The deed is in your name. You own the building. You own the business. This is all you."

I'm not even really listening anymore; I'm too enchanted by all the beautiful baby furniture around me. The tags say things like 'hand carved' and 'made with love'.

"You brought me to a baby store?"

Lana gives a little wave and walks to the back of the store, disappearing into the back somewhere. Looks like she's going to give us some time alone to look around.

"Is that okay?" Ryder asks, looking a little unsure. "I thought maybe you'd like to get a head start on some of your shopping? I know how much you love being prepared."

Tears are forming in my eyes when I step into him and wrap my arms around his waist.

"Thank you, Ryder. This is amazing."

Ryder hugs me back tightly, placing a kiss on the top of my head. "You're welcome. Now let's pick some stuff out. You decide what you like and I'll keep track." He pulls out his phone, ready to take notes for me.

We spend an hour in the store, and when we're done, I've picked out all the major furniture and some extras. I have a beautiful hand carved crib, the most amazing rocking chair, dressers, and more baby clothes than I can count. Lana takes our list, promising to arrange the delivery and get back to me with a date. And she won't take my credit card, assuring me it's already taken care of.

After we promise to visit and say our goodbyes, Lana takes us to the front of the store and locks the door behind us.

"You bought your neighbor a store?" I finally ask, as Ryder helps me into the car again. "And convinced her to come in on a Sunday so I could pick stuff out?"

"Yes and yes," he says after getting in on his side. He starts the car and pulls away from the curb. "She used to watch us for free when we were kids. Dad didn't make a lot of money, so he worked all the overtime he could to make ends meet. If it weren't for Lana's kindness, Hunter and I would've had to fend for ourselves in the evenings so Dad could work, or we would've been homeless. She was like a second grandmother to me. When I heard she was laid off and in danger of losing her home, I paid off her mortgage and bought her this store. She's always had a thing for babies and this opportunity came along at the right time."

Have I been selling Ryder short all these years? I always assumed he only thought about himself, but I'm learning today that's not the case. He's been looking after me so well this last little while, and now I learn he's set his old babysitter up for life when she lost her job. It makes me wonder what else I've been missing about Ryder while I was busy noticing the funny guy who's always up for a good time.

"That's really wonderful, Ryder. She's lucky to have you."

He shrugs. "I was lucky to have her," he says. "I saw my Gran every summer and anytime she could visit, but Lana was the adopted grandma who was around all the time. They're both important to me."

We continue driving in silence for a while before Ryder says anything else.

"So, there are a few things I need to warn you about before we get to our next stop," he says, with a hint of hysterical laughter in his voice.

Uh oh. Maybe I spoke to soon. Where could Ryder be taking me that has him feeling crazy?

31

That Damn Medusa and my Boner Freak Out

Ryder

THIS VISIT TO SEE my Gran could go one of two ways: either she loves Denise and wants to keep her forever, or she loves Denise but scares her away with her 'interesting' personality. Either way, she loves Denise, so at least I don't need to worry about that.

"On Sundays, I usually go visit my Gran in her retirement community, Peaceful Pines," I tell Denise. "And she can sometimes be a little bit much for people."

"You visit every Sunday? That's so sweet."

"Almost every Sunday, and it's not as sweet as you'd think. Gran isn't like those sweet old ladies you see knitting sweaters in TV shows."

"Okay," Denise drawls. "So what is she like, then?"

"Well, there's not a good way to explain it, so you'd better wait and see for yourself. I wanted you to know that you shouldn't expect any typical grandmother type behavior during this visit."

"Alright, I will keep an open mind." She looks confused, and I suppose I could give her a better warning, but the truth is, I never know what to expect when I visit Gran.

One time I came to see her, and she'd gone sky-diving with the ladies from her book club. Another time I showed up to a hundred old people in their bathing suits, painting their bodies with glow paint, getting ready for an early-bird rave. And yet another time, she and her friends had stolen a bunch of flatbed shopping carts from the hardware store and were having races around the parking lot.

Side note: If I ever need to move to a retirement community, I hope it's one like this.

I pull into the visitors' parking lot at Peaceful Pines and shut off the car.

"This might be a longer visit, if you want to bring your bag with you this time. Gran is still in independent living, so when I visit I do her deep-cleaning and change her sheets and stuff. She hates it when I do, but I like to help her out."

Denise reaches into the back seat for the bag she put there while I get out of the vehicle. I'm walking around the front to open Denise's door for her when suddenly at least twenty little old ladies and men jump up from beside the other vehicles parked around us.

"Fire!" I hear my Gran yell, and then I'm being pelted with a seemingly never-ending barrage of water balloons. What the fuck? That's sticky. And gooey. Shit! That's not water, it's Jell-O.

"Gran!" I yell. "I surrender. Stop! Call them off. Gran, help!"

The barrage stops shortly after my screaming does, but it has less to do with Gran taking pity on me and more to do with the geriatric gang of misfits running out of balloons.

"Gotcha good, you little peckerhead," Gran's best friend, Gladys, yells while she laughs at me. "You're going to be washing Jell-O out of your pubes for weeks!"

"Joke's on you, Gladys," I blurt. "I had a full body wax yesterday. I don't have *any* body hair *at all*." I slap my face with my palm as I finish talking. I know what's coming next.

"No shit?" Gladys says, one hand on her hip and the other pointing at my crotch. "Well, whip it out. Let's have a look."

"Gladys, you old pervert. You're not looking at my grandson's dick." Gran turns to me. "You can show it to me, though, Ryder. It's nothing I haven't seen before. Remember the first time you got a little boner, and you came running out, all worried, and showed it to me? Poor little fella. You thought you were turning into a statue."

I scrub a hand down my face. Why would she say that now? When I called earlier to say I was bringing Denise, it was so that Gran would know *not* to embarrass me. Apparently, she has other ideas. God, I hope Denise is still in the car and didn't hear Gran talking about my first boner. The sound of the car door closing tells me she most likely did, though.

"Turning into a statue, hey? That's a weird thing to assume." Denise is laughing. "Why on earth would you think that?"

I flash a dirty look at Gran. "Yeah, Gran. Why would I think that, I wonder? Any ideas?"

"Oh, don't look at me like that. You're the one who was so gullible." She turns to look at Denise now. "I may have told him a little fib about my mean old neighbor being Medusa, and that if she caught him in her yard, he would slowly turn to stone." She shrugs. "Lying to children has always been one of my favorite hobbies."

Both Denise and Gladys are laughing at me now.

"Hunter threw my ball into her yard, so I had to go get it, and she saw me. I don't think I've ever run so fast. I thought I was in the clear when I didn't turn to stone that day or the next, so I forgot all about it. But then when I got into some of Gran's reading material and popped a woody a few days later..."

Denise is leaning with her arms on the hood of my car, with her forehead resting on her arms. Huge laughs are coming from her and she's shaking with the effort. I walk over and pick up her purse and her bag and point towards Gran's building.

"Alright ladies, let's take this inside. Denise, this is my Gran, Delores, and her best friend, Gladys. Gladys and Gran, this is Denise. Gladys and Gran live next door to each other." I make quick work of the introductions. From how this visit has started, I have a feeling it will be in our best interest to get out of here before these old birds do something even more ridiculous. "This won't be one of my longer visits because Denise and I have a dinner to get to later."

Gladys and Gran walk arm in arm to Gran's little cottage, both of them still giggling at both my childhood embarrassment and my current sticky state, leaving me to take care of Denise while she gets her laughter under control. Once she's standing up straight, I lace her fingers with mine and lead her toward Gran's cottage.

"I can't believe you thought you were turning into a statue," she says with a shake of her head. "That's hilarious."

"You know," I lean over and whisper in her ear. "I can still get as stiff as a statue. I'd love to show you later."

Her mouth drops open, and she stops walking. I chuckle a little at the look on her face.

"I'm teasing you, Denise. Come on, let's go see what else Gran has planned to embarrass me and corrupt you. If you think that statue story was bad, wait. I'm sure she has many tricks up her sleeve."

"You ass," she says through a laugh. "I can't wait to hear more embarrassing stories. And I hope you don't think I'm keeping them to myself later, either. I'm sure the guys would love to hear about the Medusa neighbor and your first boner freak out."

She laughs the entire walk to Gran's place, and I don't think I could love a sound more. Except the sounds she makes when I make her come. I love those the most. Even the thought of them is getting me hard.

I stop outside Gran's place and let Denise go in ahead of me. I need a minute to stop myself from turning completely into a statue. That damn Medusa.

32

Gran And Gladys, the Dirty Old Ladies Club

Denise

"So how do you know Ryder, dear?" Gran is the cutest little old lady. She's wearing a bright purple, two-piece track suit with white, high-top, Air Jordan sneakers. Oddly enough, even the fact that she's wearing a trucker hat that proudly reads 'fuck bitches, get money' across the front doesn't detract from her cuteness. She's brewing a pot of tea and while the kettle boils, she asks me to get the tea cups from her little china cabinet in the living room.

"I manage the band," I say, while I find the teacups. What the hell? These teacups are not what I was expecting. They look like normal bone china teacups, but besides the beautiful flowers and gilding along the edges, each cup has a different curse word printed in gold calligraphy. "Um, Delores? Are these the teacups you want us to use?"

"Call me Gran, dear," she says before she comes out of the tiny kitchen and looks at the cups in my hands.

"Oh, yes. Of course. Aren't they great? I found them at a local craft fair. Well, it was more like a kink convention, but they also had a variety of vendors, not the usual BDSM fare. One can only buy so many whips and restraints, you know. This place doesn't have nearly as much storage as I would like."

"Gran!" Ryder is coming inside, finally. He didn't come out and say it, but I think he needed a minute to 'soften the statue'. "This is Denise's first time visiting you. Don't scare her away with your kink convention stories. She's not ready for that much information yet."

He looks over at me and mouths 'sorry', before going over to his Gran and giving her a kiss on the cheek.

"Now, I hate to ask, but do you still have my joggers or something else I can change into? I need to get out of these Jell-O clothes and I need to shower. I can't believe you would ambush me with balloons filled with a gelatinous dessert."

"You're lucky we filled them with Jell-O and not aspic. I imagine you'd have liked balloons filled with meat jelly even less." She chuckles. "Besides, it's not like it was my idea. Gladys came up with it, and she's the one who posted the sign-up sheet in the bingo hall."

"I did not, you old bat!" Gladys screeches from the hallway, where she's come out of the bathroom. "I still have the sheet if you want to see it, Ryder. It says 'help me drown my grandson with Jell-O balloons and wipe that smug look off his stupid face'. You're certainly not my grandson. And thank goodness for that, or the dreams I've been having would really be inappropriate. *Ha-cha-cha*." She fans herself with her hand while she looks Ryder up and down.

Oh my god, Gladys announced that she has sex dreams about Ryder. She's eighty years old if she's a day and she is having sex dreams about her best friend's grandson. Ryder runs a palm down his face and shakes his head. I choke on my spit while I try not to laugh. Visiting with Gran might be hazardous to my health. How many times can I choke on nothing before I die?

"I'm going to grab a towel and throw my stuff in the wash, Gran. I won't be able to do all your cleaning for you today. I don't do my best work in my underwear."

"No, I should hope not," Gran says with a wink to me. "Tell me he at least gets fully undressed when he's getting up in them guts. He's not one of those men who leaves his socks on, is he?"

I choke again, and a huge laugh bursts out of me. What do you say when someone's grandmother inquires about their grandson's sex habits? When she clearly enunciates 'getting up in them guts'? Even if I know for a fact he gets fully undressed, it's not like I'm going to tell her that. Luckily, Ryder chimes in to save me because my mouth is working, but no sounds are coming out.

"Gran! For fuck's sake. Can you please behave for five minutes? I need to wash this Jell-O off before you start being insane, okay?" He comes over to me next and whispers, "I will be so quick. If I weren't covered in sticky goo, I wouldn't leave you alone with her. Don't let them gang up on you. She and Gladys have a way of making people say things they don't want to. I swear, they should work for the police doing interrogations."

I laugh from nervousness, not humor. Well, it's partly from humor. I'm feeling a morbid curiosity over what this crazy granny will say next. But even though I'm not really keeping any secrets, the idea of discussing my sex life with Ryder, with his own grandmother, against my will, has my palms sweating and my heart beating a little too quickly.

"Please hurry," I joke, but not really. "I'm a little scared."

He nods once, his tongue poking out and playing with his lip ring, before turning and running to the bathroom. I think this will be the quickest shower of his life.

"So Denise. Now that we got rid of that pain in the ass, party-pooper grandson of mine," Gran says to me with a sweet smile. "Can I offer you some whiskey with your tea?"

Shit. I don't want her to know that I'm pregnant, since she clearly thinks Ryder and I are together. Maybe I am keeping secrets after all.

"No, thank you." Hopefully that's good enough for her, but I have a feeling it won't be.

"Oh come on now, a little nip won't hurt ya. I won't even tell Ryder you're encouraging his old granny to drink," she says with a wink.

I laugh at her attempts to blackmail me. "I seriously doubt he'd believe that I could pressure you to do anything. You seem to be the one in charge here."

"Ha! Good eye, girlie. I like you. Now you need to drink with me. Let's have a toast. To keeping my dumbass grandson in the dark." She goes to pour some whiskey into the teacup she's selected as mine; the one that says 'Bitch'.

"No, Gran. Really. I can't."

She gives me a knowing look. "Hmm. That's what I thought. So, spit it out. How far along are you?"

"What?" I splutter. "How did you know?" I'm thinking that maybe Gran is a witch. How else would she be able to tell I'm pregnant from my declining whiskey? It's the middle of the afternoon. Plenty of people would say no to whiskey at this time of the day.

"Oh, lots of reasons," she says. "Gladys and I both knew as soon as Ryder drove up with you. Isn't that right, Gladys?" She looks around for Gladys and finally finds her down the hall, holding a glass up to the bathroom door, trying to eavesdrop on Ryder in the shower. "Gladys, what the hell are you doing? He's not talking in there. You won't hear anything."

Gladys sighs heavily and comes back to where we're standing in the living room. When she stands next to Gran, you can see that they consulted each other when they got dressed today. Their tracksuits are the same brand, different colors, and they have the same white Air Jordans. Gladys doesn't have a hat, though. I guess only Gran is down with fucking bitches and getting money.

"I'll have you know that I'm like a bat, but for peckers. I can tell how big a man's dick is using echolocation. Also, I was trying to hear if he was whacking it. Don't think I don't know why he sent you in here alone, young lady. I saw that stiffy he was trying to rearrange. And good for you. I hope for your sake he knows what to do with it."

What is up with these women? They're more sex crazed than hormonal teenagers. I can't even come up with responses to anything they're saying. I'm too shocked that these cute, blue-haired, little old ladies are talking like this.

"Well? Was he?" Gran asks her.

"No, I don't think he was. At least, if he was, he was super quiet about it."

"Well, thank goodness for that. I taught that boy better than to beat his one-eyed custard chucker in someone else's shower, especially when he's a guest for the afternoon." She taps a finger on her lips. "Although I suppose he *is* uncomfortable. All that pent up 'energy' and nothing to do with it." She finger quotes 'energy' because she definitely means something far more sexual in nature.

"You know what?" Gladys says to Gran. "I agree. Let's go for a walk. Leave these two kids alone for a little while." Gladys wiggles her eyebrows at me.

"That's a great idea," Gran says to Gladys. "We'll be back in half an hour. Put the sheets in the wash when you're finished with your pants off dance-off."

Before I even catch on to what they're getting at, they've walked out and shut the door behind them. I'm standing alone in Ryder's Gran's living room, and I'm positive she left so that Ryder and I can have sex. I don't think I've ever been flabbergasted before, but I am definitely feeling flabbergasted right now.

I grab my project bag and pull out my female genitalia embroidery, to give me something to focus on. Before I can start, though, Ryder is coming back down the hallway wearing a pair of gray sweatpants with the waistband of his boxers peeking out over the top. The view is enough to make my mouth water.

He looks around and when he doesn't see anyone else, he asks, "Where did Gran and Gladys go? I thought for sure Gladys would be here trying to get a peek at me when I got out of the shower."

I put my embroidery down beside me and look up at him. He dried off like a guy, meaning he hardly dried off at all, and there are little rivulets of water running down the separation of his abs, down the V of his adonis belt, and soaking into the waistband of his boxers. I swallow hard before I tear my eyes away.

"They, uh, they went for a walk?"

"What? Why would they do that?"

"Well." I laugh a little, because this sounds so ridiculous, even in my head, that I'm not sure Ryder will believe it. But he knows his Gran, so maybe he will. "Gladys was eavesdropping at the bathroom door to see if she could hear you masturbating. And to use her special bat powers to find out how big you are." I gesture vaguely toward his cock.

"Oh, for fuck's sake. She's got a one track mind." He shakes his head and gives a rueful laugh. Ryder doesn't seem as surprised as I was. Gladys must be batshit crazy on a good day for this to be par for the course.

"She said she knew you were rearranging your hard-on when you sent me in here first. So she figured you'd be taking care of yourself in the shower..." I trail off, not really wanting to say the rest out loud. "Your Gran said something about a custard chucker?"

Realization dawns in his eyes. "Oh fuck," he says, running his hand down his face again. I have a feeling that's a gesture he makes a lot when he visits Gran. "They went for a walk because they think we should have sex, didn't they?"

I nod my head, torn between laughing hysterically and being shocked into silence.

He comes over and moves my embroidery out of the way before sitting beside me.

"I'm sorry," he says, shaking his head and blowing out a breath. "I didn't think I'd be in the shower long enough for them to get that out of hand. They must have organized that whole Jell-O fiasco to get you alone for a few minutes."

I can't hold it anymore, and the laughter pours out of me. "Do you really think they considered using aspic instead of Jell-O? Could you imagine?"

He laughs. "I suppose I *should* be thankful that it wasn't meat jelly."

"She also gave me the 'Bitch' teacup and told me she knew I was pregnant. That she and Gladys had it figured out as soon as you pulled in the lot with me in the car."

"Yeah, I guess that makes sense." He looks at me and chuckles a little. "I rarely bring anyone here, besides Aiden. And Gladys and Gran nearly scared him off."

"I could see that. Aiden is pretty quiet compared to them. Those women are hilarious."

"Hilarious is one word for it."

"Your Gran must be the reason you're so much fun. Although, I think she has you beat in the dirty mind department. And I didn't even think that was possible. She told me to put the sheets in the wash when we were done with our 'pants-off dance off'."

He looks at me, and this time I can see the heat in his eyes. "If you could read my mind right now, you wouldn't say that." Ryder licks his lips and leans in a little closer. "If I said even half of the things that seeing you in this dress has me thinking, you'd never question how dirty my mind is again."

"Oh," I say, surprised at how quickly the tone of this conversation has changed. His voice has heat already flooding my core.

"Ever since you came down the stairs at your place, all I've been able to think about is what's under this dress," he whispers against my ear as his hand traces circles on my thigh above my knee, sending sparks blazing along my skin. "But my Gran must be crazy if she thinks I'm doing anything with you here in her house, when I know she's outside waiting to jump in and catch me with my pants down. Literally."

He gives me a quick kiss on my lips and whispers, "shhh," before standing up and tiptoeing to the front door. He throws it open and two old ladies with guilty looks on their faces come tumbling in, only to be caught by Ryder, one in each arm, as they all crash to the floor in a heap.

33

Hairlessness Inspections for Science and Stuff

Ryder

"When were you going to tell me about knocking up this lovely lady?" Gran has recovered from her stumble into the house, all traces of embarrassment at being caught long gone.

"Yeah," Gladys pipes in. "You know how long we've been waiting for you or Hunter to inject someone with your baby gravy so we can be great grannies?"

Yet again I'm shaking my head, running my hand over my face. I haven't talked to Denise about Aiden's plan yet, but even if we were to pretend that the baby is actually mine, I don't think I'd be able to include my Gran in the lie. I'm too close to her to lie about that. Not that I think it would matter to her either way.

"Gran, the baby isn't Ryder's," Denise says. "It's a complicated situation with an ex-boyfriend, and Ryder has been helping me. He rescued me from the asshole last night."

"Is that so?" Gran's face is unreadable as she looks between me and Ryder. "What happened?"

"I broke up with him last week, before I knew about the baby. Last night I told him I was pregnant, and he freaked out. Started screaming at me, insisted the baby wasn't his, accused me of cheating, broke a ton of picture frames, nearly destroyed my embroidery collection, and broke a lamp. Ryder came in as he was closing in on me."

"Aiden and I were both there, so after I made sure Denise was safe, I brought the dude outside to Aiden. He and Devon tried to follow him home, but he lost them somehow. So, for now, we are all taking turns hanging out with Denise, so she isn't alone. At least until we find Andrew, and Denise figures out how she wants to proceed."

Gladys sips tea that smells suspiciously like straight whiskey out of a teacup with 'whore' emblazoned in gold letters across the side. "Well, I'd say the solution is obvious."

"I'd have to agree with you on that, Gladys." Gran says, sipping her own whiskey and tea concoction from her teacup, but instead of 'whore', hers reads 'cunt' in golden cursive. God, I love my Gran. She is her own brand of crazy and it's so much fun. Even if it can be a little embarrassing sometimes.

"And what is this oh so obvious solution?" I ask. I know the solution that I'm rooting for. It's the one that ends with me and Denise together, raising this baby with Andrew dead in a ditch somewhere. Of natural causes, of course.

"You need to step up, Ryder," Gladys says with an exasperated sigh. "This guy doesn't seem to want this baby. And he sounds like he would be a shit father, anyway. Tell people it's yours and that's the end of it."

"Well now, that's not the end of it," Gran adds. "You can't tell people it's your baby, without actually acting as if that baby is yours. You'll have to be the father."

"I can't let him do that." Denise jumps in before I have the chance to say anything. "I can't trap him into raising another man's baby."

"Oh, bullshit," Gladys spits. "Genes aren't the only thing that make a man a father. I know firsthand that loving the mother and treating her and her family right has a hell of a lot more to do with it than a little swimmer making it to the finish line does."

"Alright. I think that's enough for now. Denise can take care of this in her own way." I look over at Denise. "For the record, though, that's the same idea that Aiden and I had."

"Oh no, I won't have everyone ganging up on me over this. It's bad enough that Devon and Xena had the same idea. I swear, if Alex and the rest of the guys come to the same conclusion, I'm going to take myself to one of those old school homes for unwed mothers."

"Don't bother," Gladys laughs. "Those places are awful. They won't even let you swear. And forget masturbating when the pregnancy hormones get the best of you and send your libido through the roof. I'm so glad my Donald came and rescued me from the one my parents sent me to when I was a young woman. We eloped and had a crazy sex filled honeymoon in Las Vegas."

Gladys' eyes get a little misty as she tells the story. She doesn't talk about her husband often, but I know she misses him. He passed about ten years ago, the year before she and my Gran both moved into this retirement community. They've been neighbors and best friends ever since.

"Well, that's something to keep in mind, especially since Andrew isn't likely to come and rescue me." Denise chuckles a little. "And even if he tried, I certainly wouldn't go with him. That ship has sailed. I'm honestly not even sure he deserves to be a part of this baby's life, but I know I need to at least consider it."

"Oh no, dear," Gladys clarifies. "The baby's father didn't rescue me. Donald was one of my best male friends. I'd always had a little crush on him, but my family didn't approve. When I fell pregnant with the baby's father, and he tried to cause me to lose the baby by throwing me down the stairs, my parents sent me away to keep me safe. Donald got wind of the situation and beat that dickhead seven ways from Sunday and sent him packing. Told him to never show his face in that town again. Then he came and found me and the rest is history. My parents certainly changed their minds about Donald after that."

That sounds almost exactly like what Denise is going through right now, and I can see from the look on her face that she's not prepared to deal with this information now.

"I'm sorry you had to go through that, Gladys. Donald was a smart man to snag you." I look over at Denise. "We should probably get going, though. Alex needs us to stop and grab something at the grocery store. Thanks for the tea, Gran. I'll come by in a few days and get my clothes, if you can throw them in the dryer for me?"

"You're going to run around topless?" Denise asks. "I don't think they'll let you in the store like that."

"I have a shirt in my car that I forgot to put on for the party last night. It's a good thing too. I never would have expected a Jell-O ambush when visiting my grandmother in the retirement community." I shoot Gran a smirk. "They said this was a respectable place when I moved you in. Who knew you'd start a gang of blue-haired miscreants and use me as the victim for most of your trouble making schemes?"

Gran gets up from her chair and comes to give me a hug. "You love it, kiddo. Besides, Hunter gets it even worse than you do when he comes to visit. Ask him about the firecracker incident next time you see him. I think you'll be impressed."

Gladys cackles from her spot on the couch. "I wonder if that boy's leg hair has grown back yet? He might have you beat for hairlessness, Ryder. Maybe you should show me? You know, for science and stuff."

I go give Gladys a hug, too. She might be a dirty old lady, but she's still Gran's best friend. I know Gran is never lonely or bored when Gladys is around. "I'm not showing you my hairless body, you perv. You can ask Denise for confirmation though," I tell her with a wink.

"I knew it! I knew you two were bumping uglies," Gran yells before spinning around to look at Denise. "Does he take care of you? If he doesn't, you be sure to kick him in the wang. This boy knows enough to know that ladies always come first. And hopefully second too, if he's doing it right." She winks at Denise.

Denise's face is so red she's about to burst into flames. I think she's finally reached her limit of old lady sex conversations. At least for one day.

"Alright Gran, we're going to leave some things a mystery for now. Denise's family might not be quite as open as ours. You can't expect her to give you a report on my sexual performance yet. Let's save something for the next visit, yeah?"

"Oh fine, you big poop," Gran pouts. Gladys is booing and giving me a thumbs down. "Denise, it was lovely to meet you today. Come back whenever you like. There are many, many more embarrassing stories about Ryder to tell you. I even have some old photos around here somewhere. I'll dig them out before your next visit."

"It was nice to meet you too, Gran. And you as well, Gladys. It's been... interesting, to say the least." Denise chuckles a little as she stands. "I can't wait to come for another visit, so I can hear those embarrassing stories about Ryder. He's always so sure of himself. I think he could stand to be knocked down a peg or two."

"Yeah, yeah. Let's get moving. I can only take so much abuse. Even when it comes from the three most beautiful women I know." I pick up Denise's bag before she gets the chance. "Gran, Gladys. Until next time."

I open the door and wait as Denise hugs Gran and Gladys. When she gets to me, I grab her hand in mine and lead her to the car.

Opening up the trunk, I pull out the Team Alex shirt I had made and forgot to wear to the party last night. I quickly pull it over my head and walk up to open the door for Denise.

"That's what you were going to wear last night?" She bursts into laughter. "I think it's a good thing you forgot."

"You know, you're right; it'll have a much bigger impact at family dinner. Especially since I had one made for Devon too and forgot to give it to him yesterday."

We're both still laughing when we leave the parking lot of the retirement complex to head back toward town.

"So now what?" I ask. "It's too early for dinner, but I thought we needed to get out of there. They had their pervert level cranked right up today. It was almost enough to make me blush. And you know how bad it has to be before that will happen."

34

Milkshakes and Bathroom Meetings

Denise

"So Alex doesn't actually need you to pick anything up?" I ask.

"Nah. I made that up so we could get out of there. Gladys is bad enough when I'm fully dressed. Sitting there with no shirt on was asking for trouble. Once she gets into the whiskey, she gets a little handsy." He laughs and makes a grabbing motion with his hands. "She's been curious about the size of my junk ever since I went to a pool party at the complex and she saw me in my board shorts. I think she thinks there is a lot more going on down there than there is."

I bark out a laugh. "You're joking, right? We both know you are more than adequate in that department. I know I sure didn't have any complaints." I clap my hand to my mouth seconds too late, leaving that statement hanging there in the air between us. "I mean... shit. This is awkward."

"We're going to have to talk about it eventually, babe," Ryder says, glancing away from the road ahead for a moment. "But for now, I can pretend that I didn't hear you say how incredibly satisfied you are with my monster dong." He breaks into laughter before lowering his voice, taking on a more serious tone.

"At least until you've decided what you want to do with the Andrew situation. Then, when you realize that I'm in this for the long haul, I will expect a full report on how you don't have any complaints. After that, I'm going to use what you consider to be my more than adequately sized cock to satisfy you every chance I get."

Holy fuck, did it get hot in here? I sneak my hand to the window controls and roll down the window a bit, pulling the front of the dress away from my body to let some air in there. Ryder smirks and looks at me out of the corner of his eye. Dick. He did that on purpose. And if I weren't starving again, I might make him do something about it. Gladys was right, these pregnancy hormones are no joke.

"Can we go to Maggie's for a milkshake?" I ask. "I'm hungry again, but the only thing I really feel like having is one of those giant milkshakes."

"Anything you want, babe." Ryder turns the car down a street that will take us past his place. "I want to stop and grab different shoes. These are covered in Jell-O, and it's starting to feel sticky."

"Thankfully sticky is all you need to worry about. Imagine what they would smell like if they'd gone with the meat jelly option." I fake gag. "So gross."

Ryder pulls up at his place and runs in to change his shoes. I don't even get out of the car because I don't trust myself not to jump him the minute I get him alone in a private place. I need to work on keeping my hormones in check. Maybe a new vibrator will help keep my mind off of Ryder's exceptional bedroom abilities? I pull out my phone and start browsing my favorite adult toy site, Fade Toys, and I'm so engrossed in my research that I don't notice when Ryder gets back into the car.

"Doing some shopping? You know, I'd be happy to help you test those out. I'm not intimidated by sex toys. I know sometimes things work better if I have a tag team partner helping me out. As long as you're happy, I'm happy."

I close the page and turn my phone off before Ryder can say anything else, my cheeks burning with embarrassment. And the worst thing is that now I won't even be able to buy one of the vibrators I was thinking of because I won't be able to use it without imagining Ryder helping me with it. So much for getting my mind off of him.

"Never mind," I say. "Let's go to the diner. I want to have my milkshake. I don't want to talk about this."

"Alright," Ryder says, driving away from the curb. "But the offer stands. With or without toys for assistance. I'm your man. Everything I have," he says as he gestures to his whole body, "is yours to do with as you wish."

I turn toward the window and bury my face in my hand, determined not to engage in this conversation any further. Even with his stupid joking tone, I want to make him pull over somewhere and fuck me against the side of the car. Why does he have to be so damn sexy? And why does he have to seem so damn sincere when he says he still wants me, even though I'm pregnant? His insistence is making it so much harder for me to do the right thing.

When we pull up to the diner, the parking lot is nearly empty. Ryder parks in a spot close to the entrance and he comes around to open my door. In the short time I've been driving around with him, I've gotten used to his whole opening doors for me thing. I kind of like it. It makes me feel taken care of. Usually I'm the one taking care of everyone else, so this is nice. I never expected Ryder would be the one who could make me feel this way. Anyone who's ever heard me complain about having to clean up after his nonsense would be shocked to see his behavior toward me now. He's made a career out of being irresponsible, after all.

Has he really, though? He bought his old babysitter a store and makes sure she's taken care of. And it sounds like he's the one who bought that cute little place for his Gran in the retirement community. It wouldn't surprise me if he's taking care of his dad and his brother too, somehow. Maybe it really was an act that he was putting on? Maybe the character of Ryder Sullivan from Sleeping Dogs is a different person than the man Ryder Sullivan? Could that be?

We sit in the same booth we had the last time we were here and we even get the same server. She comes over with menus and gets our drink orders. Vanilla milkshake for me this time, and Ryder gets a coffee.

"So what are you thinking of for the baby's room?" Ryder asks. "Are you going to find out the sex of the baby and do the room up for a girl or a boy? Or were you thinking something better?"

The server brings our drinks then and I notice she does the same napkin routine as last time, attempting to slip Ryder her phone number. Ryder's reaction this time is much different. He picks up the napkin and hands it to her.

"I'm here with this beautiful woman and I would appreciate it if you didn't pass me your phone number again. It's presumptuous of you to assume that I am interested in calling you when I am clearly here with someone else. You have no way of knowing the nature of our relationship, but regardless of what it is, it's not polite of you to attempt to discreetly pass me your phone number while I am clearly with someone. I'm sure you're very nice, and I'm going to assume you meant no offense, but I think we would all be more comfortable if you sent us a different server for the rest of our visit."

The server stammers something that sounds like it might be an apology while shoving the crumpled up napkin into the pocket of her apron. She goes behind the counter and whispers to another server, who nods her head in agreement. I guess she'll be taking over our table.

"That wasn't really necessary," I tell Ryder. "We're not together. It's okay if you take her number."

"No, it's not okay. She doesn't know we're not together. Plus, I want us to be together. I'm not looking for anyone else, for any reason. I'm serious when I say I'm going to take care of you. I'm going to prove to you I am the man you need in your life to help you with everything. I know you don't actually need me, Denise. I don't think you need rescuing. But I care for you, and I want to be here for you. I'm going to do everything I can to show you I can be that man for you. You take care of everyone and everything else. I want to be the person who takes care of you." He reaches across the table, grabs my hand, and brings it up to his lips. After kissing my knuckles, he places my hand back on the table.

"I need to run to the bathroom," I blurt, before sliding out of the booth and scurrying to the back hallway, where the restrooms are located. Once inside, I wet some paper towels and use them to cool my face.

Ryder is saying all the right things. What I wouldn't give to have someone taking care of me for a change. I've never been able to rely on anyone, even when I wanted to. People aren't wired that way, in my experience. They say they'll take care of you, but it doesn't work out that way. Even my parents did the bare minimum. Oh sure, they provided the home, food, clothes, and education, but they were seriously lacking in the nurturing and loving departments. I can't even remember the last time my parents hugged me.

I finish cooling my face and dab it dry with a fresh paper towel. I'm about to leave the restroom and head back to the table, when original server comes in.

"Oh," she says in surprise. "I didn't know anyone was in here."

"That's okay," I say. "I was on my way out."

I try to walk around her, and she stops me with a gentle touch on the arm. "I'm really sorry about what happened before," she says. "What your boyfriend said was actually a real wake up call for me. I've been pulling the same crap for ages. He was the first one to ever call me out on it, though. You wouldn't believe the number of men who pocket the number and call me later." She laughs a humorless laugh. "I don't even know why I do it. It makes me feel good for a few minutes when we hook up, and then I feel like absolute garbage for days afterward. Everything has been going shitty for me for so long that I liked the boost it gave me when the guys took me up on my offer. But, anyway. You don't want to hear about that. Gah. I'm so embarassed." She sniffles and wipes her eyes with the back of her hand. "I'll let you go now. I'm really very sorry. Please tell your boyfriend thank you for me. I think I really needed to hear that."

There's something about this girl that hits me right in the feels. It could be the pregnancy hormones and mothering instincts kicking in, but in the spur of the moment, I decide I'm going to help her.

"What's your name?" I ask.

"Umm, it's Ivy. Why?"

I fish around in my purse until I find a business card and hold it out to her. "I will be looking for an assistant coming up soon. I manage the band Sleeping Dogs and need someone to take over some tasks that I normally do while the band is on the road. I'm three months pregnant and I will need to have this person trained up and ready before the baby is born. There are some parts of my job that I won't be able to do while I stay home with the baby. I have a feeling about you. So if you think you might be interested, call me at that number, and we'll set up a proper meeting. You know, at an office. At the very least, at a table in the diner instead of the restroom."

She laughs at my joke. "I... thank you. I don't know what to say." Her eyes well up with tears again. "I will definitely call you. Thank you so much."

She wraps her arms around me in a tight squeeze, and I hug her back. I have no idea why, but I want to take care of this girl. She feels like a little sister to me, and I've never met her in my life. So weird.

"Well, Ivy. It was nice to meet you," I say as I drop the hug. "But I need to get back to my milkshake before it melts. This baby has been craving it since the last one I had. Be sure to call soon. I do a lot for the band, and whoever takes some of that on is going to have their hands full. I need to make sure that you'd be able to handle it before we come to anything."

She nods her head as I turn and walk out the door.

I must be crazy. I had a more complex vetting process when I hired Alex to be the chef at Connor's place. And I basically asked the server who hit on someone she thought was my boyfriend, right in front of me, to be the new me while I take time off for the baby. Baby brain is real, y'all. That's the only thing I can think that would cause this. I'm chuckling to myself and shaking my head a little when I slide back into the booth with Ryder.

"Everything okay? You were gone for a while. Is it your stomach again? Are you going to be sick? We can skip dinner and rest at your place if you want."

"No, no," I say around my straw after I take a big slurp of milkshake. *So good.* It's not completely melted, but it's soft enough to get through the straw easily, which is nice. I don't like a milkshake that's too thick to drink. "I'm fine. Just having a mental breakdown, maybe? I gave my card to the server who hit on you. Her name is Ivy, by the way. She apologized to me in the bathroom, and I got this weird feeling that I'm supposed to help her. I thought I would talk to her about maybe taking on some of my duties with the band when I take time off with the baby. Maybe she could take on traveling with you guys and I can do what I can from home or something? I don't know, it's not a very well thought out plan. Which is so unlike me, I have to laugh. Isn't that crazy? These pregnancy hormones are really messing with me."

Ryder looks at me with his eyes wide. He opens his mouth like he's about to say something, but instead shakes his head and takes another drink of his coffee.

"I know! It sounds so crazy, but we had an entire conversation in the bathroom. I didn't promise her the job or anything, told her to call me soon and we can arrange to talk somewhere less bathroom-like. I have this feeling that she could be fantastic at this, you know?"

It doesn't make sense, but at least Ryder knows enough to not doubt me on this. Even though I'm known for being in control and having everything planned, I've actually done plenty of things because of gut instincts before, and they've worked out okay. Approaching the guys at that house party and demanding they take me on as their manager was one of the best decisions I ever made, and I did that on the spur of the moment. I'd even had a few drinks when I did it, and that turned out great.

"I trust you, Denise." Ryder finishes his coffee. "I know you wouldn't do anything that would harm the band, so I will back you with whatever you decide."

"Thanks. That means a lot. I know it's weird, since I normally make lists upon lists before making a decision, but every once in a while I get a gut feeling and I have to follow it."

"I know exactly what you mean," Ryder mumbles to the table. I wonder if he intended for me to hear that. "Well, should we get going? Has the baby's milkshake craving been satisfied?

Connor said he wanted us to come a little early today. He probably has some sort of speech planned about the engagement."

I make an exaggerated groan accompanied by an over the top eye roll. "Again? Didn't we sit through a speech *and* a song last night?"

"You know, I was thinking the same thing. I've had about as much of their love as I can stand." Ryder laughs and fakes gagging. "We get it. You love each other. Give it a rest, already."

Ryder throws a couple of twenties down on the table to pay for our drinks and we make our way to the door, still chuckling and cracking jokes about Connor and Alex. As much as we tease them, though, we'd never begrudge them their love.

35

Surprise!

Ryder

YOU EVER MADE A plan and then regretted it when it's much too late to cancel? Because it took many people to help you pull it off and there is no way to turn back? No? Just me? Great.

At least I was able to stop at home and change not my shoes, but also my clothes. I can never look at Jell-O the same way again, thanks to Gran and her merry band of geriatric miscreants. I swear that retirement community is more like a summer camp for delinquent kids than it is a relaxing place for old people to spend their golden years.

We're on our way to Alex and Connor's place, for what Denise thinks is our normal Sunday family dinner, when in reality we're throwing her a party to welcome the baby to the family and to let her know she will have all of our support, no matter what.

Except she told me she didn't want to tell anyone else yet, and this ensures that now everyone knows. And it was my idea. And there is a very good chance she's going to rip my balls off for going behind her back to make this happen. Visiting my Gran was mostly a way to keep her distracted while everyone else decorated and did all the actual work of putting the party together. I was more of an idea man on this project, but that doesn't mean all the blame doesn't lie squarely on my shoulders if this goes sideways.

"Looks like everyone else is already here," Denise observes as I pull up to park beside Travis's truck. They parked all the other vehicles in front of the garage or along the driveway, but left the spot closest to the door available for us.

Real subtle guys.

This isn't a surprise party, necessarily. It's a party that will be a surprise for the recipient, namely Denise. No one is planning to jump out and yell surprise at her. I hope they won't, anyway.

"Hey, so, thanks a lot for coming to visit my Gran with me," I say, grabbing her hand before getting out of the car. "I'm glad you guys got to meet each other. You are the two most important women in my life. Well, there are five of you, if we include Lana, Alex, and Gladys. I'm sure I'd face much worse than meat jelly if Gladys didn't make the cut." I laugh. That Gladys is a character, it's a shame her grandkids don't visit her more. "I want you to know that no matter how dinner goes down tonight, I really care about you, and I want to support you in whatever you choose to do."

I drop her hand and get out of the car before she asks questions. Apologizing in advance was a coward's move, but I can't bear the thought of her being angry with me. I suppose if I were smarter I wouldn't have planned this party if I really didn't want her to be mad, but no one's ever accused me of being smart. The best I get is that I'm not as dumb as I look, as Aiden so kindly pointed out this morning.

I go around and open the passenger door and help Denise out of the car, taking advantage of how she's allowing me to hold her hand as I walk her to the door. I open the door to the house, ushering Denise inside in front of me, and we are greeted with the coolest sight.

Hundreds and hundreds of beach ball sized helium balloons in black, silver, and white decorate the entire front entryway and continue down the hallway past the dining room and on toward the kitchen.

"Wow!" Denise looks impressed. "They really went all out to celebrate their engagement again, didn't they?" She whispers. She doesn't know this is for her and her baby, and not for the newly engaged couple. "Let's get in there. We're the last ones here."

She drags me by the hand to the dining room, and before she says hello to anyone, her friend Xena sees her.

"You're already here!" Xena yells. "I told you they'd be early. Pay up, Tiny Dancer." She holds her hand out to Devon, who rolls his eyes and slaps a twenty-dollar bill into her palm. "Clearly, I know them better than you do. That must make me an honorary member of the band or something, right? I play a mean rendition of Hot Cross Buns on the recorder. I'm sure it would blow you all away."

"That's enough, Princess," Devon tells her. "Let's allow our guest of honor some time to get accustomed to her own party."

Denise looks around, finally noticing that everyone is looking right back at her. And then she sees the banner on the wall. It reads 'Welcome to the family, Baby! We love you already,' and it's surrounded by even more helium balloons. She spins around and jabs a finger into my chest.

"Did you do this?"

I take her hand in mine and rub my chest. What? She jabbed me really hard. It's probably going to leave a mark.

"Um, sort of?" I can't leave my friends hanging out to dry. "I came up with a plan, and while I kept you busy today, Alex and Aiden did the rest. Well, with all that they've accomplished, I would assume everyone here helped."

"Wait? So you planned to have a bunch of elderly people attack you with Jell-O filled balloons to keep me distracted? And your Gran and Gladys acted like a couple of pervs to keep me occupied?"

"Nope, I can attest to the fact that Gran and Gladys are as pervy as you experienced, probably even more so. You wouldn't have had much directed at you since you're a woman, but if you'd been a man? Shit. I've never blushed so hard in my life as when I visit them." Aiden shudders at what I'm guessing is the memory of the first time I brought him with me to visit Gran. She had recently taken a lap dance class at the senior's center and she insisted on giving him a demonstration. And then Gladys had to show him her moves, too.

He's never fully recovered.

There's a reason I spend most of my visits cleaning her house instead of talking. Some things a grandson doesn't need to know or bear witness to.

"So the visit was part of it. In hindsight, I should not have warned Gran I was bringing you. That's what gave her time to organize the Jell-O fiasco."

Denise is looking down at her feet and shaking her head. I can't see her face so I can't tell what she's feeling right now, but I really hope she isn't furious with me. For a guy so intent on proving how reliable and *trustworthy* I am, I sure didn't wait very long to show her I'm not.

Waxing my whole body might prove to not even be the dumbest thing I do *this week!*

"Denise, I'm so sorry." I start my apology. "I thought it would be nice for you to know how much support you have with all of us behind. I wanted you to see that you will have more help tha—"

She cuts off my apology when she launches herself at me, grabbing fistfuls of my hair and pulling me down for a kiss. I shake off my surprise and wrap my arms around her, pulling her body close and kissing her back with everything I have. I lift her off the floor and turn to take her out into the hallway. And that's when the whistling starts. Assholes won't even let us kiss in peace. Not that I let that stop me. I push Denise against the wall, softening the kiss until I pull away and rest my forehead against hers.

"You make it so hard to stay away from you, you asshole," she says, lifting her lips and kissing me again, a quick brush of her lips against mine. "I don't want to force you into life with a baby."

I pull her into a hug and hope that I can reassure with my words. "You're not forcing me into anything, Denise. I would consider myself the luckiest guy on earth if you let me share a life with you and your baby. Let me love you the way you deserve to be loved. You *and* this baby. I want it all with you. I want to watch you grow this baby, and then give birth, and then everything that comes after. Late night feedings, horrifying diaper explosions, unexplained spit-up, first smiles, first steps, first day of school. Let me be the one to do father-daughter or father-son events. And most importantly, let me be the one you turn to when you need a partner, a friend, and a lover. I want everything, always."

36

Gran and Gladys: Bad Bitches

Denise

"You don't need to answer me right now," Ryder says. "Let's go back in and enjoy your party. You can think about what I've said later. For now, let our friends show you how much they love you, too. Take a minute here to relax and then come back in when you're ready. I'll go fend off the wolves."

He kisses me deeply one more time, not as needy as before, but a slow tasting of me that stops my breath. Ryder pulls away slowly and my lips follow as though his lips are pulling me forward. I kiss him this time, my hands reaching up and weaving into his hair, pulling him close once more.

"Ewww, gross. They're still kissing out here in the hallway." Xena interrupts our kiss with her oh so hilarious assessment of the situation.

"Jesus, Ryder. Get a room. You still have one downstairs." Connor yells. "But keep it down. We don't want to listen to you two fucking while we're here trying to have a perfectly respectable party."

"Fuck off," Ryder yells back. "I'll see you in there," he whispers to me, with one more kiss before going back into the room.

"Well, that looked like some pretty steamy kissing to me." Xena leans against the wall with me. "Want to talk about it?"

I nod my head and lead her through the kitchen and out to the deck. Heat rises in my cheeks when I look over to where Ryder and I sat that first time, when he made me come with his fingers.

"So?"

"So, I don't know." I answer honestly. "He says I wouldn't be forcing him into anything, but I still feel like I'm trapping him. I don't want to bring someone into this baby's life to have him duck out when it gets too hard. But he sounded so sincere when he said he wanted it all. He even included vomit and dirty diapers on the list of what he wants to be a part of. So it's not like he's going into it with this rosy view of cute, chubby angel babies who never cry or get messy. He sounds like he knows what he would be in for."

"Then why don't you let him decide for himself what's good for him? Why don't you let him love you like he so clearly wants to?"

"Because I can't!" I whisper yell. "Because I have to be the one to take care of everything, otherwise it won't get done. How can I rely on someone else to do some of it? Especially someone who's been as unreliable as Ryder? Do you know how often I've had to step in and rescue him from stupid situations he's gotten himself into? Or paid people off to get photos deleted? What if he goes back to being that guy?"

"That's a fair question. But how do you know that any other guy in the future wouldn't turn into that guy? I'm sure you never would have even considered being with Andrew if you had any notion that he'd turn out the way he has. The fact is, you have no way of knowing what will happen in the future. Anyway, according to Devon, Ryder was acting that way to take his mind off not being able to have you."

"Oh? Devon said that? And since when do you have long conversations with Devon?"

"Don't change the subject." Xena snaps. "We're talking about you, and your control freak tendencies. I got news for you, darling. You won't have much control once you have a baby around. Those things run on their own schedule and have their own ideas of what's best."

I'm about to answer when I hear the buzzing of my phone from inside my purse. Everyone I know is here. Who would text me now? I put my finger up to Xena to show her I need a second and pull my phone out of my purse. The lock screen shows me I have a text from Andrew.

"Ugh, it's Andrew," I say, rolling my eyes.

"What the hell does he want?"

"Ugh. Who knows? I'll read it later." I'm about to put my phone back in my purse when Xena grabs it from my hands and swipes the screen to get to the message.

"Uh, Denise? Maybe you should look at this now. Why would Andrew send you a picture of an old lady napping?" She turns my phone around so I can see the picture up on the screen. It's a photo of Ryder's Gran, and it looks like it's taken through a window. She appears to be resting on the couch.

"That's Ryder's Gran."

As I grab my phone to get a closer look, another message comes through.

Andrew- Tell your boyfriend he took something from me, so now I'm going to take something from him.

"What the hell does that mean?" I whisper. "What did Ryder take from him?"

"Uh, hello? Ryder took you. At least that seems to be what dickhead here is thinking." She gestures to the phone in my hand.

Oh shit! Suddenly, I realize Andrew is going to do something to Gran.

"Do you have your car?" We need to get to Gran before Andrew does something stupid. He wouldn't actually hurt her because of me, would he? "I don't want Ryder to freak out about his Gran. We can call your brother and have him meet us there. I'll call Ryder once Kaden has Gran safe, and they have dealt with Andrew."

"I do, but my keys are in my purse in the dining room. I can't go get it without people noticing. What should I tell them?"

"Crap. Let me think." What can we do now? We need to get out of here, and fast. "Got it. Tell them I have a headache and you're grabbing pills for me. Grab a bottle of water too, to make it more convincing."

She nods. "Okay. I'll be back in a minute." Xena turns to go back inside.

"WAIT!" I yell, loud enough to stop her in her tracks. "Meet me out front instead. Go get your keys and move fast before anyone notices you're going the wrong way. I'll call Kaden right now." Xena nods her understanding and disappears through the door.

I pull up Kaden's contact information and press the call button.

"*Kaden Cross,*" he says by way of greeting.

"Kaden, it's Denise. I need you to meet me at the retirement community outside of town, Peaceful Pines, it's called. Do you know of it? Meet me at cottage number three. My ex-boyfriend sent me a photo implying he's going to do something to the lady that lives there, so bring as many of your cop buddies as you want."

"*Shit, Denise! I'm going to have to radio this in, but I will meet you there. DO NOT go in until I get there. Do you understand?*"

"Yes, of course, Kaden. I'm not stupid, you know."

"*No, you're a control freak, and that's worse. Promise me you won't go in.*"

I cross my fingers behind my back, even though there's no way he can see me doing it. "I promise I won't go in until you get there. Now go." I hang up as I get to Xena's car. Moments later, Xena runs full speed out the front door. The car beeps as she presses the unlock button on the key fob.

"Let's go, let's go, let's go. They're on to me. Run!" She's panicking as she opens her door and starts the car. She's backing up and buckling in at the same time. "Devon was giving me a look. He knows I'm up to something. I'm such a terrible liar." She bangs her hand on the steering wheel, spins it so we turn to face the right direction, and peels out of the driveway.

"It's fine. I figured they'd find out eventually. I actually expect your brother will call him after he radios for backup. Let's use your 'my brother is a cop' powers for good right now and get there as fast as possible." I give my seat belt a tug and make sure it's in the proper position as she stomps on the gas pedal and sends the car speeding down the highway.

The city passes by in a blur as Xena expertly maneuvers her car through all the stops and turns necessary until we're pulling into the parking lot at Peaceful Pines. As we're getting out of the car, Kaden pulls up and blocks the path to the cottages with his police cruiser.

"I told you to wait until I got here, Denise. Looks to me like you were about to go walking right in with no idea what you're getting yourself into."

I pull out my phone and show him the photo and message from Andrew. "This lady needs help. Why don't you and your little partner," I wiggle my fingers at the blonde police woman who's gotten out of the passenger side of the police cruiser, "go make yourself useful. Cottage number three."

Kaden looks at the photo and grunts a noise at his partner. They both draw their weapons and, using that crouch run that you sometimes see cops in movies use, run up to the Gran's door and bang on it.

This would be exciting if I wasn't on the verge of pissing myself with fear.

"Police. Stand back," Kaden yells at the closed door. And then blondie takes a step back, gives the door a good kick, and it flies open. Kaden ducks in first and his partner follows.

I wait patiently for approximately ten seconds until I can't stand the suspense anymore before breaking into a run. As I get close to the cottage, I'm greeted by the sounds of laughter. Correction, *hysterical* laughter. What?

"What the hell is going on in here?" I yell as I run inside. I take in the scene and see that Kaden is the one laughing hysterically while his partner rolls her eyes a little and hides a smirk. Gran and Gladys are sitting side by side on the couch, pretty as you please, drinking what I assume is whiskey out of her naughty teacups.

"Oh hello dear," Gran says to me. "I didn't know you were coming back already. What happened to your party? Can I get you some tea? Oh, who's your friend?" She looks behind me to where Xena is standing.

"I'm Xena, and I would love some tea, if it's not too much trouble." She steps into the living room to move toward the kitchen when she literally stumbles on the reason Kaden is laughing so hard.

Right there, in the middle of the floor, is Andrew. Hogtied in a beautiful pink rope with what looks to be an intricate series of knots. He looks furious, but he's not saying anything. That's probably because he has a matching pink ball gag in his mouth, though.

"Do you like my handiwork?" Gran asks as she gets teacups out for me and Xena. "I've been learning the art of Shibari—you know, Japanese rope bondage?—ever since I saw a demonstration at the kink convention where I bought these cups." She holds up the cups she selected for us. One reads 'trollop' and the other reads 'tart'. "I was hoping I'd get to use that rope on a gentleman caller, though, and not an intruder. Maybe this sexy officer would like to stay after this and let me practice?" she asks Kaden with a waggle of her eyebrows.

He chokes on a laugh. "Sorry, ma'am. We need to get this guy down to the station as soon as possible. Thanks for the invitation, though."

"That's... I have no words, Gran." I pull her into a hug, while also frisking her and checking her over to make sure she's not hurt. "I guess we didn't need to rush here to rescue you, after all. You had it under control."

"Oh no, Gladys here gets most of the credit. This little fucker had a knife pointed at me and was saying something about making me pay for what my grandson has done when Gladys came crawling in from the back room and used her stun gun on him." Gran toes Andrew in the side with a look of disgust on her face.

Gladys holds up a hot pink stun gun that Kaden promptly takes from her. "Got him right in the ballsack. From the smell, I think he's probably as hairless as Ryder is down there now. Not that I would know that for sure, since he wouldn't even show me."

"I told you to stop trying to look at my grandson's dick, you perv. You're way too old for him. Plus, he already has this beautiful lady right here looking after his cockular needs." She stops and points at me, waggling her eyebrows, as she's so fond of doing. "How else do you think she got my great grandbaby in there?"

Andrew thrashes around on the ground at my feet, muffled words straining to escape from around the ball gag. I can't make out anything resembling a word, but the cadence of his frantic grunting suggests he's saying, 'I knew it', and 'you slut'. So I kick him while Kaden and his partner are securing Gladys's stun gun. And then I kick him again, for good measure.

"What the fuck is going on here?" Ryder's stunned voice comes from the doorway.

Oh, shit. I didn't think I'd have to explain myself until long after this mess was over.

Here goes nothing.

37

Andrew Did What?

Ryder

"Oh, hi, kiddo." Gran walks past the officers, and the body tied up on her floor, to give Ryder a kiss on the cheek. "I thought you said Denise's party was today? Shouldn't you be over there enjoying some cake or something? Sorry we didn't make it. We got caught up, as you can see."

"Well hello there, handsome." Gladys has spotted Devon standing behind me. Not that he's hard to notice. The man had to duck his head to get through the door. And turn sideways, for crying out loud. "How would you like to stick around and let us practice our Shibari on you?"

"Don't be ridiculous, Gladys." Gran chides her friend. "You and I don't have enough rope between us to tie up that monster. Good lord boy, where'd they get you from? From the size of you, I'd say your poor mother's coochie still hurts. Mine hurts looking at you, but I'd say that's for an entirely different reason." She winks salaciously.

"Devon, have you met my Gran, Delores? Gran, this is Devon. He works as security for the band. And I don't think it's very polite of you to talk about how he destroyed his mother's vagina. At least not during the first meeting."

"It's fine, dude," Devon tells me. "My mom talks about how I destroyed her vagina all the time. It's why I'm an only child.

Apparently you don't get over giving birth to a fifteen pound baby naturally." He turns to Gran. "It's nice to finally meet you, Delores. I've heard good things from this guy right here." Devon steps aside to reveal Aiden standing behind him.

"Oh, Aiden, honey. Glad you're here. I learned some new lap-dance moves at the seniors' centre that I need to show you. I even learned some nice knots in Shibari that I can use, so you're not tempted to run away like you did last time. Once I get my ropes back from that idiot on the floor, that is."

"Everyone shut up!" I bellow. Why are they talking about Devon's birth and Gran's lap dancing skills, when there is clearly something more important going on here? "Can someone please explain to me why the hell Andrew is gagged and tied up on the floor? And why did I have to find out from Devon that you two had snuck out of the party and run over here? To what? Rescue my grandmother?"

"Well, yes. But as it so happens, it's Andrew who needs rescuing from Gran and Gladys." Denise says with a smile. "Gladys says after her work with a stun gun that he probably rivals you in the downstairs hairlessness department."

Gladys interjects, "Got him right in the nuts! And then Delores tied him up with some of her fancy knots."

Denise hands me her phone with a text message screen pulled up. On it I see a message from Andrew saying he's going to take something from me since I took something from him, and before that there's a pic of my Gran on the couch.

"You came here to hurt my Gran, you son of a bitch?" I storm over to where Andrew is still tied up on the ground and kick him before the cops can get to me. "What was your big plan after that, idiot? Did you think Denise was going to see that you'd hurt a sweet little old lady—sorry Gran—and then she wouldn't be able to resist you?"

"I think that's enough now," one of the cops says. "I'll cut these ropes off and we will take this guy to the station. You ladies will all need to come in to make statements as well."

"Wait!" Gran yells. "Don't cut my rope. I can untie it. I paid good money for that stuff."

I let Gran and the cops figure out the Andrew situation on their own, and I pull Denise aside.

"Are you okay? You're not hurt, are you?" I ask.

"I'm totally fine. Gran and Gladys had it handled before we even got here."

I blow out a relieved breath, then pull Denise in for a hug. "I can't believe you would run in here like that? You should have told me. I would have come with you. Andrew could have seriously hurt you."

"I wasn't intending on rushing in here alone, Ryder." She pulls back and looks into my eyes. "I had already called Kaden, I mean Officer Cross, to meet us here before we left Connor's house. He pulled up as we did." She points to the male cop; a good-looking, muscular guy, with a short, conservative style haircut, and tattoos covering his arms and part of his neck. He looks like the kind of guy Denise should be settling down with. He's the right mix of wholesome and edgy. *I think I hate him.*

"You wanted *him* here? And not me?" The sickness I feel sneaking up on me is a jealousy like I've never experienced before. Maybe she didn't really feel anything for me. At least not like I feel for her.

"What? No. It's nothing like that, Ryder. Kaden is Xena's brother. I wanted to make sure he'd be the first cop here. You know, in case Andrew had hurt Gran and I had to accidentally on purpose fatally wound him."

"I would have backed you up." Xena peeks her head between us. "It would definitely have been in self-defense. No jail time.

You guys wouldn't have had to worry about your baby being born in prison or anything."

Suddenly, a weight crashes into me from the side, knocking me down and taking Xena with me. Luckily, I was able to push Denise back far enough that she didn't fall too. Not that I want Xena to get hurt, but she's not the one who's got a baby to worry about, after all.

"I knew it! You asshole. I knew it was your baby this whole time. You took her from me. She was mine. I was going to make her into the perfect woman. I should have known she was like every other slut I've been with. That baby is going to be born all fucked up from the drugs you guys do all the time. If it even make-"

I finally wrestle my arms out from underneath me and I slam my fist into Andrew's mouth before he finishes that awful thought. Unfortunately, Xena's brother pulls him away from me before I get any more punches in.

"Yup, you're right." Denise spits at him. "I'm a slut and I'm having Ryder's baby. Are you happy now?"

"Hey now, y'all need to stop talking about my future granddaughter-in-law like that. She's a nice girl, and she's going to be giving me a great grandbaby soon. But I expect the two of you to get married first, you got that?" Gran comes over and hugs Denise. Looking deep into her eyes, she tells her, "I'm so happy to have you in our family, young lady. You're full of piss and vinegar, the sort of girl my Ryder needs to keep him in line. But I won't tolerate anyone calling you a slut, even if you're saying it yourself."

Aiden reaches his hand out and I take it, accepting the help up off the floor. Devon has already picked up Xena and is currently looking her over, checking for injuries, I expect. Her brother is glaring at him during this inspection, but his hands are full with pulling Andrew off the ground.

Not sure how Andrew thought that attack was going to go, considering Kaden handcuffed him as soon as Gran untied the ropes. After knocking me down, all he did was roll around on top of me and yell out his little rant about Denise and the baby.

"We're going to take this guy in and get him processed. Ladies, and Ryder, come down to the station and we'll take your statements." Kaden turns and squints at Devon. "You and I have some things to talk about later."

Kaden and his partner walk Andrew out to their police cruiser, and Aiden leaves behind them. I watch through the window and Andrew's head 'accidentally' slams into the side of the car as Kaden helps him into the back seat. I let out a small chuckle before turning to Denise.

"He could have hurt you," I whisper, taking her hands in mine. "I was so scared when Devon showed me the message from Kaden telling him what you and Xena were up to."

"You were more worried about me than you were about your Gran?" Denise whispers back. "She's the cute old lady. Andrew could have really hurt her."

I raise my eyebrows and scrunch my nose, tilting my head a little. "Well, that doesn't really appear to be the case now, does it?" I point over to where Gran and Gladys are winding up Gran's pink rope. "They look like they can take care of themselves. You should have let the cops handle it. Or at least told me and let me come with you. You can't be running off doing dangerous stuff like this with a baby on the way. Especially not anything that involves Andrew, now that you really know the kind of person he is."

Denise's face suddenly turns stormy, telling me I've said exactly the wrong thing.

"Listen, Ryder." Denise puts her hands on her hips. "If I want to deal with a problem myself, a problem that is my fault, let's not forget, then I will do so. It's not like I was rushing in here to play hero. I called the police. I didn't come alone, and I was perfectly safe the whole time. I don't need you butting in and telling me what I can and can't do because you think you're in love with me. The last thing I need after Andrew is another guy thinking he has a say in how I run my life." She pokes her finger into my chest and turns. "Xena, let's go. Can you drive me home?"

Xena turns from where she's talking to Devon. "Uh, yeah, sure. Okay." She turns back to Devon and says something too quietly for me to hear. Not that I'm listening, anyway. I have a feeling I've really screwed up with Denise. And we were finally doing so well, too.

Way to go, Ryder. Why can't I go any length of time without fucking everything up?

38

Who Does He Think He Is?

Denise

"WHO THE HELL DOES he think he is? He starts acting more responsible and suddenly he's telling me what to do? Like I haven't been the one keeping him out of trouble all these years?" I'm pacing back and forth beside Xena's car because I can't stand the thought of sitting still yet. Adrenaline is coursing through my body, and I can't seem to unclench my fists. "First Andrew and now Ryder. Why is it men think they can tell me what to do? Where are they getting this from?"

Kaden and his partner, her name is Rhea, according to Xena, are standing outside of their cruiser, watching me while I rant and rave. Aiden is standing with them, his mouth hanging open slightly as he takes in my display. I'm not usually this emotional, so some of it is probably because of pregnancy hormones, but certainly not all. Ryder has only been a responsible human being for a week. He has no business calling me out for one little thing.

Well, not that little of a thing, I guess. But it's not like it was that dangerous, really. It's not like Andrew had a gun. Of course, I didn't expect that he'd have a knife. And I certainly didn't expect that he would attempt to hold Ryder's Gran hostage with it.

What would have happened if Gladys hadn't been there with her stun gun? Could this have had a much worse outcome?

Andrew getting zapped in the balls is hilarious. Gran being hurt or killed is not.

"Do you think Andrew really intended to hurt Gran?" I ask Xena. Not that she knows Andrew at all, but she has good people sense. She can usually tell what kind of person someone is after talking to them for a little bit. "Could someone I dated for a year have hidden that kind of crazy from me for so long?"

Xena doesn't answer right away. Instead, she comes to the passenger side of the car and opens the door for me. She gives her brother a wave before getting into the driver's seat and starting the car. When she gets us back out onto the highway, she finally talks.

"I think Andrew came out here with a knife for a reason. He sent you that text and photo for a reason. The more you look at it, the more it seems his intention was to hurt her. His text said he would take something from Ryder, because he thinks Ryder took you from him. And I highly doubt that Andrew came here with a knife, thinking he would force Gran to be his grandmother instead of Ryder's."

"I..." I'm at a loss for words. I huff out a breath and lean back into my seat, crossing my arms over my chest. "Fuck."

"Yeah, pretty much," Xena says. "So, what are you going to do about it?"

"What *can* I do about it? I screamed at Ryder in front of his grandmother and some of our friends. I accused him of being like Andrew. You know, the guy who tried to attack his cute, little, perverted grandmother?"

"That one is going to be difficult to come back from. Plus, why would you even say that? I'd hardly put being concerned for your safety and wanting to dictate how you look and who you're friends with in the same category."

"I DON'T KNOW!" I drop my head back and huff a breath. "I wasn't thinking clearly. Seeing Andrew tied up and hearing about how he threatened Gran freaked me out. How could I let this happen?"

Suddenly, Xena cranks the wheel and the car skids to a stop on the side of the road, forcing me to slam into the seat belt and back into my seat.

"What the fuck, Xena?" I look over and see her shooting daggers at me with her eyes. If I didn't know she was human, I'd swear flames were about to come out of her pupils and singe off my hair. In case I'm not being clear, she is pissed off. At me, apparently.

"You didn't *let* this happen. This was not something you could have controlled. No matter how much you think you keep everyone in line, you cannot control another person's behavior. Andrew's actions are not your responsibility. Do you hear me? This. Is. Not. Your. Fault. Period. End of story." She lets out a breath and safely pulls the car back onto the road, like nothing ever happened. "So, am I taking you home, or should we go give our statements right now?"

"I... I... Statements, I guess." I stammer, still not sure what actually happened. Xena can be scary, even without her sword.

"All I'm saying is you need to learn to let some things go. This is a perfect time for you to practice. You can't control everything when it comes to that baby, so you better get used to it now."

We sit in silence for the rest of the drive to the police station. Giving our statements is short and sweet, thanks to Kaden being there. He makes sure we're brought in right away and makes the process as easy as possible. He also lets us know Andrew spewed out his plan during the drive back to the station, despite being advised of his rights, so the case against him is pretty airtight. Andrew apparently has a lawyer with him now and he is preparing to sign a confession soon.

At least that dickhead is taking responsibility for something. Meanwhile, I have to wrap my head around the fact that both

Gran and I have said, out loud, that the baby is Ryder's. When we know that it really isn't. I have a feeling I should go talk to Gran without Ryder there. She seems like she will give me honest advice. And if she doesn't, I'm sure Gladys will.

When we walk out of the police station, we find Devon waiting in the Escalade.

"What are you doing here?" Xena asks him. "You don't need to make a statement, do you?"

"Nah, I'm waiting on Aiden. He wanted to come here and talk to Kaden's partner. She brushed him off back at the retirement community and he wanted to come find her and take another shot." He puts his hands over his heart and flutters his eyelashes. "I think our little man is finally growing up. He has his first crush."

We all laugh until we see Aiden come out of the police station behind us, hands in his pockets and a frown on his face.

"Uh oh," Xena whispers. "Looks like he got shot down again."

"Hey Aiden," I say. "Thanks for coming out to check on us at Ryder's Gran's place. We're going to get going now. I'll see you guys later."

I walk back to Xena's car and wait while she says a quick goodbye to the guys.

"Home?" she asks, when she makes it to the car.

"Yeah, I'm done with today." I need some time to go over everything that's happened. At least with Andrew in jail tonight, I won't need anyone staying over to look after me, and I'll get some time to myself.

39

Help Me Be That Guy

Ryder

"WELL, KIDDO," GRAN SITS next to me on the couch and pats my knee. "You've made a right mess of this one, haven't you?"

I groan. "Ugh, don't remind me. What am I going to do, Gran? Pretty sure Denise hates me now. She compared me to Andrew. *And that was after* he came here and threatened you with a knife. That's bad, isn't it?"

"Yeah, that's pretty bad. But you were acting like a right little prick, weren't you?" She laughs. "That girl has more independence in her little finger than I've seen in most women's entire bodies. And here you thought you could try telling her what she can and can't do. I always thought you were smarter than that, but you sure proved me wrong."

"Dumb as a bag of hammers, this one," Gladys says as she smacks me on the head from where she stands behind the couch. "Tea?"

I take the cup she's offered to me. This one reads 'dumbass' and I'm positive she chose it on purpose, for me.

"How many of these cups do you have?" I ask Gran. "I don't think I've seen the same one twice."

One big sip of my 'tea' has me sputtering. "Dammit, Gladys. This is *not* tea!"

"That's better than tea, young man. Whiskey will put hair on your chest."

"I'm not ready for hair on my chest, Gladys. I paid a nice lady a lot of money to torture me with hot wax and rip it all out. If it grows back too soon, it'll all be for nothing."

"I don't believe you actually did that," Gladys says. "What's that thing the kids are saying these days? Pics or it didn't happen?"

"For the last time, Gladys. Stop trying to see my grandson naked. You're about ninety years too old for him, and he already has that nice Denise to think about."

"Ugh, Denise. What am I going to do about that, Gran? How will I win her trust? It's like she thinks I might be worth something and then I say or do something stupid and she thinks I'm an idiot all over again." I slurp back my whole cup of 'tea', savouring the burn as it slides down my throat. Now that I'm not expecting tea, it's not actually that bad. It's not the vodka that I normally drink when wallowing in my misery, but it'll do for now.

"Well, I'd say step one is that you need to stop being an idiot."

"Thanks, Gran," I say, my voice dripping with sarcasm. "Why didn't I think of that?"

"If you have thought about it, you sure haven't worked too hard to actually do it. What have you done to show her you're worth her time? To show her that letting you into her life in a meaningful way isn't going to end up in her having someone else to take care of, other than this baby?"

"I know I wouldn't want to be facing having a baby alone, with the one man showing interest being the one who needs more taking care of than an infant." Gladys offers from her spot next to me on the couch. I'm book ended by old ladies who are taking turns berating me. This is not how I expected this evening to go. "Incompetence is not an attractive trait."

"So far, I've taken her shopping at Lana's for all the baby furniture. And bought it all and plan to be there when they deliver it to set it all up for her. I've talked to her about how she wants to do the nursery so I can have that all done before the furniture gets there. And I threw together a small party for today to welcome the baby to the family and to show Denise that she will have more support than she can handle. So what else do I need to do?"

Gran and Gladys both look at me, eyes wide and mouths open.

"You've done all that already?" Gladys asks.

"You're not as dumb as you look after all," Gran adds.

"Why does everyone keep saying that? Do I really look that dumb?"

"Well, you know," Gran starts. "You're a good-looking fella, you have muscles, you're almost always smiling, and you do a lot of silly stuff to make people laugh. You don't exactly come across like a rocket scientist."

"I guess I didn't think acting like an idiot for so long would convince people that I actually am an idiot." I huff out a breath and sink back into the couch. "Maybe I am as dumb as I look."

Gran pats my knee. "No, you're not. You've got a good head start on making that girl realize you're a good man. We need to figure out what else you need to do to make her really believe it. She's in a complicated situation."

"But did you notice she didn't deny your gran or that dipshit when they said the baby was yours? She even said it herself."

"That was to get Andrew off her case and out of the picture. All of our friends have come to that same conclusion. The easiest way to get Andrew out of her life is to let him believe I am the father, since he already thinks she cheated on him with me. That wasn't a declaration of her love for me, an expedient way to cut him out of her life for good."

"While that may be true, you can't deny that she feels something for you. I can tell by looking at that girl. She lights up when you're nearby," Gran tells me.

"And you're the same way with her," Gladys adds. "I've never seen such a dumb smile as the one you have when you look at her. It makes me want to puke. But in a good way."

"You really think so?" I ask Gran. I know I look like an idiot when I look at Denise, but does she really look at me the same way? "You've met her. How do you know she doesn't look like that all the time?"

"Well, before you opened your big, dumb mouth earlier, she was looking at you like you hung the moon. Of course, then you tried to tell her what she can and can't do and she rightfully put you in your place. And by rightfully, I mean you completely deserved it. She's a grown woman, and she's been taking care of you and the rest of your idiot friends for what, fifteen years? She's more than capable of taking care of herself."

"You're right, Gran, she is capable. But I want her to know that she doesn't have to do it alone. I *want* to take care of her. Nothing would make me happier than to be the one she turns to when she needs support. *That's* the guy I want to be. So how do I do that? How do I be that guy?"

"Alright kiddo, I have a plan. It won't be easy. Are you sure you want to do this? Being a parent is a lifetime commitment. Even if you and Denise somehow don't work out, you will still be this baby's father. Do you understand?"

My own mother abandoned me when I was a kid. I know what that feels like and I would *never* subject a child to that, whether or not they have my blood. Being with Denise feels like the most natural thing in the world. It makes me feel capable, like maybe I can actually be the man that I want to be, for her, and for the baby.

"Yes. I understand. Better than anyone, I know what it's like when a parent doesn't love you enough to stay. I wouldn't try to become this baby's father if I didn't intend to be there for life, no matter what happens."

Gran claps her hands together and stands up. "That's all I needed to hear. Give Gladys your phone and she'll start making the calls. You, come with me."

Confused, I give Gladys my phone, and I take Gran's hand. She grabs her purse and leads me out the door toward her car.

"We have some shopping to do. Get in."

Gran's never steered me wrong before, so I'm going to trust that she knows what she's doing. If she can convince Denise to trust that I want to be that baby's father, and that she's not trapping me, I will do whatever Gran tells me to.

40

Take Control of What I Can

Denise

XENA DROPPED ME OFF at home about an hour ago. She offered to stay and hang out, but I really wanted to be alone, so I sent her on her way. I've had a shit few days and I need time to process.

As soon as I get into my house, I go straight upstairs to shower. After being in Gran's place, that close to Andrew after he went off the rails, and then spending some time in the police station, I feel the need to scrub myself clean. How did I ever let Andrew touch me? How did I not see his craziness from miles away? I stand under the shower spray and use a loofah and my favorite coconut body wash to scrub my skin until it's pink. And then I stand under the spray until the hot water runs out.

I still have Ryder's shirt and even though I should probably wash it, I decide to wear it again anyway because it's comfortable, and it makes me feel good. After towel drying my hair, I throw it up in a messy top knot and run to my dresser for pants. I was in the cold shower long enough that the chill has soaked into my skin, so I grab a pair of comfy joggers and throw on some thick socks to top off my stellar outfit. I wonder if this would meet Andrew's approval? The nerve of that guy. Thinking he could turn me into what he wanted. And I almost stayed with him for the baby.

And we're back to the baby again. Gran and I both told Andrew that the baby is Ryder's, and Ryder didn't even flinch. He says I wouldn't be trapping him if we got together, but I feel so guilty about it, anyway. He didn't choose this. Ryder happened to realize that he has feelings for me at an inopportune time, and he feels like he should step up, since Andrew is an asshole. That's not a good basis for a relationship, especially not one with a kid involved.

I go downstairs and grab my embroidery kit out of the office. I left my current project in Ryder's car, so I'll need to start something new and I have the thing. Ryder mentioned how much he liked some of the other pieces I've made, so I will work on a little something for him. Before I can decide what it will be, my phone rings from my purse on the hook by the door. Because I rush to answer, I don't notice that it's my mother calling. I probably would have let it go to voicemail if I had.

"Hello?"

"*Denise. What's this I hear about you having Andrew arrested?*"

"Hello, mother. How are you?" She's never been one for small talk and I like to irritate her by putting off whatever questions she asks until she's at least greeted me.

"*Yes, hello Denise. How are you? Now about Andrew?*"

"What about him, mother? I didn't have him arrested. He threatened my friend's grandmother with a knife and the police arrested him when they arrived. That's what happens when you commit crimes, mother. The police arrest you."

"*Yes, Denise. I'm aware. But I was told that you were the one who called the police. Which is basically the same thing as having him arrested. His mother is furious with me.*"

"I called the police because he sent me a message threatening Ryder's Gran. What should I have done differently? Allowed him to hurt her?"

"You know he was doing that to get your attention, darling. He wanted to win you back. I didn't even know you had broken up with him. Why would you do such a thing? You know how close your father and I are with his parents. This could ruin our friendship."

"Mother, Andrew has been trying to change me into someone I'm not. And when I dumped him for that, he refused to believe it. He showed up at my friends' engagement party and tried to cause a scene outside. Then when I brought him to my place to break the news of my pregnancy, he freaked out and started breaking stuff. He might have even hurt me if Ryder hadn't shown up and gotten him out of my house for me."

"Well, you should be glad for him wanting to make you a better person. And why did I have to hear from Andrew's mother that you're pregnant with that Ryder man's baby? How would you expect Andrew to react? After you cheated on him and got pregnant with that trashy man's baby? But luckily for you, he's agreed to forgive you and take you back. So you need to call the police immediately and drop the charges against him so you can get back to your life with him. And it's past time you leave that silly job and do something better with your life. Now that you and Andrew will get married, you can stay home and raise the babies."

I snort an incredulous laugh. I can't believe I expected more from my mother. She learned that I'm having her grandchild and the only thing she's concerned about is how my relationship with Andrew makes her look. She didn't even congratulate me or ask me how I'm feeling. I should have realized when she introduced me to him it wasn't in *my* best interests that she did so. My parents have always been selfish, and not with looking after me when I was sick as a kid, apparently. This isn't how family should be. This isn't how *my* family is going to be.

"Mother, I want you to listen to me carefully." I enunciate slowly. I've finally had enough and she will hear what I have to say. "My relationships are not your concern. You are my mother, you are supposed to support me, but since you can't seem to do that, I think it's best we not talk for a while. Now, before that happens, I will tell you a few things. First: Andrew is not coming back into my life for any reason. If you choose to have him in yours, I will not be there. Second: I am having Ryder's baby. If I am going to be with anyone, it is going to be him. And third: I like myself the way I am. I am not changing for you or for anyone else. If I make any changes, they will be because I want them, and not because anyone else has told me I should. Now, if you can deal with these things, then I would be happy to see you sometime soon to discuss what your relationship with your grandchild will be going forward. But for now, I don't want to talk to you, and I don't want to hear anything else about Andrew. If the next thing out of your mouth isn't an apology, then I will hang up."

"*Well, I never-*"

"Alright mother, I guess that's your decision."

And then I hang up the phone. On my mother. After telling her to butt out of my life for the first time in thirty-six years.

Rolling on the high from finally telling my mother off, instead of quietly rebelling and avoiding her as I've done up to this point in my life, I head into my office and sit at the computer. I think it's time to contact my lawyer and see if there is some way to keep Andrew out of my life for good. If Ryder wants to be with me, I need to know that it's not because he thinks it's a way to keep me safe from Andrew. If I can prove to Ryder that Andrew can't get to me or the baby, then I will believe him if he says he doesn't feel obligated to be with me to keep me safe.

The Law is on Our Side

Ryder

GRAN'S PLAN INVOLVES ME in a three-piece suit, but since it's late on a Sunday, we have to settle for dark jeans and a fitted button-down shirt. It's fancier than I usually get, so even though she wanted a three-piece suit, she concedes this looks pretty good too.

"We can save the three-piece for the actual wedding," Gran says, as she pulls up in front of Denise's place.

Oh, didn't I mention? Gran's plan was a well thought out proposal. Well, a somewhat planned, last-minute proposal that has about an eighty-seven percent chance of failing, but a proposal the same. However, the jeans and button-down shirt are a vast improvement on my last proposal. Then again, pretty much anything would be an improvement on being half naked with my dick and balls popping out the top of my boxers.

Gran is more well connected in this town that I am and within two hours of leaving her place I have a plan, help from Aiden and Devon (thanks to Gladys calling them from my phone), and a ring. I also have a team of assorted friends setting up a location for the proposal to happen.

All I need to come up with on my own is what to say. And a way to get Denise there.

"Well, Gran." I let out a deep breath and wipe my sweaty palms on my jeans. "This is it. Wish me luck."

Gran reaches out and grabs my hand. " Tell her how you feel, kiddo. Tell her what you told me. You've been acting like a fuck up for a while now, but underneath that, you are a good man, with a good heart, and I know you will take care of that girl and that baby. If an old lady's opinion matters at all, I think you will make an excellent husband and an even better father."

I lean over the console and pull her in for a hug. "Your opinion means the world to me, Gran. Thank you for everything. I'll see you there."

She pats me on the back before I pull away and get out of the car. Aiden and Devon walk over to me. They were nice enough to drive my car over to Denise's house for me and Devon passes me the keys now.

"You ready?" Aiden asks. "There's no room for confusion now. Make sure she knows you're an option, and then she can decide if you are the option she wants."

"What if she doesn't want me? What if I ask and she says no?"

"That is a distinct possibility, especially based on your past behavior," Devon says. "But I don't think that's what's going to happen."

I send them off to the location too, leaving me standing alone in front of Denise's place. Good thing she has her curtains drawn or she would have seen us all having a meeting in her driveway. It'd be pretty hard to deny something was going on if she looked out and saw us standing there chatting for no reason.

While walking up to her front porch, I nearly wear holes in my pants from wiping my sweaty palms so much. Not to mention I've almost ripped my lip ring out three times in the last minute and a half, from pushing it back and forth with my tongue. I wish I'd thought to bring flowers, but we had them all delivered to the venue. At least I remembered to keep the ring with me.

The jeweler Gran knows specializes in alternative style jewelry, which is how I could find the perfect ring for Denise. It's black gold, with a multicolored stone that the jeweler somewhat condescendingly informed me, is alexandrite. If I didn't want this particular ring so badly, and if this dude wasn't friends with Gran, I might have punched him in the face for that. But I kept my temper and left with the ring that I'm now going to propose with.

Gran's plan, the one that everyone has helped to put together, is that I convince Denise to come with me somewhere else to talk and then I propose there where everyone else is waiting. That public proposal worked for Connor and Alex, but my situation with Denise is different. For one thing, there's a good chance she is going to say no. And for another, I have to make her believe that she's not trapping me into something I don't want. Neither of those situations are things that require an audience.

When I raise my hand to knock on Denise's door, it flies open and I'm standing there, looking like I'm about to knock on her face.

"Oh!" she says in surprise. "I was coming to find you. I called, but Gladys answered and said you were out with your Gran. Oh, she also told me to tell you she's disappointed with the lack of dick pics in your phone. She was hoping to 'get a peek at the goods'. That woman is obsessed. You should show her your dick and get it over with."

I laugh. Of course Gladys would snoop through my phone looking for dick pics.

"Fucking Gladys," I say, shaking my head. "She is persistent, I'll give her that."

We stand awkwardly for a minute.

"So, can I come—"

"Do you want to come—"

We both laugh.

"Yes, I'd love to come in, thanks."

Denise turns and walks inside, and I follow. When I close the door, I make sure to lock it. Even if Andrew is supposed to be in prison, I'd rather be safe. And by that, I mean I want Denise to be safe.

"So, I have some awesome news," Denise starts. "But first, do you want anything to drink? Are you hungry?"

While it's true that I haven't eaten much today, I'm so nervous I don't think I could get any food down if I tried. I flick my lip ring back and forth and shake my head no.

"Come sit." She sits on the couch and pats her hand on the spot beside her. "So, I talked to my lawyer today. Apparently, you don't need to claim my baby as yours in order to keep Andrew away. Since he's already denied that the baby is his, and since I don't plan on naming him on the birth certificate, it's unlikely that he'll come after me for custody. Add to that the fact that he is going to jail, and that I'm getting a restraining order against him, there's no way he could get custody even if he tried. Isn't that great? Now you won't be stuck with me!"

What? Is that what she's been thinking this whole time? She thought I was pretending to have feelings so that I could keep her safe from Andrew? That doesn't even make any sense.

"I don't understand," I say softly, after an uncomfortable silence. "You think I've been faking things since you told me about the baby?"

"Well... yeah, I guess." She doesn't seem so sure now. Thank god. This is my opening and I plan to make the most of it.

"Denise, I've only ever pretended to *not* have feelings for you. My feelings for you are very real. In fact..."

42

That's My Forever Penis

Denise

Ryder is dressed nicer than I've seen in a long time, with his dark jeans and white button-down shirt. Truthfully, I'm having a hard time concentrating on what I'm saying because all I can think about is ripping that shirt right off of him so I can see the nipple rings that are poking through the fabric. He took out the barbells he had in his eyebrow, but I'm happy to see that the lip ring and nipple rings are still in their rightful place.

"Denise, I've only ever pretended to *not* have feelings for you. My feelings for you are very real. In fact..."

Wait, what's happening right now? Pay attention, Denise. This feels important. I watch as Ryder slides the coffee table over and kneels on the floor in front of me.

"The first time I saw you, I knew I wanted you. I was young and dumb, of course, and we hadn't even spoken, but something about your confidence as you walked around that party called to me. It didn't hurt that you have always been the hottest woman in the room, no matter where you are." Ryder laughs a little. "I really thought I was going to take you home that night. Did you know that?"

"I had an idea. You were pretty much devouring me with your eyes the whole night." He looked great then, too. And I wanted to go home with him. But I wanted to manage the band more, so that was my priority.

"When you told us you were going to be our manager, I figured I should step back. After all, I couldn't very well have a one-night stand with you if you were going to be around all the time afterward. And forget having any kind of relationship. By the time I realized I couldn't get you out of my head, you'd made us so successful there was no way I could risk a relationship with you. What if I screwed up?"

He takes my hands in his, brushing his lips against them softly.

"You have no idea how difficult those first few years were for me. Once I got to know you, I wanted you even more. You're the strongest, smartest, and most amazing woman I've ever known." He smiles. "But if you tell Gran that, I'm afraid I'll have to deny it."

I giggle. "Yeah, I'd say Gran is quite a bit stronger and smarter than me. And a hell of a lot more devious, too."

Ryder laughs. "She is absolutely more devious. The Jell-O balloons weren't the worst thing she's ever done to me. And she's gotten so much worse since she moved in at Peaceful Pines. That Gladys is a bad influence."

"And a bit of a perv, too. I keep thinking I'm going to have to fight her, the way she keeps angling to get a look at what's mine." I laugh, and then it hits me. I've said that Ryder's dick is mine. Maybe he didn't notice?

He looks at me with a smirk and raises an eyebrow. He noticed alright.

"Never mind. Please continue." I gesture for him to move on.

"We're going to revisit that," he says with a chuckle. "But back to what I was saying first. I've wanted you all this time, for all these years. The first while I was an idiot, and tried to get you out of my head the way an idiot would. Then, for years after that, I kept up the act because it was easier to do that than to face the thought that you could never want me back."

Ryder looks down and takes a deep breath. "But then you said that you had wanted me for some of that time too, and I began to hope. I started to think that maybe we could be together after all."

He pulls up one leg so that he's down on one knee. Oh shit!

"Denise, I want to be with you. Today, tomorrow, and for the rest of our lives. I want to be the man you turn to when you need help, and the one who makes you laugh when you're sad. I want to be the one who cheers the loudest when you are successful, and the one who stands back and says 'that's my girl' to anyone who'll listen when you do something amazing. And I want to be the father to your children." He stops and puts a hand on my belly. "This one, and any we may have in the future. Wherever you are is where I want to be. Because I love you. I've always loved you, and I always will love you."

He pulls a small box from his pocket, opening it and holding it out to me. Inside is the most beautiful ring. It's black, with a multicolored stone being held up in the center by tiny, anatomically correct, black hearts. It's the most 'me' piece of jewelry I've ever seen.

"Please say you'll be my wife. Denise, will you marry me?"

I stare at him blankly, switching between looking into his eyes and looking at that gorgeous ring. This is not the reaction I was expecting from Ryder when I told him about the lawyer's good news. I figured he'd breathe a sigh of relief and run off somewhere, jumping for joy that he didn't have to take responsibility for me. But he's sitting here after telling me he loves me, that he's always loved me, and he wants to marry me? Not that he wants to marry me, but he also wants to be a father to my children. Not this baby that I'm currently having, but with any kids *we* might have in the future.

Together. *Our babies. The babies that I will make with him.*

"Uh, Denise?" He asks.

Shit, how long have I been lost in thought?

"YES!" I blurt before tackling him to the ground and smothering him with a kiss.

"You will? You'll marry me?" Ryder doesn't wait for my answer before sealing his mouth to mine, his tongue stroking gently against my own. I nod my head as he fists my hair in his hand and forces us back to a sitting position, with me straddling him.

He breaks the kiss and leans back, taking the ring out and throwing the box behind him. I give him my left hand, and he slides the ring on before pulling me in for a kiss again.

I feel him getting hard beneath me, so I say the one thing that makes sense to my addled brain.

"So this dick is actually mine now? Forever?"

43

She's All Mine

Ryder

I BURST INTO LAUGHTER at her question, and she laughs right along with me.

"Yes, Denise," I say when the laughter finally subsides. I grab her hips and drag her pussy against my rock hard cock. "This dick is all for you, for as long as you want it. "

She looks at me through her lashes, hands running up my chest. Then she grabs at the opening of my shirt and pulls hard in opposite directions, sending buttons flying everywhere. Her eyes pop wide open and she giggles. Fuck, I could listen to that all day. It's not a sound Denise often makes, and I'm thrilled she's making it for me. I cup her face in my hand, running my thumb along her jaw, and her giggles stop with a sharp intake of breath.

She's mine now, and I can hardly believe it.

I'm going to avoid pinching myself, in case.

"Well then," she says, lowering her mouth to whisper in my ear. "I think I would like my dick right now, please."

"I thought you'd never ask." My dick has been trying to escape my jeans since she said she'd marry me, and I'm sure he's going to have a permanent zipper imprint if I don't set him free soon.

Denise scrambles off my lap, standing up and reaching a hand out to pull me up off the floor. Instead of taking it, I reach up and slide down her jogging pants, removing one foot at a time, until she's standing in front of me in purple cotton panties and my t-shirt. Of all the clothes she wears, seeing her in my t-shirt is the biggest turn on.

"I need to taste you again," I say, while getting to my knees and settling her onto the couch again. "It's been way too long since I've had my mouth on this pussy and I think we need to fix that right now."

She's already wiggling out of her panties, so I kneel in front of her and take over, slipping them down and off her legs. I place myself between her knees, reaching under her legs to grab her ass, and slide her to the edge of the couch. With a slight growl, I bury my face in her wet heat. She writhes beneath me as I lick and suck her clit.

"God, babe. You taste amazing," I moan against her.

"More, Ryder," she groans between heavy breaths. "Don't stop." She grabs my hair and pulls me closer, grinding herself against my face.

"Fuck yes. Take what you need. Fuck my face, like that." I slide two fingers inside, feeling her clamp down around them as her orgasm builds. I look into her face in time to see her crash over the peak. Her whole body spasms with her release, her back arching off the couch as she throws her head back, my name escaping her lips on a whisper.

So. Fucking. Hot.

"I need to get inside you."

She nods her head. "Yes, yes, fuck me, Ryder."

I stand up and push my pants and boxers down, kicking them off my feet and sending them flying like an overeager teenager. My dick aches, and I palm myself, soothing the zipper imprint I knew would be there. With my other hand, I reach over my head and rip my shirt off, leaving me standing in front of Denise, completely naked.

"Like what you see?" I chuckle, stroking my cock while Denise watches me with hunger blazing in her eyes.

I can swear that she growls when she sits up and pulls me to her with one hand on my ass and the other on my dick.

"Fuck," I moan when she licks the head of my cock tentatively, as though she's taking a taste. "That feels... oh..." I trail off into a moan when she pulls me right to the back of her throat, cupping my balls with one hand while the other grips my ass and pulls me deeper.

She controls the pace with her hand on my ass, her fingernails digging in and causing little bursts of pain to temper the pleasure she doles out with her mouth. Three slow strokes is all I can take.

"That feels too good, babe. I'm going to come too fast if you keep doing that," I say, gently removing my cock from her mouth. "And I don't want to come in your mouth. Not this time," I add with a smile.

I reach down to relieve her of my shirt that she's still wearing and throw it behind me. I look around and find my pants, dragging them over and grabbing a condom from my pocket. Stepping closer to Denise, I rip it open and roll it down onto my dick.

"I want you like this," Denise says, turning and placing her hands on the couch cushions, her ass in the air in front of me. "Fuck me hard."

I step into her, grabbing my cock and sliding the head through her wetness, using it to stroke her clit and make her moan.

"You like it a little rough?" I ask, punctuating it with a crack on her ass from my palm. Her only answer is a moan as she pushes back against me. Gripping her hip and lining up with her entrance, I wait for an answer. "Well?"

She wiggles back, trying to get onto my dick, but I lean back, denying her, and myself, in the process. After a few more moments of push and pull, she finally gives me the answer I'm waiting for.

"Yes, Ryder. Rough. I want it rough."

I slap her ass again and slam into her, feeling her contract. I massage her ass a little before slapping it and slamming into her again. The groan she makes matches my own.

"Your ass looks so gorgeous like this, babe. Just a little pink from my hand." I slap her ass again with my dick completely inside her, feeling her clamp down on my cock so hard I see stars.

"Oh fuck," I moan. "Touch yourself for me, Denise. I need to feel you come."

She reaches a hand down and starts playing with her clit, and I can feel her body respond immediately. I grab her hips in both hands and pump into her slowly, matching the pace her pussy makes as it throbs around me.

"Harder," she pants, her fingers dancing faster on her clit.

I slam into her, grinding against her at the bottom of my thrust, the rhythm slow, but hard, until I feel her start to come undone.

"Oh, god, I'm coming," she groans. "Yes, yes."

Her release spurs me on, my balls tightening. I thrust faster until I'm following her over the edge. I fill the condom, coming so forcefully I can hardly stand. Fireworks spark behind my eyelids and my dick pulses.

"Fuck, babe," I moan, as I finally still against her, the aftershocks from both of our orgasms still coursing through our bodies. "You're so fucking amazing."

I slide out of her, and she collapses forward onto the couch with a giggle and lays down.

"You're not so bad yourself, Ryder. Come here." She holds her arms out to me, inviting me to lie with her.

"One sec." I go to the kitchen and take care of the condom, stopping to grab a bottle of water from the fridge before going back to Denise. I roll over the back of the couch and stop myself with my elbows, shy of crushing her, making her laugh.

"Thirsty?" I ask, sliding down beside her and opening a water bottle for her. She sits up a little and grabs it, taking a long drink before handing it back. I finish it off and lean over her to put the empty bottle on the floor.

Denise snuggles against my chest, her fingers idly playing with one of my nipple piercings while I twirl her hair through my fingers.

"I love you, Ryder," she whispers against my neck.

"I love you too, babe. Always." I kiss her forehead, allowing my body to fully relax. I can finally call Denise mine. And I'm so thankful to her for giving me this chance.

We must doze off because the next thing I know, an hour has passed and we're interrupted from our post-sex snuggle by my phone buzzing repeatedly. I wrap my arms around Denise and roll her to the back of the couch so I can slip out from underneath her, kissing her as we move. Without getting up, I stretch out far enough to grab my pants and drag them to me to get my phone. A look at the screen makes me groan. I have thirty something messages from Gran and all of our friends asking where we are.

"Do you feel up to going out for a bit?" I ask after flailing around and finally getting myself back on the couch. "I was supposed to propose to you at the beach and everyone is there waiting for us."

Her eyebrows lift. "You planned a beach proposal but came here to ask me instead?"

"I know it's not as romantic as you deserve, but I didn't want to put you on the spot in front of everyone after what you've been through the last few weeks. Gran planned the beach thing. I went along for the ride, worried about what I'd say to you." I look down and lower my voice. "Plus, I wasn't really sure you'd say yes."

I risk looking up at her and see her smiling.

"That was so thoughtful, Ryder. I honestly preferred it this way. I've always felt a proposal should be a private thing." She leans forward and kisses me softly. "Now, about this beach thing. What should I wear?"

Well, She's No Elvis, But...

Denise

WE PULL UP TO a large house on the lake about half an hour out of town. It's a beautiful spot where most people build enormous houses on small properties. My parents have one, and it's disgustingly pretentious. People from all over the country come here to summer at Westborough's not-so-well-kept secret, but this place has a huge piece of property surrounding it and the neighbors' homes are so far away I can't even make out lights through the trees.

"This place is gorgeous," I tell Ryder when he opens my door for me. "Who lives here?"

Ryder smiles and reaches for my hand. "This is Gran's lake house, where my brother and I used to spend half of every summer with her when we were kids. I've been having it renovated for her these last few months and the contractor finished work last week. My grandfather bought this property and built this house around sixty years ago. Even when people started building those enormous houses on the other properties, they kept this normal sized house and refused to sell off parts of the property, despite having plenty of offers over the years. Now it's a beautiful, private hideaway close to the city. It's one of my favorite places."

I adjust the black body-con dress I'm wearing underneath a vintage, cropped, off-the-shoulder Mötley Crüe t-shirt before wrapping my arm around Ryder's waist. We make our way around to the lakefront house. There's a screened-in porch facing the lake, and I can imagine how beautiful it would be to sit out there and watch the sunrise. But before my imagination can take me any further, I notice all of our friends gathered on the beach, closer to the water.

They've taken a wooden pergola and strung it with twinkle lights, filmy curtains, and flowers. The effect is ethereal. That our friends all got together and did this in such a short amount of time has me a little misty eyed.

"Wow," Ryder says, awe clear in his voice. "I should have told them all to piss off and proposed here. This is beautiful."

"Do you think they'll be disappointed that you asked before we came?" I ask with a laugh.

"I guess there's only one way to find out."

The pathway ends where the sand starts, so I stop to take off my heels. Holding Ryder's arm for balance, I slip them off and drop them in the grass. Walking in sand in heels is asking for disaster. I'm a pregnant lady, after all. I don't need to be taking unnecessary risks.

"There you are!" Gran throws up both hands and waves them around. "What do you think? Not too shabby, if I do say so myself."

Noises of protest crop up here and there from the rest of our friends, and I hear snippets of people taking credit for their own parts in bringing it all together. Gran waves them off with a smile and is met with chuckles in return.

"Hey, Dad," Ryder says, reaching out his hand when his dad is the first to come up to greet us.

"Get that out of here, son." Ryder's dad smacks his hand out of the way and pulls him into an enormous hug. "It's so good to see you."

Ryder hugs his dad with one arm because he refuses to let go of my hand.

"Dad, you remember Denise, right?"

"Of course," he says, stepping over and pulling me into a hug, too. "How are you? This boy behaving for you? Or do I need to get in there and start smacking him around a bit?"

I laugh and am about to refuse his kind offer when another older man pipes in.

"Save some for me," he says, walking toward us. "I've been trying to slap this one around ever since we met. Even if he is teaching classes for free at my gym."

"Pops!" Ryder extends his hand and is again pulled into a hug instead. "It looks like the guys really outdid themselves with getting everyone here."

"Not everyone," Devon says, stepping up to join our little circle. "Your parents had something else to do tonight, Denise. I'm sorry." He gives my arm a reassuring squeeze.

"That's fine, Dev. Thanks for trying. I've sort of kicked them out of my life for now, anyway. Their opinions on the whole Andrew situation made me realize that they're not good people. Definitely not the kind of people I want around our baby."

Ryder's head snaps toward me. "Our baby?" He smiles.

"Yeah. Should I not—"

Ryder pulls me into a kiss, dropping my hand in favor of cupping my face while he kisses the hell out of me. I have a feeling I shouldn't be getting so hot and bothered standing in the middle of his dad and Alex's grandfather, but when Ryder's kissing me, I can't focus on anything else. The man can kiss, that's for damn sure. I grab the front of his shirt, pulling him closer to me, and through a fog of lust, I think I hear whistles and cheers coming from our friends.

"Alright, lovebirds, save the kissing for after. That part comes at the end of the ceremony." Gran pulls us apart and grins. "Now let's get this show on the road."

"Oh Gran," Ryder starts. "About that..."

"You proposed already, and she said yes?" she asks with a wink. "I knew that was going to happen. So this isn't a surprise for Denise, it's also a surprise for you."

Ryder looks at me with his eyebrows drawn and shrugs. "I have no idea what's happening," he says. "You?"

It's then that I notice the decorated archway set up a little way down the beach, almost at the edge of the water. I point it out to Ryder.

"What do you suppose that means?" he asks.

Everyone walks to the archway, taking seats in chairs that are lined up facing it, with a group on each side of what looks suspiciously like an aisle.

"Well, if I'm not mistaken, I'd say this is a surprise wedding, and we are getting married right now." I can't keep the grin from spreading across my face, especially when Ryder's look of confusion turns into a smile big enough to rival my own.

"Get your ass down here, Ryder." Gran yells from beside the arch. "We don't want to wait all night to start the party, do we? You took your sweet ass time getting here, and it's already getting late."

Ryder leans over and kisses me, smiling against my mouth, and asks, "Are you ready for this?"

"More than ready," I say, kissing him right back. "Let's get married."

One more kiss and he's on his way to his Gran.

Devon steps up beside me, offering his elbow. "May I have the honor of walking you down the aisle?" he asks, handing me a teardrop shaped bouquet of exotic-looking black and white flowers. All I can do is nod because I don't trust myself to speak without crying. Having a friend like Devon to walk me down the aisle takes away some of the sting of not having my parents here for me. My friends truly are the best family I could ever hope for, and they prove it to me more and more each day.

Music starts from somewhere off to the side and I notice that Connor, Travis, and Johnny have guitars out and they're playing an instrumental piece that I've never heard before. A hauntingly beautiful piece that makes me float down the aisle until I step in front of Ryder and smile up at him.

"Friends, thank you for joining us this evening, to witness the marriage between Ryder and Denise." It's Gladys. Gladys is performing the ceremony. My mouth drops wide open and I couldn't be more shocked if I tried. "Close your mouth, dear," Gladys whispers to me with a wink. "He already knows it fits."

Ryder snorts out a laugh, and I barely suppress a giggle. This should be an entertaining ceremony, if nothing else. I can't think of a better way to marry the man who makes me happier than I've ever been, than in a ceremony filled with love and laughs.

"Now then, since it appears our bride and groom have *already* been up to no good," Gladys says while gesturing to Ryder's open shirt and its missing buttons, "it's probably best if we make this short and sweet so we can let them get back to it."

The small crowd laughs and I can feel my face heat. Obviously, they all know we're not virgins on our wedding day, but I don't really need Ryder's family knowing exactly what we were up to before we came here tonight.

"You look beautiful when you blush." Ryder leans in and whispers in my ear. "I especially like it when I make you come and your whole body blushes." He leans back and winks.

That's not fair. He's fighting dirty now. He's sporting a little smirk on his lips, knowing that he's sent a rush of heat through me. What a lovable ass, getting me all turned on when we can't do anything about it. Two can play this game, though. I lick my lips slowly and drag my eyes down his body and back up again, settling on his face with the best 'fuck me' eyes I can muster. He swallows roughly and turns his back to the crowd, trying to subtly adjust his dick in his jeans.

"Oh, no you don't. It's too late now, Ryder," Gladys says, loudly enough for everyone to hear. "You've had years to show me your dick. In front of your bride, during your wedding, is neither the time nor the place."

"I—what? No, I wasn't..." Ryder sputters and everyone laughs.

"It's okay, babe," I say between laughs of my own. "I'm sure lots of grooms get cold feet and try to show their junk to their grandmother's best friend during the wedding ceremony."

"Okay, let's move on now." Gran says from her front-row seat. "I've got some dance moves I want to show Aiden after this." She turns and wiggles her eyebrows at him where he's standing as Ryder's Best Man. "I'm wearing my new thong, too."

"Gee, Gran. I can't wait," he deadpans, to more laughs from the crowd.

Xena is standing beside me as maid of honor. "You know Gran," she starts, and I see Devon shake his head the tiniest bit from where he sits next to Gran. "Devon can probably show you a thing or two if you're interested." She adds a wink and a little finger wave for Devon before laughing.

"You're going to pay for that, Princess," Devon says with a chuckle. "But first, let's get this wedding over with. You have no idea how uncomfortable it is for me to have to sit on two of these stupid folding chairs." I hadn't even noticed, but Devon is spread across two chairs, one ass cheek on each seat. It must be tough being as big as he is sometimes, but seeing him sitting like that is hilarious.

"Okay, so I was told that these two would have their own vows to say to each other." Gladys attempts to get us back on track. "Aiden, the ring. Ryder, you're up. Make some promises and make them good ones. The police gave me back my stun gun and I ain't afraid to use it." She pats the fanny pack she's wearing over her silver tracksuit. This must be what constitutes formal wear at Peaceful Pines. Gran is wearing a gold tracksuit to match.

I pass my bouquet to Xena when Ryder takes my hands, pulling me from my thoughts of the elderly residents of Gran and Gladys's retirement community. He rubs his thumbs across the backs of my hands for a moment and his tongue peeks out to flip his lip ring from side to side.

"Denise," he starts. "No one warned me I would need to say vows tonight, so I hope I don't repeat too much from my brilliant proposal earlier this evening. Although, Denise *is* the only one who heard it, and she'll be hearing variations of this for the rest of our lives, so..." Our friends and family all laugh. "I never believed this day would come. I dreamed it might, but I've not exactly lived my life as the type of man who deserves a woman as amazing as you, so I never dared to hope it could actually happen. Thank you for taking a chance on me, for loving me, and for trusting me to be your partner in life. I will do everything in my power to be the man you deserve. I promise to never stop loving you, never stop supporting you, never stop wanting you, and to never stop making you laugh. I love you, and my heart is yours forever."

His eyes are shiny, the tears pooling and dampening his lower lashes. But his smile is brighter than it's ever been, and I can see how happy he is that we're finally together. He shakes a little as he slides a matching black gold ring onto my finger with my engagement ring. My heart pounds in my chest, the excitement of the moment catching up to me.

"And now you, Denise," Gladys says to me. "Your turn for promises. I like you too much to threaten you with my stun gun. Nevertheless, make sure they're good ones, hey? Xena, pass her the ring."

A chuckle ripples through the crowd, starting with me and Ryder. We're making our vows under threat of electrocution by a geriatric officiant dressed in a silver tracksuit. This wedding is definitely one of a kind. I shake my head and huff a little laugh.

I take a deep breath, trying to calm my pounding heart, and begin. "Ryder, I love you. I've loved you for a long time, even though I tried to deny it. Even when you were screwing everything up, and being impossible to deal with, I knew that I'd never find another man like you. You make me laugh, you keep me sane, and I can always be myself around you. You're the home I want to come back to every single day for the rest of my life. I promise to support you and help you succeed, to rein you in when you need it, and to tell everyone to shut up when they tell you to fuck off." I give a warning glare at all of our friends and am met with a chorus of chuckles. "I also promise to trust you to take care of me when I need it, and to relinquish *some* control when it's necessary." Another laugh comes from the crowd. For some reason, they think I'm a control freak. Jerks. "Ryder, my heart is yours, always. I love you."

45

Gran's Gift

Ryder

HOLDING DENISE IN MY arms as we dance to Etta James' song *At Last*, our bare feet sliding in the sand, I know for a fact that I'm the luckiest man in the world. This beautiful woman is my wife, we're having a baby, and the future is something I'm looking forward to now, more than I ever have.

"You smell like coconut," I say as I lean over to nuzzle Denise's neck. "I love how your shampoo reminds me of summers at this place. You smell like sunshine, and fun, and unconditional love."

She rises on her toes and kisses me. "That's because I love you unconditionally, Ryder. You're mine now. And I'm not letting you go."

"Um, I believe that's my line, Mrs. Sullivan." I pull her head against my chest and smile into her hair. "I am never letting you go. You or this beautiful baby we're having."

"Hey, who said I was changing my name? Denise Sullivan? That's a lot of 'S' sounds in a row." Her face scrunches up a little. "I'm not sure how I feel about that."

"You're right. I could change my name to Lathan? Ryder Lathan? That sounds okay, right?" I don't have a problem changing my name. I want to have the same last name as my wife, regardless of what it is.

288

"No," she says. "You're pretty famous. It would probably be bad for your career to change your last name. I was joking anyway. I can't think of anything I'd like more than taking your name. Especially since it also gives me a feeling of separation from my parents."

I can't believe her parents wouldn't come to their daughter's surprise wedding. I've met the Lathans once or twice, though, and I guess it shouldn't surprise me that much. They're incredibly stuck up. They always looked down their noses at Denise's career, not to mention at the rest of us in the band. They're probably feeling humiliated at the thought of their daughter marrying me.

"Hey Bro." I feel a tap on my shoulder that breaks me out of my thoughts. "Mind if I cut in with my new sister?"

"Hunter!" I pull my little brother in for a hug. "You made it."

"Yeah, finally. I had a client at the shop for a late appointment and I couldn't cancel. I tried to get here earlier, but you know how it is."

Hunter owns his own tattoo shop downtown, close to Xena's coffee shop. He's always booked out months in advance, so it makes sense that he couldn't cancel.

"We get it. No problem. This was a last-minute thing. Hell, Ryder and I didn't even know we were getting married tonight." Denise gives me a quick kiss. "But I would love to dance with you, Hunter. It's been so long since I've seen you. How are things going at the shop?"

Denise and Hunter start dancing, their conversation continuing as I walk away to look for Gran, to thank her for putting all this together. And for surprising us with the matching wedding bands we needed for the ceremony. Not sure how she pulled that off, but I've long given up trying to figure out how she works her magic.

I find her standing over with Aiden and Gladys, and Aiden's face is so red it's practically glowing in the dark.

"What's going on here?" I ask when I make it over to them.

"I showed Aiden some of my new moves, and he's overcome with lust, I think," Gran says with a sly wink in my direction. "I'm afraid I may have ruined him for other women."

Poor Aiden is shaking his head and muttering to himself. Gran has always had a soft spot for him, but it's because she can't resist teasing him. She says that his blush is her favorite shade of red. He acts like it's a hardship, but I know he secretly loves the attention he gets from her. She's the family he never had.

When his family died in that car accident, he cut himself off from all his extended family. His dad's parents refused to believe anything bad about their son, and his mom's parents died before he was born. He had no one until he met me and the rest of the guys in the band. And now Gran. I'm more than happy to share her, too. She's a lot for one man to handle.

"Thanks for all this, Gran. Everything was perfect."

"Oh, my sweet boy. It was my pleasure. We can have something bigger and fancier after Denise has the baby, if she wants the whole white dress, church deal." She digs around in the pocket of her gold tracksuit, pulling out a set of keys. "Here. Keys to the lake house. I'll take care of the paperwork tomorrow."

She places the keys in my hand, pats me once, and turns to go.

"Wait, Gran. What is this?"

"I told you, weren't you listening? Those are the keys to the lake house. I'm giving it to you and your wife. It's a perfect place to raise kids. But make sure they all get swimming lessons and water safety courses as soon as they're old enough."

"I can't accept this, Gran. This is too much. And what about Hunter? Wouldn't it be good for him to raise his family, too?"

Hunter and Denise come to join us. "She already talked to me about it, Ryder. I think you should have it. I live at the shop, anyway. As long as you invite me over to hang out, I think you and Denise having the lake house is perfect."

"Gran?" Denise asks. "It sounds like they said you're giving Ryder the lake house? That's not true, though, right? You're letting us stay for a bit. Like a honeymoon?"

Gran snags Denise around the waist and squeezes her gently. "I'm giving it to both of you, love. You're married, you'll both be on the paperwork. This is where I spent all my happiest moments with Ryder's grandfather, as well as with my son and my grandsons. I want you to experience that kind of happiness too, with my great grandbaby. Besides, Ryder bought me my little cottage at Peaceful Pines, and I think you know how much fun I have there." Gran chuckles as she lets go of Denise. "There's no one here to play pranks on. All the neighbors here are stuck-up dickwads. I enjoy being with my friends in the retirement community. It's like summer camp, but with dentures and mobility scooters instead of braces and bikes."

Denise bursts into tears, pulling Gran in for another hug. "I wish my family was like you, instead of the selfish, stuck-up assholes they are. You've met them, I'm sure. They have a house here at the lake, too. How else would you know all the neighbors out here are stuck-up dickwads?"

"Well now, honey, don't cry. I *am* your family now. And there's no one more like me than me," Gran says with a chuckle while she pats Denise's hair. "The closest you can get, other than me, is Gladys."

"And I'm your family now, too," Gladys says through tears, wrapping her arms around both Denise and Gran. "Even if you've shattered my dreams of seeing Ryder's dick by marrying him and making him your forever penis."

Everyone around us laughs. Except me. I'm glad Gladys is finally going to give up her quest to see my dick. I have plans for it for the next forty years or so, and those plans involve Denise.

"Yes, Gladys," Denise says, stepping out of the hug and back next to me, where I wrap my arm around her. "That was a pretty integral part of the deal, I'm afraid. You'll have to set your sights on someone else's dick. Maybe Aiden?"

"Whoa, hold on a minute." Aiden protests. "I have all I can handle with Gran showing me her lap dance moves. I don't need Gladys trying to get into my pants now, too."

"I don't want to get in them, Aiden," Gladys clarifies. "I want to *see* what's in them. I need to know if it lives up to all the hype. But it can't be Aiden, anyway. I have heard no hype about his trouser snake at all."

Aiden shakes his head, wandering off to find someone else to talk to. He may be the oldest guy in the band, but that doesn't mean he's interested in octogenarians. Not that I've ever seen him really interested in anyone. He had a few hook-ups like the rest of us, but nothing that ever came close to serious. He spends all of his spare time volunteering with the domestic violence shelters, so it's not like he'd have time to date, anyway. I wonder what was up with that cop earlier, though?

"Want me to show you the house?" I whisper in Denise's ear as I wrap my arms around her from behind. She's been trying unsuccessfully to hide how tired she is, but the yawns are becoming too big not to notice. This woman has had a long day, and I need to take her to bed, to sleep this time. Not that I wouldn't rather make love to my wife, but she looks like she wouldn't last long enough to enjoy it.

"I would love that," she whispers, turning in my arms to kiss me. "I don't know how much longer I can keep my eyes open."

I take her hand and lead her up the stairs to the porch.

"Everyone," I yell. "Thank you so much for coming tonight. And thank you for putting everything together. Denise and I have had a long day, as I know some of you have as well, so we are going in now. I need to get my new wife to bed."

We turn as one, and go into the house to the soundtrack of our friends' and relatives' cheers and whistles. I guess Gran and Gladys aren't the only pervy ones of the bunch. I'm not all that surprised, really. There's a reason we all like each other, after all.

"Come on, babe. Let me give you the lowdown on the house while I show you to our bedroom." I take Denise's hand and pull her up the stairs behind me. "There are two bedrooms, plus the master up here on the second level. Our bedroom has a master bathroom, plus there's a full bath and a half bath in the hallway for the other rooms to share. There are also two bedrooms, plus another full bath and another half bath downstairs on the main level."

We turn right at the top of the stairs, and I open the door that leads to the master suite. One renovation I had done recently was a wall of windows overlooking the lake, plus a small, private balcony for the master suite.

"This is beautiful, Ryder," Denise says, taking in the view of lights across the lake. During the daytime, you can't see any other houses from here, but at night their lights twinkle across the water, creating an image that appears to mirror the stars. "Do we really get to live here?"

"Only if you want to," I say, wrapping my arms around her and enjoying the view. "We can live anywhere you like. As long as we're together, the rest is details."

46

I Never Piss Myself

Denise

Six Months Later

"What the fuck, Ryder?" I jump when Ryder leans over my chair and kisses my forehead. "You scared me. I wasn't expecting you home for another hour."

"The guys and I cut out early today. Since we postponed the tour, there's no need to rush to complete this album."

Ryder sits beside me in the other Adirondack chair on the private deck of our master suite. I have several giant pillows under my ass, because if I didn't I'd never be able to get off this chair by myself. Ryder keeps trying to bring a different type of chair out here for me, but I want no part of it. To me, that feels like I'm letting this pregnancy defeat me and I'm not about to let that happen, not this close to the end. I'm due next week, so I'm pretty sure I can deal with this chair for at least that long.

"Are you hungry?" Ryder asks. "I can order something. Or I can throw together something if you prefer. I invited the three musketeers for dinner, too."

Gran and Gladys took Lana under their wing at the wedding, and they've been inseparable ever since. We bought Lana her own cottage at Peaceful Pines and now the three of them spend all their time terrorizing younger visitors and causing mayhem. So far no aspic filled balloons, though. Thank god.

He grabs my hand and kisses my ring finger, the one that is missing my wedding rings. I've been a little swollen the last few weeks, so I took them off. I miss them. They're on a chain around my neck for now, but I can't wait until I can wear them again. Ryder wears his every day without fail. He says it's because he's so proud to be married to me; that he needs to make sure everyone knows. I'm sure part of it is that he's having a hard time kicking his old ladies' man image. He doesn't need to worry about that, though. I trust him. I know that no matter how many groupies are throwing themselves at him, he'll be coming home to me.

"I'm starving," I say, beginning the process of rocking myself out of this damn chair. "Let me come down and help you make something. I'm feeling like a big salad. Or maybe some spaghetti. Or what about burgers?"

I rock and rock until I lean forward far enough to grab the railing in front of me and pull myself up to standing. And then I feel a pop before a rush of liquid runs down my legs. I look down in horror.

"Oh, fuck. I'm pissing myself," I tell Ryder, my eyes wide and my voice low. The liquid is still flowing and since I'm wearing a sundress, there's nothing there to catch the flow except for my thin cotton panties. "I've never pissed myself before."

Ryder rockets out of his chair, coming to my side. "Um, babe. I don't think that's piss. Has your back been hurting today?"

"Look at me! I have a twenty-pound turkey strapped to my stomach. Of course my back has been hurting." Did I really marry this dumbass? What the hell was I thinking?

"You're right, babe. That was a dumb question. Let me get the water started for you and then I'll come help you into the shower, okay?"

He runs inside, and I hear the water start. I strip off my dress and panties right there on the deck, dropping them with a soggy plop in front of my chair before making my way into our bedroom. Ryder comes out of the bathroom to find me rummaging through my drawers, looking for something to wear.

"Why don't you go ahead in the shower," Ryder says, coming up behind me and placing his hands on what used to be my waist. "And I can find you some clothes? You must be uncomfortable standing around naked."

Rage flares in my chest, and I spin around, belly first. "What are you saying, Ryder? You can't stand to see me naked? I disgust you with my giant belly, and pissing myself? Fuck. You're such an asshole."

I storm to the bathroom and step into the shower. The warm water washes the pee from my body and quells the rage I feel toward Ryder a little. I don't even know where that anger came from. Ryder hasn't been able to keep his hands off me since the wedding. We have sex all the time, and he's constantly telling me how sexy I am.

"Hey babe," I call out. "I'm sorry. I think I'm hangry or something. You know I didn't mean that."

He comes into the bathroom and sets a stack of clothes on the counter for me. I watch him strip out of his own clothes, then join me in the shower. Strong arms wrap around me from behind, and his hard cock tells me he's more than satisfied with the way I look. I lean back into his chest, ready for some shower sex, when I feel my stomach tighten.

"Did you feel that?" I ask.

"Yeah, babe, I did." he says, reaching for the shampoo bottle. He squeezes a little into his hands and massages it into my hair. "I'm pretty sure your water broke on the deck, and that you're going into labor. I'm going to help you wash up and get dressed, and then we're going to get you to the hospital."

Ryder read every baby book I bought, and then he read some more that he bought on his own. He's been the most calming influence throughout this entire experience. If it weren't for him, I'd have been freaking out going through this alone. If Ryder thinks I'm in labor, then I'm most likely in labor.

My parents still haven't called, except for one time a couple of months ago, when they asked if I was ready to forgive Andrew. They think if I forgive him he will have his sentence reduced and he'll be out of jail sooner. Right. As if I want that to happen. I'm sure I don't need to mention they reacted poorly to the news of my marriage to Ryder, and we haven't spoken since. Good riddance, I say. I have a much more supportive family now, and I can't imagine ever going back to the cold, unfeeling ways of my old one.

Ryder has put a little conditioner in my hair and he's rapidly rubbing me down with a loofah and body wash when my stomach tightens again.

"Ow, shit," I say. "That one hurt."

"That was pretty fast, babe. Have you been feeling your stomach tighten like that before now?"

"Well, sort of. But not as bad. It's been happening for a couple of days."

"A couple of days!" he yells. "Shit. Why didn't you tell me? We need to get going."

He turns me around carefully and tips my head back, massaging the conditioner out of my hair. Reaching past me, he turns off the shower and steps out to grab me a towel. While he's helping me dry off, I feel my stomach tighten again.

"Ow, fuck!" I yell, trying to control my breathing for a few moments. "That was bad."

"Hi, kids." Gran's voice comes up the stairs. "We're here!"

"Gran," Ryder yells. "We're upstairs. Denise is in labor. And her contractions are coming right on top of each other."

Less than a minute later, Gran, Gladys, and Lana are joining us in the bathroom. Ryder has helped me kneel on the bathmat in front of the shower.

"Son of a fucking bitch asshole cocksucker!" I scream after another contraction. "This is not normal. What the fuck is happening? Why is my vagina on fire?"

"Okay, Ryder. You're up," Gladys says, somewhere off in the distance. "You kneel behind Denise. Get ready to catch that baby."

"Excuse me. What?"

47

Want to Play Catch?

Ryder

"What?" I scramble into a kneeling position behind Denise, like Gladys said. "What do you mean *catch*?"

"Pay attention, dumbass." Gladys smacks me on the head for looking at her instead of Denise. "That baby is coming now. And you're going to catch it when it does. Put your hands here." She moves my hands into position, where I can see something is already making its way out of Denise. Holy shit, is that the top of the baby's head? "And let it happen, Dad."

I focus my attention on Denise while Gran, Gladys, and Lana scurry around, coming in and out of the room for a moment, before Gladys gets down in front of Denise.

"Alright sweetie," she says in a calming voice. "On the next contraction, you're going to push for all your worth. We've got you. Everything is going exactly as it should. Are you ready? Now push."

Denise bears down, pushing with no sound, and suddenly there is a tiny head resting in my hands.

"On the next one, the rest of the baby is coming out," Gran says quietly in my ear. "You'll use one hand to hold the head and the other to cradle the body, okay? Then you'll bring that baby right up to your chest and hold her there until you hand her to

Denise. You've got this. I'm so proud of you." Gran kisses my temple.

"Denise, babe, you are so amazing. You're the strongest person I've ever met. I love you so much baby, you're doing great."

"Ryder," Denise yells through panting breaths. "Shut the fuck up."

"Okay, Denise," Gladys says. "This next one could be the last. I want you to take a deep breath, hold it, and push like you're pooping out the biggest turd of your life. Don't worry if you shit on Ryder. Skin washes. He'll be fine."

Denise huffs out a laugh. Leave it to Gladys to add humor to the situation.

I hear Denise take her big breath, then she tenses and starts pushing. Gran reaches near my hands and pushes around where the baby's coming out. A moment later, a baby is sliding into my arms and I'm pulling it up to my chest, like Gran said.

The sounds of relieved sobs echo through the bathroom, coming from both me and Denise. Her shoulders have slumped a little.

Gladys comes to me and checks over the baby, making sure everything is as it should be.

"It's a girl, babe. We have a beautiful little girl," I say through my tears.

Gran and Lana busy themselves tidying around us and laying towels out. Denise turns over carefully, with Gran helping her keep her foot from catching the umbilical cord.

"Ryder, come here." Gran directs me to slide the baby into Denise's arms, and then to move behind Denise so she can lean against me while she lies on the floor.

Gladys takes over my position between Denise's knees. "You aren't quite done, love," she says to Denise. "You still need to deliver the placenta, but the good news is that the hard part is over. You should be able to relax a bit and let your body do the rest."

Lana is using a cool washcloth to wipe Denise's brow and telling her what a great job she did.

Gran leaves the bathroom and comes back with a soft blanket to drape over Denise and the baby and an extra one to wrap around my back. I guess going from being nice and warm inside your mom to freezing out here in the open air would be quite the shock. At least the hot water from our shower warmed the bathroom a bit before this all started. There's still a little steam on the mirror, too, which gives me an idea of how fast this actually went.

Gran helps Denise get the baby latched on for her first feeding and then stands beside us, admiring the baby.

"Oh, isn't she a beauty," Gran says, with a hitch in her voice. I don't even have to look at her to know she's crying as much as I am.

After a few minutes, Gladys wraps something in a towel and places it on the counter above our heads. Gran, Gladys, and Lana each take turns kissing me and Denise, and then they leave the room.

"I gave birth on our bathroom floor," Denise chuckles.

"That was definitely not in the birth plan," I laugh, kissing her cheek. Denise's control freak tendencies were in full swing when she wrote that birth plan. It's probably good for her that things didn't go exactly as planned. I'm sure it's the first of many times she'll need to go with the flow where the baby is involved.

"Definitely not," she agrees, looking down at the baby. She has chubby little cheeks, and a shock of black hair like Denise that will probably stick straight up once she's all bathed. "So, what are we going to name her?"

"Cole," I say without hesitation. "I see all that black hair and that's all I can think of."

"I like that. Cole Delanys. D-E-L-A-N-Y-S. After your Gran, Lana, and Gladys. Thank god they showed up when they did today."

I tilt her face toward me and kiss her on the mouth, awed that she would name her baby after three of the most important women in my life.

"Knock, knock," someone says at the open bathroom door. "I hear someone and their new baby need a quick checkup and a ride to the hospital. We'd be happy to help with that."

Two female paramedics walk in and start fussing over Denise. I take the opportunity to get up and find some clothes, because I've only just realized that I've been naked this entire time.

I refuse to take the warm blankets away from Denise and Cole, so all that's available to cover myself with is a hand towel. I do my best to cover my dick with it and head into the bedroom to get dressed. While I'm there, I get something for Denise as well.

Once the paramedics have finished, Denise gets dressed, and we take the ambulance to the hospital while Gran, Gladys, and Lana follow in the car. Denise checks out fine, but they want us to go to the hospital so that she and the baby can see a doctor. Often the doctor will want a first time mom to stay overnight there too, so we're not sure if we'll be getting back home tonight. I don't care either way, as long as they know I won't be leaving my girls' sides, so they'd best be prepared for me to stay, too.

48

The One I Needed All Along

Denise

I WAKE UP IN our comfy king-sized bed to the sounds of Ryder's voice. When I open my eyes, I see that he's standing in front of the window, looking out at the lake, and rocking Cole in his arms while singing her a lullaby. We've been home for two days after our one-night stay in the hospital and I can already tell he's going to be an amazing dad.

"Morning, babe," he says without turning around. "How'd you sleep?"

I sit up and stretch while he walks over to me with Cole. Her black hair has a slight curl to it, which makes it stick up in a fuzzy little halo.

"I slept pretty well, actually." Ryder slides Cole into my arms and then sneaks in behind me on the bed so I can lean against him while I feed her. He's been my chair during every feeding, either holding me, or massaging my shoulders, or running his fingers through my hair. "In between all the feedings, that is. Thanks for getting up with her this morning and letting me catch a little extra sleep. I feel like I've been awake for a month."

"I'd feed her for you if I could, but sadly, my boobs are not equipped for that. Damn these useless man nipples." He laughs. "They're for show."

"Well, it's a good thing you've decorated them so nicely then, I suppose. I can't say I'm sad about how you look with those nipple rings."

"Hold up, lady. Don't objectify me. At least not yet. The doctor said your lady bits are out of commission for a while. You can't get me all excited and then leave me hanging." He's joking, of course. He loves it when I objectify him.

"I figured you've been lacking in character lately. Thought I could help you out by giving you a case of character building blue balls, for old times' sake."

Ryder laughs and kisses me on the neck. He scoots me back against him a little more so I can lean back, then he wraps his arms around me and helps me hold Cole. She doesn't eat a lot at a time yet, so she pops off my breast in a few minutes. As I'm getting my shirt fixed up, there's a knock on our bedroom door.

"Hello?" Ryder calls out.

"We couldn't wait any longer. Please, can we come in and see Denise and the baby?" It's Alex. She's been impatiently waiting for me to go into labor since the day she found out I was pregnant.

"Come in, Alex." I say.

The door opens and the first thing I see is a baby bump. Alex's baby bump, to be exact. She's around six months along, but she's having twins, so her belly is huge. She waddles over to the bed and sits beside me, pushing Ryder's foot out of the way.

"Move it, Dad. Auntie Alex needs some baby time," she says, while wiggling her arms toward me and the baby.

With some effort, Ryder gets his foot loose and slides off the bed to greet the rest of our visitors. Everyone is here.

"Oh my god," Alex says, the tears already welling up into her eyes. "She's so beautiful. And that hair! No wonder you guys picked Cole. I've never seen hair that black before. Well, except maybe yours, Denise."

Without waiting for her to actually ask, I slide Cole over into her arms. Alex has been dying to hold my baby, and I don't want to know what would happen if I made her wait longer. I know firsthand how crazy those baby hormones make a person.

"Gran said you 'caught' the baby?" Devon asks Ryder. "What does that mean?"

I lift myself off the bed to give Alex some time with her niece and walk over to where Devon, Ryder, Aiden, Connor, Travis, and Johnny are standing. All my guys in one spot. Five uncles and one daddy, all for Cole. My heart swells.

But that doesn't mean I won't fuck with them a little.

"It means that I pushed a human out of my vagina, and Ryder stood by and grabbed her as she came out. Then he snuggled her while I got situated so that I could hold her."

"But, didn't your clothes get all, you know, gross and covered in baby goo?" Devon's face shows exactly how he feels about baby goo getting on him. He's most definitely not a fan.

"Uh, actually," Ryder says, rubbing his hand through his hair. "We'd gotten out of the shower, and it all happened so fast I couldn't even get dressed before she was born."

"So you were naked?" Connor asks with a snort of laughter. "So your naked body got covered in baby goo?"

"It's not like it shoots out of a cannon or something, guys. Plus, it was worth it to be the first person to hold her. Not even a doctor held Cole before I did." Ryder grins, and I can almost see the hearts in his eyes. That man is so in love with his daughter. There's no way she won't be a daddy's girl with how much he's going to spoil her. He's already wrapped around her finger. She can't even whimper without him running over to pick her up.

"It was worth it for me, too," Gladys says, coming over to join us. "I finally got to see Ryder's dick. It's pretty okay, I guess. Not nearly as big as I was expecting from all the rumors I'd heard."

Ryder chokes on air and the rest of the guys laugh. "I didn't even think of that. Is that why you stepped up like you did? To see my dick?"

Gladys is the one who talked us through the entire birth. Without her, Gran, and Lana, I don't know what we would have done. Hopefully called 911 and had them try to talk us through it. But it sure was nice having someone beside me who seemed to know what they were doing.

"No, dipshit," Gran says while smacking him on the back of the head. "Gladys used to be a midwife. She was the best possible person to have around for an emergency childbirth."

"Gladys, how would you like to move in to my house until our babies are born?" Connor interrupts. "Thinking of Alex giving birth to twins has me so freaked out."

"Hold on a minute here." Ryder raises his voice to be heard over everyone's chatter. "What do you mean my dick is 'okay, you guess'? My dick is amazing. Ask Denise." He points at me as I try to sneak away from the conversation. "You love my dick, don't you, babe?"

I stop in my tracks. "Yes, dear. You have a very nice dick. Uh, I'm going to check on Cole and Alex now."

Everyone bursts into laughter as I spin around and walk back to the bed. Just as I reach Alex, a pair of muscular arms wrap around me from behind, and I'm carried out to the balcony, the door closing behind us, closing us off from our visitors.

"You love my dick." Ryder states, spinning me around and wrapping his arms around my waist. "Admit it."

"Yes, Ryder. I admit it, I love your dick." I chuckle. I don't get his insecurity. If ever a man had a reason to be proud of his penis, that man is Ryder. "I love it so much I'm going to make you shove it down my throat after everyone goes home."

He pulls me against him, and I feel his reaction to that statement. He's getting hard already.

"You're killing me, babe," he says, grinding his dick against my hip a little. "And as great as that sounds, I can't let you do that. You had a baby and your body needs to rest. The last thing you need is my dick in you."

"Ugh," I pout. "You're no fun."

He cups my face and tilts my chin. I meet his lips with my own in a gentle kiss.

"I love you so much, Denise." He whispers. "You amaze me every day. And I promise, once your body is healed, and you're ready for sex, I will give you orgasms as often as you can stand. I can't wait to get my mouth on your pussy again."

"What?" He can't mean that. He watched the baby come out of me. I look down at my feet. "You're not grossed out by it? After seeing the birth?"

"What? Are you crazy? How could I be grossed out? That was the most beautiful thing I've ever seen. I need to worship that pussy, because it is a goddess, like you. I'm going to have to start referring to it as 'Pussy the Goddess', or 'Goddess Pussy', or maybe 'Goddess'."

Ryder's hand reaches around the back of my head, his fingers threading through my hair, and he tilts my face to meet his again. He seals his mouth to mine, his tongue diving in and exploring my own. My belly melts in a puddle of heat and I can feel my pussy throb, which I must admit feels a little uncomfortable at the moment. I guess there's something to this whole waiting a while before initiating sex again. Ryder softens the kiss before pulling away and resting his forehead against mine.

"There is nothing that could happen that would make me want you less, Denise. You are the sexiest woman alive, and that isn't based on your appearance. Everything about you makes me love you more every single day."

God, I love this man. Who knew that the one I wanted for all these years was actually the one I needed all along?

The End

Keep Reading for a Sneak Peek of Skip a Beat (Sleeping Dogs Book 3)

Not today, Man-bun. Not today

RHEA

"I'm sorry, Sir? I don't think I heard you correctly. Did you say 'suspended'?" I can't be suspended. I follow all the rules. Out of every officer in the precinct, I'm the only one who does every single thing completely by the book. "Are you sure you're talking to the right person?"

"Unfortunately, yes, I am talking to the right person. I personally don't agree with it, but I can't do anything about it. You are being suspended for excessive use of force. Turn in your badge and gun. You're suspended without pay for thirty days pending adjudication by the Police Commission."

"I understand, Captain Ross, Sir," I say numbly, removing my badge and gun and placing them on the Captain's desk. My movements feel jerky and stilted, and my voice doesn't sound quite like my own. "I take full responsibility for my actions, and I'm prepared to take whatever punishment the commission sees fit."

"Listen, Rhea." Captain Ross takes his glasses off and rubs the bridge of his nose with one hand. "This situation won't resolve itself easily. There is a good chance that you won't be allowed back on the force. Between you and me, the guy making the complaint, Frank Martin, is friends with the mayor. I'm already feeling pressure from higher up to fire you and get it over with."

Frank Martin? The abusive husband Kaden and I brought in? "I don't understand, Sir." Why would they want to fire me? I do my job, and I do it well. "We were responding to a domestic disturbance call. He was screaming so loudly at his wife that the neighbours were concerned enough to call us. He pushed her down the stairs right in front of me. I couldn't leave him there and risk him doing worse, could I?" What the hell did they expect me to do in a situation like that?

He heaves a heavy sigh. "No, you're right. You couldn't allow it to continue. It's that this is now a whole thing, and unfortunately, it's usually the person who isn't friends with the mayor that gets shit on in these situations. I'm only telling you this so that you spend your time wisely during your suspension. You may need to consider a different line of work when this is all said and done. You're a good cop, Rhea. You got unlucky this time."

"Oh." All I've ever wanted to be was a cop. Every decision I made regarding education and extracurricular activities was made with that goal in mind. I don't even know what I would do if I couldn't be one anymore. Why the hell does it always have to come down to politics and popularity, even in police work? It seems like every day it becomes less about right and wrong and more about who knows who. I'd be lying if I said being a cop has lived up to my dreams of what it would be like.

"I'll do what I can for you. You're the best cop I've got, and I'd hate to lose you."

"Thanks, Captain. I guess... I guess I'd better get going then. I look forward to hearing from you when this is all cleared up."

I'm sure nothing will come of this. I did everything the right way. They can't fire me because someone doesn't like me. Can they?

"You too, kid. Take care." He grunts and shuffles some papers around on his desk. "Send Cross in here, would ya?"

I'm barely two steps out of the captain's office before my partner, Kaden Cross, jogs up.

"So, how did it go?" He asks.

I've been worried about this meeting since the captain's secretary booked it with me. I've never been brought in front of the captain before. If it's possible, Kaden has been even more concerned. I'm not one to step out of line, so the captain wanting to see me was big news around the precinct.

"Oh, not too bad," I say, my voice dripping with sarcasm. " Off to start my thirty day, unpaid vacation now. Captain wants to see you, by the way."

What am I even going to do with myself for 30 days? I foresee a lot of trail runs in my future. Maybe I should get a pet? Like a cat. Or a snake.

"You're suspended? What the hell for?"

"Remember that domestic disturbance call we went on last week? When I arrested the older guy for pushing his wife down the stairs right in front of us?"

"Yeah, I remember. That guy was a dick. All 'Do you know who I am?' and 'You're going to regret this'. Such an asshole."

"Well, that asshole is friends with the mayor. And he's saying I used excessive force when I took him into custody. Now I'm suspended for thirty days, and the whole issue is awaiting adjudication by the police commission."

"What? That's bullshit. I was there. You barely even touched the guy. It was a textbook arrest. You were even gentle when you put the cuffs on. You're the most by the book cop anyone in this precinct has ever seen. I don't think you could break a rule if you tried."

"You know that, and I know that, but apparently it doesn't matter. It's okay, though. I'm sure it will all work out. There's no way they'll fire me for something that didn't happen. Right?"

"I guess." Kaden doesn't seem as confident as I feel. "What will you do if they do fire you, though? You've always wanted to be a cop."

"That's a damn good question. I guess I have something to think about while I'm on my unplanned vacation. That'll give me something to do other than run, at least."

"Well, worse comes to worst, I'm sure we can convince Xena to hire you at Bump & Grind. Maybe you could even get her to stop threatening people with that stupid foam sword she has behind the counter and save me some money." He shakes his head.

Here at the precinct we have a sword jar instead of a swear jar and Kaden is the only one who has to contribute. Every time we get a call about his sister threatening her customers with a sword, he has to put money in.

"You gotta admit, though, it is pretty funny seeing her swinging that thing around and then seeing the looks on her customers' faces. And aside from you having to put five bucks in the sword jar every time it gets called in, it's not really harmful. We all know that it's not a serious threat that we really need to respond to."

"Whatever. I still think it's unfair. It's not my fault my sister loses her mind any time someone calls her 'Warrior Princess'. If anyone should have to pay five bucks when she pulls out that sword, it should be our parents. They're the ones who named her after that character Lucy Lawless played, not me."

He crosses his arms and frowns. "And besides, she really should be arrested for that one of these days. She's becoming a menace."

Kaden follows me into the locker room, where I empty my locker into my bag. No sense changing here. I'll take off my uniform shirt and wear the tank I have underneath when I go. No one could think I look like a cop while I'm wearing a tank top with Wonder Woman on the front.

"She's only bothering you, Kaden. Everyone else thinks it's hilarious. You probably need to drop it. It's a lost cause."

"Gah!" He says, while shaking his fist to the sky melodramatically. "I know. It's so damn irritating. I need to figure out a way to get back at her. That might make me feel better. At least for a little while, anyway."

"Alright, you keep me posted on that." I give him a little wave with my keys. "I'm going to head out. You should probably go see the captain now. He may need to assign you a new partner. Or maybe he'll make you ride a desk until I'm back, because you made him wait so long."

"Oh, shit." He jumps and starts jogging away. "I'll call you later to check on you."

I shake my head as I walk out of the precinct. All those years I spent dreaming of being a cop, I never pictured my partner being someone like Kaden. He's got the muscular body I imagined a male cop should have, but that's where any resemblance to my imaginary partner ends. I always thought my partner would be incredibly smart and serious, and Kaden is... well, Kaden is smart enough, but he's rarely serious. But we've been partners since the beginning and I wouldn't have it any other way. He's the brother I never had.

Really, he's the brother I do have. When he found out that I grew up in the foster system and that I don't have any real family, he made me a member of his. His sister is one of my best friends. I get invited to every holiday dinner and every birthday.

His parents fill a stocking for me on Christmas, for crying out loud. I might as well me Rhea Cross instead of Rhea Ryan. The third, unrelated, Cross sibling.

And that's how I know, no matter what happens with this suspension and adjudication, I will be fine. Even if I'm not Kaden's partner, I will still be part of his family. And family takes care of family.

Stepping out into the sunlight to get to my car leaves me blinded for a moment and before I acclimate to the brightness, someone has walked up beside me and started talking.

"Diana Prince, just the person I was hoping to see," he says to me, using the name of Wonder Woman's secret identity. Maybe wearing this tank wasn't such a good idea after all. "I was hoping to ask you something the other day after you arrested my friend's ex-boyfriend over at Peaceful Pines, but I didn't get the chance. And I haven't been able to get in touch with you since then, either."

It's the hippie-looking, long-haired guy who was with Devon the day I arrested some idiot who got himself tied up by two little old ladies while attempting to take them hostage. As if today wasn't bad enough, now I have to deal with this random guy who keeps trying to ask me out. He was trying to talk to me that first day, and he's been around the precinct a few times since. What's it going to take for him to get the hint that I don't want to go out with him? I mean, he has a nice-looking butt, but get a clue man. I don't have time for this.

"Oh hey... you," I say, already walking away. I don't even know the guy's name, I've been referring to him as 'Man-bun' in my head, because of the way he always wears his long hair in a high bun. "Can't talk now. I'm swamped. So many things to do. Catch you later." I speed walk to my car, arms and hips swinging, unlocking the door with the fob before I'm even close to it. Without a single look back at Man-bun, I throw my bags in, jump in the driver's seat, and start it up, already speeding out of the parking lot before I've got my seat belt on.

"Not today, Man-bun. Not today." I whoop, turning my car toward home, leaving him standing in the parking lot with his mouth hanging open. "You and your exceptionally nice ass are going to have to find someone else to date."

KEEP READING IN SKIP a Beat (Sleeping Dogs Book 3)

Keep Reading Sneak Peek of Santa's Baby (coming late 2023)

Chapter One

PHOEBE

Of all the ways I ever imagined spending the Christmas of my thirty-first year I can say with certainty tracking down the Santa Claus who impregnated me was not one of them.

Yet here we are.

"This place is nice, Phoebe," Gavin says, walking into the living room and setting down a box marked "Lincoln." "Maybe the owners won't ever come back from their trip abroad so you can buy it. The furniture is pretty sweet." My idiot brother then flops face down on my fully furnished rental's overstuffed blue velvet couch and groans obscenely. "Oh, man. I could do dirty things to this couch."

It's not every day I rent a place sight unseen, so you can imagine the relief I felt when we got here and the place looked exactly like it had in the photos. That I could find a fully furnished place on such short notice, right before the holidays, was a miracle in itself. Finding a nice place in a safe neighborhood? Yeah, there had to have been some divine intervention involved for that to happen.

"Ew, don't be gross Gavin. And get your stinky ass off the couch. You're filthy."

"Is that any way to treat the guy who helped you move?" He dragged himself off the couch. "Speaking of which, didn't you promise me pizza and beer as payment for that help?"

"Ha! Nice try, kid. I'll order pizza but you're sticking with soda until you're of legal age. Plus, you still need to drive home so I wouldn't let you drink even if you were old enough."

Gavin is eighteen, my much younger sibling from my mom's second marriage. My bio dad left mom when Lane was born and I was still a few months shy of two years old. Needless to say, after being with such a bastion of paternal fortitude, it took Mom a long time to find another man worth taking a chance on. I was twelve when she started seeing Dennis, and fourteen when they married and Gavin was born.

Like most teenage boys, Gavin's all raging hormones and unrestrained snark. But, despite his many annoying traits, he has the biggest heart and he's one of my favorite people. When I found myself left at the altar almost a year ago no one was angrier than Gavin. He stormed around the hotel, hoping to run into my newly ex-fiance so he could unleash his teenage fury. It's probably a good thing he never found him, though. I doubt it would have been a fair fight.

Seventeen-year-old Gavin was a short, scrawny little shit. Eighteen-year-old Gavin is almost six and a half feet tall and packed with muscle. He's never said so, but I'm pretty sure he started working out after the wedding disaster so he'd be ready if he ever saw my ex again. After a year of protein shakes and lifting weights, not to mention a huge growth spurt, Gavin is formidable. It still wouldn't be a fair fight, but the advantage would go to Gavin, not Webster.

I almost feel guilty for not being as upset as he was about the situation. It was a shock when I got the text telling me he wasn't coming, but not marrying Webster Day was for the best. It was a dick move, but in the end, he made the best decision for both of us.

"No way, Lane said she would drive home." Gavin jumps up off the couch and yells down the back hallway, "Isn't that right, Lane?"

Oh, shit. Despite being one of my favorite people, I may have to murder Gavin if he wakes up Lincoln. That thing they say about never waking a sleeping baby? Yeah, that's totally true.

"Shhh. Will you shut up already?." I slap my hand over his mouth. "Lincoln is sleeping."

He looks so sheepish I might actually believe he felt bad about it if I didn't know better. There's no way Gavin would leave here without saying goodbye to his nephew, even if said nephew is barely old enough to see past his own fist. Gavin is sure Lincoln recognizes him, though, and is so proud of that fact. I believe it, too. Lincoln always seems calmer when his Uncle Gavin is holding him. And Gavin never misses a chance to hold him, even if he has to make his own chances.

"Too late," Lane says, coming out of the back hallway with a tiny baby snuggled in her arms. "Little guy was awake when I tried to sneak into his room to drop off a box. I think he sensed me because as soon as I walked in an unholy rumbling started coming out of his little rear end. You need to do laundry, by the way. I rinsed everything and left it to pre-soak." She looks down at Lincoln with a grin and singsongs, "Isn't that right, Linky? Mommy has to do laundry. Yes, she does. She's lucky Auntie Lane changed you and the sheets instead of running away and letting her deal with it."

My heart swells watching my little sister snuggle my baby and not for the first time since I came up with the plan, I second-guess my decision to move back to Westborough. What am I going to do without my family around to help me for the next three months? This was a terrible idea. But if I want Lincoln to at least have the chance to meet his father, this is where I need to be. And my sense of right and wrong won't let me entertain the thought of not trying to find his father. There's a man out there who doesn't know he has a son, and that doesn't sit right with me. I want him to at least have the choice of whether to be involved in Lincoln's life, even if he ends up being a dickhead like my father and chooses to have nothing to do with him.

"Hey, hey. I can see your brain working from here." Gavin is back on the couch, getting his sweaty teenage boy smell all over it. Whatever, I'll Febreze it when he leaves. He can't stink it up too badly in such a short time, can he? "Everything is going to be fine. Tell her your news, Lane. I can't handle seeing her cry."

I reach up and touch my cheeks, and sure enough, they're wet. "Sorry if my feelings offend you, you little twerp. I'm going to miss you guys, that's all. I'm allowed to be sad about that."

He jumps up off the couch and wraps me in a sweaty hug. "I'm going to miss you too, Feeble," he says, using the nickname he called me when he was little and couldn't quite get his little mouth to say Phoebe. "But you won't have to miss Lane."

I blink a few times and pull myself out of his embrace. "What's he talking about?" I ask Lane. "What are you talking about?"

Gavin takes Lincoln from Lane, snuggling him tightly to his chest, and takes him into the kitchen. I hear the cupboard doors open and close and the water runs in the sink. Sounds like Uncle Gavin is making his nephew a bottle.

"I didn't tell you because I knew you'd try to talk me out of it, but I'm staying with you. You have the third bedroom I can sleep in. I even got myself a part-time job at a coffee shop. I'm staying to help you with Lincoln so you can focus on finding his dad. It will be easier to track him down if you don't have to bring Lincoln with you everywhere you go. Plus, I can't be away from you guys for that long." Lane's eyes are shiny with unshed tears. "I just can't get enough of those midnight feedings," she jokes.

I chuckle. "Are you sure? You don't have to put your life on hold for me, Lane. I love you for wanting to do this, but you don't have to stay."

"I know that," she says, wrapping her arms around me. "I want to stay."

"You're the best sister I could ever ask for," I choke through a sob. "I couldn't have made it this far without you."

And it's true. The seemingly endless months of my pregnancy with Lincoln would have been so much harder if it hadn't been for the help of my brother and sister, and, of course, my mom and stepdad. I won't tell Lane and Gavin, but after living back home with my parents for the last year, and having my family around all the time, I was a little scared to be on my own with Lincoln in the city. I loved living here with Webster, but being on my own with a baby is different. The excitement of Westborough seems almost scary when I think about protecting my son from unseen dangers. I tried to play it cool, but I'm thinking I didn't do such a good job of it if Lane secretly arranged to move here with me. I've never been so happy to be such a shitty liar.

"Are you guys done with all the girly feelings out there? Me and the big guy want to come chill on that sweet-ass couch but we don't want your emotional breakdowns cramping our manly style."

Lane and I both burst into laughter. After one more squeeze, I let her go.

"Yeah, we're done," I call out. "I'll order that pizza now so you can get on the road."

"About that," he says, walking back to the living room with my son in the crook of his arm. "Mom told me to spend the night and drive back in the morning. She doesn't want me driving alone at night in the winter. I don't know what she thinks I do after work at home. It's usually pretty late by the time I get out of the market."

Lane sits next to him on the couch, her eyes on Lincoln. "There's a big difference between driving five minutes in Fallbridge at ten at night and driving on the highway at two in the morning. Especially in the middle of winter."

"Yeah, yeah. Okay, Mom," he teases. "I'm already staying the night. Happy?"

"You bet," she says while ruffling his hair, taking advantage of the fact that he has his hands full feeding Lincoln. "We just wuv you so much, Gavvers," she adds in a baby voice. "We would hate it if anything happened to you."

"Hey, no fair. Hands off my hair. Do you know how long it took to get it like that?"

They sit side by side, alternating between cooing over Lincoln and bickering with each other while I busy myself with ordering the pizzas and unpacking some boxes. The best part about finding a fully furnished rental is how little I had to pack to come here. It would have sucked if I'd had to move my furniture out of storage for such a short stay. Three months isn't long enough to justify renting a moving van. With this rental house, all I needed was some boxes in the back of Gavin's truck and I was ready to move in.

I just hope three months is long enough to find Lincoln's dad.

The doorbell rings, and Gavin hops up to grab the pizzas. "Oh, thank god. I'm starving," he says, spreading the boxes down on the coffee table and flipping one open. "I'm a growing boy, you know." He grabs two slices and stacks them.

I bring plates and napkins out from the kitchen. "We know, Gavin. You tell us every time you get even the tiniest bit hungry."

He wiggles his eyebrows, and grins before shoving the pizza sandwich in his mouth.

"So, Phoebe. Why don't you tell me how you plan on finding this guy? All you said before we came was that you're moving here for three months to look for him. Do you even have any idea where he is?"

I heave a sigh. This is the biggest problem with my plan. It sucks. When you get blind drunk after being left at the altar and hook up with someone you just met, it would be a lot easier to move on with your life if you didn't get yourself pregnant in the process. Failing that, it would be nice if you remember the name of the person or any detail about them other than he'd been dressed as Santa Claus for a Christmas party that was being held at the same hotel as your wedding. The only things I have to go on are the big red velvet coat I stole when I crept out of there in the wee hours of the morning, still drunk from the night before, and a picture I snapped of him with his face mashed so far into the pillow you can't tell with any accuracy what he looks like.

Why did I take his jacket, you ask? I guess I thought my walk of shame would feel less shameful if I covered my wedding dress with Santa's jacket. It didn't. But I made it back to the room without being seen, packed up, and headed home with no one finding out I spent what should have been my wedding night with a stranger.

Until a month and a half later when I got the shock of a lifetime, ensuring that *everyone* would eventually know *exactly* how I spent that night.

That's right.

My fiancé left me at the altar and the first thing I did was run out and get impregnated by Santa Claus.

Talk about Ho Ho Ho.

WANT TO KNOW WHEN Santa's Baby is available? Get the Roomie Review. Sign up at chantalroome.com/newsletter

Books by Chantal Roome

Sleeping Dogs the complete collection
The men of Sleeping Dogs have had their fair share of women, but now that they're a little older, and a little wiser, they're looking for something more meaningful than the one-night stands typical of their past.

Second Chance (Sleeping Dogs Book 1)
She's an unemployed chef afraid of being burned by love again. He's a world-weary rock star tired of being used. Can a second chance at first love heal them both?

Face the Music (Sleeping Dogs Book 2)
She's a serious control freak of a band manager. He's a jaded joker of a rock star. Will a jealous ex and surprise pregnancy tear them apart before they start?

Skip a Beat (Sleeping Dogs Book 3)
She's a disgraced ex-cop looking for a career change. He's a moody drummer trying to keep his demons at bay. Can vandalism and ill-conceived revenge plans be the glue that mends their lives and binds them to each other?

Only the Best (Sleeping Dogs Book 4)
He's a romantic, guitar-playing tattoo artist looking for true love. She's an emotionally and physically scarred photographer who keeps people at a distance. When one wants true love and the other wants one night, can friendship and a fake relationship ever be enough?

Way off Base (Sleeping Dogs Book 5)
She's a single mom struggling to rebuild her life. He's a reluctant rock star tired of being alone. Can they repair a foundation of lies to build the life they both want?

CHANTAL ROOME WRITES CONTEMPORARY romantic come-dies and is the author of the Sleeping Dogs series of cinnamon roll rock star rom-coms. She loves writing love stories with just the right mix of sweetness, humour, and sex. When she isn't writing, she's drinking way too much coffee, binge reading romance, and living out her own second chance romance with her husband. She's also a mediocre mom to two frustrating, but hilarious and endlessly loveable kids, and one dog who has eaten every toy he's ever been given.

Keep in touch with Chantal on social media

Visit Chantal's website at: www.chantalroome.com

Get the Roomie Review Newsletter chantalroome.com/roomiereview

Join my readers' group facebook.com/groups/theromcomroome

f facebook.com/chantalroomeauthor

⊙ instagram.com/chantalroomeauthor

𝓟 pinterest.com/chantalroome

♪ tiktok.com/chantalroomeauthor

🐦 twitter.com/croomeauthor

g goodreads.com/chantalroome

BB bookbub.com/authors/chantal-roome

www.ingramcontent.com/pod-product-compliance
Lightning Source LLC
Chambersburg PA
CBHW051216190726
48288CB00006B/1989